BY ROBERT JACKSON BENNETT

A DROP OF CORRUPTION

A
DROP
OF
CORRUPTION

...

AN ANA AND DIN MYSTERY

ROBERT JACKSON
BENNETT

NEW YORK

Published in the United States by Del Rey, an imprint of Random House,
a division of Penguin Random House LLC, 1745 Broadway, New York, NY 10019.

DEL REY and the CIRCLE colophon are registered trademarks of
Penguin Random House LLC.

Some of the maps and art were originally published in *The Tainted Cup*
by Robert Jackson Bennett (New York: Del Rey, 2024).

Hardback ISBN 978-0-593-72382-1
Ebook ISBN 978-0-593-72383-8

Printed in the United States of America on acid-free paper

randomhousebooks.com
penguinrandomhouse.com

1st Printing

First Edition

Book design by Edwin A. Vazquez

The authorized representative in the EU for product safety and compliance is
Penguin Random House Ireland,
Morrison Chambers, 32 Nassau Street,
Dublin D02 YH68, Ireland.
https://eu-contact.penguin.ie.

To the Spaniards—*Mantente amable, mantente tonta.*

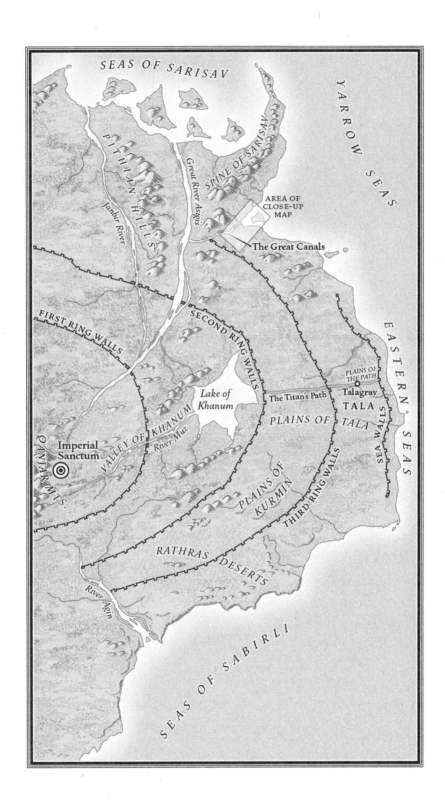

SEAS OF SARISAV

YARROW SEAS

PITHIAN HILLS

Janbir River

Great River Asgis

SPINE OF SARISAV

AREA OF
CLOSE-UP
MAP

The Great Canals

FIRST RING WALLS

SECOND RING WALLS

EASTERN SEAS

Lake of
Khanum

PLAINS OF
THE PATH

The Titan's Path

Talagray

TALA
TALA

PLAINS OF

VALLEY OF KHANUM

River Muz

Imperial
Sanctum

QANTAR MTS.

PLAINS OF
KURMIN

THIRD RING WALLS

SEA WALLS

RATHRAS DESERTS

River Agin

SEAS OF SABIRLI

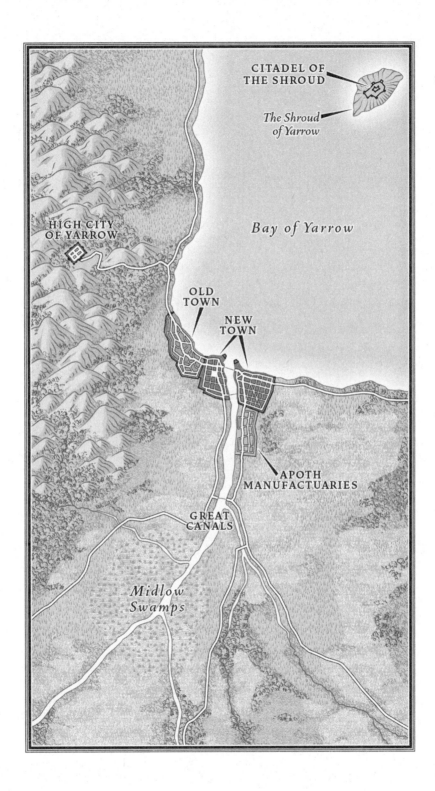

CITADEL OF
THE SHROUD

*The Shroud
of Yarrow*

Bay of Yarrow

HIGH CITY
OF YARROW

OLD
TOWN

NEW
TOWN

APOTH
MANUFACTUARIES

GREAT
CANALS

*Midlow
Swamps*

MILITARY RANKS
OF THE
GREAT AND HOLY EMPIRE OF KHANUM

(from highest to lowest)

CONZULATE

PRIFICTO

COMMANDER-PRIFICTO

COMMANDER

IMMUNIS

CAPTAIN

SIGNUM

PRINCEPS

MILITIS

A DROP OF CORRUPTION

BEFORE THERE WAS MEMORY, BEFORE THERE WAS HIS-tory, there were the leviathans: the colossal, monstrous creatures that lumbered ashore each wet season and went wandering the plains, bringing death and panic with them. For centuries, the folk of the land lived at their whim, and knew only fear and suffering.

Then the people of the Valley of Khanum learned the secrets of shaping flesh and root and branch—secrets rendered from the blood of the leviathans.

They altered their bodies. They made themselves brilliant, and strong. And when they emerged so transformed from the shadows of that valley, they began to change all the world before them.

First, they devised methods to bring down the leviathans. Then they conquered the petty tyrants, who ruled the highlands where the leviathans could not venture. And thus, the Empire of Khanum was born.

For six hundred years, the Empire has spread and survived—but only barely. The first people of Khanum died out long ago, and the Empire lost much wisdom and cunning with them. Each year, the leviathans still come ashore. Each year, all the arts and genius of the Empire must be mustered to hold them back. And all the while, harmony, equality, and progress must be maintained, for without them, the Empire shall unravel.

Within this Empire serves Dinios Kol, who is assigned to the Iudex, the imperial institution for administrating justice. His mind is altered so he forgets nothing. He acts as assistant investigator to Ana Dolabra, a woman so brilliant she lives most of her days blindfolded and rarely leaves her rooms, for fear that common life shall overwhelm her mind.

Together, they are tasked with the investigation of imperial deaths of an unusually difficult or dangerous nature. He investigates and remembers; she analyzes, evaluates, and spies hidden truths in all he witnessed.

Together, they bring justice to the Empire.

I

...

THE
VANISHED MAN

CHAPTER 1

▴ ▴ ▴

I'D THOUGHT THE JUNGLES OF THE EASTERN EMPIRE TO
be oppressively hot, but as I sat in the prow of the little canal boat and
felt the sweat slip down my brow, I decided the north was, without
question, far worse. The final leg of our journey had been almost entirely shaded by the dense tree canopies, yet even in the coolest shadows, the jungle underbrush perpetually steamed, as if all the world
was just shy of boiling. My blue Iudex coat had been soaked in sweat
from collar to cuff for nigh on three days now, so much so that I left a
wet print where I sat. Not a fine first impression to make for the officer waiting for me.

We made one last bend around the canal and finally approached
the Yarrowdale waterfront. Even at this early hour, the piers were
swarming with vessels: tiny fishing junkers and lumbering barges
and merry little oyster cogs—as well as some unusual craft I'd never
seen before.

I eyed these as we approached the piers. They were unwieldy, low-
bellied boats with thick stonewood walls fastened to their sides, yet
the walls sparkled with glints of hammered iron. I realized they were
stubbled with arrowheads lodged deep in the wood, the shafts splintered or cut away. It was as if each craft had withstood a half-dozen
volleys mere moments ago. An odd sight in so quiet a place.

I disembarked, my bag thrown over my shoulder, and stood on
the busy waterfront, peering about for the imperial officer assigned to
meet me here.

Yet no one appeared. There were the fisherfolk, lined at the piers and looping nets about their arms, half-naked with their pale flesh burned dark from the sun. There were a number of indigents, filthy and with matted hair, who sat at the edge of the waterfront bowed like religious supplicants. There were many Engineers, returning from the canals so mummified in mud you could hardly spy the purple of their uniforms. And last were the many Apothetikal soldiers, who stood on guard with their crimson Apoth capes about their shoulders and their spears clutched tight in their hands, watching the crowds with hard, brittle eyes.

I noted their pose, their tension. Strange to see Apoths assigned to guard duties: they were usually more concerned with tinctures and reagents. I glanced again at the scarred armored boats rigged up along the piers, and wondered exactly what had been going on here in the port town of Yarrowdale.

I waited for twenty minutes at the piers, the air roiling and steaming, the jungle beyond sighing as the wind tousled the trees, but I did not see my officer. I silently cursed the Empire's much-delayed and always-confused communications. Perhaps they'd told them the wrong day.

I trudged off, my bag on my back, headed for the Yarrowdale ossuary, for that was where the corpse was stored. Yet as I started down the road, I paused.

Just past the start of the road there was a small hillock, dotted with barri trees with thick turf gathered about their roots, and there, lying in the middle of the turf, was a young woman, wearing a hooded cloak with her fingers clasped over her belly like she was deep in restful slumber. Her trousers and boots were so congealed with mud they were now little more than clods of soil, but the color of her cloak was Apoth crimson.

And there, at her breast: a few winking heralds. The bars of an imperial signum, just like myself.

I had been told an Apoth signum would be waiting for me here. I approached her, hoping I was wrong.

I'd planned to clear my throat to wake her once I was near, but when I was within ten span of her she spoke aloud, her Yarrow accent as thick as pudding: "Can I help you?"

"I was told I was to meet an Apoth signum here," I said. "Might that be you?"

She opened her eyes and looked at me. She was quite young and short, a pale, pink-skinned, broad girl, with short, greasy hair stuck to her scalp. Her eyes were very round, and the whites of them had a greenish tint to them—a common feature of Yarrow folk of the region—but the flesh about them was purpled, as was the flesh of her ears and nose: a sign of significant augmentations. It was likely the girl could hear every beat of my heart and smell every drop of sweat upon my body.

"Oh!" she said. She looked me over, still lying flat on the grass. "I thought you'd smell more expensive."

"I . . . What?"

She propped herself up on her elbows. "I have been smelling the breeze, waiting for you. Inner ring officers always have a very expensive aroma. Lots of oils in their hair, and their skin so perfumed. Yet you do not smell as this." She squinted at me. "So. You are the Iudex officer who is here to help us with our mysterious dead man?"

"I am," I said. I gave her a short bow. "I am Signum Dinios Kol, Iudex Special Division."

She looked me over but said nothing.

"And you are?" I asked.

"Did you eat dried fish on your journey here?" she asked.

"I beg your pardon?"

"Dried fish. Did you eat a slice or two of this today? Perhaps one spiced with coriander?"

"I . . . well, yes? Why?"

"Mm," she said, nodding sagely. Then she stood, bowed, and said, "Signum Tira Malo, Warden of the Apothetikals. I apologize for not giving you a finer greeting, Kol. The true Empire lies a long way from here. Sometimes we forget its touch."

"Is it common for Yarrow officers to just lie about on riverbanks in the morning?"

"Lie about?" she said. "I was attempting to dry." She extended an arm into the sun, and ghostly flickers of steam arose from her sleeve. "I have had a long night's work on the canals and in the swamps, trying to comprehend more about how our dead man came to be so very dead. It was dirty work, and useless, but will get dirtier still." She looked over my shoulder. "I thought there'd be two of you."

"My immunis shall come in her own time," I said. "I presume there are lodgings assigned for us?"

"Of course. My comrades shall take care of her, when she comes." She nodded toward the folk I'd taken to be indigents, seated at the waterfront. I realized now they were also bound in Apoth cloaks, as muddy as they were. "But before we go—would you prefer to vomit here, out of doors, Kol? Or would you prefer to wait?"

I stared. "I'm sorry?"

"The scent of fish on your breath," she said. "It is not decent. I think the fish has turned sour, and whoever served it to you spiced it so you could not taste it. I give it, oh, about an hour until your stomach starts burbling, and then it shall come up." She turned to me, smiling lazily. "It will not be helped by the ossuary. It is a difficult place, even if one's stomach is as still as stone. And especially given the state of our dead man."

I pressed my hand against my stomach, thinking she had to be wrong. But then there, in some crevice of my belly: did I feel the slightest unpleasant flutter?

I glared at her. "You make many assumptions, Malo. I am fine, and ready to begin our work."

"Are you," she said lightly. "Very good, then! Let us go to the ossuary and do our filthiness there."

THE YARROWDALE OSSUARY did not put me at ease: between the low, vaulted ceilings and the distant mutterings of other Apoths, the building felt much like a catacomb, and worst of all, the dank air reeked of a vaguely musky yet awful scent.

"You are a lucky man, Kol," Malo said as we walked its passages. "You know this?"

"Why is that?"

"They recently did a purge of our samples," she said. "Tossed out all the ones well past their term, for we can only preserve them for so long. The air in here is now like a spring meadow, compared to how it was last month."

I pressed a knuckle to my nostrils. "How can anyone bear it?"

"A simple answer." She stopped to grab a cart on high spoked wheels and began pushing it along with us. "Most don't."

I looked Malo over as we walked. She did not seem bothered by our surroundings in the least: she sauntered along, chewing languidly on a piece of hina root—a minor stimulant—which gave her mouth a blackish tinge. She'd hung her cloak up at the door, and I saw now that she sported not only a short sword sheathed at her side, but two knives in her belt, one in her boot, and a little one sheathed at her wrist. I wondered exactly what her duties were, to require such strength of arms.

Finally we came to a little cupboard door at the end of the hall. "Here he is," she sang.

She opened the cupboard door. I braced myself, yet the only thing within was a wooden box, about ten smallspan tall and three span wide and long: not much larger than a Legionnaire's shield. Malo grasped the box and slid it out onto her rolling cart, the spindly spokes of the wheels creaking with the new weight.

I studied the shallow wooden box.

"I had thought," I said slowly, "I was coming to review a body."

"A what?"

"My orders said I was to review the body of an officer found in a canal, who is suspected to be a victim of violence."

"Ohh," she said thoughtfully. "Well. Then someone has made a mistake! For I did not say we had a *body*. I told my superiors we had found *remains*. I chose the word most carefully."

There was a silence as I continued looking at the small, flat box on the cart.

"So," I said, sighing. "I take it he's not just very short."

She grinned, her teeth now black as Rathras grapes from the hina root. "No such luck. Shall we take a peek?"

WE MOVED TO a circular, laboratory-like room, with a wide, bronze table beneath a row of glimmering blue mai-lanterns. The air here smelled strongly of lye and other cleaning reagents. A drain was set in the floor beneath the table, with a pinkish halo of stain on the stone about it: a place often cleaned, I supposed, but never truly clean.

Humming, Signum Malo slid the box from the cart to the table, then walked to the shelves and donned a large leather apron and gloves over her muddy, crimson Apoth's uniform. "You might want to get a chair," she said. "This can take time. I am a warden, and thus trained in many Apoth arts, but most of what I do is tracking and, ah . . ." She mimed firing a bow and arrow. "Resolving disputes, I should say?"

I parted my soaking cloak and dumped myself into the chair, my sword swinging at my side. "I'd thought a warden's tasks were keeping valuable reagents and precursors safe, not combat."

"Well, we don't get any Legionnaires for protection out here. We are far from the Empire proper, and there are no leviathans this far north. Yet it makes a crude sense, does it not? For what are human beings, if not walking bags of valuable reagents and compounds?" She grinned. "Why should I not track them, and bleed them of some critical reagents when deemed fit?"

She returned to the wooden box on the table, twisted three bronze clasps running along a seam at the side, then tugged at the top. With a loud clattering, the top and walls fell away.

Within was not a body, nor anything resembling a human limb, but a large, oblong brick of a very unusual moss, with stiff, bonelike tendrils all densely grown together. The brick was perfectly rectangular, having grown to fill the interior of the box—or so I supposed.

Malo gently pushed the brick of moss off the bottom slab of wood until it rested free on the table.

I stared at the brick of moss, my thoughts lingering on that word: *remains.*

The powerful, musky odor in the room intensified, and with it rose an unpleasant burbling in my stomach. I kept my face still but thought, *Damn it all, she was right about the fish.*

"Won't be a moment," said Malo.

Humming, she paced to a shelf and picked up a tray carrying many small knives and a large, corked blue pot. Then she returned to the brick of moss, uncorked the pot, and poured a thin stream of oil over the brick with a flamboyant flick, like a cook greasing a hot pan. Then she corked the bottle, set it aside, and began rubbing the oil along the brick with her gloved hands, massaging it into the many crevices of the tendrils.

"How does this work?" I asked.

"The moss?" she said. "You've not seen it before?"

"Most of the bodies I've reviewed have either been quite fresh or long since gone."

"A lucky thing, for you," she said. "It has always been called *ossuary moss*—though it is not truly a moss but a predatory fungus. It lives in hollows in the earth, lining the chambers there, waiting for creatures to fall in. When they do, the moss stings them, paralyzing them, and slowly grows to swallow them, like a cocoon. That's when the *truly* fun stuff happens." She grunted as she shifted the brick. "It secretes a fluid, cleaning the organism of the many pestilences that cause rot. Almost like curing it, really, so it can then consume all the tissues, with no waste. The breed we've altered no longer consumes flesh, of course. It simply leaves us with a sample that stays fresh for up to two years."

I glanced at the many cabinets lining the hall behind me. "Samples?"

Malo grinned at me. In the darkness of the laboratory, with her eyes and nose stained so purple, her face had a skeletal look. "We are Apoths, Kol. We make use of many tissues. Some of them our own."

There was another putrid wave of musk. The oil had now soaked into the moss's hide until it attained a slightly translucent sheen. I glimpsed a ghostly white mass at its core.

"Please tell me what you know about the murder," I said.

She chuckled bleakly. "A more pleasant subject, maybe. But only somewhat."

"DEAD MAN'S NAME is Immunis Mineti Sujedo," Malo began, "of the Imperial Treasury. Hailed from the second ring of the Empire as a member of a Treasury delegation, here to confer with the king of Yarrow on *high imperial business.*" The words dripped with poisonous sarcasm. "He was last of his delegation to come, arriving just over two weeks ago—the tenth of the month of Hajnal. He was met at the waterfront by Apoth guards, seemed in good health and high spirits, and was escorted to his lodgings. Just as we shall do for your immunis, when she comes."

I paused. I had already known much of this, but not that last bit. "Why was he escorted by guards?" I asked.

"Because he was here to talk about taxes," she said. "And everybody hates the tax man—especially here in Yarrow. Which is no safe place."

The sight of the armored boats so stubbled with arrowheads flashed in my mind.

"I see," I said quietly.

"Guards got him moved into his rooms," continued Malo. "Then he visited the Treasury bank in the city, again escorted by guards. He did some business there and returned just before sunset. When he got back to his lodgings, he said he was not feeling well after his journey. He seemed to be weak of stomach."

I nodded sternly, trying not to think of my own rebellious innards.

"He had the guards send a notice to his Treasury delegation leader saying he would be staying in that night," Malo said. "Then he called for dinner, yet ate little, and went to bed. He was due to visit with the other members of his delegation the next morning, but . . . he did not appear. A message was sent to Sujedo's rooms, requesting his presence. When there was no answer, the guards went in and found the man had . . . Well. He'd been abducted in the night!"

"Abducted?" I asked, surprised. "The orders I was given indicated he'd gone missing."

"That is not as anyone here would put it," she said. "*Gone missing* would make one think he disappeared while moving from one place to another. But a guard was posted at his door all night, and the door itself remained locked throughout, and the man never left the room. The only sign that anything had gone amiss was his bed, which showed signs of a struggle and was bloodied and mussed."

"Bloodied?" I asked.

"Yes, as if he'd been attacked or stabbed as he slept. Stranger still—the windows of his room were all still locked from the inside! No signs of tampering, no breaking, nothing. No one has any idea how the attacker got in or out. And besides the man himself, nothing within had been taken. I went to his rooms and gave the airs there a good sniff." She tapped her purpled nose, apparently indifferent to the oil on her gloved fingertip. "I can track a squirrel through wet forest for over a league with little more than a tuft of fur. Yet when I went to Sujedo's room, I found *no* scent but his, and those of the servants. He was alone in his chamber for all the time before we found him gone. How he vanished from it, I cannot say."

I glanced at the brick of moss, now gleaming with oil. "And when and where did you find the remains?"

"We discovered them on the fifteenth of Hanjal, five days after his arrival and disappearance," she said. "So, ten days ago now, in case you have forgotten what date it is with all your travels."

I gave her a small, cold smile. "I didn't."

"Of course not. We found all the bits some twelve leagues away from his lodgings. The journey to the exact spot is long, hilly, jungle-dense, swampy. And that is *after* you leave the city of Yarrowdale, with many eyes watching. A tricky path to walk undetected, let alone with a body." She spat a stream of black spittle to her right. It landed directly in the drain below the table: a feat of astonishing accuracy. "I am beset by impossibilities. How might this man be stolen from such a place with no one noticing? How could he reappear in such a state, so far away? We wardens could not answer any of it." She shot me a wry look. "How happy am I to have you Iudex here to work your magic. I much prefer hunting ratshit smugglers in the jungle to this."

A flatulent puff arose from the tendrils of moss. The stench in the room was now nothing short of horrid.

Malo sniffed the air. "Smells done to me," she said. "Let us see . . ."

A final gust of reek from the brick, and then, slowly, it began to soften, starting with a sinking indentation in the center, then growing until the corners wilted and drooped, and then, gently, the mass of pale tendrils began to unfurl.

Malo began plucking at the drooping tangle, wielding a pair of tongs like a cook fluffing a kettle of rice. "Ah, yes. Come!"

I joined her beside the table. She plucked again at the dissolving moss, and a form began to emerge at the core.

No, that wasn't right: not one form, but three.

First there was a hand, the fingers curled as if gripping an invisible ball. Its fingernails were the color of tea, and were darker than the flesh, which was a pale gray. It was ragged at the wrist, the delicate bones there ending in shattered splinters, their spongy marrow permeated with dark stains.

Next to that, a chunk of torso, headless and armless. Most of the left shoulder and rib cage, but not much else. It had been thoroughly disemboweled, as if all the organs had been scooped out by a giant spoon. Ribs emerged from the pale flesh like straw frets at the edge of a gentryman's paper fan. Somehow, ridiculously, the left nipple remained, dark and pebbled, along with a brambly tuft of black chest hair.

And there, lying just below that on the bed of moss, was a jawbone, fleshless and perfectly severed from whatever skull it had once hung to. Much like the marrows of the fractured wrist, the crevices of the teeth were dark with sediment and stain.

"That is all they've found of him," said Malo. "All they ever could fish out of the canals of our missing Treasury man Sujedo. Sad, is it not?"

I stared at the severed pieces, my nostrils swimming with the odor of the moss, and now the stench of rot.

The sour fish in my belly rolled over yet again.

I turned, staggered to the drain in the floor, knelt, placed my hands on either side, and vomited directly down it, coughing so mightily my whole body began to ache.

"There it is," said Malo appraisingly. "You seem very practiced! That is the most precise vomit I have ever seen."

I resumed my position over the drain and retched again.

CHAPTER 2

...

WHEN I HAD GOTTEN HOLD OF MYSELF, I RETURNED TO
the table and stared down at the fragments of flesh.

I had never had to work with such shattered parts of a person
before. Still, it was my job as an Iudex investigator to memorize it: to
engrave all I saw in my memory, and then report my experiences to
my commanding officer.

I reached into my engraver's satchel at my side, slid out a small
glass vial, and uncorked it. I shut my eyes and inhaled deeply from it,
letting the aroma of the nectarous oils bathe the interior of my skull:
a blessing after what I'd just been through. With this scent in my nostrils, I could better anchor all the memories I'd engrave here, and
quickly recall them later.

I opened my eyes, looked down at the pitiful remains of Sujedo,
and focused.

I took in the shape of the remains, their color, the way they had
been contorted; how the bones had been broken, how the skin had
curdled, the wend and weft of the flesh. As my memory had been enhanced to be perfect, these awful sights would remain with me until I
died. But such was my lot in service to the Empire.

I dabbed at my mouth with a handkerchief. "Why didn't we find
more of him?" I asked huskily.

Malo slid off her apron and gloves. "We've many reaper-backs in
the Yarrow canals. My thinking is, one found him floating and made
a meal of him."

"Reaper-backs?"

"A turtle. Slightly smaller than a man. Very pretty shells, but very carnivorous. Can take an arm off in a single bite. Or, well . . ." She gestured at Sujedo's remains. "More."

"What makes you so sure they're what did this?"

"The organs, or the lack of them. Reaper-backs have a tongue for them. After the smugglers, the turtles are the second most dangerous thing on the Great Canals. And they are much harder to kill."

"How exotic. Do we think he fell prey to one of them?"

"Possible. But it's more likely, I think, that he was fed to them to try to dispose of him."

"Why?"

"Because of this," she said, pointing to the outer edge of the shoulder, where the arm would ordinarily connect to the chest muscles.

I peered at it, fighting another rumbling in my stomach. Yet I saw what she meant: the bone and ligaments there were not torn and ragged, but queerly smooth.

"A cut," I said. "Like sawing. He was cut into pieces before he entered the waters?"

"That is our conclusion," said Malo. "Perhaps to better attract the turtles, or . . . perhaps the killer simply enjoyed butchery. I am unsure. Yet look closer at the hand."

I leaned in and studied the preserved hand. There was a discoloration at the joint, I thought: a stripe of flesh both too dark and too pale in parts. I spied a hint of tiny lacerations in the stripe, in patterns that made me think of something fibrous.

"He was bound," I said. "By the wrists."

Malo nodded, slightly impressed. "Yes. Fibers in the wound, too. Looks like from a rope of some kind. Very dark, very coarse. Tar soaked." She tapped her temple, beside her purpled, augmented eyes. "Canal-rigging rope, as far as I can see."

"Canal rope," I said quietly.

"Yes. He must have strained against them greatly to make those marks."

"Was there anyone unusual seen at his lodgings?"

Malo shook her head. "There is the rest of the Treasury delegation, who come and go in their work with the Yarrow king. Then there are the servants—the maids, the cook, the footmen. And then, of course, the guards assigned by we Apoths. They all say they saw no one unfamiliar, nor strange."

I pondered this, then sniffed at my vial again, anchoring the sight of the bruised wrist within my mind. "Can you turn over the other pieces for me, please?"

She did so, gingerly turning the jawbone and the fragment of torso like they were fine crockery I had a mind to purchase.

There was something on the back of the torso, I saw, on the shoulder blade: a circular patch of missing skin, excised from the flesh, about the size of a talint coin.

"What's that?" I asked, pointing.

"We don't know," said Malo. "Not a turtle bite, though, as that takes off more than skin. The skin was cut off or shorn away."

"Did Sujedo have any identifying marks?" I asked. "Scar, blemish, or tattoo?"

"You mean," said Malo, "could they have cut skin away to make it hard for us to tell who he was?"

"Yes. Did he?"

"No," she grunted. "But if he was murdered, and if the murderer knew anything about the man, they would've been aware that identifying him would be simple."

"Why's that?" I asked. Then I frowned. "Wait. How *did* you identify these body parts as belonging to Sujedo, given that they lack nearly all identifying features?"

She looked me over like I had just said something very foolish. "Because he was Treasury," she said flatly.

"And what does that mean?" I asked.

Another prolific yet incredibly accurate spit. She squinted at me. "I thought you Iudex knew everything. Yet you don't know the Treasury arts?"

"Treasury officers serve in civilized cantons," I said tartly. "Which are not places I often visit in my duties."

She grunted like she found this explanation wanting. "Treasury officers above the rank of captain have augmented blood. Comes from a little cultivated organ implanted in the armpit." She tapped her own to show me. "Treasury banks handle all manner of protected materials. Safes, vaults, lockboxes ... Like reagent keys. You know these things? The little trinkets that give off a pheromonal signal, telling a portal to open?"

I nodded, stone-faced, for I was indeed familiar with these.

"A Treasury officer's blood is like the same," said Malo, "opening protected things when they grow near, or at a touch."

"And you found the right kind of blood in these bits."

"These body parts didn't have much blood in them, but they had enough for our tests. They contain the blood of a Treasury immunis. Since we are only missing one of those ... well, must be Sujedo."

I turned this over. "We seem to be missing quite a bit of him," I said. "So that makes me wonder ..."

"Could some madman carry Sujedo's severed hand into a Treasury bank to open a safe, or some such?" asked Malo. She snorted. "Give us Apoths some credit. We can detect dead blood, sure, but the protective tests about the vaults are designed to respond to a high concentration of *living* tissues. Not dead ones."

I stood over the shattered remains, tabulating all of this information.

"So," I said. "In sum ... we do not have all of Sujedo's body."

"Obviously," said Malo.

"And we do not have any witnesses for his abduction, nor his death. Nor do we have any idea how either was managed."

"We do not."

"In fact, we do not actually know *where* he died. Or when. Nor do we have any suspects whatsoever."

"You are beginning to see my relief," Malo said dryly, "that you Iudex are here to work your magic."

I pondered how to move forward. "The only two places Sujedo went during his time here were to the bank and to his lodgings. Yes?"

"Yes."

"And what business did he do at the bank?"

"Stowed away some papers in a safe," she said. "I had the Treasury clerks there pull it. It was his orders, along with sheets of numbers. Tax things. Nothing particularly interesting."

I dabbed at my mouth with a handkerchief, hoping my pallor hid my dismay. It was one thing to be dropped into such a location to work with bare pieces of a body, yet the more I learned about this murder, the less trail there seemed to follow. How strange it felt to be presented with a death so puzzling, and yet also so utterly blank. Yet I would have to rummage up something to report on before Ana arrived, or I'd hear no end of it.

I sighed, then said, "I suppose you'd better take me to his lodgings, please."

CHAPTER 3

⁂

YARROWDALE WAS A PORT TOWN, GRIPPING THE BAY OF
Yarrow like a growth of barnacles about the curve of a cliff, then fun-
neling south to cling to the Great Canals linking the bay to the River
Asigis, and all the wealth of the Empire beyond. I had viewed many
maps of the city during my trip here, engraving the layout in my mind.
As we exited the ossuary and started off, I summoned them out of my
memory.

The rambling sprawl mostly fell into three distinct pieces, moving
from southeast to northwest along the side of the bay. At the southeast end was New Town, built by and for the many Iyalets of the Empire, for there they refined and shipped out countless priceless
precursors and reagents through the canals. Northwest of that was
Old Town, the original home of the Yarrow kings and their folk,
though they had left that place long ago. And finally there was the
High City, built in the ranges far northwest of that, where the current
Yarrow king resided with all of his royal retinue, removed from the
bustle of industry that now consumed the land of his ancestors.

The ossuary, being an Apoth facility, was situated in New Town,
and as Malo and I passed through it the place seemed all cheerful,
rambling roofs and rollicking movement, the damp lanes packed with
tradesfolk and pack animals and imperial officers—mostly Apoths,
going by the rivers of crimson cloaks surging about me. Tall, flowering fretvine buildings were piled up on either side of the street, the
sea-facing sides blooming with bright green moss, like slices of toast

layered with a curiously green butter. A band of pipers and drummers played at a crossroads ahead, and danced merrily when tossed a talint.

It was much like many imperial cities I had seen in my service, in other words, yet every path sloped down to the north, toward the Bay of Yarrow. And though the bay was hidden from my view, the awareness of the ocean was all about me: the murmur of waves, the scent of salt and seaweed on the air, and the hot, rumbling winds that came coursing down from the east.

I shuddered as we walked. It had been over a year since I'd ventured this close to the sea. Even though these waters were different from those in the East, I wished to look away from them.

"Something wrong?" asked Malo.

"I don't much like the sea," I muttered. "Nor being so close to it."

"Ahh. You are a true imperial, then, eh?" she said.

I shot a glare at her and wiped my brow. "And you are not?"

"I am Yarrow, born and raised," she said. She waved at the jungle-draped hills about us. "For better or worse. But do not fret yourself. Though we're seaside and the wet season approaches, we've not had a living leviathan in Yarrowdale since before memory."

I suppressed another shudder, now at one word of hers in particular: *living.*

IT TOOK NEARLY an hour of walking to reach Old Town. There the fretvine houses of New Town receded, and in their place stood tall, somber buildings of pale stone all stained faint green. Stone buildings were quite rare in the Empire, and these were of beautiful make, with a coral design running atop their roofs and coiling about their columns; yet many leaned at angles, or slumped in places, pooling water on their porches and overflowing with bundles of dark green growth.

"This is Old Town?" I asked dubiously.

"Used to be the high seat of Yarrow, many years back," said

Malo. "The place of the king and his noble court. Do you not find it impressive?"

I eyed a tumorous growth of mold crawling up one wall. "It seems rather lived in."

"That is one term for it," she conceded. "The craftsmen of the old courts grew these towers from a type of sand, full of tiny bugs. You could add things to the sand, put it in a mold, and the bugs within would make it harden into that shape. But the stone did not age well. Didn't settle right. And many things leaned."

I dodged a stream of water trickling down from the roofs. "So I see."

"Yes. Then the Empire came, and made their deal with the king, and bought the land here. The Yarrow court abandoned this place, moving to the high holy city above, and took with them the arts of how to maintain these stones. Now it rots. As do all their people who dwell here."

"The king simply left his people here? With no arrangements?"

"Yes?"

"Why would he do so?"

She paused and looked back at me, studying my face as if suddenly worried I was some reckless cretin. Then she shook her head and we continued on.

I followed her through the warrens. There was a somber air in this place: the people here were thin and unhealthy, and there was the ever-present echo of coughing.

A thought occurred to me.

"Beg pardon," I said. "But—the Treasury delegation was lodged *here*?"

"It's as I told you." Malo grunted as we climbed a short, awkward stair. "No one loves the tax man, Kol. Don't want him to stay, stick him somewhere shit. The king of Yarrow apparently delights in torturing the Treasury officers they send to speak with him, and requested they stay here. Now—step fast. We are in a dangerous area. I don't want anyone seeing your very pretty face, assuming you're a rich man who paid for the shaping of it, and knifing you for your talints."

"I did not pay for my face," I said, nettled, but Malo was already moving.

WE FINALLY CAME to a tall stone building, rising high above the leaning sprawl of Old Town. It was easily the finest of the stone towers, spanning six stories, with an ornate, coral skin dotted with many small windows, yet despite its scale and artistry, it, too, was green with fungus and greatly aged by the coastal weather.

"That was his room," Malo said, pointing. "Up there."

I looked up, shadowed my eyes with a hand, and squinted. She appeared to be pointing at one window at the very top.

"Sujedo . . . was housed in that highest room?" I asked.

"Yes," she said.

"So he didn't just disappear from a locked room," I sighed, "but from a locked room four hundred span off the ground."

"Thereabout. Quite a trick, no? Plucking a man from such a high room, with the windows locked and all, and no one saw nor heard a thing . . . I cannot ken it."

I slid a shootstraw pipe from my pocket, stuck it in my mouth, and chewed on it, letting the taste of the tobacco calm my mind and stomach. "And I suppose he didn't just fall out, being as a body striking the ground tends to produce a lot of noise and notice."

"And a big stain," she added. "Of which we have found none. Nor can I smell blood anywhere about this place—except within Sujedo's rooms."

I sniffed my vial, engraving this sight, and we entered the tower.

The rooms were guarded by three Apoth militii, who stood gawking in the hallways as Malo unlocked and opened the door to the dead man's rooms for me. I paused in the entryway, taking it in. It must have been a stately place once, yet now it was musty and sodden. Rivulets of water wriggled across the rounded ceiling, leaving trails of mold in their wake like the slime of snails. Running along the curving outer wall of the suite of rooms were six rounded windows peering southeast, all shut, all locked. The doors of the cupboards in the corner were open but their shelves appeared totally bare.

Yet what drew my eye most was the mossbed sitting by the wall, with a dent in the fern pillow, and a wide brown stain crawling across the sheets: perhaps enough blood to fill two sotwine pots, if not more. A serious wound, then. And from the positioning, it would indicate a wound to the torso, perhaps the kidneys or liver. Fatal if untreated.

I grunted, thinking. Then I noticed: merely standing in the hall made me put more weight on my left foot than the right.

I squatted and placed my shootstraw pipe on the floor. It teetered for a moment, then decisively rolled to the left.

"We tilt, yes," said Malo. "As many buildings in Old Town do. The Imperial Engineers have sworn this building should not fall over anytime soon, but it is worse the higher we go."

I debated how to proceed. "Who else has been in here so far?" I asked.

"Lots of folk," said Malo. "Sujedo's guards. Me and the other Apoth wardens. We confirmed nothing was removed from the rooms. We placed everything we found on the table."

I put my pipe back in my mouth, suppressing a cringe. Though she surely thought that made my job easier, she was quite wrong.

"Are any of the Treasury delegation members present?" I asked.

"I had instructed them to make themselves available, but apparently they're busy today. Meeting with the king, you see," she said with a false awe. "Or, more likely, his many courtly busybodies."

"Who is lodged on either side of this room?"

"The room to the west is empty. But the room to the east is occupied by Sujedo's colleague Immunis Valik."

"Who heard . . . ?"

"Nothing."

"And the guard outside never saw anyone leave Sujedo's rooms?"

"Except for maids and servants, no."

I sucked my teeth for a moment, thinking. I slid my vial from my engraver's satchel, sniffed it, then stepped inside the room.

First I reviewed the bed, studying the crinkle and bend of the sheets, and the way the fern pillows were piled atop one another.

"The topsheet's gone," I said.

"We took it to extract the blood upon it," explained Malo. "For we'd also found a dribbling of piss in the chamber pot. We distilled the scents of both and found they came from the same man—and, when we found Sujedo's corpse, we matched it to him. It is his blood, and his piss."

"And you found no other sign of an intruder? No hair, nor blot of different blood?"

"Nothing," she said.

Frowning, I moved on.

There was a large table set against one wall, and, as Malo had said, it was piled high with all the items they'd apparently discovered during their search. I grimaced as I approached it. Moving everything from its location made estimating its value to the investigation much more difficult: a knife found hidden behind a pillow is much more interesting than one packed away in a bag. But there was little to be gained from criticizing the work of the locals.

"We have reviewed these as well," said Malo. "The clothes have a strong smell of citrus and mold. It made figuring out all the scents in here far trickier. I assumed the killer used it to cover their deeds."

I bent low and sniffed. She was right: there was a bright flash of lime, followed by the unpleasant aroma of rotting wood. Curious.

I sniffed my vial again and reviewed Sujedo's items one by one. A small mai-lantern; three Treasury uniforms, two standard white, one dress gray; a box of ceremonial heralds, along with cuff fasteners and other jewelry; three belts—two brown, one black; a bag of ashpens; a bag of coins, totaling sixty-three talints and four coppers; and an extensive bag of tinctures and vials of powders, mostly for managing pains of the head. Which made sense: like many in the Treasury, Sujedo had been an axiom—a person cognitively enhanced to be preternaturally talented at calculation—yet such an augmentation came with side effects, often leading to a truncated life span. As my own memory was significantly augmented, I knew this well.

I looked at all this for a long while, engraving each item in my memories. Then my eye fell on the final item on the table: a small rectangular piece of what appeared to be bare iron. I picked it up and turned it over in my hand. It was heavy, smooth, and cold.

"Don't know what that is," said Malo. "We found it on the floor. Looks like simply a plug of iron."

I studied it. It was about the length of my finger and seemed wholly unremarkable. Yet it was smooth and unmarred, as if it had been fashioned to be this shape and size. It bothered me.

"Where did you find it?" I asked.

She pointed to the wall with the windows. "Over there."

I put the piece of iron in my pocket, then went to the wall and studied the floor, then the windows. I'd thought the iron might be a bit of broken component from the window but found nothing: all the shutters were both whole and securely fastened shut, using an iron sliding lock. The locks slid back and forth easily enough, but once they'd been fastened, the window didn't jostle. Though the rest of the building leaned and leaked, the windows held fast.

I opened one window and stuck my head out, squinting through the sea breeze. A deathly drop yawned below me, made all the more alarming by the tilt of the tower. The idea of anyone going in or out of these windows was utterly mad.

I looked about, squinting again as the ocean breeze struck my face. I could see the cheery peaks of New Town to the east and south, the Apoth works puffing steams and smokes. Canals coiled all about them in slashes and tangles, each teeming with rippling ship sails. To the south and west I glimpsed some of the steaming, sprawling expanse of the jungle, cut through here and there with tiny farms and vales, and then, to the northwest of us, mounted atop a high clutch of hills, was a clutch of bone-white towers.

The High City: the domain of the king of Yarrow. It seemed smaller and more distant than I'd seen in the maps. I couldn't help but think of it as a spirit kingdom from the stories, a place where playful sprites would lure children with a piper's song.

Then, with great reluctance, I finally looked north.

The Bay of Yarrow unrolled before me, the afternoon sunlight glinting merrily off the vast waters.

And there, leagues away in the ocean, stood . . .

Something.

It looked a little like a tent, tall and pointed and swirling like the ones you might find at a canton fair, and though it was quite far away, its enormous scale was still evident, rising hundreds of spans out of the water, taller than anything I'd ever seen save the sea walls of the East. It glowed slightly in the midday sun, a soft, viridine glimmer. I narrowed my eyes, wondering what it was made of; perhaps vines or grasses, so closely grown they seemed to form shifting panes of green glass. Protected within this green cocoon, I knew, was the citadel at its center. I imagined I could almost discern the shape of walls and roofs somewhere within it.

"How bright it looks today," remarked Malo, joining me at the window. "They say it gets brighter as the wet seasons approach, and darker as the leviathans slumber. The year has worn on faster than I'd thought."

"That's the Shroud?" I asked quietly.

"It is. Perhaps the most valuable thing in all of Yarrowdale, and the thing people fear most. And who can blame them? We are taught to fear the leviathans as children. It is only natural to fear their grave-yard."

I gazed at the Shroud, hypnotized by its movements, its surface roiling and undulating in the bright sun. It almost seemed to beckon to me.

"Sujedo didn't have shit to do with the Shroud," said Malo. "*Nobody* wants anything to do with that, except for we Apoths. Seen enough here?"

I coughed, muttered, "Yes," and gladly turned away. Though this investigation already offered no end of puzzles, I took solace in knowing it would have little to do with that unearthly place.

CHAPTER 4

∴

I THEN INTERVIEWED THE STAFF OF THE OLD TOWN tower, the maids and washerfolk and servants and cooks. Sujedo had come and gone so briefly, however, that most hadn't even seen the man.

"I assisted him to his rooms, sir," said the porter, an elderly man named Hajusa. "He was most kind, and agreeable." An impish glint crept into his eye. "He even gave me a silver talint for my trouble. Not exactly to the rules, however," he said, placing a finger alongside his nose.

I gave him a conspiratorial smile, then asked him to describe Sujedo.

"Oh, he was a handsome man," Hajusa said. "As many from the inner rings are. Thick hair, black and curling. Pale eyes. He was rather short, however. I'm not as tall as I used to be, but I was still taller than he . . ."

"Did you see anyone else coming or going from the building that night? Anyone at all?"

"Only servants, sir, and no one untoward. This is the finest building in all of Old Town. Used to be the palace of the king, in the ages before the Empire." He attempted a haughty pose. "We hold ourselves to a high standard here."

"Do you know what business he was coming here for?"

"Oh . . . well, I assumed it was the adoption of the realm," he said uncertainly. "Making Yarrow a proper imperial state, I mean."

His face was guarded now, and his eyes no longer met my own.

"How do you feel about that?" I asked. "You can speak honestly. I know little of it."

"Well. I . . . suppose it's always been coming. All that was decided decades ago, by kings who were long dead before I was born." He attempted a deferential smile. "But it's not my place to speak on the stuff of kings, of course."

I glanced at Malo, who shrugged and extended a hand—*What else did you expect?*

I thanked him and moved on.

NEXT WE SPOKE to the maids, who were both of Pithian or Yarrow stock, with eyes as green as Malo's and a greenish hue to their gums.

"He was polite, sir," said one woman. "Quiet, sir. Didn't talk much at all, sir."

"Very neat," said the other. "Very spare. And very sick. Hadn't touched a drop of his broth when I went to collect it."

They nodded one after the other, again and again, their cadence so regular I was reminded of a child's wooden toy dancing at the plucking of its strings.

"What time did you go to collect it?" I asked.

"Oh . . . evening, or thereabout," said the second woman. "After dinner. It was dark out. The gentleman was lying on the bed, eyes closed, breathing hard. I left in a hurry, worried whatever he had might be catching. He did not seem well . . . His hand twitched, I recall, his fingers flitting against his belly."

"His hands shook?" I asked.

"Just the one hand, yes," said the first maid. "Like a palsy, almost. Beating against his belly. Like my mam had, before she faded and perished."

"And the windows," I said. "Were they open then, or closed?"

The maids thought about it.

"Closed," one said finally.

"Yes, closed," said the other. "And locked. I remember he had the lamp on, on his table, for it was very dark by then. We left him, and then in the morning . . . well, the gentleman had disappeared, leaving nothing but blood and savagery behind!"

"And no one heard anything?" I asked.

"Nothing!" she said.

"It was as if a spirit had whisked him away," said the first. "Stolen out of his bed, like a sea spirit snatching up children from the old tales." She paused. "You don't think that's what it *was*, do you, sir?"

I paused, surprised to be asked if a specter from a folktale might be our culprit. "In my experience, ma'am, regular people are more than dangerous enough."

"You think it's mad, for us to talk of spirits," said the second maid archly. "But given what they do with the Shroud out there in the bay . . . perhaps the ghosts of those things linger, and hate us, for all we make from their flesh."

"What about this bit of iron?" I asked, holding it up. "Did he have this?"

They peered at it and shook their heads.

"Never seen that before," said one.

"Not once," said the other.

I pressed them more, until Malo began yawning where she leaned in the corner. I let them go.

LAST WAS THE GUARD who had accompanied Sujedo through the city, an Apoth militis named Klaida.

"It was a very common day, sir," he told me. "The immunis came. Moved in. Then I took him to the bank and waited outside the vault, for I'm not allowed in."

"How long did you wait?" I asked.

"Oh, less than a few minutes, sir. I believe he was just making a deposit at the vaults. He had a bag with him, of about this size." He gestured with his hands: about two span wide and tall, and a half span thick.

"Big enough for more than documents, then?"

"Yes, sir. He had something inside and left it there. The Treasury clerk there can tell you more—his eyes fluttered just as yours do, sir."

I perked up at that. "He was an engraver?"

"Yes, sir. Likely has to be, to remember all who come and go to the bank. Immunis Sujedo then came out, I took him back to his rooms here, and that was that."

"He didn't mention what he put in the bank, I assume?"

"No, sir."

"Did he talk at all?"

Klaida thought about it. "He asked me about my wife, sir. I remember that."

"Your wife? What did he ask?"

"Just how she was faring. I thought it an odd comment, given that I hadn't told him about her at all—nor that our wedding had been only two weeks ago. But the immunis pointed out that I had my ring on my thumb, and I kept touching it like I wasn't used to it, so it must be new, he guessed. It seemed a clever thing, to know so much from just a glance. I supposed it was just something Sublimes like you, ah, could do, sir."

I frowned. While nearly all Imperial Sublimes exhibited some unusual behaviors—myself included—axioms were not known for their social competence. Usually, the more they worked with more abstract numbers, the more aloof they grew.

I asked about the plug of iron. Like the others, he did not know of it.

"Did he show any symptoms besides his claims of stomach pain?" I asked. "Perhaps a palsy or tremor to his hands?"

"Palsy . . . no," said Klaida, thinking. "But . . . he did tap against his leg, over and over again, as he walked. Like drumming. Like he had a tune in his head and couldn't help but beat its rhythm against something. It was a little strange, sir. Does it mean anything, sir?"

I sighed and thanked him for his time.

FOR MY FINAL task I reviewed the vacant room beside Sujedo's. I had old Hajusa unlock it for me, though he paused as he opened it.

"We've not had many people stay in this chamber for some time, mind, sir. The room is quite wet. The way the tower leans, you see, all the water tends to gather here . . . In fact, all the rooms on this side are tricky to maintain."

He opened the door and I peered within. It was almost an exact copy of Sujedo's room, but every surface was overgrown with curling mold. The bed was bare wood with no moss mattress, and it, too, had been devoured by greenery. Even the closet was furred over with growth.

I looked to Malo, who stood at the door. "Smell anything unusual here?" I asked.

"Am I to be your hound?" she said. "But—no. Nothing but mold. It is the same as all the other molding rooms on this side of the building. We searched those when we first looked for Sujedo. There was nothing."

I thanked Hajusa, he locked the room back up, and we departed.

CHAPTER 5

∧ ∧ ∧

IT WAS LATE AFTERNOON WHEN WE FINISHED UP AT Sujedo's lodgings—too late for us to venture to the Treasury bank and interview the clerks there—so Malo and I began the long return to New Town.

"So?" asked Malo. "Have you dug out some clue or hint that I have missed?"

"I've hardly been here a day," I said.

"Then that is a no. How kind you are, to allow me my pride." She cocked her head, listening. "But let us dine, then. For I've had no food all day, and I can hear your stomach rumbling even now."

I paused, feeling faintly violated. "You can?"

"Yes. You need broth. Otherwise you shall be of no use to me tomorrow."

We turned onto the main street to New Town. Yet just as I was beginning to find the idea of a bowl of soup appealing, we heard a high voice behind us: "Ah—Signum Kol? Signum Dinios Kol?"

We stopped and turned. A short woman in an elegant but simple gray dress was wandering down a lane after us, hand raised. Again, she called out my name, her voice high and tremulous, like a distressed person seeking help.

I studied her, perplexed. As far as I was aware, there was no one in Yarrowdale who should know me, nor indeed know that I was here, save for my commanding officer and Malo.

I looked to Malo, who merely shrugged. "*I* don't know her," she said. "Do you?"

"Not at all," I said.

We watched as the woman approached. I thought I saw something to her eye—a sharpness, perhaps—that gave me pause. "Yes?" I said as she came before me. "Can I help you?"

She smiled broadly and bowed, panting. A leather satchel hung from her neck, with many small rolls of parchment carefully sealed with wax within. "I'm so glad I caught up to you, sir," she said breathlessly. "And I thank you for stopping. I am Sorgis Poskit, with the Usini Lending Group."

Again, I glanced at Malo, who looked as baffled as I.

"All right?" I said.

The woman smiled again, seemingly deaf to my confusion. "You may be more familiar with one of our ancillary offices, Signum Kol," she said. "Specifically, the *Sapirdadi Creditor's Body*?"

My breath went cold in my lungs. I fought to keep my face even.

"Oh," I muttered. "I had not expected to . . . to find you here in Yarrowdale."

"The Usini Lending Group has offices all throughout the Empire, sir," she said sweetly, bowing again. "As you are a client of ours, I was wondering if I could perhaps have a word with you."

I WALKED WITH the woman a far ways, mindful of Malo's keen ears. Then I turned, looked her over, and tersely said, "I apologize, ma'am, but I was not aware any civilians were knowledgeable about my duties in Yarrowdale. Especially given the importance of my work here."

"The Usini Lending Group manages much credit within the Iyalets," Poskit said, still in that saccharine tone. "It is our prerogative to maintain awareness of where our clients are stationed at any given moment."

Of course, I thought. The one institution that was more capable than the Iyalets themselves, naturally, were the Empire's money-lenders.

Still trying to maintain some level of haughtiness, I said, "Even those of Special Division?"

"Oh, *especially* those of Special Division, Signum Kol." Something glittered dangerously in her gaze. "Given the type of work they do, that is. I wished to discuss the terms of your father's final line of credit with you."

"Why?" I demanded. "I thought the situation simple. He got sick, took out an enormous loan to pay his medikker's fees, then died. I have been punctually paying down that loan ever since—correct?"

"You have been doing so under the *conventional* terms, yes, Signum Kol." Madam Poskit's smile became positively treacly. "But now you have been posted here, to Yarrowdale, which is not yet formally part of the Empire—and is, as I am sure you are aware, exceedingly dangerous."

I realized what she meant. "You're going to demand a higher loan payment of me," I said, "because I've been posted to a place where I might *die* before I can pay you off?"

"I do not *demand* anything, sir," Poskit said, feigning outrage. "It is simply part of your liability allowance! One your father agreed to, if you recall."

"My *late* father," I said heatedly.

A tiny, sympathetic pout. "As you say, yes. Very sad. We also have not yet taken into account the manner of your new assignment, Signum Kol. The Empire's Special Divisions often experience high changeovers in personnel, you see. So many are dismissed because of their inability to keep up with their demanding duties. Or the officers quit out of stress, or they fall victim to . . . other circumstances."

"You mean they get killed," I snapped, "in service to the Empire."

"Oh, I cannot say, sir!" Poskit said. "I simply observe the actuarial reports. Thus, I wished to inform you that these two liability allow-ances have been applied, and your line of credit is now subject to a new payment scheme." She produced a tight roll of parchment and handed it to me. "The details are there, along with information regarding the first required payment." A flash of her treacly smile, and she bowed. "I apologize for interrupting you, Signum Kol. I would not wish you to pay any penalties in your labors for this! Good day." With that, she turned and strutted away.

I watched Poskit go, stunned. I looked down at the roll of parchment in my hand, my blood burning in my veins.

No. No, I would not look at it. Not now, anyway.

I stuffed it in my pocket and rejoined Malo at the corner. I found her leaning up against a fretvine wall and idly staring out at sea.

"Who was that?" she asked.

"Nobody important," I muttered.

"Didn't look like nobody important."

"Can we keep going, please?" I asked. "I am quite hungry."

She bowed. "Of course."

MY FATHER HAD BEEN, in his own way, a man of some talent. He had been talented at being born to a moderately prosperous family in the Outer Rim; talented at fathering children on my mother, to the point that it eventually killed her; and, last but not least, talented at choosing the worst possible investments and political interests to give his money to, eventually achieving total bankruptcy.

This was why I had become a Sublime in the first place and labored as an engraver for the Iudex: the Empire paid well for such servants, granting generous dispensations and eventual lands in exchange for the penalties to our well-being. By bearing witness to corpses and killers—and indeed, becoming a killer myself—I had intended to pay off my father's enormous debts and eventually earn enough to move him, my grandmother, and my sisters out of the dangerous Outer Rim and into the third ring, behind the safety of imperial walls.

But then the man had sickened and died, yet not before he incurred more debts made under even more odious terms. This meant that even though I now had an imperial position that paid quite well, I was still nearly as impoverished as I had been when I first applied to become an engraver.

Yet even more galling than my own destitution was what this had done to my future: though I considered myself a reasonably skilled Iudex investigator, I secretly dreamed of serving in another Iyalet, in another service, in a canton far from here.

As I trudged through the streets of Yarrowdale, my heart felt shadowed. If my father's new debts were to follow me about the Empire like a ghostly lamia from the children's tales, then my dream of a new service would remain just that: a dream, and nothing more.

CHAPTER 6

∧ ∧ ∧

MALO AND I DECAMPED TO A DINGY TAVERN CLOSE TO my own rooms in New Town for dinner, a map of the canals laid out on our crooked, damp tabletop.

"Sujedo disappeared here," I said as I touched the area in Old Town. I squinted in the dim tavern light, then drew a line southwest to the canals. "And then, a week later, he was found here . . . twelve leagues away."

"Far too far to carry a body, as I have said," Malo said around a mouthful of scallops.

"Is there anything unique about where they found him?"

"The spot is close to one of the smugglers' camps. Here." She drained her cup of sotwine and pointed to one stretch of canal. "The smugglers constantly move about in the jungles to the west there, and we wardens raid them all the time, recovering stolen reagents. At first I assumed they were the culprits, but this did not fit at all."

I took a delicate sip of broth, hoping it would calm my still-mutinous stomach. "How long's all this smuggling gone on?"

"Decades. Since the Empire set up their Apoth works here. People pay a lot of money for reagents, and grafts and cures. Calcious grafts for broken bones, warding grafts for immunities . . . If you can survive stealing it from an Apoth storehouse or barge—and if you can get to the River Asigis to the west and sell it to the bargefolk there—you can be rich."

"Do these smugglers ever kill?"

"They did not use to," she said. "But it has gotten much worse in the past two years. Sometimes a barge disappears, and we never find the crew. Sometimes they shower the Engineers and their beasts of burden with arrows, then snatch up cargo in the chaos. We are no less merciless, however."

I studied her face and did not doubt it.

"Why hasn't the Empire ever taken care of it?" I asked.

"For one thing, Yarrow isn't the Empire," she said dourly. "Or not yet. Though the Treasury delegation was working to change that. But until that time, King Lalaca is still technically the ruler of this realm. That makes enforcing imperial rules harder."

I lifted the bowl to my lips, rethought it, and put it back down. "But there's more."

"Yes. For a lot of smugglers are Pithian and Yarrow folk." A cold smile. "Like me. And like me, they know the jungle and the waters. That is why so many wardens are of Yarrow stock. Who else could hunt them?"

"How do you feel about that?"

"About what?"

"Any of it. About the Empire taking over Yarrow. It's been in the works for almost a century, yes?"

"I think what most Yarrow folk do," she said simply. "I think it was the king's agreement, made with the Empire for the king's lands long ago."

"Are they not your lands, too?"

A trim smile. "Spoken like one who has never known a king."

ANOTHER MAP, another near-nameless stretch of jungle. Malo popped her last scallop into her mouth and surveyed me skeptically. "So. You are . . . Special Division? What is that, exactly?"

I grimaced, recalling my unpleasant discussion with Madam Poskit. "Every Iyalet has a small set of floating officers. Personnel sent to handle complex or unusual situations. Engineers, Apoths,

Legion—and Iudex. This death was deemed unusual. Thus, here I am . . ." I attempted another meager sip of broth. ". . . in all my glory."

She rubbed the rim of her bowl with one mud-stained finger, then sucked the oil off it. "If you can find how a dead man can pass through walls, I shall call you glorious indeed."

"Let's hope. Please be at my lodgings at sunrise, Malo. Then we shall see what task my commanding officer will put us to. Though I suspect she'll send us to the Treasury bank."

"Will she be able to make sense of any of this?" asked Malo.

I finished my cup of weak sotwine and gave it thought. "In all honesty," I said, "there's a very good chance she'll have it sorted by nightfall."

Malo stared at me. "What?"

I shrugged.

"You speak honestly?" she said.

"Yes. I give it . . . oh, six out of ten odds that she'll know the solution by at least tomorrow morning. Maybe seven."

"If it takes so little for her to comprehend it, why come here at all? Why not send a letter?"

I thought about it. "Probably to try new food. Or maybe just to punish me."

CHAPTER 7

∆ ∆ ∆

MY LODGINGS WERE LOCATED IN THE MIDDLE OF NEW Town, set among the many Iyalet offices managing the many imperial works in Yarrowdale. It was one of the more modest buildings, but pleasant enough, yet as I approached, I noticed the porter boy standing outside, pacing and fretting in the lane.

When he spied me he scurried over, his face flushed. "Signum!" he called. "Signum, sir, are . . . are you Iudex? Can you help me, please, sir?"

"Perhaps?" I said, perplexed. "What's this about?"

"It's, ah, the other Iudex officer, sir."

Instantly, my heart sank. "Oh. What's she done?"

"She's on the patio, you see, and the . . . the smell, sir. She's eating, but . . . but the *smell* of it, it's awful, and I don't know what to do!"

I sighed. "Please lead the way."

I followed the porter around the side of the building. The wind rose ever so slightly, and I caught the powerful, noxious aroma of rotting sea life. We rounded the edge, and I came to a stop.

A flagstone patio was laid out on the hill, overlooking the bay, complete with wicker chairs and table. It must have been a merry sight once, but no longer, for it had been turned into a graveyard of oyster shells.

Nearly half of the patio was obscured by piles of glistening carapace and crust and nacre, the pools of the oysters' cloudy liquor baking in the waning afternoon sun. I could hardly begin to count them;

they had to be from several hundreds of oysters, at least. The heaps of shells rose gently to curl about the tea table in the center of the patio, almost like an embankment, and it was there, beside a soaking sack of unshucked shellfish, that my commanding officer Immunis Ana Dolabra sat hunched, plying another mollusk with a dull knife.

"They're all starting to turn," whined the porter beside me. "We've already had complaints from the officers in the other quarters! The patio shall reek for days if we don't clear it up soon, but she won't stop or move elsewhere, and the things she has said to me, sir . . ."

I watched as Ana pried open the shell, freed the flesh from within, tipped it into her mouth with a slurp, and tossed the shell over her shoulder. Though my stomach had mostly recovered, this sight—along with the aroma of such fetid sea life—set it rumbling again.

Ana's pale head shot up. She sniffed, then slowly turned to face me—though she could not see me, for her eyes were bound up in a thick red blindfold. As usual.

"Din!" she said merrily. "You're back!"

"I am, ma'am," I sighed. I dismissed the boy, then stepped about the heaps of shells, my boots crunching on the flagstones, until I came to stand behind her. "But, ma'am, the proprietors have asked me t—"

She raised a finger. "First! Tell me, Din—how far a trek is it down to the sea?"

I eyed the coastline. "A few leagues. Maybe less. But wh—"

"I have a request," she said. "I would like to see if you could go down to the waters there, preferably to a spot far from seaweed, and fetch me a pail of seawater." She grinned so wide the corners of her mouth almost touched her ears. "I'm tasting the city, you see. The region. The *seas*."

I scratched my eyebrow with a thumbnail, awaiting the rest of it. "Are you, ma'am."

"Oh, yes. The oysters absorb what's about them as they grow, you know. I can taste where they're *from*." She wielded the dull little knife with all the deftness of a midnight murderer and popped open another shell with a wet click, the liquor running down her fingers. "All it needs is a little salt. If you were to take a pail of seawater and slowly boil it, we would be left with the purest sea salt. And what a thing it would be, to taste the flesh of the sea itself, seasoned with its own salt! It's too poetic for us *not* to. Yes?"

"I did not think your appetite for oysters was so tremendous, ma'am."

"Oh, I'm not actually hungry, Din. Really, it's that each oyster is *different.* You can taste in each one which reef they came from, which side they grew upon, which waters they flourished within. They are like melodies of the ocean itself rendered in flesh." She tilted her right ear to the coast. "Just listen to it. I've never been so close to the sea . . . All about me the world is bright with patterns. I can hear the heartbeat of the ocean in the wax and wane of the waves. I can feel the wind unspooling from its wild tangles out over the waters. And now I taste those waters, and all that dwelt in them." She grinned savagely as she pried the lump of gray flesh from the bottom of the shell. "I wonder . . . is this the closest I'll come to tasting a leviathan's flesh? Did these oysters absorb a hint of their essence?" She noisily sucked it back. "For I've heard whispers that *some* parts of the titans are edible, if properly bled . . ."

I grimaced. Though I did not know the manner of Ana's cognitive alterations—and indeed, she'd always been irritatingly coy about what they were—she'd always shown a predilection for pattern spotting that far surpassed obsession. From ancient history to masonry to the speckling of colors in the human eye—and now, apparently, oysters—Ana was perpetually hungry for new, obscure information to dissect and analyze, so much so that she often went about blindfolded, claiming that to perceive too much of the world made it difficult to focus on what she found interesting.

"Would you be ready for my reports of the day, ma'am?" I asked loudly.

She flicked the spent oyster shell away, and it went clattering over the heaps. "My, my. You seem impatient. Has your day not proceeded well?"

I grimaced as I thought of the little roll of parchment in my pocket.

It felt like I was carrying around a bombard charge with a lit fuse. "No," I said. "It has not."

"You mean you did not relish the experience of sailing upriver for six days through rough weather," she said, grinning, "all to come here and peer at clammy corpses? Our home is wherever the dead are found in difficult or delicate circumstances, Din. You should feel quite at ease here! Tell me—what is the situation? Shall our predicament be difficult, or delicate?"

"I'd say both, ma'am," I said. "But at the moment, it seems more difficult than delicate."

Her brow furrowed. "Truly? I didn't read the wrong orders, did I? It's the *Treasury* man, yes? Found dead in a canal?"

"That is only somewhat correct, ma'am. But yes."

Her brow's furrows grew until they became small hills. "I would have thought this would be simply a *delicate* case, given that it's a Treasury man dead. Yet you say the death is also *difficult*? Do you not have any concept of how it was done?"

"None," I said. "The man apparently vanished from his rooms. There is no motive, nor culprit, nor anything of use. Just a bloodstain in a bed, and little more."

She nodded, head cocked. "Hum! Well. Perhaps this *is* a good one. How exciting." She wiped her mouth on the back of her sleeve and stood. "You know, you are not a stupid person, Din."

"Thank you, ma'am," I said, pleased.

"Or, rather, not an *unusually* stupid person."

"Thank you, ma'am," I said, far less pleased.

"You often quickly catch a whiff of what's going on, even if you don't yet have the full picture. It's only when you're really very befuddled that I know the work might offer some mild entertainment." She stuck her arm out. "Come! Take me back to my rooms and let us discuss this. And bribe that irritating little porter child however much it takes to have him clean all this shit up."

———

I LED ANA back to her rooms, which were arranged as she always preferred: all windows tightly shut, her bed in the far corner, her countless books stacked beside it, her musical instruments laid against the wall—she was favoring a Pithian lyre during this trip— and a tea set and iron stove dominating the center of the chamber.

I shut the door behind her. She removed her red blindfold, blinked her wide, wild yellow eyes, and pushed back her bone-white forelock as she looked around. "This room is a little *too* big, Din," she said. "It shall take me time to grow acclimated."

"Would you like me to cover the windows with rugs, ma'am? That could block out more light."

"No, no. The light isn't the issue, but the size . . . Too much for me to look at. But I shall manage." She paced a wobbly circle and waved to the teapot. "I asked the porter to procure me the roots of some Yarrow sprinklefoot—I'm told the leaves add an interesting aroma to the tea. Might you oblige me a cup? You can brief me on our intriguing pile of human parts as you do so."

I slid the appropriate vial from my engraver's satchel, sniffed at the fragrance of nectar, and began speaking as I went about brewing her a pot of tea, my eyes shivering as I regurgitated every aspect of everything I'd seen that day. Ana listened, blindfolded again to focus, yet she sat not on a chair or on her bed but sprawled on her side on the floor, one long, pale digit tracing the curl of the fretvine surface: a curiously girlish pose, despite her somewhat older age.

It was very late when I finished my report. I could glimpse the pale moon peeking through the gaps in the windows, and the sounds of the port had died away, drowned in the rumble of the seas. I had to flick the mai-lantern in the corner to awaken the grubs within and set them glowing, and soon a soft blue light filled the room.

Ana sat still for a long while, the now-cool cup of tea clutched in her hand. Then she began rocking back and forth: a telltale tic that she was thinking hard.

"I begrudgingly admit," she finally proclaimed, "this murder is more promising than the last couple we've dealt with."

"Then you *do* think this was murder here in Yarrow, ma'am?"

"Oh, certainly," she said. She turned over to lie on her back. "It is most definitely murder. Our dear dismembered Sujedo did not have a fit of the heart, tumble into the tides, and get eaten by wandering turtles. I think he was killed, and I think the manner in which it was done tells us a great deal."

Ana tossed back the tea, then threw the cup aside and held her hands up, fingers splayed, like a troubadour about to begin a tale-telling. "Imagine it! Imagine Sujedo seated on a canal barge, floating upriver. An arrow from the brush would have been quick, grisly, and—apparently!—not uncommon for this place. Or as he disembarked from the barge and made his way into town—someone could have bumped into him and put a blade in between his ribs while no one saw. That would have been easy, too. Or, as I think you know well, perhaps one could serve the man a slice of dried fish, laced with poison undetectable through the powerful flavor of the aged meat . . ."

I glared at her. "Your point is taken," I said. "Death would be an easy thing to deliver in a place like this—is that it?"

"Of course. If the point of all this was the man's assassination, there would be simpler ways of getting it done! Methods that would have assured his death and still offered safety to the murderer. So—why choose this?" She rubbed her hands together like she was about to tuck into a meal. "I feel akin to the disappointed maiden during her first night in the marital bed—the more I pull at what I find, the more I find to my liking! Let us begin, then."

ANA THEN ASKED me many questions. What had been the skin color of the remains? What had been the length and girth of the fingers on the severed hand? How big had the shoulder been? And the jaw? Since I had memorized the sights in the ossuary, I was able to show her the exact size of all I had witnessed, gesturing with my hands as she allowed the barest slice of her yellow eye to peep at me under her blindfold.

She moved on to my trip into Old Town. Had anyone reported seeing anything unusual about Sujedo's gait, or any other physical affectation? What was the color of the mold growing in the vacant room beside Sujedo's? And what buildings had been around the tower from which he'd vanished?

I answered these to the best of my ability. When I finished, Ana simply sat there, sipping her tea and thinking, one long, white finger still following the threading of the fretvine floor. "So . . ." she said. "The shoulder had a patch of skin removed. Deliberately."

"Think so, ma'am. It was a very circular shape."

"But the Apoths can't tell us what it was."

"No, ma'am. They seemed to find nothing unusual about it."

"Interesting . . . And they found Sujedo's piss and blood—but nothing of any intruder?"

"No, ma'am."

"Yet the man's clothes had a *citrus* smell, you say?"

"They did. Signum Malo assumed that was done to cover up the sce—"

"Quiet," she snapped. "I am thinking! Hm. You say Sujedo also tapped his leg as he went about his business . . . And he asked the guard about the man's *wedding*, you say? Despite being an axiom?"

"Yes. I thought that very odd, too."

"Being as axioms are usually as socially cognizant as a wet fucking brick, yes," she said. "It is quite damned odd."

I pursed my lips, for Ana's own grasp of social decorum was often nonexistent, but refrained from comment.

"I've no idea what to make of the tapping bit," Ana continued. "Unless the man had some kind of affliction. But one last question, Din, to help me build the scene in my mind . . . The porter said *all* the rooms on the leaning side of the tower were difficult to maintain. Yes?"

"Yes, ma'am?"

"Then," she said softly, "would that mean there is likely a vacant room *below* the one you saw, as well?"

"Ah . . . that is likely, ma'am. But I confess, I did not ask to see it."

"No matter," she murmured. "Malo told you she and the other wardens had searched all the rooms and found nothing. It can wait.

Now. You couldn't talk to the rest of the Treasury delegation—correct?"

"Correct, ma'am. They were busy with the king of Yarrow, as Signum Malo told me."

"So you do not know anything of the dead man's history or personal nature."

"Only what the Treasury has already shared."

"And there is no information," she asked, "suggesting that Sujedo met with any of his colleagues on his brief day in Yarrowdale?"

"No, ma'am. He was ill and did not have business with them until the next day."

"But isn't that also very strange?" she asked softly. "His colleagues were housed directly next door. Even if he was ill, there seems to have been ample time for them to talk to him, or he to they . . ."

"Don't know, ma'am. Some did worry what he had was catching."

Ana sat very still, the fronds of her alabaster hair trembling as a draft rushed through the room. "We shall have to interview his colleagues, then, and soon. Though interviewing the delegation might be tricky, apparently."

"Yes. This business with the king of Yarrow . . ."

In an instant, she shed her air of dreamy reflection, and her face twisted into an expression of poisonous condescension. "Business!" she scoffed, and ripped the blindfold from her head. "Business, yes! But business long done! That pot of shit soup has been bubbling for years now . . . What *do* you know about all that fucking nonsense, Din?"

I hesitated, unsure what she wished me to say. "I know Yarrow is a tribute state, ma'am—one the Empire both does and does *not* quite run."

"And?"

"And . . . that puts us in a spot, for it produces the most valuable reagents in all the Empire."

"Quite correct! Squeezed from dead leviathans out in the bay like juice from an aplilot, then rendered in countless Apoth facilities on the shores. A very tricky, very ghastly, very deadly business." She cocked her head. "Ah! I meant to ask—I assume you have seen it, Din?"

"Seen . . . ?"

"The *Shroud*, of course! You have seen it out in the waters?"

"Yes, ma'am."

"Describe it for me, please. I am most eager to hear of it."

I reluctantly did so, describing the great, green, fluttering form floating out in the bay, and the hint of a citadel hidden in its depths, though as I spoke the entire thing began to feel less like a structure and more like some great parasite, attached to the horizon and bleeding the whole of the world.

"How fascinating," Ana whispered when I finished. "A design both amazing and horrid—but it is also invaluable, as it gives us the alterations we need to keep the leviathans back each wet season." She sprawled out on the floor again. "Allow me to enlighten you on the situation, Dinios. For history, as always, has predetermined much of the circumstances here."

I sighed, nodded, but said nothing. When Ana talked history, asking questions simply made things last longer.

"THE TRUTH IS that we are all here, Din," Ana began, "*all* of us—including the extremely dead Sujedo—because of a quirk of *geography*. The currents of the Eastern Seas, you see, render it impossible for our ships to haul dead leviathans southward. And to the north, the Spine of Sarisav makes accessing the deltas of the Great River Asigis with such a burden impossible. So, just over ninety-two years ago, the emperor began looking about for a new port city on the eastern coast . . . and decided there was only one option—the Bay of Yarrow, tucked away in the Pithian Hills. At the time, it was a crude backwater, run by petty, vicious tyrants calling themselves kings. And when the Empire came parading in, and the emperor's mighty agents requested to palaver with the king of Yarrow, well . . . the king, along with everyone else in the Empire, likely thought them mad.

"The Empire negotiated for peaceful imperial rights within Yarrowdale," she continued. "The right to build, the right to conduct trade. The king of Yarrow demanded a huge ransom, and got it— though he also agreed that in one hundred years, the region would come *directly* under the rule of the Empire and become a formal canton. Perhaps it seemed an easy deal at the time. The king did not wish to fight the Empire, and one hundred years probably felt like an eternity to folk leading such short, brutal lives." She grinned savagely. "And he was *lucky*, of course. If it had been the early days of the First or Second Empire, when the race of the grand Khanum was strong and populous, they'd have simply marched in and torn him and his forces to pieces!"

My skin crawled, but I said nothing.

"Yet then," said Ana, "neither the king of Yarrow nor anyone else predicted what the Empire would do over the next decades . . . For then we brought the Engineers, and the slothiks, their great beasts of burden. And we carved tunnels and channels through the Pithian Hills . . . until we made the Great Canals, connecting the Bay of Yarrow to the Great River Asigis, thus tapping all the wealthy markets of the inner Empire."

"Ah. So then the deal didn't look nearly as good?" I asked.

"Oh, it got even *worse*. For back in those days, no one dreamed that the Empire would eventually slaughter leviathans so efficiently. Yet once we learned those arts and developed a way to render miracles from the titans' flesh, the Bay of Yarrow became the natural home for such works."

"The Shroud," I said quietly.

"Exactly. Now the value of the city is *astronomical*. And in less than a decade it shall all be transferred over to the Empire itself! And the king, well . . . he would *very* much like to back out of the deal his great-great-grandfather made. He wishes to extort more money, more resources, more agreements from the Empire. Which means every day is a fucking temper tantrum with him! Goddamn autocrats. They really are hardly better than shit-stained children."

"But can't the Empire simply take the realm whenever we wish? Could the Yarrow king really be a threat?"

"On the field of battle? Not at all. But the Yarrow king still commands the loyalty of his landowners in the west, which gives him some strength of arms—and their forces would assuredly *not* fight a pitched battle! They know the terrain, the jungles, the rivers. And worse, we have many grand and delicate things to defend here. The Apoth works, the Shroud, the canals . . . We spend piles of treasure and blood every year just *maintaining* them, so that they in turn maintain the Empire. It chills the heart to imagine what would happen if any of this was exposed to combat!"

"So the murder of Sujedo . . ."

"Yes, the abduction and murder of a Treasury negotiator sent here to make sure the damned deal is proceeding as planned *is* rather alarming. Is this some ploy of the king's? If so, why target Sujedo? What would his death accomplish? We do not know. Thus, we must proceed delicately—but quickly."

"DO YOU HAVE any ideas how it was done, then, ma'am?" I asked. "Or who is behind it?"

"For the latter, no," Ana said, tilting her head. "But for the former—somewhat! To begin with . . . that piece of iron you found, Din. Do you still have it?"

I took it from my pocket and held it out to her. She removed her blindfold and snatched the piece from me, turning it over in her hands, and even sniffed it.

"No one spotted Sujedo with it," I said. "And no one knows where it came from. It seems to be nothing so far."

"Hmm," she said softly. She held it up close to her eye, then turned to her iron stove, muttering, "Let us see, then . . ."

She flicked the plug of metal at her stove. With a loud clang, it struck the side of the stove—and, for a fleeting moment, it stuck fast.

I stared, mouth agape. Then the piece of metal slid down the side of the stove—very slowly, in a strange, stuttering, scraping movement—before finally clattering to the floor.

"What . . ." I said faintly. "How did it . . ."

"It is lodestone," she said. She bound her hand up in the folds of her dress and picked up the iron, for it was now hot from the stove. "Or it was *made* to be lodestone. Though it has lost some of its strength."

My eyes fluttered as I searched my memory, summoning information. "The rock that sticks to metal?"

"Certain metals, yes. But if you rub a piece of those certain metals upon true lodestone for long enough, the metals shall eventually gain some lodestone properties. This piece of iron was made to be lodestone, but it has lost much of its power . . . But not all." She turned to me, grinning. "And *what* were the locks of Sujedo's windows made from, Din?"

"Iron, ma'am. Is . . . is that how the murderer got into the rooms? They climbed to the very top of the tower, and used lodestone to undo the locks from the outside to get in?"

"I don't think it's as simple as that. For Malo spoke truth to you today—we are beset by impossibilities. How was no person found within that room? And how was his body found so far away days later? We reconcile these impossibilities, and we are left with the answer."

"And . . . what might the answer be, ma'am?"

"The answer, Din," she said, "lies in asking the right *questions*. We should not be asking 'How did the killer get into and out of those rooms?' but rather . . . which rooms was Mineti Sujedo in, and when, if any at all?" She grinned widely. "Tomorrow, go to the Treasury bank and interview the engraver there about Sujedo's visit. But I really want *practical* things from them—Sujedo's girth, his gait, his height. Make the engraver *show* you. Make him point on your shoulder . . ." She stabbed her own scrawny deltoid with a narrow digit. ". . . to show how tall the man was, for example. Am I clear?"

"Yes, ma'am."

"But before you go to the bank, best send a message to the Treasury delegation and schedule a meeting with them at their lodgings in Old Town. The man you wish to get hold of is Prificto Kardas. He is the one running that operation. I wish to talk to him personally. You shall likely have to catch him quick before the goddamned king and his people gobble up all their goddamn time. Got it?"

I sighed deeply as I added this to my list of tasks. "Yes, ma'am."

Ana inspected me closely. "Hm," she said slowly. "How else was your day, Din?"

I hesitated, for she did not usually ask such plainly personal questions. "I had thought I had described almost all of it, ma'am."

"Yes, but you said nothing of your *emotional* well-being, Din. This is our fifth investigation in but a year and a half. We are chewing through the stack at quite a clip! Yet I know not all souls fit easily to such labors."

I suppressed a sigh of relief, for I'd almost thought she'd known of my new money issues. "I am well-accustomed to how this works now, I think, ma'am," I said.

"Oh, are you? And how shall it go?"

"Well, first there is the pleasant puzzle, yes?" I said. "The how, and the who. Then all the dirty drudgery, wherein I follow folk about or dig through their refuse. And then, inevitably, either a rope or the slam of an iron door, and tears."

She cackled evilly. "Ah, child . . . If this one is as simple as that, I shall be overjoyed! It already has a rotten scent to it. Still—is this work not as *glamorous* as you wished, Din? Did you think the life of a civil servant was going to be a grand and theatrical role?"

"As long as it pays, ma'am, I shall serve whatever role you desire."

"What a mercenary statement!" she said. "I'm surprised at your cynicism, Din, given your valiance in Talagray. I am tempted to ascribe it to your illness." She looked me over. "You are pale. And need rest. But before you retire, go and check the post for me, please. I suspect I'll have a few letters that have been sent ahead."

"It's well past sundown, ma'am," I said. "Are you sure the post station will be open?"

"This is Yarrowdale, child," she said. "Home of the *Shroud.* They receive and send orders all day and all night here. Go and get my post, and then you may rest."

I bowed. "Of course, ma'am."

"Note that I said *rest,* Din!" she called as I retreated. "And nothing *else!*"

I shut the door.

CHAPTER 8

▲ ▲ ▲

ANA PROVED TO BE RIGHT: AS I WALKED THE SHORT DIS-
tance to the Yarrowdale imperial post station, the city about me was
still thriving and thrumming. The manufactuaries and breweries and
fermentation stills clung close to the canals, each resembling giant
ceramic pots with many little spouts and spigots, each one leaking
threads of silvery steam into the night sky. In the sparkling light of
the mai-lanterns, the sight reminded me of shrines in the third ring,
their cauldrons releasing fumes as worshippers tossed in pellets of
faithwood.

I fetched the post—a small bundle of letters that had been re-
routed from all over the Empire—and trudged back to our lodgings,
a mai-lantern swinging from my hand. I slipped the letters under her
door one by one but paused on the third package of parchments,
which was slender, thick, and utterly black.

A message from Ana's commanding officer, surely. She received
one about every two months. I shuddered and quickly put it under
the door as if the parchment was poisoned. I had only met Ana's commanding officer once, when he had first offered me my position in the
Iudex Special Division, and I fervently wished to avoid meeting him
again. I hardly wanted to even touch the man's writing, if the word
man was even appropriate for a being of that nature.

Once this was done, I tottered into my rooms, shut the door, slid
off my boots, and set my mai-lantern down on the floor. I rubbed my
face, grumbling, and debated the task before me.

You've put this off long enough, I thought. *No more to it, then.*

I slid Madam Poskit's roll of parchment from my pocket, squatted by my lantern, and read it slowly, squinting to make its tiny writing legible to me.

The terms proved even worse than I could've imagined. A full two thirds of my monthly dispensations would now be going to service my father's debts. Most of the remaining third, of course, would be sent home to support my family, which meant I was now living off a scant handful of talints a day.

I crumpled up the parchment and tossed it away. I would have to grow accustomed to eating rice and lentils until this investigation was over; presuming that this was enough to get Madam Poskit to remove me from the burden of her dreadful liability allowances, that is.

I sat in the dark, longing for something good to savor, if only for a moment.

"Fine," I whispered. "Fine, fine."

I went to my bags, opened my satchel, and reached into a tiny compartment in the back. I slid out the slim slip of parchment there, so carefully folded and so carefully stowed away. Then I unfolded it by the mai-lantern with trembling fingers, as if I handled not mere parchment but some holy writ from a sacred tome.

The letters at the top of the parchment did not dance for my accursed eyes, for they were bright and big and black: *TRANSFERRAL PETITION FOR THE IYALET OF THE IMPERIAL LEGION.*

I gazed at the petition and all my answers written below. I had answered it over the course of many nights, meticulously shaping each letter with each agonizing twirl of the ashpen. An imperial officer could petition to be transferred to another Iyalet only after two years of service in their first assignment; in but a few months I could submit this form and leave Ana for the grand ranks of the Legion.

My heart quickened at the thought of it. Though all the Iyalets of the Empire were admired, it was the Legion that held the greatest respect, for it was the Legion that fought back the leviathans each year, holding them at the sea walls, raining fire and death upon them with bombard and ballista. It was they who bore the entirety of the

Empire upon their backs, these noble warriors adorned in black and silver. It was their suffering and toil and service that ensured that our civilization persisted for another season.

Those who donned the sable uniforms saved untold lives every year, whereas I, in the Iudex, merely looked upon the dead, and could do little else.

Yet as my gaze lingered on the parchment in my hands, I knew the time to apply would come and go. The life of a Legionnaire was deadly work, and Madam Poskit's contract would never allow for such a transfer. No matter how much I'd paid already, I would have to stay alive, and keep paying, and keep serving the Iudex: to deal only in the dead, and the small, petty-hearted people who'd killed them for one foul reason or another, while in the East, along the sea walls, the greatest of us fought and died, and gave for their nation.

I folded up the petition, the parchment creasing at its familiar folds and bends, and stowed it away again in my satchel. Then I sat there in the dark.

I thought of my brief service in Talagray, and the Legionnaires I had known there. One soldier burned bright in my mind: Captain Kepheus Strovi, with whom I'd spent only a handful of days, yet in my augmented mind it felt akin to a lifetime.

I placed my hand on my mossbed and let my eyes flutter in my skull. My thoughts sang with the touch of him, the smell of him. The way he slept so restlessly in bed, as if in combat with his pillow; the slow, lazy, confident smile he wore when facing the day. The caress of his hand, the drip of his sweat, the press of his heel in the small of my back.

My eyes stopped fluttering, and I returned to the present. I leaned my head against the corner of the bed. Not for the first time, I wondered: were such eternal memories a blessing, or a plague?

The sea thundered on the shore outside. The smell of salt filled my chamber.

Rest, Ana had told me, *and nothing else.*

I slid my boots back on and left.

———

THE FIRST SOTBAR I found in Yarrowdale that night was of a distinctly Apoth bent: there was one table of crooked-looking young princepii, for example, who eagerly reviewed an array of glass tinctures to augment their evening. Many of the other Apoth militii present were Yarrow, with green eyes and thick beards, quaffing common sot with an enthusiasm that bordered on suicidal.

But I was not here to drink. Even though I ambled up to the bar and purchased a small pot of sot, I had other aims tonight.

I gauged the crowd as I sipped. The men here were not to my liking—the Yarrow boys were too bearded, and the Apoth princepii too reedy—so, a bit downcast, I reviewed the women and found some suitable candidates. A few had already cast eyes at me.

I pinned my hair back, took another sip of sotwine, and went to work.

I moved throughout the crowd in slow, familiar steps as I went about my dance: waiting for the right look, the proper fleeting glance, before approaching with a small smile; then, my eyes fluttering, I'd recall the best greeting, the best clever comment; or the right movements, or the right positioning; or when to look them in the eye, or look away; or when to let my hair fall in my face, and when to pin it back again.

To others, the dance might have seemed artful, yet to me, it was routine. I had memorized this method over the past year as I'd moved from place to place: much like picking a lock, some combination of these gestures and exchanges worked to win the right attentions. Or perhaps that was not quite it: perhaps I was more like a man dabbing bloods and scents upon his flesh as he stood before a darkened wood, waiting for some predator within to pounce on him and spirit him away.

The one who moved most boldly was a Yarrow girl, about my own age, pink-skinned and tall and well-built, with a wild mane of fair, frizzy hair, and green-tinted eyes that were no less wild. Her senses had been augmented like Malo's—there was the telltale purpled flesh about her eyes, nose, and ears, almost as though they'd been painted with purple ink—but I still thought her lovely, or lovely enough. She approached me gladly, the collar of her Apoth uniform unbuttoned and askew, and she gestured to my cup and said in Pithian: *"Ki iha mire lai koi hai?"*

Though I did not speak Pithian, I caught the nature of the comment and bought her a pot of sot.

We talked, somewhat: she spoke very little imperial standard—her speech was almost entirely monosyllabic—and I knew no Pithian at all. But we laughed at each other's outsized gestures as we tried to explain ourselves, and each knew what the other was saying.

Finally she leaned close, her green-stained eyes shining, and she said something in Pithian and cackled.

"Ahh. What was that?" I asked, smiling.

A silver-haired medikker nearby rolled his eyes and said, "She said your face is so pretty, but she is worried it is like a small horse."

"What? She said what now?"

"It is a local expression, and a depraved one at that—she means, she is worried she might crush it while riding it." He shook his head and muttered, "Damned Yarrows . . ."

I turned back to her. She was watching me with a greedy gleam in her eyes.

"Can you take me away from here?" I asked.

She grabbed me by the hand, and we left.

I'D HEARD IT said that engravers are good lovers, for they remember what people want. I'd come to think this true, not just by the responses I'd witnessed when coupling—for such things, as I knew from my own experience, could be faked—but from how often I was invited back. Yet though I was attentive that evening, and grew passionate when I sensed she desired, and ferocious when she asked, I knew these acts were mere labor I paid for the moment after.

Afterward: when all was spent, and the shuddering grew still, and the sweaty limbs atop my own grew cool. Only then I could hold them and make the world small for me.

No more debts or moneylenders. No more bodies and blood. No more trivial little people burdened with hearts both vicious and dull. Only then, perhaps, the absence of Kepheus would burn a little less bright, and all would be small and controllable.

I lay there with my arm cast across her pale breast, my face lost in her auburn hair. I let the silence steal over me like a cloak.

Suffocate me, I told it, *and let me sleep.*

I tried very hard not to listen to the voice in the back of my head: the little one that pointed out that Ana had ordered me specifically *not* to do this; the one that stolidly reminded me that Ana knew that I spent about half my evenings in someone else's bed, and did not appreciate it.

Let me go, let me go, I told the little voice. *I am owed something good, let me go.* Yet now sleep would not come.

I sighed where I lay. Then the girl—I realized I still did not even know her name—stirred and rolled over to look at me.

I cracked an eye. Her grin had returned, as had the wild light to her eyes.

"Is all well?" I asked her warily.

She said something in Pithian—*"Ika hora, dubira, aukiha"*—and reached down and took my wick in her hand and massaged it. When it did not respond quickly enough to her liking, she sat up—still grasping me—gave me an appraising look, and nodded at the door and said the four words again.

I took the meaning immediately: *Another round, or you can go.*

"Ohh," I said, somewhat crestfallen. "Really?"

Her eyes shone yet more brightly, and the cadence of her massage quickened.

I took a breath, estimating how much work I would have to do to earn peace tonight. "Well. If you insist."

CHAPTER 9

▲▲▲

JUST BEFORE DAWN I SLIPPED OUT OF THE GIRL'S HOUSE to return to my own lodgings, exhausted and tottering. A fog was crawling out of the bay, so thick it was hard to see more than fifty span down the road, yet I'd engraved the path in my mind and knew the steps, even if I half-sleepwalked them now.

When I finally approached my lodgings, I heard a voice ring out of the fog: "What have *you* been up to?"

I stopped and spied Signum Tira Malo sitting on the stoop a few span down from my door. She smiled at me, her teeth dark from yet another lump of hina root.

"You've been waiting at my door?" I said, surprised.

"You said sunup," she said, and gestured to the overcast skies. "The sun is almost up. I must say, I was confused to hear no heartbeats within your lodgings, nor the whisper of any breath. But to see you now, and . . ." She sniffed the air as I approached, and grinned. ". . . and to catch the *scent* of you, all is clear."

I scowled at her. "Do you pry in the affairs of all who walk this street?"

"I do no prying! Would you have me stop up my ears and nose to keep your privacy? But do not feel shame, Kol. If anything, I am amazed."

"What?"

"Why, you were so serious and frowned so much yesterday, I wondered if you had any blood in you at all. Yet obviously, you have that, and more—if it's not all spent! How have you already managed to bed another? Have you even been here a full *day*?"

I felt heat in my cheeks as I unlocked my door. "I am going to change my clothing, Signum," I said firmly. "I will be back shortly."

"You will also want to wash your undercarriage," she said. "You do not need a warden's nose to smell all that." She sniffed again. "But do I find that scent *familiar*? Was it someone I know?"

I shut the door with a snap.

THOUGH IT WAS hardly morning, a line was already forming at the Imperial Treasury bank, with dozens of merchants, tradesmen, workers, and no shortage of Apoths queuing up to deposit their earnings.

"Don't know if you ever work with Treasury folk, Kol," Malo said as we approached it. "But these officers . . . they are very different."

"How might you mean?"

She considered it. "They are so fine and clean," she said, "I am unsure if they have assholes."

"Ah. Noted."

I showed the line of people the heralds pinned to my cloak, and they parted for me to enter the bank with Malo following. The front area was a curious space, being composed of stalls with vine mesh walls that prevented the customers from physically touching the Treasury representative on the other side, while money and papers were passed back and forth through a narrow slit in the bottom. I saw that Malo was right, for the Treasury officers were indeed different: most were pale, soft of face, tastefully bejeweled, and dressed in the pale gray or white uniforms of the Imperial Treasury—all immaculate and unstained, of course, for Treasury officers rarely ventured out of their offices. I watched them preening and whispering behind the vine mesh, feeling like I observed a menagerie of dazzling, caged birds.

I began my inquiries, and they brought us the officer who had been on duty when Sujedo had visited: a young, slender Rathras signum named Tufwa, whose long hair poured down his back in a shining cascade.

"Oh!" he said after our introduction. "Special Division, is it? How impressive! The Treasury Special Division merely manages the most inflammatory of bankruptcies. You must feel a great deal prouder to go about putting the world to rights for the Emperor's justice."

"Thank you," I muttered. "Now—Immunis Sujedo?"

"Yes, a terrible business . . . That was the tenth of the month of Hajnal." His eyes fluttered as he summoned up the memory: a rather unsightly tic of all engravers, including myself. "Immunis Mineti Sujedo arrived in the late afternoon to store materials with us. Presented his credentials to the front princeps, who delivered him to me. I tested his blood authorities and confirmed his station. Then I took him to the Iyalet vault to access his safe, as he requested. We store all confidential materials there, for imperial business."

"How did you confirm Sujedo's blood authorities?" I asked.

"With a balmleaf pad," said Tufwa simply.

I waited for an explanation. When none came, I said, "And what's that?"

Tufwa frowned and said, "I take it you have not attended many Treasury banks?"

"People don't often get murdered in banks. They're usually rather difficult to escape from."

Tufwa looked me over like I was now a great deal less impressive. Then he went to his desk and brought back an unsightly specimen: it appeared to be a small clay tray filled with moist earth, yet growing over the earth was a strange, fleshy pad of gray-white fungus. "You simply place your hand to the pad . . . Go on. It won't hurt you."

I did so. The flesh was cold and moist. As I took my hand away, the pad turned a dark, mottled color before slowly turning back to gray-white.

"This response indicates you do not bear the correct blood authorities," said Tufwa. "If you had been a Treasury officer of deserving rank, it would have changed to a corresponding color."

"More secure than a reagents key," explained Malo, "for people lose keys but usually don't lose their blood."

"Exactly," sniffed Tufwa.

"And it performed correctly for Sujedo?" I asked him.

"Of course. I remember, after all."

I sniffed at my vial, anchoring this fact in my mind. "What was Sujedo's business in the Iyalet vault, then?"

"After his death, the wardens requested I pull his box. It contained his orders concerning the king of Yarrow. Tax projections, mostly. Nothing terribly surprising, but nothing we might want circulating. He had good reason to store it."

"It was stored in a regular safe?"

"No, not at all," said Tufwa. "We used one of the Treasury officer boxes. I shall show you."

He led us down a narrow stone passageway ending in a tall stone-wood door reinforced with iron, with another balmleaf pad on the edge. Tufwa placed his hand upon the patch and kept it there for a good while; then we heard a click within the door, and it opened.

"This is the Iyalet vault," he said, entering and gesturing about, "expressly for imperial use."

We followed him in and were confronted with stacks upon stacks of wooden safes with complex locks, yet all of them bore the same patches of strange, fleshy balmleaf.

Tufwa gestured to one stack of safes in the corner, which were each adorned with the symbol of the Treasury: the coin set in the hexagon. "That is where Sujedo stored his materials," he said. "Third box from the bottom. Such boxes are made to open solely for senior Treasury officers."

I stooped to study it. "And he had no issue opening this one?"

"None. I pulled the box and placed it on the table here for him to open. He put his hand to the lock, and the box opened for him, and I left him alone to make his deposit. It was all quite simple enough."

I turned, studying the cabinets and safes around me. There had to be dozens, all of varying sizes. I half wondered what it would be like to pop one open, grab the talints from within, and dump them on treacly Madam Poskit to pay off my father's loans once and for all. A stupid thought, yet it gave me an idea.

"Sujedo was alone in here?" I asked.

"Yes," said Tufwa. "I left him here to make his deposit, as is procedure."

"How long was he inside?"

Again, a fluttering to his eyes. "Less than five minutes, I should say."

"Did he touch or alter or open anything else?" I asked.

"We have not searched for that," said Tufwa warily. "Opening the boxes of the other Iyalets is forbidden unless there is an emergency."

"If you were to search, how might you do so?"

He pointed to the corner, where a very complex-looking set of scales were set upon a tall table. "These scales are to the highest Apoth code, meaning they can measure a single grain of salt. We would weigh each box, and if the weight of any has changed, we would summon the owner. If they do not come within the designated time, only then are we authorized to open it ourselves."

"And you, being an engraver, remember the weight."

"I do. But that, as I said, is only for emergencies." He sniffed. "And I do not believe one has been declared yet."

"The guard who accompanied him reported that Sujedo carried a bag with him, one about this large." I showed him, mimicking Klaida's movements exactly. "It sounded as if it were too large a bag for simple documents. Yet when Sujedo left, the bag was empty. So . . . what might he have deposited?"

"I cannot say," said Tufwa slowly. "I do recall the bag, and recall its size . . . but I am not sure I'd say it held something beyond documents. This is the Treasury, after all. We manage quite a *lot* of documents."

I frowned, thinking and trying to ignore Tufwa's impatient fluffing of his hair. "Please tell me of Sujedo's appearance," I said at last. "Height, weight—all of it."

Tufwa did so, eyes fluttering. Sujedo had been a thin man, he told me, and small, with thick, curling black hair, and rather pale eyes that weren't quite one color or another—gray eyes, perhaps. His skin had been gray, like that of all Sublimes and peoples who had undergone significant suffusions; he had been right-handed and had exhibited few scars, though little of his skin had been exposed to Tufwa's gaze, of course.

"How tall was he?" I asked. "Can you show me exactly?" I grimaced, recalling Ana's orders. "I mean—can you show me how tall he was compared to me?"

"I mean . . . I can? If it is necessary." He stuck his arm out, eyes fluttering, and touched about halfway down my shoulder. "That tall."

I nodded, feeling slightly humiliated. None of this was a surprise, really: the porter had said Sujedo had been short.

Tufwa watched me irritably, as if wondering what other idiotic questions I had for him. "Anything else?" he asked.

"No," I said, bowing. "Thank you, Signum."

MALO AND I trudged back through New Town together, dodging the pack animals and the streams of Apoths flooding out to begin their day.

"So what the hell was that?" asked Malo as she stepped around a heaping mound of feces.

"Mule droppings, from the look of it."

"How amusing. I meant your questions back there. Why was I awake so early for that? What did that teach us?"

"I've no idea. My immunis asked me to ask, so I asked. I will now give her the answers. Then we shall move on, to more questions, and hopefully more answers."

Malo shook her head. "I thought the Iudex moved in ways more interesting. Is it always like this? For if so, I shall not look forward to Yarrow becoming a full canton and getting its own courts."

"Take comfort. If we make a horrid mess of this, you may get neither."

We rounded the corner to my lodgings, the gulls wheeling and laughing overhead. I knocked at Ana's door, heard her voice within singing, "Come!" and we entered.

Ana's rooms, as always, had turned into an utter mess overnight, with books lying open everywhere and papers covering nearly every surface. Ana sat in the middle of the floor, blindfolded, her Pithian lyre in her lap. She turned her head toward us. "Ah! Din. Good morning. And . . . unless the sound of feet has confused me, there is another with you?"

"Yes, ma'am," I said. "This is Signum Tira Malo."

Malo bowed and muttered a quiet "Good morning, ma'am."

"Ah, very pleasant to meet you!" said Ana brightly. "I've two questions I wished to ask you, Malo. Is that all right?"

"Ahh. Certainly?"

"Excellent. The first—would you be *true* Yarrow, Malo? Born and raised?"

Malo looked quite uncomfortable at that. "Well. Yes?" she said. "As much as one could be, ma'am."

"Then could you possibly point Din in the direction of a place to procure another Pithian lyre?" asked Ana. She laid a hand on the instrument in her lap. "I've one here, but the Yarrow court is rather renowned for their duets, as you no doubt know. I believe I have a method of attaching two together so that I can attempt a duet on my own, but I would naturally need to have a second to do so."

Malo stared at her, boggled. "I . . . Yes, certainly, ma'am."

"Yes," said Ana, grinning. "Now for the second question . . . You're a true warden? Augmented and all?"

"Yes?"

"I've always wondered—is it true that wardens can tell a lie by the way a person's heart beats? Or detect if they are in love, or at least significantly aroused? I should think that'd make parties *very* interesting to attend, yes?"

There was a beat of painful silence.

"Uhh," said Malo. "Sometimes?"

"We have just come back from the bank, ma'am," I said quickly.

"Oh? Very good! Before you say more of it, Din, I have one question that has weighed most on my mind." She set aside her lyre. "Tell me—was Sujedo ever *alone* in the Treasury vault at any point of his visit?"

Malo and I exchanged a worried glance.

"Yes, ma'am," I said. "He was."

"I see, I see ... Intriguing! Very good work, both of you." She stood and blindly walked over to me, hand extended. I met it with my forearm, and she grasped it tight. "You can tell me the rest on the way. Let us all go to Old Town, to speak to the Treasury prificto, and review where at least one of these many crimes took place."

"Many crimes, ma'am?" said Malo, surprised.

"Oh, yes," said Ana. "I believe many deeds were done on that day, the tenth of Hajnal." We walked down the porch to the New Town lane. "The disappearance of our man in white was but one of them. We shall see!"

CHAPTER 10

．．．

WE RETURNED TO THE TOWER IN OLD TOWN AND wound up the many stairs to find the top floor now filled with senior Treasury officers darting from room to room, their arms overflowing with scrolls and parchments. We were directed to the largest chamber, positioned on the far side of the tower from where Sujedo had been housed. Two Apoth guards were stationed before it, and they inspected our heralds closely before opening the doors for us.

Dominating the room within was a large, long meeting table, so piled up with papers that it was difficult to spy any bit of actual table. Nearly a dozen senior Treasury officers were positioned about it, shuffling through the parchments like a gold miner might seek a glitter among the mud. So absorbed were they in their tasks that none noticed our arrival.

Only two officers reacted to us: a young Treasury signum, seated off to the side, and an older man at the head of the table, who sat crooked in his chair as he cast a rather weary eye over the proceedings. His skin was gray, indicating significant alterations, and he—like Ana herself—was of Sazi origin, with long, dark, braided mustaches that pooled about his collarbones. There was something wry and ironic about his face, like he knew a great many secrets and found all of them slightly ridiculous.

He looked up as we approached, then smiled brightly, as if he not only had expected us but was overjoyed at our sight. He turned to the signum and jerked his head—*We're done here*—and they stood and walked to greet us, he with his white Treasury cape dashingly coiled down about his forearm.

"Ahh," he said. "Iudex, is it? About poor Sujedo? Finally, what a relief." Again he smiled, this time so warmly I found myself disarmed: an unusual thing, since I was often guarded about such high officers. "I am Prificto Umerus Kardas, leader of the Imperial Treasury delegation. This is my assistant, Signum Gorthaus."

We bowed in return, and the young woman bowed back, though I noted the heralds on her breast: the eye set within a box, indicating she was an engraver, like myself. It was unusual to see so many Sublimes of my sect in one city, but then, Yarrowdale was a valuable place, with many valuable things to keep track of.

"Good afternoon, sir," I said, bowing once more. "I am Signum Dinios Kol of the Imperial Iudex, and this is my investigator, Immunis Ana Dolabra."

"A pleasure," said Kardas. "Always happy to see another Tala officer! It is with the deeds of those on the Outer Rim that all of our safety is secured." He then turned to Ana. "Ah . . ." His eye lingered for a fraction of a second on her blindfold; then he bowed low, took her by the right hand, and kissed one pale knuckle. "Always a delight to meet a member of the old country."

I stared, startled not only by the boldness of the gesture but also because I was aware of how rarely Ana washed her hands. Yet I realized that, as the two were both Sazi and hailed from the inner rings, there might be some sense of greater kinship between them.

Ana grinned back her predator's grin. "Of course, sir. Though it has been a long while since I've laid eyes upon the homelands."

Kardas glanced again at her blindfold and gave a charming laugh, as though in on the joke. "I apologize for the state of things." He gestured at the table of whispering officers behind him. "My officers are busy folk and burdened with heavy tasks."

"It is no trouble at all," said Ana. "I thank you for making time for us, Prificto Kardas. Though I do not believe we shall take up too much of your time here."

I frowned slightly; I'd expected a full interview with all the delegation, which would normally take hours.

"Then come," said Kardas. "Let us sit and discuss these troubles,
and hope we find some answers!"

WE LEFT THE MEETING room to adjourn to a small parlor. The
chairs there were very fine, upholstered in rich silks and comfortably
cushioned. It would have been a pleasant place had it been in a different building, but just like Sujedo's rooms, Kardas's chambers were
musty, moldy, and slightly foul-smelling.

"I also apologize for the environs," said Kardas as he sat. "I'd serve
you tea, but . . . well, the way the building tilts makes it difficult to
pour. King Lalaca, you see, specifically requested we reside in this . . .
structure? Hovel? I lack the word. Yet it was apparently the grand
house of his ancestors many decades ago."

"I cannot see it, sir," said Ana. "But it does not *smell* grand."

"I agree. As with all things concerning King Lalaca, there was a
cynical play. If we refused to house the delegation in these chambers,
he would have proclaimed it an insult and refused to meet with us.
Now he makes us stay in this dreary place and forces us to meet with
go-betweens with nothing useful to say." A weary smile. "I sometimes
feel we shall sooner see the blessed Khanum walk the earth again before we make any progress."

"It must be a dreadful situation indeed, sir," said Ana, "if the king
is proving resilient to even your talents."

Kardas smiled, puzzled. "Talents? What might you mean?"

"I assume, sir," Ana said, "that you are a Sublime? Specifically, an
emitias?"

The prificto regarded her warily. As he did, I glanced at his heralds
but could not spy the symbol of the pear within the oval in the center:
the sign of the emitias Sublimes, who were preternaturally skilled at
reading human emotion, so much so that it was rumored they could
smell and react to human pheromones.

"What makes you say such a thing, Dolabra?" he asked mildly.

"Well, I have met all manner of Sublimes in my day," Ana said. "But only four have ever kissed my hand upon greeting me—and they have all been emitiasi. It's a gesture I always respond so well to, but most others don't have the gall! Yet they sense I desire it, as if they read my very mind."

"You assume so much," said Kardas, "simply because I kissed your hand?"

"Well, there is that, and I hear absolutely no surprise in your voice at the sight of my blindfold, nor the rest of my appearance. You seem an unusually socially deft officer, in other words! Suspiciously so. And such an augment would make sense, sir, you being a diplomat."

There was a tense silence. Then Kardas smiled broadly and laughed, so much so I was nearly bowled over by his charisma: an emitias indeed, then.

How strange, I thought: emitiasi were broadly distrusted among other imperials, given their skills for manipulation, and were not often appointed to positions of high leadership.

"True enough!" Kardas said, laughing. "I am as you say. But those of my commanding rank do not often reflect their Sublime status. We tend to dispense with such formalities."

"And you'd be doubly inclined to do so when serving as a diplomat," said Ana, grinning, "as you're likely capable of reading much in any human reaction! Not something you'd wish to remind the king of Yarrow of, true?"

Another charming laugh, though this one was slightly nervous. "Yes, perhaps so. You seem quite shrewd, Immunis. I am now more assured that this awful matter with poor Sujedo shall be resolved quickly!"

"Let us hope," said Ana. "Now—to questions, sir?"

"TO BEGIN WITH," Ana said, "what might be the subject of your disagreement with the king of Yarrow?"

"Ohh, a very familiar one," Kardas said, sighing. "The disagreement here is the same as it always is with the great and the wealthy. It is *taxes.* Within less than a decade, the realm of Yarrow shall become a full imperial canton. Its people shall gain the right to vote for Imperial senators, and the protection of the Legion—yet they shall also have to pay Imperial tax. My delegation's task is to audit, review, and assess the value of all economic activity in Yarrow before that handover occurs, to ensure a smooth transition. The king, however, is also the *largest* landholder in all of Yarrow. Thus, he will be subject to the greatest tax."

"Ahh," Ana said. "Yes, that would definitely put him in a snit, I should expect."

"Correct," sighed Kardas. "The king is proving to be a master of evasion, if not outright punishment! For a good time we made progress, meeting during the first week of the month for the past two or so years. Yet in the most recent months, it has all stalled out. I am forced now to pursue him, like a spurned lover. Yet I have only been appointed as lead of the delegation in the past year. Signum Gorthaus has served here throughout." He gestured at the signum behind him, who gave us a tired smile.

"All other officers serving on the delegation are axioms, I take it?" asked Ana.

"Correct, it being Treasury work," he said. "Though I now admit, I do worry that such a nature might make my officers easy prey."

"Prey?" asked Ana.

"Well, we are in treacherous environs, Immunis," said Kardas. "To see dishonesty in another's bearing requires some perceptiveness for ordinary people, but even more for a Treasury axiom."

Ana paused. "When you say 'treacherous environs,' sir," she said, "how treacherous might you mean?"

"Well—we have already been the subject of one attack," said Kardas. "Another does not seem *un*likely."

"Are you suggesting, sir, that Sujedo's death might have been an *assassination*? Perhaps by King Lalaca, or his agents?"

"I do not know. But I know the king disdains our task here. Violently so."

"Would killing Sujedo disrupt or damage or delay that task?" asked Ana.

"Disrupt? Perhaps. But it would not delay or end it. If the king wished that, well . . . I would be a much better target rather than Sujedo, yes?" A watery smile crossed his face. "Yet still I live. So far."

WE THEN ASKED Kardas the usual questions: what was seen, what was heard, and what any of his delegation knew. As Malo had suggested, Kardas and his people knew nothing.

"We did not see him," he admitted. "Immunis Sujedo arrived very late, then sent us a note saying he was ill and would visit us in the morning. Then he was simply gone, his bed horribly bloodied, and no one could give us any answers. Nor could they find any sign of him at all, for days!"

"Besides Sujedo's disappearance, did any of that behavior seem strange at all, sir?" asked Ana.

"Possibly," said Kardas. "None of the rest of my delegation fell ill. But Sujedo was, ah . . . a very *inner* ring sort of person."

"Meaning . . ."

"Meaning," drawled Malo, "the fellow was softer than a jellied egg."

Kardas shot her a look. "True enough, yes. He was exceptionally skilled at managing ledgers, but he was not, I should say, robust. A trip of that sort likely wearied him."

"But you knew him personally, sir?" said Ana.

"I did," said Kardas. "But only somewhat. He was rather new to my section."

"But you had *met* him before."

Kardas slowly furrowed his brow. "I . . . Well. Yes? Why?"

"Had the rest of your delegation met him?"

"Yes. Again—why?"

"I beg your pardon, sir, but if I might ask . . . Do you have an engraver on staff here? One who might have also met Sujedo?"

Kardas glanced at Signum Gorthaus. "I do. Why?"

"I am simply testing a theory about his disappearance," said Ana. "If it is true, then we can cut to it, and save your valuable time, sir."

The prificto extended a hand to his signum. "Gorthaus, I believe you served with Sujedo some six years ago—correct?"

The young signum bowed in her seat. "Correct, sir."

"Then, if you would kindly oblige?"

She shot to her feet. "Certainly, sir."

"Excellent," said Ana, grinning. "Another engraver makes this much easier. Now. Please summon a memory of how *tall* Sujedo was, Signum."

Gorthaus blinked uncertainly, then did so, eyes fluttering. "Yes, ma'am."

"Now . . . hold out your hand to show *exactly* how tall the man was."

Again, Gorthaus blinked but did as Ana asked, holding out her hand as if touching an invisible man on the crown of his head. "That tall, ma'am."

Kardas's eyebrows had now arched so high they were halfway up his brow, but he stayed quiet.

"Din here has been to the Treasury bank today and spoken to the Treasury engraver there," explained Ana, gesturing to me. "He asked him to display how tall Sujedo had been when he visited the bank. Now, Din—please show them the height Signum Tufwa indicated."

I stood and approached Gorthaus's outstretched hand, feeling slightly ridiculous. My eyes fluttered as I summoned the memory, and I pointed on my shoulder to where Tufwa had touched; yet the spot I touched was a full four smallspan lower than the height Gorthaus was now indicating.

"Is there a difference in height, Din?" Ana asked.

"Ah . . . yes, ma'am," I said. "Tufwa indicated the man was four smallspan shorter."

"I see," said Ana softly. "How fascinating."

"I don't understand," said Kardas. He anxiously bit the tip of his thumb, then asked, "Are . . . are you suggesting that Sujedo was *shorter* that day at the bank?"

"Allow me to test further," said Ana. "Tell me, sir—was Sujedo an attentive man? Quick to notice things about people, and ask questions?"

The prificto now looked bewildered. "Ah . . . no, I would not say that of him, Immunis."

"And yet," said Ana, "the Apoth guard who accompanied him reported that Sujedo was clever, charming, and noticed several details about him that ordinary people would have missed. Does that sound like him, sir?"

"N-no. No, that does *not* sound like him."

"I see," said Ana. She was now oozing smug satisfaction. "Well, then, sir—what would you say is *your* assessment of all these reports of Sujedo? The height of the man, and his strange behavior?"

Kardas turned this over. "I would say everyone has made some mistake," he said finally, "and been looking at the wrong person entirely!"

Ana's grin widened. "Exactly. *Exactly!* I would say the same thing myself. In which case, the conclusion is obvious."

There was a beat of silence.

"To me," muttered Malo, "the conclusion is not obvious at all . . ."

"I'm afraid I agree," said Kardas.

"Well, we are now faced with two impossible proposals," said Ana. "Signum Malo—you say it was impossible for someone to be stolen out of a locked room in the top of a tower, then moved across the city and the jungle and the canals without anyone noticing. Yes?"

"I do," said Malo.

"And you, Prificto," said Ana, "you say now that it is impossible for all these witnesses to have seen the man you know to be Sujedo, correct, sir?"

"I . . . suppose," said Kardas.

"Then one can only conclude," she said, "that Sujedo was *not* stolen out of that room and spirited away to the jungle—because he was never *in* it to begin with. Because the man who arrived in this city claiming to be Sujedo, and indeed moved into his rooms and slept in his bed, was someone *else*—a complete and utter impostor."

CHAPTER 11

∧∧∧

"I CANNOT COMPREHEND THIS," SAID KARDAS SLOWLY. "I thought Sujedo's remains had been found. Are you suggesting he was *not* kidnapped? *Not* murdered?"

"Oh, no, sir," said Ana. "Sujedo *was* kidnapped and murdered. But not under the circumstances we have thus imagined."

She leaned forward, her posture akin to a reedwitch telling fortunes at a canton fair. "Listen, sir," she said. "Imagine now Sujedo's journey north to this city. He came upriver through the canals, the very last man to join your delegation. But he did not complete that journey! Along the way, he was attacked—snatched up, and kidnapped—and you *never* received news of it, for his attackers moved too quickly for anyone to notice. They bound him in the jungles—by the wrists, as Malo had noticed—and took a sample of his blood and urine and undressed him. His clothes were then removed and quickly tailored to fit a *new* man . . . this impostor who arrived here claiming to be Sujedo. I suspect he likely also applied other alterations—a dye for his hair, perhaps, or powders or graft colorings for his skin. The illusion was likely quite good at a distance. They also doused his belongings with lime and mold, just in case a warden might sniff him out and realize his clothes held the aroma of another man."

Ana sat back in her chair, luxuriating in the moment. "Thus, he arrived in Yarrowdale, purporting to be Mineti Sujedo, displaying his heralds, carrying his documents, and mimicking the missing man's bearing. He brought Sujedo's belongings into his rooms when the rest of the delegation was not present, then quickly departed to do business in the city. He returned, invented a reason not to see any of the delegation in person to ensure that his ruse was not detected—he claimed he was very sick—and hid away. He then used Sujedo's blood and piss to provide false evidence that the true Sujedo had been present, and fabricated a scene of abduction. And then he vanished! But in truth, I suspect, he actually *escaped,* slipping out from underneath everyone's nose to vanish into the night!"

There was a thunderstruck silence. The tip of Kardas's thumb remained wedged between his front teeth as he sat there, boggled.

"Why in hell," said Malo flatly, "would someone do all that, ma'am?"

"I have my ideas about why," said Ana, "but I would prefer to prove the *how* first."

Kardas stopped biting his thumb and shook his head. "All this seems absolutely mad, Immunis! How would no one notice that this man wasn't Sujedo?"

"Well, Sujedo was expected, and this man had the uniform, the heralds, yes?" said Ana. "He had all of Sujedo's documents, he was able to wield his blood privileges to get into the Treasury bank, and he knew what to say and how to act. And he took great care—no, perhaps *improbable* care—to avoid being seen by anyone who might actually recognize Sujedo. Though his time here was brief, I think every moment of it was carefully planned."

"Then how was this not discovered during the investigation of the disappearance?" said Kardas, looking to Malo.

Yet Ana broke in: "Because as you say, it was mad to suggest! Why go about asking if the man in the room really *had* been Sujedo, especially if your primary task was trying to find the fellow? And once you found the body and identified it as the missing man, why ask then?"

"And how *did* he disappear," demanded Malo, "given that he had vanished from a locked room?"

"That is far simpler! He vanished with this," said Ana. She produced the lodestone from her pocket. "This piece of iron was found in Sujedo's chambers. It has been manipulated so it has the properties of lodestone. It attracts and sticks to iron. I recalled there was a prison break in Medullaria years ago, enabled by a prisoner being snuck a lump of lodestone—for with that, he was able to manipulate the slide locks of his chamber from the *other side of the door.*"

She said this triumphantly and was met with a bewildered silence.

"Might you elaborate, Dolabra?" said Kardas.

"My proposal is that this impostor had two of these lodestones," said Ana. "One he placed on the interior lock of the window. He then climbed out the window, clung to the side of the tower, shut the window, and used the *second* piece of lodestone to guide the lock back into place *through* the wooden shutter. The piece of iron on the interior eventually lost much of its lodestone properties and dropped to the floor—where it was found, briefly puzzled over, and set aside. Thus, our impostor made his exit and sealed it up behind him, leaving no trace of himself nor his disappearance."

"And then what," said Malo, "he climbed down the *entirety* of the tower?"

"No," said Ana. "For Sujedo's room is next to a vacant room, is it not? Closed due to water damage?"

"Yes," said Malo. "But the guard was standing just next door to it. He did not see anyone exit through that room."

"True," said Ana. "But there is another vacant room *directly below that one,* yes? One that was *unguarded?* All the impostor needed to do was climb one room over and *down,* slip through *those* windows, and vanish, leaving behind a chamber that appeared to have never been violated in any way. Then, days later, after Sujedo had served his purpose, his kidnappers killed him, butchered him, and—as Signum Malo said—did with his body simply as one does on the canals."

"Found a hungry turtle," Malo said quietly, "and served him up."

"Indeed," said Ana. "But the turtles were not as hungry as expected—and thus, we found him."

Kardas sat back in his seat, stunned, the tip of his thumb hanging mere inches from his lips. "Do . . . do you have any evidence for this theory, Immunis?" he asked faintly. "Or is this all conjecture?"

"For now, it is conjecture," Ana said. "But as I said, I think evidence is easily found."

"Found where?" said Malo.

"In the vacant rooms just to the side and down from Sujedo's chambers," Ana said smoothly.

"But . . . but we looked there, ma'am," said Malo. "We searched all the rooms when we first searched for Sujedo. We found nothing."

"You looked too quick, I think. Let us look again."

WE TROOPED DOWN the leaning hallway, then down one flight of stairs, me leading Ana by the arm. We had the porter unlock the door to the vacant room below, and once again I was back in the musky, reeking air, dimly lit by a blade of daylight slicing through a crack in the windows.

"The shutters, Din," said Ana. "Check them, please."

I did so, studying each one, yet when I touched the first shutter on the right, it opened easily, even though it appeared to be locked. I peered at the lock and spied a seam running through the iron.

"The lock's been sawed through, ma'am," I said. "Looks like it's closed, but the lock does nothing."

"That is one bit of evidence, then," said Ana. "I am guessing our impostor's lodestone trick only works through barriers with *another* piece of lodestone on the other side. He had to use a less elegant method to get in here . . . but let us look for more." She sniffed the air. "The mold in this place likely regrows when stepped on or touched. But where it has been disturbed, one may see indentations . . . I say *one*, but in reality, only Malo's eyes can discern anything at all. Signum—do you see anything?"

Malo gazed about the room, her bright green eyes narrowed. Then her mouth fell open. "Yes," she said softly.

"And what do you see?"

"I see . . . footprints," she said. "Maybe from when they first searched the room, but . . . but there is another string of disturbances, leading . . ." She walked to the eastern wall, then studied it, squinting. "There is a brick here, in the wall, that has been disturbed. I can see it in the mold about it."

"Din—remove that brick with your sword," said Ana. "But *carefully*. This is a very clever person we are dealing with. He may have prepared for us."

I drew my sword, the bright green blade glimmering even in this room, and delicately slid its point into the side seam of the brick. Using my sword as a lever, I pushed the brick until it tumbled out of the wall, and stepped back.

For a moment, nothing happened. Then Malo narrowed her eyes, studying the gap from ten paces away.

"It is clothing," she said. "Or was."

"Was?" said Kardas.

Malo unsheathed a knife, walked to the gap, and speared something and held it up for us to see. It appeared to be a soft, black, drippy substance almost like tar.

"It has been treated with a reagent," she said. "So it was consumed and decomposed rapidly. But . . . there is something else."

She dropped the clump of black, then reached into the gap once more and used her blade to flick out something small and twinkling, which tumbled to a stop at my feet.

I squatted to look at it. "A Treasury herald," I said. I searched my memory to identify it, and realized it matched one of the many heralds upon Kardas's breast. "The same as one you wear, sir," I said to him.

Kardas leaned forward to look at it. "Th-that is the herald of the Order of the White Clove," he said faintly. "For great service to the Treasury."

"And Sujedo, I take it, was also a member of that order, sir?" said Ana.

"Y-yes. He was."

"Then the conclusion is clear," said Ana. "The impostor snuck out of Sujedo's rooms, climbed down into this one, changed *out* of Sujedo's clothes, and hid them away in this wall—for he knew he would be in terrible trouble if caught with an officer's clothing—yet he first treated them to ensure that they rotted beyond recognition."

"But why bother?" said Kardas. "We found the herald. We know the clothes are Sujedo's."

"Not to disguise the clothes," said Malo. She spat a stream of black spit out the open window. "But to remove scent. Hair. Skin."

"Yes," said Ana. "We are in a city of Apoths. Any trace of a human can be used to track them. He had to be sure that even if we did find his leavings, we could not use them. And all the hair and blood and urine he left in the room above—that was Sujedo's own! In other words, this man knows the nature of Apoths and wardens, and was almost unfathomably careful to only leave behind things he *wished* to be found."

"By hell . . ." muttered Malo. "What a person this is."

"Yes!" said Ana. "A marvelously brilliant creature. Having made his way to this room, I think the impostor then changed into a different set of clothes—probably those of a servant. Simple, undistinguished apparel. He then simply walked downstairs and slipped out. To where, I do not yet know."

A silence as we all absorbed this.

"But . . . but why do this at *all*?" asked Kardas, frustrated. "Why go to all this trouble? Why kidnap and butcher poor Sujedo, then pretend to be him for . . . for what, only half an afternoon, and then fabricate this scene?"

Malo's whole body went stiff. "The vault," she whispered.

"Correct!" said Ana triumphantly. "This impostor, pretending to be Sujedo, was left *totally alone* in the Iyalet vault of the bank for . . . oh, well, several minutes at least. And I think those several minutes were the *entire point* of the kidnapping, this complicated façade, all of it. He went to these great lengths solely to get into that exact place, at that exact time." She sniffed. "The question is—what did he *do* there?"

We all stared at one another in horror.

"Well . . . well, what *did* he do there?" demanded Kardas.

"Oh, don't ask me," said Ana. "I've no idea! I suppose we'll have to open up all the damned boxes to figure that out, yes?"

THE ENTIRE SCENE dissolved into pandemonium. Malo sprinted away without another word. Kardas began crying for his assistants to get to the bank, and soon the whole building filled up with the stamp and pound of Treasury feet as the delegation panicked. Soon it was just myself and Ana, slowly descending the crooked stairs as she clung to my arm.

"Better get me back to my rooms, Din," she said. "My head is beginning to pound from all that mold and conversation. I am unsure which one was worse! And you, I think, shall need to go to the bank to see what is found, or rather not found."

"Certainly, ma'am," I said. "But . . . you truly think this was just all about a bank robbery, ma'am?"

"In all honesty, I've no fucking idea *what* this was about anymore! But I am most curious to find out."

"I see . . . But there are two things I can't make sense of in all you said."

"Good!" she said. "I appreciate it when you throw rocks at my ideas, Din. Keeps me from going too far up my own ass. Proceed."

I coughed. "Yes . . . First, why all this show with the disappearance? If he wished to get into the vault, why come back here and keep pretending to be Sujedo, instead of simply running with what he'd taken?"

"I think the answer to that will depend on what was stolen from that vault," said Ana. "But the likely answer is that by making his exit so inexplicable, our thief obscured the true crime entirely. I mean, *no one* has been looking at the bank for nearly two weeks! Instead, people have been wandering around calling Sujedo's name out in the street. A wonderful defensive play, really."

"Perhaps, so," I said. "But I also wonder—how was this impostor able to wield the blood authorities of a Treasury immunis?"

"Yes . . . that troubles me most out of all of this. There are three potential answers, I believe. The first and simplest is that he himself actually *is* a Treasury immunis—but that is unlikely, for why then would he bother to pretend to be Sujedo? We shall discard this possibility," she said with a sniff, "as it is tremendously stupid. The second, of course, is that when they captured Sujedo, they removed the cultured organ that granted him his Treasury authorities and implanted it in the impostor. But that is a very tricky and deadly operation. Swapping an organ is not simple work, even for an experienced medikker. It would take time, and the kidnappers would have had to move fast, otherwise Sujedo's absence would be noted."

"And the third possibility?"

She shrugged. "The third is that our impersonator managed to somehow transport the blood of Sujedo with him through means I have not yet devised! A bottle of Sujedo's blood hidden on his person, say, would not have worked. It takes the touch of a *living* hand bearing the proper authoritative blood, as you witnessed. We shall have to investigate further."

We exited onto the Old Town streets, which were still ringing with the shouts of the departing delegation.

"The glow of my triumph fades," said Ana quietly. "And much troubles me. I dislike hearing Kardas suggest that the king of Yarrow might be involved . . . and, to be frank, I dislike Kardas himself being present. An emitias? In such a delicate place? And to learn that he has been so profoundly *unsuccessful* in all his labors? It bothers me. Yet . . . we are staggering around in the dark. We know nothing of this impostor—his name, his nature, his origins, his goals, nothing. And I am disturbed by his depth of knowledge."

"How do you mean, ma'am?"

"Well—the fucker simply knows too much! He knew about the delegation's schedule, the bank, the safes! I would guess that the pool of individuals who know about any one of those subjects is quite limited. Let us derive the size of that pool, Din, and then go gazing in it."

CHAPTER 12

∴

I FOUND THE TREASURY BANK IN NO LESS OF A STATE of pandemonium than the delegation's tower. All bank business had been shut down, and dozens of laborers and officers were milling about in the street, making futile demands for their money. The guards at the door were so rattled that they first denied me entrance, but I finally forced them to look at my heralds, and they allowed me in.

I wound my way through the bank and found Kardas and his Treasury officers within the Iyalet vault, observing as a panicked Signum Tufwa slid out each vault box and weighed it on his fancy scales. Kardas paced about the vault in a small circle, arms crossed, occasionally biting the tip of his right thumb. The nervous tic had so completely taken him over that the nail of his right thumb now bore small indentations from his incisors.

"I don't even know how it could have happened!" Tufwa was saying. "Our balmleaf locks don't open if the privileged blood is even *slightly* decayed! It shouldn't have been possible, it shouldn't!"

Malo and two other Apoth officers lurked at the back of the vault. Judging from the sheer amount of mud and weapons on their bodies, I guessed they were wardens as well. Malo looked up as I approached. Her face was wan and taut, with no sign of her usual breeziness. "They are doing a basic check first," she said. "He looks at all the boxes that were opened in the week before the tenth of Hajnal, to see if the weights of any have changed since then."

"But so far," said Kardas, "all seems true and proper." He glanced at me sidelong. "Did your immunis really conceive all this just from hearing *one day* of your reports?"

"She did, sir," I said.

"How amazing," he said softly. "What an astounding woman. I almost regret hoping she's wrong."

We continued watching as Tufwa weighed box after box. The day stretched on and on, broken only by the click and clack as Tufwa slid the boxes in and out of their shelves. I idly wondered if Ana's speculation about our impostor had been incorrect.

Then Tufwa placed one box upon the scales. He read its weight, then twitched, his long curtain of hair rippling.

I stepped close. "What is it?"

"Ah . . ." He peered at the scales, as if wishing he did not see what he now saw. "This . . . this box is . . . changed."

"Changed?" asked Kardas. "Changed how?"

"It is four stone heavier than it was after it last received a deposit, sir," said Tufwa.

"*Heavier?*" I said. "Someone has *added* something to it?"

Tufwa's eyes fluttered as he summoned up his memories. "Yes. Though I do not know how. This safe was opened for a deposit on the second of Hajnal. It has not been opened since. Not . . . not by my memory, at lea—"

"Wait," said Kardas. He darted forward, his white Treasury cape fluttering behind him. "This is not a Treasury box. It's an *Apoth* box."

"Wh-what?" said Malo, startled.

Kardas pointed to the sigil on the front: the drop of blood set in a hexagon. "See for yourself. It belongs to your Iyalet, not mine. Are we to presume that this man dressed up as a Treasury officer and committed murder and torture . . . but not for riches or money or talints at all, but . . . but for something in a single *Apoth* box?"

Malo stared at the safe as if the sight of her Iyalet's insignia horrified her, but she said nothing.

"What was in it?" I asked Tufwa. "Do you know?"

Tufwa, trembling, shook his head. "I am permitted to know what safes are in use, and for whom, but not what is deposited. Too many confidential reports and materials are stored here."

"Then who opened it last that you recall?"

Another fluttering of Tufwa's eyes. "A . . . an Apoth Immunis. Rava Ghrelin, of the Medikker Fermentation Division here in Yarrowdale. He made the deposit on the second of that month. Bank protocol dictates we should summon him first before breaking open the box ourselves."

I looked to Malo, who gave a panicked shrug. "No idea who the hell that is," she said. "But that division does very serious work. Yet far more disturbing . . . that safe should have been even more secure than the Treasury box."

"Why?" I asked.

"We Apoths don't grant blanket access to our officers, like the Treasury does," she said. "You want to be able to use our boxes in the Iyalet vault here, you got to give us *individual* tissue samples. Spit is easiest. But just in case you've got someone else's spit in your mouth, we also ask for piss. Less likely to have someone else's piss in their belly. Then we apply reagents to the samples, swab it on the balmleaf substrate for the safe, and it's done. All this means that box should have been one of the most secured things in all of Yarrow."

I realized why Malo seemed so dismayed. "And . . . it shows no damage? No panel removed, nor hinges severed?"

"Not that I can see."

"So . . . it would seem someone simply came, pressed their hand to the balmleaf lock, and . . . it opened for them. Is that how it appears?"

"Yes," she said faintly.

There was a long, uncomfortable silence.

"By hell," said Kardas. "Are we to believe that this impostor appears to have had not only the blood privileges that allowed him to open a Treasury box . . . but *also* those of an Apoth? Specifically, for access to *this one* box?"

No one said anything.

"Then our impostor has . . . has a spectrum of magic blood within him?" Kardas asked. He laughed miserably. "A mix of them, like some kind of mulled wine, that allows him to open nearly any damned safe he chooses, no matter how it is warded?"

"That," said Tufwa, "or he is the greatest bank robber I have ever heard of."

I looked to Malo. "We need the owner of this safe here," I said. "This Ghrelin. And we need him talking. If we can't find him, we open the damned box ourselves."

"R-right . . ." said Malo. She looked back at her two wardens. "Fetch him here. Tell him we have some questions about the contents of his safe, but no more than that."

"And please check the other safes," I said to Tufwa as they left. "It's possible the man broke into them as well. I doubt it, but we will need to know."

CHAPTER 13

⌄⌄⌄

AGAIN, WE WAITED. THE SUN SLOWLY SLID THROUGH THE
sky until it hung heavy over the western hills. Tufwa and his colleagues continued to work, opening up safe after safe. Eventually they
finished, with nothing else found: only the weight of the safe belonging to this Immunis Rava Ghrelin had been changed.

Finally we heard the whine of the gate hinges, followed by the
clack of the locks of the great bank door. Then the wardens returned,
followed by a third person.

He was a tall man, and delicately built, with pale gray skin and
eyes so gleaming black they had the look of fresh tar. His head was
quite hairless, but this did not surprise me: many Apoths who worked
with reagents preferred to simply alter their scalps so their hair did
not grow at all, rather than cleanse and sterilize their hair every day
after their work. Perhaps in compensation for this, his face had been
ornamented with paints and powders, a common practice of some
Kurmini men: a blush of brown to his gray cheeks, and lines about his
eyes. Yet despite these graceful touches, his face bore a look of anxiety
akin to that of some caged creature startled by an intrusion into its
paddock.

I looked to Tufwa as he entered. He gave me a slight nod—
That's him.

"I shall let you take the lead on this, Signum," said Kardas quietly
behind me. "I believe you have more experience with questioning
people . . ."

"As you wish, sir," I said. I stood as the man entered, moved to intercept him before the vault, and studied his heralds as he approached. The axiom symbol twinkled at his breastbone, the spiral set within a square: a man with a mind for calculation, then.

I bowed low to him. "Good afternoon. Would you be Immunis Rava Ghrelin, sir?"

"I am," he said warily. "And you are?"

"Signum Dinios Kol, of the Iudex."

"Iudex? I wasn't aware that we had Iudex in Yarrowdale, being as this region is not yet formally part of the Empire."

"I'm with Special Division, sir," I said. "We are only assigned to high-priority situations."

Ghrelin slowly nodded. Then his gaze flicked to Kardas, and he studied the prificto's heralds. "Ah. That . . . that Treasury officer, the missing one. Is that it?"

"Correct, sir," I said. "I'm afraid I have to ask you a few questions about your business at this bank. Would you like to sit?"

He thought about it. "No," he said finally.

"All right," I said, somewhat taken aback. "Might I ask what your duties are here in Yarrowdale, sir?"

"What does this have to do with my vault box, Signum?" he demanded.

"I am unsure at this moment, sir. But I must know before we continue further."

His mouth compressed into a tight, bloodless line. "I am part of the Medikker Fermentation Division. We are responsible for designing new alterations, grafts, and suffusions to amend issues with the human body. Is that what you need?"

"Issues such as . . . ?"

He waved a hand impatiently. "Such as combating disease, or deformations, or chronic injuries and the like! Now tell me—why am I here, please? What is going on with my box, Signum?"

I studied his expression. He now seemed cold and imperious, yet there was something brittle about his eyes. I felt he was trying to read my own expression, as if I were a medikker myself and he wished to hear news of a family member's prognosis.

I thought: *He already knows.*

"I am afraid that we've had a breach in the defenses of this bank, sir," I said. "One box has been tampered with, and only one—yours."

His dark eyes leapt back and forth between me, Kardas, and Malo lurking before the vault. "And . . . what was stolen?"

"We do not yet know, sir," I said. "The Treasury weight check actually indicates it contains more than it should."

"So . . . you are proposing that someone *added* something to my box, rather than stealing from it?"

"Again, we do not yet know. We were hoping you could open it for us to inspect it—though I would like to know what was in it before we do so."

Ghrelin struggled in silence for a moment. His cheek began to twitch, as did his arms and fingers.

Then he did something very curious: he dropped his right hand and began tapping erratically with three fingers against his belt buckle, creating a *tap-tap-tap* noise. Yet though this tapping continued, he neither wept nor broke into a rage.

"How did this happen?" he whispered.

"We're attempting to discover that, sir. We suspect it is in connection with the capture and murder of a senior imperial officer."

He swallowed. "Papers. It . . . the box contained papers. But it also contained reagents, to be shipped to the inner rings. A messenger was scheduled to arrive here, open the box, take the papers and the reagents, and board a barge for the inner rings."

"I see, sir. And . . . what kind of reagents or materials would this have been for?"

He looked at me, startled, like I had distracted him from some deep reflection. Again, I felt him trying to read my expressions.

"Healing grafts," he said.

"Mere healing grafts, sir?"

"Yes. But a formula that was still in development and was not fit to be produced at scale." He suddenly spoke very quickly. "It was proving effective against many respiratory diseases. Drop cough, cavley, irtius, jharelia, more. These are very common diseases that kill thousands each year, especially children and the elderly. With this new formulation, we . . . we hope to change that."

Malo and her wardens were slowly standing up behind me.

"I see," I said. "Then would you come with us, sir, and open the box? We would very much like to confirm what has happened to it."

He swallowed and nodded, his hand still tapping on his belt. "Certainly."

THE VAULT WAS utterly silent as we entered. All the Treasury and Apoth officers watched Ghrelin, who anxiously teetered over to the table with the box, his trembling hands still tapping on his belt; yet Ghrelin himself took no notice of any one of us, and stared instead at the box itself, as if it held some deadly weapon he dreaded.

"I believe you'll just need to put your hand against the balmleaf there, sir," I said.

"Of course," he said quietly. "I have done this countless times myself, Signum."

Yet he hesitated, his fingers still rapidly tapping on his belt.

"Very good, sir," I said. "But—please, once it's been unlocked, allow me to open it. Just in case."

"In case of what, Signum?"

"I cannot say. But—just in case, sir."

Ghrelin glanced around at the room, taking in the many officers who were with us. He opened his mouth as if to object, then thought better of it, took a breath, and pressed his hand to the balmleaf lock.

The balmleaf turned a faint brown color. There came a click from somewhere within the box.

I stepped forward to open it for him; yet Ghrelin was faster, and to my surprise, he anxiously reached out and flicked open the box's lid to peer within.

I began to demand he stop, yet then Ghrelin screamed and staggered backward, as if all too eager to get as far away as he could from the box.

"Oh, hell!" he cried. "By Sanctum! What . . . what is that! Who is that, who is *that*?"

We all gazed at him, bewildered. Then I approached the box.

Inside it sat a lumpen, withered object, rounded at the top and rippled at the bottom, and covered all over with dark, wrinkled flesh, like that of a cut of meat left in a smoker pot for a very long while. It was quite large, being about a span tall and three quarters of a span wide. I only realized what it was when I saw the protuberance of a crooked nose in the middle, and below that two delicate, paperish lips; and there, on either side, shriveled, shrimplike appendages that could have once been ears.

"Ah," I said softly.

I heard Prificto Kardas whisper beside me, "What in *hell*?"

Then Malo: "Oh, fuck."

It was a head. A severed human head that had been mummified or preserved, with nearly every feature still intact save its eyes, which must have been removed, for the sockets now sat empty. The surreality of the sight was so intense that I almost laughed.

Yet the maddest thing was the small piece of parchment tucked between the dark, paperish lips; for written there in very small, careful handwriting, were ten words:

For those who sip from the marrow
Te siz imperiya.

I stared at the words, astounded.

Malo shook her head, made a quiet *tch* sound, and said, "Well. I am afraid I am going to have to ask you all to leave the bank. And quickly, too."

"Wh-what?" demanded Prificto Kardas. "What do you mean, Signum?"

"We wardens have a procedure for when an organic substance is used as a tool of sabotage or tampering," she sighed. "And a goddamn head qualifies as a substance, and sticking one in an Iyalet vault is most definitely tampering. We shall have to all troop in here and make sure it is not a carrier of infection—and then try to figure out whose fucking head that is."

"But . . . but where is it?" asked Ghrelin faintly.

"Where is what, sir?" asked Malo.

"Where . . . where have all my materials gone?" he asked, panicked. Then his voice grew to a shriek: "Where has it all gone, *where has it gone?*" One of the Treasury officers went to comfort him, but he violently shoved her back, shouting, "Don't touch me! Don't you know what's been done to me? Don't you understand *what's been done?*"

Then he burst into tears and collapsed to the floor, his face buried in his hands.

CHAPTER 14

∧∧∧

I LEANED AGAINST THE WALL OUTSIDE THE TREASURY bank, chewing my pipe as late afternoon slowly blended into evening. Within, I knew, the Apoth contagion crew was subjecting the severed head to no end of tests, not only to identify it but also to ensure that it held no contagion or dangerous issue. As they'd been in there for nearly three hours and there'd been no alarm yet, I assumed all was safe, or at least as safe as a bank with boxes of severed heads could possibly be.

For the twentieth time, I debated if there was anything I could do besides wait here. I had no one else to question, really: after his collapse, Immunis Ghrelin had been rushed to a medikker's bay. Though I had told them I wished to speak to him further, they rather curtly informed me that I'd need the approval of his superiors first. I did not love the sound of that, for it only deepened my misgivings about what might have been in that box.

I took my pipe out of my mouth and tetchily studied it. Chewing it was no substitute for its smoke, and though this habit of mine was dreadfully expensive, now seemed a good time to indulge.

I squatted, reached into my satchel, and took out my kindling bag and a tiny clay pot. The pot was no larger than my thumb and held a stiff, lumpy little mushroom. I speared the mushroom through with a splinter of treated wood; a thread of smoke unscrolled from within it; then the splinter of wood suddenly danced with a tiny, merry yellow flame.

I held it to the tip of my pipe, sparked the tobacco, and took a long pull from it, relishing the hot billow of smoke in my lungs. Then I placed the firestarter pot on the brick pathway and stomped on it, killing its flame. A foolish thing, perhaps, to waste it on a single pipe; but the taste of the tobacco calmed my nerves and thoughts, and I thanked Sanctum as the fumes poured from my lips.

Then the door of the bank opened and a figure emerged, wearing an immense mask wrought of glass and slickly shining algaeoil cloth, with a long metal snout: a warding helm, to protect against contagion.

A voice came from within the helm, sour and resentful: "You look like you're having a pleasant time."

The person undid the fasteners on the back and slid the helm off to reveal the sweaty, pink, furious face of Malo.

I nodded to her and spoke, my words animated with smoke: "How goes it?"

"How do you think?" she snapped.

I nodded sympathetically, then sat down on the ground along the bank wall and gestured for her to do the same. Growling, she sat beside me and leaned her head back.

"It is a head," she said. "And *only* a head. It has no secret plagues or contagion within it. A relief, I suppose! But . . . it is not Sujedo's head."

"As I thought," I said. "Being as that head still had its jawbone. Any idea when we'll discover whose it is?"

"We already know. It apparently belonged to an Apoth princeps. A Princeps Traukta Kaukole. He died about two years ago."

My mouth fell open in surprise before I realized how they must have identified the victim so quickly. "Ah. Fellow had a banded tooth?"

"Oh, yes. Here in Yarrowdale, we make sure to track all the bits of our people as best as we can."

A banded tooth was a false molar that had been grown in a reagents tank with a unique striping pattern running across the enamel. When an officer received such a tooth, the pattern was assigned to their name, so if their corpse was ever discovered in the future, it could be speedily identified.

"And how did this Kaukole die?" I asked.

"He was assigned to the management of an Apoth barge that shipped out of here—but the barge vanished en route, along with the entire crew. We never found the barge, nor any sign of their bodies. We eventually marked them all as dead." She spat bitterly onto the bricked pathway leading to the bank. "We assumed smugglers were behind it. One of their first attacks before they became more violent."

"And our impostor . . . took the man's head, and preserved it for two years?" I asked, mystified.

"So it seems!"

"Only to leave it here for us to find, while robbing the bank?"

"So it seems! And he used a very specific art to preserve it, a method of dehydration commonly practiced by we Apoths. But I've no idea why he would do such a thing, or indeed do any of it at all! Unless he does it to send a message, stating that he is a smuggler himself, and . . . he now takes credit for this man's death? And perhaps many others?"

"Like a hunting trophy," I said quietly. "Except the prey he hunts is us?"

Malo made a gesture at the sky, beseeching the attention of one of the elder pantheons. "How I dislike the reversal."

"The note it held. Did I read that right?"

"I assume you did," said Malo. "It said—*For those who sip from the marrow, Te siz imperiya.*"

I turned this over. I had no idea what the first words about the marrow meant, but the final three words were in Old Khanum, an ancient language almost no one spoke anymore, as nearly all the Khanum had gone extinct ages ago; yet they seemed to echo the Emperor's common dictum, *Sen sez imperiya*, which roughly translated to *You are the Empire*, the ancient motto empowering all imperial citizens to make the Empire their own in their own way.

But this message was an inversion of that. Not the standard *You are the Empire*, but rather . . .

"*I* am the Empire?" I said out loud.

Malo laughed bleakly. "Apparently!"

"A skull with words in its mouth," I said. "Stating that it is the Empire . . . It's a message, too, clearly. But I can't make sense of it."

"If you can make sense of this, Kol, it would make me think you have a worm in your brain." She lay back on the brick pathway.

"What will you do with the head?" I asked.

"Once we are done testing it, we shall treat it as a body of one fallen in war. We'll place it in a gilded box, with signs and offerings of reverence from his commanding officers and Iyalet, and have it sent home to his family. They will have already received his lands and dispensation, given that we declared him dead long ago. As if that could ever be enough. Yet still—I am half-tempted to curse you, Kol."

"Pardon?"

"You have come here and not only *not* solved the murder of Sujedo—you have revealed more crimes that may be far worse! The only thing we can think to do is haul in every smuggler and jungle ruffian we know and see what they can tell us about this Kaukole's death—or any movements of this bank robber, should he truly be a smuggler. Though given what we have seen of him so far, I am not optimistic that we shall learn much." She yawned. "Perhaps Tufwa is a good drawer. Maybe he can sketch his likeness . . ."

I looked at Malo sympathetically. All her brash barbarism had melted away, and now she was little more than an exhausted girl sprawled in this empty courtyard. Only a little younger than me, but she seemed at that moment very young.

I held out my pipe. "Care for a puff? Might help."

"Gods, no." She made the sound of hawking something up and spitting it out. "Though this day is ill fated, I will not resort to smoke. Inhaling fumes is terrible for you. I shall keep to my hina root."

"Makes your teeth black."

"So does smoke."

I shrugged and puffed on my pipe. Again we lapsed into silence, listening to the calls of the Apoths in the bank.

"So, this man . . ." I said. "This man somehow hears news of the Treasury delegation and keeps close observation of their movements. He figures out when the last member is going to arrive. He kidnaps the fellow and comes into Yarrowdale and spends the entire day pretending to be this man, just so he can get into the Treasury vault—through means we still can't comprehend. Yet he doesn't just take his prize, whatever it was. Instead, he very calmly places a withered, severed head in the box, along with his inscrutable note. Then he shuts it, returns to his masquerade as Sujedo . . . and then fabricates his own murder before vanishing into thin air. Is that the full spill of it?"

A dreary silence as Malo thought. "It seems so," she said.

I took one last puff of my pipe, then tapped it out on the bricks. "All for healing grafts," I said. "For a cough. It makes no damned sense."

"Perhaps he knows someone who is sick?" said Malo.

"I doubt it." I stood, dusted myself off, and carefully stowed the remainder of my pipe away.

"Then what are you thinking?" Malo asked.

"I think something is wrong," I said. "But I don't yet know what." Then I bade her good night and started back up the path to Ana's lodgings.

II

...

AND ALL
THE WORLD
A SAVAGE GARDEN

CHAPTER 15

⟨ ⟨ ⟨

ANA SAT PERFECTLY STILL IN THE DARK OF HER ROOMS AS she absorbed my report, plucking absently at her Pithian lyre every few minutes. When I finally finished, her fingers retracted from the strings, and she slowly turned her blindfolded face toward me, her mouth open in outrage.

"He left . . . a fucking *note*?" she asked, incredulous.

"It, ah, appears so, ma'am. Along with a head."

Ana's grumbling stretched on and on. She seemed to have entirely forgotten I was there.

"Ah, ma'am?" I asked. "Are yo—"

"I mean," she thundered finally. "He left a *note*! I just . . . I just can't fucking believe that he had the audacity to leave a *note*! It bothers me terribly!"

"I, too, was bothered, ma'am," I said. "Though mostly by the sight of the hea—"

"But frankly, this whole thing *reeks* of audacity!" She ripped her blindfold off, shot to her feet, and began pacing the room like a convict just told of an extension to their sentence. "Can you imagine how many yards of guts it takes, Din, to prance into such highly guarded institutions with little more than confidence to aid you? Aware all the while that simply running into the wrong person at the wrong time would instantly result in your violent arrest? Why, a delegation member might have traipsed back to the tower for any number of reasons, spied this fucker sauntering about, and said, *Hey now, who the hell are you?* Such a thing would be especially dangerous here in this city, which is so crawling with soldiers wary of violence, each empowered to cut anyone down without so much as a peck on the cheek! And now—this! A fucking *note*! I feel we needn't bother looking at faces to find this man, Din! Just keep an eye out for the fellow with testicles large enough to cause back deformities, and we shall have our culprit!"

She sat and began furiously tuning her lyre.

"He is no thief, Din," she proclaimed. "Nor is he a smuggler. For smugglers don't leave notes—and they especially don't leave *political* notes."

"Political?"

"Yes! Are you so ignorant of your imperial history, Din? The bastard quotes the emperor himself!"

"He does?" I said, puzzled. "I thought the statement was *Sen sez imperiya,* rather than—"

"Oh, damn it all!" she fumed. Then she cleared her throat and appeared to recite from memory: "*And thus the emperor said to his advisers, 'We have seen many empires fall, for they did not extend past the breath of their emperors. They decayed, and grew unjust. If I wish this new empire to last, I should not declare to my people that I am the Empire. Rather, I should say to them, You are the Empire. And with that blessing, they shall make a realm for the ages.'*" She sniffed. "That is from *The Letters and Conversations of Ataska Daavir, Fourth and Final Emperor of the Great and Holy Empire of Khanum.* The sixteenth letter, if I recall."

"All right . . . but what's he suggesting by quoting this in a note?"

"Hell if I know!" snarled Ana. "But it's quite a fucking statement! Especially here, in Yarrow, where the status of the Empire is a bit of a big damned question!" She raised her hands and mimed shoving something away. "I disdain it. I disdain it so, all this fucking spectacle! Nothing irks me more than a showy murderer, as if their wretched deeds were some mystical marvel!"

"And the first lines, ma'am?" I asked. "The bit about sipping from the marrow?"

Her face relaxed, ever so slightly. "Yes . . . *For those who sip from the marrow*. That is most curious. It is not from any text I am aware of." She cocked her head. "Hm. Marrow . . . marrow, in this city of blood."

I glanced at the veiled window and spied a slice of moonlit waves in the bay beyond. A dull horror crawled over me.

"You think this has something to do with titan's blood, ma'am?" I asked quietly. "Or the Shroud? The very place where they extract the blood?"

"Perhaps. For in a way, do we not all sip from the titan's marrow, in one fashion or another?"

I shuddered but did not answer.

Ana's yellow eyes were now as narrow as a knife's edge. "You know, there was an imperial proposal I read about ten years ago that referenced marrow . . . A bunch of Apoths got very alarmed about the Shroud, claiming that our whole system for rendering reagents and precursors was terribly fragile. Which it is, of course! We are rather like those clans in the ancient wastes who could only fell beasts during the rainy seasons and had to find all sorts of horrid ways to make the flesh last through the dry months. Rather than hauling a dead leviathan to Yarrowdale to bleed of its ichors once a wet season, these Apoths proposed removing a piece of one's marrow and bringing it inland, so it could—perhaps!—continue excreting blood. Thus rendering this whole horrid fucking process moot."

"What happened to these proposals?"

"Nothing. Dealing with leviathan entrails is a catastrophically dangerous business. What kind of a mad fucker would wish to climb inside one and go poking about? Whole thing got shelved. Perhaps the reference is coincidental. Or perhaps our culprit is simply mad. I cannot tell."

She lapsed into a grudging silence, and for a while she simply rocked back and forth, and would say no more.

"Then . . . how shall we proceed, ma'am?" I asked.

Ana's yellow eyes danced in her skull as she thought. Then she blew a snow-white forelock away from her face and said, "Well, first—you're going to buy me that damned Pithian lyre, Din."

I paused for a moment, puzzled. "Oh. The second one. Because you wish to—"

"To play my duets, yes. I simply *must* have something entertaining to focus on! Ordinarily I'd let my mind go burrowing into all manner of books and research, but I feel I have to keep my faculties mastered for this one. Get me my damned lyre, Din, or I swear by the emperor's buttocks, every time you report back to me, my mood shall be blacker and blacker!"

I nodded. As bizarre as it was, this was better than her asking me to purchase illegal psychoactive substances: a far more common request. "You shall have it tomorrow, ma'am."

"Good! Next . . . I see four fronts to attack on this one." She stuck four knobby fingers into the air. "First—the safe. Not the Treasury one, but the *Apoth* one."

"You're wondering how the impostor got access to that one as well?" I said. "Kardas even speculated that the man had magic bloo—"

"No!" she spat. "Do you not see? By leaving that head in that goddamned box, this fellow was telling us two very important things about him!"

I paused, and slowly all the disparate pieces tumbled into place. "Ah. He intentionally left a head with a banded tooth," I said. "A marker that only an Apoth would know of."

"There's that," she said, "*and* the head was preserved with an art known well to the Apoths! And here is another critical bit of information—for Malo *told you* how people get access to those safes! They are *given* it. Do you not see the obvious answer to this, Din?"

My skin rippled with chill. "He's an Apoth, then," I said softly. "And he's one that was once given access to that very box."

"Exactly! This would explain many things, but also his skill with disguises—for who is better at shaping flesh than an Apoth? For with those arts, he could grant himself a little thickness of face, or a tuft of hair as needed."

"And his abilities with the Treasury tests . . ."

"I assume having a great deal of Sujedo's blood available would help with passing those!" she said. "I'm still not quite sure he pulled that off, though . . . There are methods of transferring blood from one person to another, but none are quick, and *certainly* not easy. Hence, I am focusing on his manipulation of the Apoth vault as opposed to the Treasury one."

"So . . . you think the Apoths can just pull a list of all those officers with access to that specific safe," I said, "and one of the names has to be our impostor?"

"Maybe, maybe not," said Ana. "Again, this bastard's smart. Infuriatingly so." Again, she began to pace the room. "Hm . . . I feel it's unlikely he's still in service. Thus, I will need a list of *all* officers who have *ever* been granted access to that safe. I don't care if it's in the dozens or hundreds, we need to check them all."

A black cloud bloomed in my mind. There was nothing Ana loved more than lists and records, but the Iyalets of the Empire were always notoriously reluctant to give up anything important. Usually I had to put Ana in a room with someone senior and allow her to frighten them witless to get what we needed.

"Think the Apoths will give us that, ma'am?" I asked.

"I'm not done yet!" she snapped. "I want to move to our second attack front before we discuss that. And this one, Din, is a bit heftier . . ." She plucked a single, haunting chord on her lyre. "For I want to know *all* of the reagent thefts that have taken place in Yarrow in the past two years."

"You want *what?*"

"It is quite simple. I want a list of every single reagent, every graft, every precursor, every *everything* that has been stolen from this godforsaken port town in the past twenty-four months! And I also want to know when and where they were stolen from!"

"But . . . but, ma'am," I protested. "Smuggling is so rife here. I can't imagine how long such a list might be . . ."

"Yet we shall have to trawl through it!" she snapped. "Do you think this is our impostor's first robbery? His first murder? Remember, Din, that the only reason we've come to realize any of this happened is that some fucking turtle satisfied its appetite and happened to leave some scraps in the waters! Without those fragments of flesh, we'd know none of this! And we now know he was possibly responsible for one of the first smuggling murders, years ago. He may well have committed a dozen more such crimes, leaving no evidence of himself behind! So. We need that list, no matter how ponderous, and I shall see what patterns may be divined in its innards."

"And the missing reagents, ma'am? The healing grafts he did all this to steal?"

"Grafts! Ha!" She made a rude gesture with her hand. "Healing grafts in-fucking-deed!"

"I take it that you, too, do not believe that was what was in that box?"

"Absolutely not," she said. "Respiratory diseases? Utter piffle. Very idea is absurd. And you told me that Ghrelin seemed unusually eager to open that box, even though you told him not to! It makes one think, naturally, there might have been something in that box he did not want any of you to see."

"Yes. So. What do you think the killer actually stole?"

"Oh, I've no idea. Something very, *very* valuable, surely. I intend to find out what."

"What could the Apoths be doing that would make them risk lying to the Iudex?"

"Something terribly dangerous, and secret. That is for certain." She paused. "Tell me . . . when you first met him, this Immunis Ghrelin seemed nervous, yes? He seemed to know, instantly, what had gone wrong?"

"Yes, ma'am. Something in the way he looked at me. Trying to understand how much I understood myself. And then afterward, in the vault, he was overcome."

"As if the damage done to him was so great," she said softly, "he could not believe it had happened . . . Interesting. And the tapping. He kept *tapping* throughout everything?"

"Yes."

"Very loudly?"

"Yes. On his belt buckle."

"With three fingers?"

"Yes, ma'am."

She whispered, "Tapping. Tapping . . ." and shut her eyes. "You engraved this tapping in your memory?"

"Of course. All I heard and saw."

"Then summon the memories, please, Din, and tap out all you can for me. I wish to hear this myself."

My eyes fluttered as the memories of the bank came swimming up within the dark well of my mind. Then I reached forward and rapped my knuckles on her table corner, imitating the tapping I'd heard and seen Ghrelin perform. Though now that I duplicated it, I realized that the tapping had repeated rhythms, echoing over and over again, mixed in among other rhythms that were totally new. It was very strange to have the sounds brought alive by my own knuckles.

Ana listened closely, eyes closed. When I finished, she whispered, "Fascinating. Very fascinating . . . Another tapping, yet again."

I watched her leaning back where she sat, her own pale digits fluttering on her knee. Then I understood.

I recalled the maid I'd interviewed, describing the false Sujedo: *His hand twitched, I recall, his fingers flitting against his belly.*

And then Klaida: *He did tap against his leg, over and over again, as he walked. Like drumming. Like he had a tune in his head and couldn't help but beat its rhythm against something. It was a little strange, sir.*

"The impostor did the same thing," I said softly. "He tapped his body, just like Ghrelin—is that it?"

"You've grown sharp, Din!" she said, grinning. "How glad I am to see that. But don't get too excited. We cannot clap people in irons at the twitch of a finger. I'd need to hear more of this tapping to see if it means anything, and the only way to do that would be to witness more samples."

"How might we do that?"

"Well, the simplest way would be to simply go talk to Ghrelin again," Ana said. "Which we are going to do tomorrow! And that shall be our *third* attack front."

"*We*, ma'am? You wish to come yourself?"

"Oh, yes. I wish to talk to this Ghrelin personally. Make a request for an interview with the Apoths first thing in the morning, Din. I doubt if we'll be able to get him alone—odds are some of his superiors will demand to be present as well—but we'll use that audience to request all our records from them. We shall listen to what Ghrelin says, see what the Apoths give us . . . and sift through the tea leaves carefully."

I sighed deeply, now tired to the bone. "And what of the fourth attack front?"

"The fourth?" she said, puzzled. "Did I mention a fourth?"

"Even when I am this fatigued, ma'am, my memory is not."

"Oh. Ohh, yes! The fourth . . ." She shrugged. "Well, the fourth is that we wait and see what this impostor is going to do next. Or who he's going to kill."

"You . . . wish to wait for this killer to kill again?"

"Well, I don't *want* to, Din. I'd prefer it if I could just toss a stone out my window and strike this fucker in the head! Yet that is unlikely. We shall pursue the threads I've laid out here, yet . . . when he makes his next move, he shall surely be vulnerable again, yes?"

"Is there no chance he's finished?"

"Oh, Din . . ." She laughed lowly. "He is not done. He's left a *note*, and a trophy with many secret meanings! He has opened lines of communication." She lay back on her bed, her fingers threaded dreamily on her belly. "The question is—who is his audience? And what form shall his next message take?"

CHAPTER 16

. . .

THE NEXT MORNING I CALLED A CARRIAGE FOR ANA, AND
together we rode to the Apoth advanced fermentation works. The sky
was dreary and overcast, the clouds low and resentful as they gathered over the hills, until they finally released a drizzling rain. All the
world felt stagnant, with little light, and no wind.

Ana—blindfolded, of course—spoke constantly as we rattled on
over the muddy roads. "Apoth fermentation works are some of the
most complex of all their facilities—did you know that, Din?"

"I did not, ma'am," I said, yawning. However many hours of sleep
I'd captured last night, they'd not been enough.

"Oh, yes. They are mostly found in the inner rings, these great,
sprawling piles of pots and pipes and telltale plants grouped about
the canals, all put together to prevent impurities and maintain nutrient concentrations . . . The materials and tissues they produce
are so complex that even I have a little trouble following the— Oof!
My, *that* was a big bump, I wonder how that brick back there got so
dislodged . . ." She then launched into a winding dissertation about
roads: one of her favorite topics.

We arrived at the advanced fermentation works just past midmorning. It was set behind a high fretvine fence, and it resembled a
dense, misshapen clutch of large fretvine orbs clumped together.
Glass windows topped each orb, and in the center of each set of windows was a chimney releasing a narrow thread of steam. With the
high fretvine fence closely circling this lumpy design, the whole thing

had the look of a complex Rathras pastry, the fluffy dough piling out of the dish.

We exited the carriage, and I paid the pilot to wait for us. We showed our heralds at the gate—Ana's took some time to decipher as she had sorted hers by color—and were admitted inside. The interior of the building was no less strange than the exterior: it was akin to being within a giant hive, with so many interconnected, bulbous chambers with railings and walkways yawning above us, and all teeming with the red coats and tunics of Apoths going about their day.

While we waited for our escort, I studied the Apoths swarming about us, my eyes fluttering as I perused my memories. I saw no face I found familiar, yet I did note many Sublimes. Nearly all of them were axioms, though here and there I did see a spatiast, or a lingua.

Then I noticed something.

"There are no engravers," I said quietly.

"What's that?" said Ana.

"There are no engravers here, ma'am. I see many Sublimes and many augmented folk, but no engravers."

"Hm! Interesting. Perhaps they do things here they don't want anyone remembering."

A militis emerged from the crowd, bowed, and asked us to follow. Ana took me by the arm, and we wandered into the sprawling hive.

WE WERE BROUGHT to a large meeting room that was dominated by a giant, circular table wrought of black stonewood. Tiny mai-lights hung from the rounded walls, and the windows above allowed in the gray, watery light of the stormy skies. In the center of the table sat a strange contraption resembling a great brass teapot, yet it had many leathery tubes protruding from its base, each one ending in a small black nozzle.

"You may sit where you like, ma'am," said the militis. "And you may feel free to partake of our percolator as you please."

"Oh, you've a percolator!" Ana said. "What might the steams do? I'm afraid I can't see any labels about the damned hoses, of course."

"Uh, yes . . ." said the militis, befuddled. "Well. This first hose here is a stimulant, and this second one is a slight sedative, for agitation. This next one offers focus, and then this fourth is physical relaxation. Finally, that fifth one there on the end is an appetite suppressor. For very long meetings, you see."

"Excellent!" said Ana. She sat, fumbled for the stimulant hose, popped its black nozzle in her mouth, and gave it a mighty suck. The brass percolator burbled and warbled; then she sat back and exhaled, releasing a roiling cloud of thick steam. "Thank you. We shall wait in comfort, then."

The militis departed, shutting the door behind him. I watched guardedly as Ana took yet another outrageous suck from the stimulant nozzle.

"Are you sure you wish to be doing that before our meeting, ma'am?" I asked.

"Oh, it's all very mild," she said, her lips blooming steam. "These reagents just give your mood a slight nudge. They're not *real* moodies, like the ones I prefer. Here. Pass me the relaxant one. Let me give that a suck. And you—you shall take this stimulant one, Din." She shoved it in my face.

The nozzle smelled faintly of boiled cabbage. I wrinkled my nose. "Not sure I wish to indulge, ma'am."

"Don't be such a damned prude. Besides, I heard you yawning. I need you awake and alert for this. Go on! Give it a suck, boy!"

Glowering, I took the hose, vigorously cleaned off the nozzle with a handkerchief, placed it in my mouth, and inhaled.

Suddenly my bones and nerves felt alight with movement, and every object in the room became clearer, like my eyes had grown larger in my head. I put the hose down as I exhaled, and though I could see the fumes leave my lips, I could have sworn they were also swilling about in my skull, urging me to twitch and dance.

"It's like drinking three clar-teas at once," I said, awed.

"I'd forgotten your skull was so virginal—perhaps the only goddamned part of you that is anymore, boy. Stop there, then. We don't want you twitching throughout this, that'd be a damned sigh—"

Then the door opened, and a small parade of officers walked in. I stood as they entered, and Ana wobbily did the same.

The first to walk through the door was Ghrelin, still tall and tremulous, his black eyes anxious, his pale pate gleaming in the light of the mai-lanterns. He glanced at me nervously as he crossed to stand behind one of the chairs on the other side of the table. There were bags about his eyes, and a paperish quality to the gray skin about his cheeks. Perhaps he was the one person here even more tired than I.

After Ghrelin came a woman even taller than him, and indeed almost as tall as I. She moved slowly and confidently, like a person of power accustomed to being waited on, each step careful and precise. Like Ghrelin, her head was almost totally denuded of hair, but she had a Rathras look to her, her features long and aquiline. Her raiment was glorious and glittering, her robes all layered in crimsons and dark yellows, which gave her the look of an autumn leaf from one of the high mountain trees of the inner Empire. As she passed below the light of the glass windows above, I caught a glint from her robes, and saw heralds denoting her a commander-prificto. It was likely she was the highest-ranking officer in the entire facility.

After her came three Apoth commanders, two men and a woman, who followed her in a tight line. I was reminded of wood ducklings swimming after their mother. The three commanders took their places behind the commander-prificto, then turned to look at Ana and me with eyes both watchful and suspicious.

The commander-prificto waited until her people were all in place before giving us a slight bow. "Good morning," she said, her voice cool and soft. "Thank you for coming. I am Commander-Prificto Kulaq Thelenai, and these are Commanders Biktas, Nepasiti, and Sizeides."

The three commanders gave us a unified, unsmiling nod.

Commander-Prificto Thelenai extended a hand to Ghrelin. "And I believe you are already acquainted with Immunis Rava Ghrelin . . ."

A nervous smile from Ghrelin, yet he shot a searching glance at Thelenai, as if to confirm that his smile did not bring reproach. It was in this small gesture that I suddenly felt I had the feel of them: Thelenai was the grand and steely queen of this realm, and he was her scurrying counselor, rushing to invent laws to match her will.

Ana and I bowed and introduced ourselves. "Thank you all for agreeing to this interview on such short notice, ma'am," said Ana, attempting a sane smile. "We felt the situation demanded a speedy response."

"Indeed," said Thelenai somberly. "This incident is one of the most disturbing in recent memory—the sensitive workings of two Iyalets so thoroughly damaged, and here, in this most sensitive of places, at this most difficult of times! We are glad to have the Iudex assist. Please sit."

Thelenai sat, and her entourage followed suit. I did the same, and Ana plopped into her seat. Yet as we all settled, Commander-Prificto Thelenai's face was suddenly washed in the light from the windows above, and I saw that the whites of her eyes were stained deeply green, just like Malo's. There was even a faint stain of green to her lips.

I studied the sight carefully. She was the first imperial person I'd seen as green-stained as a native Pithian. I made a note to ask Ana about it later.

"If we could, ma'am," Ana said, "I would like to begin by setting some expectations. We have only recently stumbled across these crimes, and we still know very little. Yet we know the Apothetikal Iyalet here is a victim, in a way. So we must question you as victims in order to begin to understand what happened."

"Of course," said Thelenai. "But in anticipation of this meeting, Immunis, I have taken the liberty of assembling some information for you . . ." She waved a hand to one of the commanders, who reached into a satchel and produced a small pile of parchments. "I thought to procure a list of all living officers who have been given access to all the Apoth safes in the Treasury bank in Yarrowdale. It seemed likely pertinent to the crime. I hope I was not untoward in assuming you might want this."

The commander brought the parchments before Ana, bowed,

and returned to his seat. Ana sat for a moment, nonplussed to have one of her requests for information not only exactly predicted, but quickly met.

"Oh," she muttered. She plucked at the parchments like they were a dish she had not ordered. "Well, ah. This is very good. I had intended to ask for precisely that."

Thelenai gave a solemn nod, followed by a puff at one of the percolator hoses: the relaxant, unless I was mistaken. "Of course."

"While we're on the matter," said Ana, "I, ah, *had* also wished to get another bit of information. Specifically, a summary of all reagent and precursor thefts of the past two years, if I could, ma'am."

"All?" said Thelenai, her breath heavy with fumes. "That is a serious request, for there are many thefts. Yet . . . I suspect you think this criminal has stolen from us before, Dolabra? Is that it?"

"Exactly so, ma'am. For the severed head this man left for us suggests he has been with the smugglers for some time."

Thelenai considered it, then gestured to one of her commanders. "Then it shall be done. I will have them sent to your quarters as soon as possible."

"Oh," said Ana. She seemed almost disappointed to find them so unwilling to put up a fight. I could have almost sworn I heard her mutter, "Well, fuck." Then, louder, "Thank you, ma'am! This is very generous."

"Of course," said Thelenai again. "We will assist in any way we can. Though I note that these will only indicate what was stolen, and not the culprits. There are, I understand, many smuggling clans in the jungles, and they all seem as slippery as eels. Now . . . you wished to interview Immunis Ghrelin about the nature of the theft, correct?"

"Correct, ma'am," said Ana.

Thelenai looked to Ghrelin, who nodded nervously.

"You may proceed," said Thelenai.

"Excellent," said Ana.

CHAPTER 17

▲ ▲ ▲

ANA CLEARED HER THROAT. "FIRST... I WOULD LIKE TO confirm the nature of the material that was stolen, Immunis," she said. "You told Din here that it was a new formulation of healing grafts, correct?"

Ghrelin nodded, his hands in his lap. "They were."

"Can you tell us more about these grafts?" asked Ana.

"Well... they are very complex. For the diseases they cure are very complex."

"I have a delight for complex things," said Ana, grinning. "Indulge me."

"Certainly," said Ghrelin. "I shall try to explain..."

He began to speak, starting with the nature of these respiratory diseases: the way they inflamed the lungs and how these infections could rapidly progress in the very young and very old. He described the difficulty in trying to treat these infections, for though they all produced similar symptoms, they could be caused by any one of dozens of contagions or diseases, and each one required a specific graft to cure.

"I see," said Ana when Ghrelin finished. She cocked her head, letting the silence hang. "And *this* is what the perpetrator killed, tortured, maimed, and deceived so many to steal?"

Ghrelin paused. His eyes danced uncertainly about the table before he sat back into a position of relaxed repose. "It was, ma'am," he said.

"Why would he wish to steal such a thing?" asked Ana.

"I've no idea, save that the cures are very valuable. Perhaps that is why."

"Did you have many colleagues working upon these grafts with you?"

"No, I did not," said Ghrelin. "I worked alone."

"I see . . ."

Ana then asked him the common stuff. Had he seen or heard of anyone unusual asking about his works, or heard of anyone else doing so? Witnessed any signs of tampering? Seen anyone following him, or found any correspondence missing?

"No, no," he said, shaking his head. "There is nothing I can recall."

Had he ever experienced any robberies before? she asked. Had any of his works been stolen, or been the subject of attempted theft?

Again, no.

"And what did you do before working upon these healing grafts?" asked Ana.

Ghrelin hesitated. Then he said quietly, "I worked within the Shroud."

A loud silence filled the room.

"You worked within . . . the *Shroud*?" asked Ana.

"I did, ma'am," he said.

"Can you tell us about that, please?"

Commander-Prificto Thelenai raised a hand. "The Shroud is a very critical and delicate part of imperial infrastructure, Immunis. It is the sole source of the purest titan's blood. We do not share much information about it, for that could make it vulnerable. I wish to know why you ask this."

"Certainly!" said Ana. "The perpetrator appears to possess intimate knowledge of all the workings of Yarrowdale, but especially of Ghrelin's projects. Thus, it's possible that not only is the culprit an Apoth but perhaps one that Ghrelin has *met* before—though he might not know it. Ghrelin has also just said he worked *alone* upon his healing grafts, so the perpetrator likely did not meet him during these labors. Thus, Ghrelin might have met them in a previous station—including the Shroud."

Thelenai glanced at her entourage. Her commanders looked back with their small, mistrustful eyes but said nothing.

"I consent," said Thelenai. "But we can only offer you a limited testimony here." She nodded to Ghrelin. "Continue, Immunis. Carefully."

Ghrelin cleared his throat, then said, "Well, I . . . I worked upon the envelope, the veil of the Shroud. The thing that gives the installation its name. The veil absorbs and destroys most contagions as it comes into contact with them, airborne and otherwise. Without the veil, the, ah . . . the *extraction* of various critical reagents would be impossible."

The sight of the Shroud flashed in my mind: huge and green and towering, and fluttering so strangely over the waters.

Ana picked up one of the percolator hoses, plugged it into her mouth, and took an enormous pull from it, the contraption whistling like a startled dove. Then she exhaled and said, "You mean, it would be damned hard to take a leviathan's carcass and bleed it of all of its bloods and liquors *without* unleashing catastrophic contagion on all of Yarrow?"

"C-correct," said Ghrelin.

"How does it manage this feat, Immunis?" asked Ana.

Ghrelin laughed wearily. "That is like asking how the emperor has lived to be four hundred and forty-one years old! It is a great achievement that calls upon many arts, and few can claim to know or comprehend it all. But in crudest terms, the Shroud is based upon a . . . a tissue found inside of the leviathans themselves."

"The Shroud is made from a *piece* of the leviathans?" asked Ana.

Again, Thelenai raised a hand. "This is a question of great secrecy. I am afraid I cannot permit discussion of it."

"Noted," said Ana, grinning. "How long did you work inside the Shroud?"

Ghrelin hesitated. Then, very slowly, his hand crept forward on the table.

"For ... for three years," he said quietly. "That is the longest one can serve there."

His fingers twitched on the table. Then his thumb, index, and middle rose high like a mantis about to strike, and then ...

Tap-tap-tap. Taptap. Taptap-tap.

Ana's head cocked very slightly at the sound of it. I saw the hint of a smile to her lips. She appeared to think for a moment, listening to the tapping. Then she said, "Tell me, Ghrelin ... can you *explain* the Shroud to me? For I've heard many things about it, but never from an Apoth, and certainly never from an Apoth who actually *worked* upon it."

Ghrelin's fingers twitched away—*Tap-tap. Taptap-tap-taptap-tap.*

"I could ..." he said quietly. "In broad terms."

"Then please," said Ana, "indulge me."

I studied her, still grinning in her enormous cloud of smoke. She wished to keep him talking, I guessed; for when he talked of his time on the Shroud, he tapped, and she must have spied some value in his tapping.

"Well ... it takes us about two weeks to move a leviathan carcass here, to Yarrowdale," said Ghrelin. "We bring it into the bay, and we ... we dock it alongside the Shroud, out there in the waters. And then we gather the veil about it." He leaned forward, still tapping, his eyes bright with a curious light. "Each body is different, you know. No two leviathans are alike. We do not know why—we comprehend so very little about them, really—but there is always variation. And we at the Shroud have only a, a handful of days to look at the anatomy, to comprehend the structure of this new thing, before it decays beyond salvage." He began speaking very fast, and tapping even faster. "There are layers and chambers to each one, you see, with different types of bloods within. And places where the blood is most corrosive, and chambers where it is purest."

"Tell me about that," said Ana softly.

He nodded eagerly, as if she'd stoked the fire in his mind. "The purest of titan's blood—or *qudaydin kani*, as is the proper name—is powerfully metamorphic. When it comes into contact with a significant concentration of living tissues, it mixes with them, forcing a strange blending. Flesh becomes as leaf, and leaf as bone, and so on. All is warped. There are places in the plains about Talagray in the East, for example, where many leviathans have been felled, and many strange and awful breeds of flowers still spring from the blighted lands ..."

I kept my face grim and stoic at that, for I had seen such sights myself.

"What do you mean by *significant concentration*?" asked Ana.

"The very air about us is alight with a scant mist of life," chanted Ghrelin, waving a hand. "But that is not enough. It takes a slight bit more. A dusting of fungi, a scraping of mold ... Though tiny to our eyes, these are enough to induce a reaction from the *kani*. It is dangerous, but terribly valuable! And accessing it is hardest of all." A wet gleam as he licked his lips, and he spoke still faster: "It ... it comes to a question of parting flesh, of navigating this immense construct of bone and ligament and chitin, wending through the whole of its being until you find the one place, the *one place* where you ca—"

"Immunis," said Thelenai softly.

Ghrelin stopped, abashed. The wild light in his eyes dimmed, and he cleared his throat and withdrew back into himself.

"We, ah, drain it of its most critical bloods," Ghrelin finished quietly. "These we ship to the canals, to be fed through the orchards there to produce precursors and be further refined. The remainder of the carcass is hauled into the seas to the east, to sink, rot, and be lost."

His tapping slowed, then stopped.

Ana sat with her head cocked. "This work sounds very dangerous, then."

"Again—very," said Ghrelin.

"Do you recall any colleagues who disagreed with it?" asked Ana. "Or held grudges against you, or it?"

"Why?" said Ghrelin, suddenly irritated.

"It is as I said. I am wondering if one of your colleagues from this era of your service might be our culprit."

Ghrelin suddenly burst out in a wild titter of laughter. The other Apoths appeared startled by it, or perhaps embarrassed. I began to sense there was something that marked Ghrelin as different from the rest of them, including Thelenai, but I could not yet divine what it was.

"You will have to forgive me, ma'am," said Ghrelin, still smiling. "But I don't think you work with Apoths of our sort."

Ana grinned back and took another long draw from yet another hose. "What makes you say that?"

"Because we are asked to suffer most," said Ghrelin, "to provide the most. The alterations we provide, they . . . they not only keep the Empire functioning, but they make it far *better*. Even here, in Yarrow. I mean . . ." He sat forward. "Do you know, Immunis Dolabra, how many Yarrow children survived past the age of five a century ago?"

The other Apoths exchanged an uncomfortable look.

"I'm afraid I do not!" said Ana cheerily.

"Two of seven," Ghrelin said. "Only *two*. Odds were that the other five perished before then. The families here had to have an enormous number of children just to sustain themselves. Now—can you guess how many of those mothers survived these births?"

Ana sucked at a hose again, wreathing herself in fumes. "Enlighten me, please."

"A little less than two in three," said Ghrelin. "Every pregnancy, every birth—for each one, the life of the mother amounted to little more than the roll of a die. Those children and mothers and fathers that lived went on to lead lives of starvation, and disease, and poverty, and violence. But today . . ." He put a finger in the middle of the table: a sole *tap*. "Today, *six* of seven children make it past the age of five. Today, *four* of five mothers survive childbirth. Today, though starvation and disease remain present in Yarrow, they are mere ghosts. Because of Apoths like myself, and those I served with, who labored, suffered, and perished within the Shroud. Thus, I cannot imagine that one of my colleagues from these labors might be the perpetrator of these horrid crimes. It is impossible."

Ana nodded, still grinning, still awash in smokes. "Fascinating. I have just one last thing to ask of you."

"Yes?" said Ghrelin.

"What do you make of the phrase—*For those who sip from the marrow?*"

Ghrelin blinked very rapidly. "I b-beg your pardon?"

"Those words were written on a note the criminal left behind for us to discover. The full phrase was—*For those who sip from the marrow, Te siz imperiya.* Does this make any sense to you?"

I watched them all carefully. The Apoths beside Ghrelin had not moved much, but at this they became stiller than stone, their eyes fixed on indistinct points on the table, as if they'd just instructed their own bodies to go dormant. Ghrelin himself paused, a sheen of sweat now crawling across his brow. Then something steeled in his face, in his eyes, and when he spoke, his words were firm and controlled.

"No," he said. "I am not familiar with that phrase."

"And it does not seem to refer to anything you know?" asked Ana.

"Not at all."

Ana nodded and shifted forward in her chair, mouth slightly open as if wondering how best to phrase what she had to say. She reached out, appearing to grasp another percolator hose—but then she raised her index and middle fingers and tapped very quickly on the table, a brief little tattoo: *Tap-tap. Taptap-tap.*

Ghrelin's eyes shot wide. He stared at Ana's hand, then up at her face, astonished. Ana appeared ignorant of his reaction, and instead grabbed the stimulant hose yet again and inhaled from it.

"There was a proposal about a decade back to find a way to do something with leviathan marrow, yes?" she asked.

Ghrelin was shaking very violently now. "I . . . I . . . I'm sorry?"

"A proposal, I said. About trying to take the marrow from a leviathan's carcass. Does that sound familiar to you, Immunis?"

Ghrelin opened his mouth to speak, but Thelenai coolly said, "We cannot comment on any proposals or business concerning the Shroud, Dolabra. I have made that clear."

My eyes stayed fixed on her face. Did I now see a worm of terror to the commander-prificto's gaze?

Ana cocked her head, savoring the statement like one might a bite of a fine meal. "Fascinating," she said. "Then I believe we are done. Thank you all for speaking to us. It has been most educational for me."

AFTER THE INTERVIEW was finished, Thelenai remained behind to speak with us.

"You will have to forgive Ghrelin's passions," said Thelenai quietly. "He is an ardent servant of the Empire, and he is still coming to terms with this crime."

"I understand, ma'am," said Ana. "The Empire's servants are dedicated folk, in every Iyalet. Yet still I worry that Ghrelin has met our murderer sometime in his past. Would it be possible for you to send me his service record?"

Thelenai studied Ana for a moment. This close, her eyes seemed even greener than Malo's. "Of course," she said. "But you do not suspect Ghrelin of any misdeed, do you?"

"Not yet, no."

"You should not. It's very rare to have someone survive the Shroud and return to labor among us. Most go to live on the lands they are awarded for their service there. As such, Ghrelin is terribly valuable. I would not deny the emperor's justice if he were to be suspected, yet . . . I feel he must be innocent in all this."

"Let us hope so. Yet I have two more questions for you, Commander-Prificto, if you are willing," said Ana.

"Certainly."

"Why are there no engravers in this building?"

Thelenai's eyes widened ever so slightly. "Ah. You have noticed. Yes—we bar all engravers from accessing the inner reaches of the fermentation works. Likewise, we permit no warden, nor anyone else with hearing augmentations, to draw near. The reason is that much of what we do here is experimental, and untested. Anything we make will take a long while to be approved for use."

"And you worry about having an engraver walk your halls," said Ana, "and memorizing every formula they see, and then secreting out something unstable to some illegal brewery?"

"Exactly."

"Then," said Ana, grinning, "can *I* tour the fermentation works, even if Din cannot? I would be most eager to see how advanced they truly are, for I am no engraver."

Thelenai paused. "Well. To begin with, Immunis, you are wearing a blindfold. While this is not terribly unusual to me, given all the stimulative afflictions of altered folk, I am not sure what value a tour could offer you . . ."

"It is no issue! I am happy to walk and listen. And smell! That can tell me many things."

"Yes. But." Thelenai's eyes flicked down to Ana's scattered heralds and back. "The issue is, I am not sure how *you* are altered, Immunis. For though you seem no Sublime, Dolabra, I cannot help but suspect you have alterations of your own. Ones that are unmarked upon you. And that I find very strange."

There was a tense silence. Ana's predatorial grin did not waver at all.

"I cannot risk it," said Thelenai. "Thus, I am afraid I will have to turn you down. Now. If you will excuse me, we have much to do in the wake of the robbery."

CHAPTER 18

▲ ▲ ▲

"WELL. THAT WAS FUCKING ODD AS HELL, WASN'T IT, Din?" asked Ana as we rode back to our lodgings.

I was not sure which oddness she meant, as the meeting had seemed to offer no end of it, so I simply said, "I would agree, ma'am."

"Why don't you go ahead and give me the rundown? Describe all you saw—every movement, every twitch."

I did so, sniffing my vials and reporting all the movements I'd seen, and occasionally echoing the voices of the people we'd interviewed. "I am hesitant to make quick judgments," I said at the end, "but from my tell of it, it seems Immunis Ghrelin is a very passionate man."

"Yes, he has all the zeal of a true fanatic," she said. "But the idea that a veteran of the abattoir of the leviathans would leave that and go into curing coughs . . . It's ridiculous. Ridiculous! What else did you see?"

I told her of Thelenai's eyes and lips, and how they were stained green much like Malo's and the other Pithian and Yarrow folk I'd seen about.

"Yes . . ." said Ana. "It's an algae, actually. Grows on the waters about these hills. It acts like a beneficial parasite, infesting parts of the body, but granting you slightly heightened immunities . . . I'm told people grow the green if they reside here for, oh, more than a decade or so, though some lakes in the Elder West can taint your eyes in a matter of days. This means Thelenai has been here for some time . . . Interesting. And interesting that she hasn't had it fixed."

"Fixed?"

"Yes, the stain can be reversed, of course, by a sultur graft applied to the eyes. Little drops you can pop in that eat the green. Not too painful . . . I wonder why she hasn't bothered! But regardless, now for the last bit—how did they react when I brought up the *marrow*?"

"They did not react at all, ma'am. Which I found very curious. In fact, I almost felt like their reaction was . . ."

"Rehearsed?" she proposed.

"Exactly so."

"Then they knew the question was coming. I dislike that immensely, Din." A mad grin crossed her face. "But! At least now we know that Ghrelin and the Apoths here are pursuing a rather conventional brand of obstruction."

"As . . . opposed to an *un*conventional brand, ma'am?"

"Oh, indeed," she said coyly. "At first I wondered if Ghrelin *couldn't* tell us. As in, he was literally incapable of doing so. For did you know, boy, that the Empire has methods of rendering certain secrets unmentionable? Grafts and arts that, when suffused into the body and mind, alter a person in such a way that they are *physically incapable* of divulging a specific piece of information?"

"I . . . had heard rumors of such a practice, ma'am, from time to time. But I thought them only rumor. It seemed far too ghastly an idea for the Empire to ever put into use."

"Oh, no," she said, laughing lightly. "It exists but is exceptionally uncommon! The process of achieving this effect is so complex that it can only be done with the subject's *consent*. They must *agree* to this methodology. A strange thing, yes? For . . . what manner of secret could ever require such measures?"

"Yet . . . you do not think Ghrelin or the others have undergone such a treatment?"

"No, I do not," she said rather sharply.

"What makes you so sure?"

"I have witnessed folk altered in such a fashion. Merely nearing the unmentionable subject causes them significant pain. I did not note such pain in Ghrelin." She flicked a hand, dismissing the subject. "It was a random aside. Ignore it for now—but do *remember* it, Din."

I blinked, thoroughly bewildered by this, for I always engraved all she ever said. I wondered why she'd said it at all, but then, Ana often said many mad things.

CHAPTER 19

▲ ▲ ▲

WHEN WE FINALLY ARRIVED AT ANA'S LODGINGS, I EXITED, paid the pilot, and helped her to her front door. There I stopped. "There are three rather large packages here waiting for you, ma'am." I stooped to look at them. "Appears to be parchments. And I see the Apoth symbol here . . ."

"They've *already* sent me the records?" said Ana, agog. "Titan's taint! I hardly know what to think anymore."

I helped her inside, then hauled the packages in and opened them, only to discover they were so overstuffed that tiny parchments came spilling out, as if I'd split the seam of a bag of rice. I hastily gathered them back up and sorted them into stacks, and though my accursed eyes struggled with their tiny writing, I saw they were the shipping manifests of every Yarrow barge that had gone missing in the past two years.

Yet one slender envelope emerged from the piles of curling parchment. I fished it out to find Ghrelin's service record within.

Ana grabbed the copy of Ghrelin's service record, ripped off her blindfold, and read it. "Hm. His tales all line up. He was indeed working inside the Shroud for three years, but that does not explain the tapping."

I bustled about her rooms as I began to brew her some tea. "Did the tapping you heard today help?"

"Oh, very much so." She tossed herself down on her bed like a truculent child. "When you first mimicked his tapping, Din, I real-

ized that portions of it felt *intentionally* repetitious. Like notes or mo-
tifs in a piece of music, perhaps. And then I thought—well, perhaps
it wasn't music! Perhaps it was *language*."

I had been trying to start the fire in her stove, but I stopped when
I heard that. "As in, a code, ma'am?"

"Precisely! And it was one I was glancingly familiar with. Here . . .
let me see if I can find it . . ."

She leapt to her feet, paced to her box of books, ripped one out,
and flipped through its pages. Then she pounced back over to me and
shoved the book in my face. "There. Look familiar?"

I squinted at the pages, the tiny text swimming before my eyes.
The book appeared to be *Histories of Forgotten Religious Orders*, and on
the page before me was a bizarre diagram, almost like music notes all
set upon one line, with blots of ink, followed by dashes, followed by
triple dots.

"It . . . does not look familiar to me, ma'am," I confessed. "In fact,
I've no idea at all what I'm looking at."

She shut the book with a snap. "Ah. I will go ahead and assume,
then, that you are *not* familiar with the Adherents of the Sallow
Fields?"

I waved wearily. "Assume away."

"Few are, these days," she said. "They are a sect of monks that
practice an unusual vow of verbal silence in their monastery. Much
like the earth spirits they claim to worship, they do not speak aloud.
Instead, they *tap*—rapping three fingers in a rhythmic, mathematical
alphabet, upon boards they hang about their necks. It's a tricky way to
talk—they have to wait one at a time to tap out their messages, otherwise it gets very hard to hear. Rather unsurprising, then, that their
order is quite rapidly dying. Think they're down to a few dozen now.
Poor sods."

"This is the code that Ghrelin was using? But . . . why is an Apoth
communicating like a silent, mad monk?" I said, frustrated.

"I don't know."

"And why would the impostor do the same thing?"

"Oh, I've no fucking idea to *any* of this, child! Why train someone in such a thing? Unless, of course, both Ghrelin and our impostor were participating in some unusual duties there on the Shroud. Duties that for some reason required *tapping*. And duties that Thelenai and her crew do *not* wish us to know about!"

"Can we translate this code of Ghrelin's?" I said. "Will it take days, or weeks, or—"

"Oh, it is a simple pattern, and easily mastered." She waved a hand. "I believe I had it all translated on the ride back today."

There was a beat of silence.

"You . . . have mastered a nonverbal language used by a dying sect of monks, ma'am," I said dubiously, "in less than a day?"

"I mean, it's not *too* technical," she said. "It's just three damned fingers tapping, it can only be so complex." She saw the skeptical look on my face. "Would you like me to translate what Ghrelin said, Din," she snapped, "or would you prefer to stand there and keep doubting me like a stubborn little prick?"

"Translate away, ma'am."

"Right . . ." She cleared her throat and said, "Unless I am mistaken, today our friend Ghrelin was tapping out the words . . . *Sorrow. Sorrow. Despair. We are doomed. It is doomed. Failure. Sorrow. What have I done. Who has done this to me. Despair. Doom. I am doomed.* And yesterday, when you first met him, his tapping was saying—*No. No. No. No. How. Cannot be. Please, no. Cannot be. Cannot be.*" She sniffed. "And that, I think, was all. Not very positive commentary, really."

A long silence, broken only by the crash of the distant waves.

"He was saying all that?" I said faintly.

"Yes. Unconsciously, perhaps, like he was trained to let every thought in his brain spill down his arm to his fingers to be tapped out. How deliciously *ridiculous*, yes?"

"I find all these mentions of doom somewhat less than delightful, ma'am," I said weakly.

"Oh, don't melt to pieces on me now, Din! We've no idea what Ghrelin was referencing. He could have been talking about his preparations for his dinner, for all we know. Yet I am most interested in one bit in particular—*Who has done this to me?*"

"I see . . . The Apoths are lying to us, but they do not know who the killer is."

"If we believe his absurd little coded tapping is true, then yes. They *very* much want us to catch the bastard, and are willing to give us anything we need to do so—*except* tell us what they're actually up to. Which makes me think they are working upon something very secret, and very dangerous—and that our killer is likely involved in it."

The silence lingered on. The tiny flame I'd placed in the stove had now turned to smoke.

"Something to do with the Shroud?" I asked quietly.

"Possibly," she said. "Two Apoths, both of them tapping. And both of them, apparently, are geniuses, of a sort . . . for one served on the Shroud itself, and indeed built the veil that surrounds it, while the other pulled off a theft of frankly absurd complexity. Then there is the mention of *marrow*, and their reaction to it. And we know the impostor did not steal healing grafts . . . So, what if what was in that box had something to do with the Shroud, or this marrow?"

I stared at her as the wood smoke filled the room, my heart flitting in my chest. "Then what shall we do, ma'am?"

"Oh—we *catch* him, Din! We worry about Ghrelin and the other Apoths later. Let us focus on our thief and see what we can find."

AFTER I HAD made her tea, I waited quietly as Ana read through the parchments Thelenai had sent. She finally took a thunderous slurp, then sat back and pronounced: "Well, Din. We are now very definitely in the *drudgery* bit of our work."

I grimaced, for I was well familiar with this speech. "How many people are you sending me after, ma'am?"

"It's a bad one this time. Not quite as bad as Logirstad, where you had to dig through that landfill, but . . . still a piece of work." She handed a piece of parchment off to me. "There are forty-three Apothetikal officers who were given permissions to that chest in that vault."

I took the page and began engraving the names, squinting to make the letters hold still for my eyes.

"You are going to have to work this list closely, Din. Corner all of them and establish their locations during the past two, three weeks. Let's see who was where."

"But we're not optimistic—are we, ma'am?"

"No," she conceded. "I rather doubt if you can just go about knocking on doors and stumble upon some squirrelly fucker with a big trunk of costumes and wigs. We are still staggering in the dark. But your work will create a spark of light, I think—and with that, we can perhaps begin a bonfire."

"I'll start first thing tomorrow, ma'am," I sighed. My feet began to ache in expectation of the sheer amount of land I'd have to traverse to find all of these folk.

Ana looked me over. "Still haven't quite settled into your role as investigator, have you, Din?"

"I look, and talk, and ask your questions. I chase your knaves and scoundrels. Is that not enough?"

"It is for me," she said. She shot me a sharp look. "But I wonder if it's enough for *you*. Mostly because your current method of emotional management is obviously not working!"

"What do you mean, current method?" I asked, perplexed.

"I mean," she fumed, "that I *know* you slipped out the other night, boy, despite my specific orders that you rest! And while I do not know where your spiritual serenity lies, I am pretty sure it isn't in another person's *bed*, or *ass*, or whatever the *hell* it is you keep getting up to in the evenings!"

I was so mortified that I nearly fainted straightaway. "Oh, by hell," I whispered.

"I'm not *personally* offended by your behavior, of course," Ana continued, "but I'd have thought it'd at least make you somewhat *happier*, given that there appear to be dozens of people willing to nightly part their legs or lips for you. I mean, thank Sanctum you've got some of the Empire's best immunities in your blood, otherwise your wick would've surely rotted off ages ago!"

"There is no need for this talk, ma'am!" I hissed.

"Oh, don't bother with discretion now!" she said. "You've all the prudence of an inebriated cow! I'm half surprised people don't gossip that you are a whore for hire, and I your pimp! It'd all be very amusing, if the reason for your consternation weren't so obvious!"

"And what reason do you think that is, ma'am?" I demanded, flustered.

"It is that you believe we do little significant in our work!" Ana thundered. "And thus, you dream of transferring to the Legion!"

I gazed at her, stunned. I had no idea she'd known of my secret wish. I wondered how I had been so obvious.

"How . . ." I said. "How did you . . ."

Ana sighed and tried to collect herself. "Your mind is easy to guess at," she said. "For you are a decent sort, Din, and a decent young man dreaming of serving our most honored Iyalet is not the most preposterous thing. And I know you did not choose the Iudex. Rather, I chose *you*. Yet tell me—do you really think you do no good in your service, child? That this duty does not *matter*?"

"I . . . I do try to think so, ma'am," I admitted quietly.

"But?"

"But . . . when we come, the deed is already done. The body is cold, the blood cleaned away. We often find the killer, but that heals nothing, as far as I can see. It only leads to a rope, or a cage, and many more tears." I swallowed. "Is it so strange a thing, ma'am, to helplessly look upon the slain and dream of instead saving lives?"

"Ahh, but you forget the emperor's most famous teaching, Din," Ana said. "Ironic given that the words are so pertinent to this case!"

I nodded glumly as I realized what she meant. "*Sen sez imperiya.*"

"Yes. *You* are the Empire, and all your deeds matter, both large and small! You know the words, but I do not think you know the lesson, not yet." She cocked her head. "I'll make a deal with you, Din. When the time comes that you are eligible to transfer to the Legion, I'll write your recommendation myself."

My face flushed, for I could not bring myself to admit that with my father's debts floating over me, even her recommendation would be of no help. "Ma'am," I protested. "You . . . you really shouldn't . . ."

"Don't be ridiculous, child," she sniffed. "I can do as I'd like, and I'd prefer an investigator who *wants* to be here. Yet I suspect that when that time comes, you may not wish to transfer."

"Why not, ma'am?"

"Because you are a reasonably smart boy. I suspect you shall come to realize what many Iudexii eventually learn—that though the Legion defends our Empire, it falls to *us* to keep an Empire worth defending."

I had no idea what to say to that, so I merely bowed my head. But then a thought struck me.

For so long, I had accepted Ana as a component of the Iudex without thought: for all I knew, she had popped from the womb bound up in blue, and with a blindfold on her head. But now I wondered: why *did* she serve in the Iudex, of all the Imperial Iyalets? Why here, when her genius could suit nearly any other department, with their own innumerable puzzles and problems?

I asked her this, and she smirked. "Hmm. I thought I had done my best to dissuade such ponderings, Din."

"It only seems fair, given that you know so much of my own mind, ma'am."

"Perhaps." She was silent for a very long time. "I shall say only—some Iudexii learn the value of justice while they serve. Others come with the conviction already *within* them. I am of this latter group."

"Why was justice so important to you, ma'am?"

"Why do you think?" she snapped. "You're not stupid. You will come to the conclusion eventually, I'm sure."

I fell silent, abashed. I was saved only by a sharp knock at the door. Ana waved a hand and said, "Go. Let us see what new madness this realm drops at my doorstep."

I went to the door and opened it to find a man holding yet another package, this one carefully wrapped in mosscloth.

"Was told to bring this round, sir," the man said. "From the music workshop. I believe it's already been paid for in full?"

"Oh, yes," I said. I took it from him, thanked him, and bowed. Then I shut the door and returned.

I set the package down before Ana. "I think you shall appreciate this, ma'am."

She frowned, puzzled, before her face lit up, and in an instant it was like she'd forgotten all we'd argued about. "Ahh! Is it? Oh, my goodness . . ." She clapped, girlishly giddy, and unwrapped the moss-cloth to reveal a small, finely made Pithian lyre. "Oh, tremendous. *Tremendous!*" She scooped it up, tuned it for a bit, then set it down on the floor next to her other one. Then she simultaneously played the same chord progression on each with her left and right hand, a strangely haunting tune. "How excellent. Did you know that the lyre duet is one of the ancient arts of Yarrow, Din?"

I nudged the fire in the stove and began making another pot of tea, this one for myself. "Is it, ma'am?"

"Yes. Some say it reflects the dominance of twins and triplets in the royal lineage here—a rather fascinating biological quirk. Led to some *very* interesting issues with inheritance, and many brothers killing brothers, sometimes at ages as young as six. Horrible shit, really!" Another simultaneous chord progression. "But it did make for such beautiful music . . ."

I watched as her pale fingers danced across each lyre, plucking out the sad, woodsy music, a dreamy smile splashed across her face as she meditated on these horrors. I thought of all she'd said but could make no sense of it. I still knew remarkably little of her history, really; indeed, I'd never met anyone who could explain her. Even Thelenai had been bewildered.

Ana had only grown close to telling me what augmentations she possessed once, back in Talagray, saying: *My situation made me amenable to an . . . experiment. An alteration. The nature of which should not bother you—for you would not be able to comprehend it.*

Yet this, like everything else, still meant very little to me.

"When are you going to tell me what augmentations you have, Ana?" I asked quietly. "And how it is you can do all you can do?"

"When I need to, you little shit," she said, "and no earlier! Now, go get some rest. Some *real* rest, this time. For tomorrow the drudgery begins!"

CHAPTER 20

⁘

FOR THE NEXT FOUR DAYS, I BOUNCED ACROSS THE BAY of Yarrow like a cricket fleeing a vole. I rode mules, horses, carriages; I floated about in canal barges and little sloops and rowboats and carracks; but, most of all, I walked, so much so that I wore a hole in my right boot and had to purchase new ones from an Apoth shop. "New material!" the man confided in me. "Mushroom leather blended with algaeoil. Very resilient!" The boots felt unnervingly soft and pliant, but they held, and I continued on in my drudgery.

Yet I found nothing. I spoke to over thirty Apoth officers of many senior ranks—captain, immunis, immunis-prificto, commander—yet all I interviewed not only gave verifiable alibis for their movements during the tenth of Hajnal, but most of them claimed they hadn't been in the bank vault in months, if not years. The more I searched, the less I seemed to find.

As I did my drudgery, Ana's chambers came to resemble a rat's nest, with pages of parchments stuck to the walls, ceiling, and floor. Soon she was quite literally cocooned by records of thefts, living in a swirling world of pilfered reagents and precursors. If she made any progress, she did not say so; she simply sat in the storm of it all, plucking at her lyres. Most unsettlingly, she had pinned the note from the skull's lips on the highest point of one wall, and worked day and night under the small, strange banner of *Te siz imperiya*.

On the third day I visited Madam Poskit at the Usini Lending Group offices. There I heaved over an enormous sack of talints, the first of many payments I'd have to make to her. She made a show of counting each coin, and when she finished she gave me her wide, treacly grin and said, "I shall look forward to seeing you again soon!" I trudged away, muttering and miserable.

On the fourth day I could bear it no longer and sought out the Yarrow girl from my first night. I could not find her, so I settled for an older Kurmini man, a Treasury officer, who had a weary charm to him. He insisted on making me a full dinner and serving me wine. I sensed immediately he was trying to replace someone lost, and consented to play his game. He wept in his sleep in the middle of the night. I didn't have the heart to tell him in the morning.

Meanwhile, the rest of Yarrowdale stayed quietly busy, moving on from the theft and murder as if it had been a fight among friends. Ships trundled up and down the canals; merchants came and went from the Treasury bank; the Shroud billowed and rippled in the bay; and I walked the many muddy roads, wondering if this might be the first investigation Ana and I might never close.

ON THE MORNING of the fifth drudgery day I discovered that the officer I had planned to interview—my fortieth of the lot—had recently been seconded to Prificto Kardas's Treasury delegation to replace the dead Sujedo. This meant, I was told, that if I wished to speak to this officer, I would have to track down Kardas and his little band of muttering number-readers.

"But they are in the west today," said the Treasury clerk guardedly. "Speaking to officials from the king's court."

"What do you mean, the west?" I asked. "Can you give me anything more specific than a direction?"

She pulled out a map and pointed to a building well west of Old Town, set high in the hills above the city. With a sigh, I started off.

I paid a handful of talints to hire a horse for this trip, and this proved a wise choice: a soft drizzle came pattering down as midmorning wore on, rendering the paths slick and unreliable, yet my mount's footing was sure and steady. The landscape unfolded about me as we traveled: behind every hill there seemed to be another, each higher than the first, and as the rain swept over us the landscape came alive with trickling creeks and chuckling waterfalls.

Then the rain broke, and a tuft of low cloud rose like a veil, revealing a structure nestled in the western peaks: a white stone citadel, shining in an errant beam of sunlight. The High City of Yarrow, I gauged. It was an almost celestial sight in this strange, wild place. Then another tussock of cloud came rolling in, and the vision was lost.

Finally I arrived at my destination, which did not appear to be anything so pleasant as a home or mansion, but rather a crude woodland fort, with parapets made from the trunks of trees, and a high stone bastion set behind the walls. Soldiers milled about on the wallwalks, tall and attired in iron mail with glittering epaulets and high, embossed helmets. Not imperial soldiers, then, but Yarrow.

I glanced back down at the path behind me. Exactly whose authority was I now traveling in? I wondered. Was I truly in the Empire at all?

I rode to the fort cautiously, relaxing only when I spied the Imperial Treasury carriages stationed before its rickety wooden gates. There were three other carriages alongside them, huge and wrought of dark wood and elaborately painted in greens and golds. These belonged to the court of the king of Yarrow, I presumed, though they were not quite as fine as I'd imagined a royal carriage might be.

It didn't seem wise to simply walk up and knock on the gates and demand entry, for this might not only bother the guards at the walls but also interrupt any negotiations Kardas was conducting within. Instead, I tethered my horse alongside the steeds of a Treasury carriage, dismounted, and leaned against the vehicle to wait.

For a moment it seemed a blessed thing, to be still in this quiet, dripping forest. Then I heard a noise, soft and shuddering.

I cocked my head, listening, then heard it again.

It was weeping. Someone was weeping nearby.

No, that was not so: it was not one person, but many.

I stood, my eyes fixed on the huge Yarrow carriages. I glanced at the fort walls and saw no soldiers watching in my direction. I quietly approached the closest Yarrow carriage.

The vehicle had two large, swinging doors in the back, but these were securely chained shut; yet there was a wide slit of a window along the top. After another cautious glance at the parapets, I grasped the corner of the carriage, vaulted up, and peered inside.

Nearly a dozen people were within, seated on the floor and bound in chains of iron. Their skin was pale and filthy, their wrists thin in their manacles, their cheeks sunken. They were a sorry sight, and they stared up at me warily.

Every set of eyes was deeply green: Yarrow folk, all of them. A few men, but mostly women and girls, and very young, too.

I asked, "Who are you?"

They said nothing. They didn't understand imperial standard, then.

My eyes fluttered as I tried to recall what snatches of Pithian I'd heard in the streets of Yarrowdale. A few whispered in alarm at the sight.

"Tu kauna hai?" I asked.

They exchanged glances. Then one girl whispered, *"Asim gi'aca gae ham."*

I frowned. I knew no Pithian myself, of course, so this was of little help to me.

Then a voice called out: *"Tusim ho!* Stop, you! What do you do there?"

I looked to my right, along the wooden wall of the parapet, and saw a man striding toward me. He was a short, broad, powerfully built creature with green Pithian eyes and a prodigious beard that was green at the roots. He wore a plain leather jerkin, a fur cape, high riding boots, and a black, cylindrical cap. Most curious, though, was his face, for the whole of his brow had been stained a dark, thunderous indigo, which made his heavy, leaden stare all the more intimidating.

"Who are you?" the man demanded imperiously. "What are you doing here?"

I stepped off the carriage and studied him as he advanced. There was a swagger to him that suggested a familiarity with battle: something in the pivoting of his hips, the easy movement of his arms. Though he bore no weapon, he approached me with all the bravery of a man fully prepared to join combat.

I glanced again at the wall-walks and saw some of the gathering soldiers sporting bows. This purple-faced man likely did not need a sword to feel the confidence of arms, then.

"I am Signum Dinios Kol of the Iudex," I said to him. "I'm here to see Prificto Kardas."

"Are you?" snapped the purple-faced man, stepping close. "You'll not find him in there. Get some distance from that carriage, now. Back away."

I did not move.

"I heard weeping, sir," I said coolly. "I thought it wise to look."

He raised his head and looked down his nose at me. "That is not your affair. Back away."

I hesitated just long enough to bother him, then took a small step back. "Why do you have those people chained in there, sir?"

"You ask impertinent questions."

"I ask obvious questions, sir. Who are they?"

He narrowed his indigo-painted eyes at me. "Hm. A blue one. I've never seen a blue one."

"What?"

"I have seen red imperials," he continued. "And a few black. And white, far too often. But never blue. You are Iudex, you say? Is that a . . . an imperial *phansi vala*? Executioner?"

"I am not an executioner," I said stiffly. "I deal in matters of justice."

"Ah. As do I. These are fugitives. They have broken their oaths to their lords and fled their sworn vows. I return them to their rightful places now."

"This is approved by the imperial powers, sir? They know of what you do here?"

He let a tiny, icy silence slide by. "I do not need their approval. For we are not *in* the Empire. You stand on Yarrow soil. You have for many leagues. Did you not know?"

I looked him over, liking what I saw less and less. "May I have your name, sir?"

He thought about it. "No."

"You won't give me your name?"

"I do not give imperials anything I do not need to. And I need give you nothing, boy."

Another tense moment. His eyes danced down to my sword at my side, then back up to my eyes. There was a greediness in his gaze, as if he wished me to draw, eager for the conflict, even though he himself was unarmed. A strange thing, I thought.

Then there was a creak and a crack to my left, and the rickety gates of the fortress opened. We both looked, and Prificto Kardas came striding out, biting his thumb as he so often did when worried. He was flanked by his many Treasury officers, their faces all flustered and downcast. Only Signum Gorthaus kept her face stoic and still, yet this was a common thing in engravers.

Kardas stopped when he saw me. A strange, shameful expression stole over him, as if he felt I'd caught him in some compromising act. "Kol?" he said. "What are you doing here?"

I bowed. "I had come to ask questions of a member of your delegation, sir," I said.

The purple-faced man spoke up: "He seemed more interested in my carriages, Kardas. Too much so."

"Ahh," said Kardas slowly. "I see. Have you two come to know each other, then?"

I shot a glare at the purple-faced man. "No, sir."

"Well. This is Thale Pavitar, Kol. He is the jari of the court of Yarrow—a role akin to a priest. He is often part of my negotiations."

"You are a man of faith, sir?" I said tartly to this Pavitar.

"I keep many ancestral oaths," the broad man said. "Without those, all is lost. True?" He grinned, his teeth flashing in his beard. I almost winced, for his teeth were misshapen and discolored: a sight quite unusual to me, for in the Empire we possessed calcious grafts that could easily amend any tooth or bone.

"Yes . . ." said Kardas uncertainly. "Well, Kol, I am sorry that you have made the trip here, for we cannot accommodate any interview at the moment." He stepped between Pavitar and me in a transparent effort to defuse our conflict. "I'm afraid we must relocate to the High City to continue our discussions, and we must be quick about it, for we feel we make some progress now."

A twitch to Pavitar's beard, as if he thought this very unlikely.

"I shall be happy to contact you when we return to Yarrowdale, though," said Kardas. "And we can conduct all interviews there."

I bowed in return, my anger simmering under Pavitar's smirk. Yet as I bade them goodbye and moved to mount my horse, more people exited the gates, and one figure in particular drew my gaze.

He was a short, pale man, thin and reedy and arrayed in fine silk clothes of a bright yellow-green color, with long locks of hair that hung well-coiffed about his neck. He was surrounded by soldiers clad in green and armored like the ones on the wall, but their helms and epaulets were of finer make, as if escorting this man was a special duty. Like Pavitar, this new man's face was painted, yet his paints were not purple, but green: a flowery, curling design that coiled about the edges of his cheeks and gathered at his mouth.

Yet it was his eyes that struck me most. They locked on me immediately and glittered with intelligence, yet it was a very cold sort: he studied me as if he were a butcher and I a sow, and he was imagining how he'd part my joints to yield the best cuts.

"Kardas," said the green-faced man, his voice soft and wary. "Who is that?"

"Ah—this is an imperial officer, sir," said Kardas, sounding uncharacteristically anxious, "sent here to look into the death of my delegation member. He shall be going shortly."

"The death of your delegation member?" echoed the green-faced man. "You mean the one so brutalized in the canals?"

"Yes, sir."

The green-faced man took a step forward, studying me. "You came all this way alone?"

"I did, sir," I said.

"With no guard, nor any escort?"

"No, sir," I said, puzzled.

The green-faced man's eyes stayed fixed upon me. He did not speak for a long time. I began to feel somewhat discomfited.

"And who might you be, sir?" I asked finally.

Kardas cleared his throat. "This is Satrap Danduo Darhi, Kol," he said. "The administrator of the court of Yarrow, and foremost adviser to the king."

I glanced back at the green-faced man, whose face remained inscrutable. That explained Kardas's anxiety, then: he likely did not wish this man to return to the king of Yarrow with news that Imperial Iudex officers wandered about picking fights with their priests. Perhaps that was why he'd tried to send me off so quickly.

I bowed yet again—this time a full bow, my brow nearly touching the tips of my boots—and said, "It is a pleasure to meet you, sir."

The green-faced Darhi attempted something resembling a smile, yet it was as warm as a stone in a mountain stream; but I noted that despite all his poise, his teeth, too, were misshapen and rotted. "It seems a pity for someone with so valiant a task to have come so far, and alone, only to be sent away with nothing! For we wish the Treasury delegation all the safety we can offer—yes? Especially after such a tragedy. I assume you have given him kind greetings, Pavitar?"

"The kindest," grunted Pavitar.

"I've no doubt. But, still . . . I am moved to grant him a token of my favor. Not all can navigate the slopes of our realm so easily." Darhi reached into his pocket and slipped out something shining and silver.

Pavitar shook his head, disgusted. "Why must you always make such a show?"

"I do it for I am a decent man, and reward decent work," said Darhi. "And it is a hard thing for an imperial to travel so far, alone." He handed the silver thing to one of his soldiers, who took it and began to trot toward me.

"Oh, no, sir," I said. "There's no need to offer me any gi—"

"Signum Kol would be most happy to take your gift, sir," said Kardas, and shot me a look.

I took the silver thing from the Yarrow soldier. It was a coin, wide and flat and bright. I hastily put it away, sensing that now was not the time to scrutinize it.

"If you are ever in the High City," said the green-faced Darhi, "show that to any Yarrow fellow you meet, and he will call you a friend. If he is of noble make, he is oathbound to grant you a service."

"A high gift," said Pavitar sourly. "One that requires *great* works to be deserving of it."

I took the comment to mean I had accomplished no such thing, but I bowed and said my thanks.

"Very good. On your way now, Kol," said Kardas nervously to me. "On your way, please."

I mounted my horse and rode back down the muddy path. After I had turned once or twice, I slid the coin from the pocket to study it.

The coin held the crude visage of a man, grim-faced and with a beard in braids, and a narrow circlet set upon his brow. Not the face of the emperor, then, as I was accustomed to seeing on talint coins; perhaps the king of Yarrow, whose face I did not know.

I glanced back up the path and saw a figure standing at the edge of the bluff, watching me: the purple-faced Pavitar, his fur cape rippling in the breeze. He gazed at me, then turned and walked away.

I WAS A LEAGUE away from Old Town when I heard a rustling from the foliage at the edge of the path, and then a voice: "There you are. Finally." Malo emerged from the leaves, her crimson hood spattered with mud and her longbow slung across her back. "I have sought you all day, sniffing your trail, Kol. Why do I find you here? Nothing good lies at the end of this road."

"So I saw," I said. "I went to try to speak to one of Kardas's people. Instead I spied something very strange."

She stopped. "Did you," she said carefully. "What was it?"

"A fortress, or perhaps a prison. And several painted men, who apparently serve the court of Yarrow."

Malo went very still. "I see . . . Come. Walk with me and tell me what you saw."

I dismounted and led my horse as I walked with her, describing the chained people I'd found in the carriage, and my confrontation with the purple-faced Pavitar.

"Ah," said Malo bitterly at the end of it. "*Naukari.*"

"What's that?"

"Those folk were *naukari.* Ancestral servants. The Yarrow of old still thrives in the west of here, living under the rule of the king. There the nobles and chief men have inherited many elder things. They have inherited lands from their fathers, and the oaths of loyalty that their fathers made to the king . . . and they have inherited people. *Naukari.* The ones bound to serve."

"The realm of Yarrow practices slavery?" I asked, surprised.

"No, for slavery means markets, and prices and such. The folk in the west do not deal in such abstract things. They keep to the old ways—one who is born to the servant of the land is also bound to serve that land for all their lives."

"There's no way out of it?"

"Only if the king or a lord or a landowner decides you are no longer *naukari.* Yet that is a rare thing. Many run away. Some, as you saw, are captured and returned." She spat rather viciously into the trees. "The purple-faced man, Pavitar, is the jari of the court. A priest, like Kardas said, but one that enforces oaths and ancestral fealty— including those governing *naukari.* That fortress you saw indeed serves as a prison, where they keep the servants who tried to flee to the Empire, before returning them to their lands."

I reflected on this dismal thought for a moment. "They were from the court of the king, you say . . . but their teeth were rotted and had to be quite painful. Why do they tolerate such a thing?"

She cawed with laughter. "The Yarrow court disdains all things imperial, Kol! They would not accept the Empire's gifts to save their own lives."

"I see. And their painted faces?"

"A sign of prestige. Certain roles at court are color-coded. Just as the Iyalets themselves bear a color. Though I do not know this Darhi. He must be new. Let me see the coin he gave you."

I gave it to her, and she studied it with her augmented eyes.

"An oathcoin," she said. "Granted by a Yarrow noble. Quite the boon!" She let out a laugh again, but the sound was black and cruel. "Imagine, an oathcoin in the hands of an imperial! Perhaps the Elder West truly has changed, for it seems this Darhi is willing to owe you a favor."

"But why? All I did to earn this was ride a horse up a damned hill."

"My guess? I think while Pavitar wishes to intimidate you, Darhi attempts to buy you." She smirked and flipped it back to me. "I *did* say you looked expensive, Kol."

I snatched the coin out of the air and glared at her. "What of Kardas? Does he happily tolerate this abuse of the Yarrow people?"

"Happily? No. But you want the world run your way, walk a few weeks in that direction." She gestured southwest. "You will find the Empire soon enough."

"It all sounds . . ." I said, but then held my tongue.

"Barbaric?" she ventured.

"It is not my place to criticize another culture, I suppose," I said stiffly.

This drew a morose chuckle. "Truly? I myself think the practice abominable. I am glad it shall die in a matter of years, when this realm is adopted by the Empire. But until then, there are many servants who flee, and risk their lives doing so." She peered up into the hills. "The ones you saw today . . . their mistake was they didn't run far enough."

I glanced at Malo and saw the disdain in her face. Suddenly it was very easy to think of her as one such child, slipping away from the demands of the soil to become a warden of the Empire.

"Did you?" I asked.

"Did I what?"

"Run far enough."

She turned her gaze on me, eyes sharp. "I sought you today to talk business. You want to do that, or you want to keep pissing the day away on things we cannot change?"

"All right. Have you found someone resembling your sketch of the impostor?"

"That? No. That was all shit and got us nothing. But I have found something *very* valuable indeed. We talked to everyone who worked the canals, everyone we could find. We heard nothing—until we came upon an old fisherman, who told us a story. One day, just before the tenth of Hajnal, this fisherman is down in the reeds with his nets, seeking a juicy prize, when he looks up . . . and he sees a boat coming down the stream."

"All right . . . ?"

"In that boat is five men. Four of them are very dirty and dressed like the jungle folk—armed, carrying bows. But the fifth man . . . he is very strange. For he is dressed all in Treasury white. And he has a cloth *bag* over his head, as if he does not wish for anyone to see his face."

I frowned, pondering this. "The impostor, wearing Sujedo's uniform, before he robbed the bank?"

"We thought the same."

"Why hide his face?"

"I do not know. It all seems mad. The fisherman was deep in the reeds, so they did not see him. He watched as they took their boat northeast, to here, to the city. We found him, asked him to show us on a map where this was, and he did so. And can you believe it? This spot is *just north* of an old smuggler's camp, one we ourselves have raided many times. Comes alive every few months. We are thinking—what if it is alive again?"

My mind began racing like I'd taken a suck from the Apoths' percolator.

"And what if that's where Sujedo was taken and killed," I said quietly, "and what if the impostor is still there?"

"Exactly. So I have a question for you, Kol." Malo's smile grew wide. "You ever been on a warden raid before?"

"WHAT!" SQUAWKED ANA. "You want to go on some kind of god-damned boat ride down some god-awful river?"

I shook water off my straw cone hat as I leaned against her bedroom door. "I think it'll be decidedly less pleasant than you make it sound, ma'am, but that's the spill of it."

Ana grumbled for a moment, then glared around at the collage of theft reports she'd stuck to nearly every surface in her room. "How many people have you checked on from the list of people with access to that safe?"

"Thirty-nine."

"Thirty-nine of forty-three?"

I spied a little black beetle crawling up my hat's brim and flicked it off. "Yes, ma'am."

"And they *all* had verifiable alibis?"

"They did. I've found not a hint of anything useful."

She screwed up her face and grumbled some more. "We're looking in the wrong damned place. But I can't for the life of me discern what the *right* place is yet. I feel it's close, like a bubble in my brain . . . something Thelenai said, but I can't recall what." She grabbed her lyres— she had rather cunningly attached the two together with a set of wires and screws—and began to pluck a moody melody. "The hell with it. Perhaps a muddy stretch of swamp is a better place to go snooping than about here. How long will you be gone?"

"Two to three days, ma'am."

"Then you may go. Have the Apoth quartermaster send me food, three chamber pots, and enough quiridine pellets to soak up the stench." Another melancholic chord. "I'll let you empty them when you return. I'd normally try to do it myself blindfolded, but after I dumped one out on that woman's pet bird, I've made a rule to avoid it. But, Din . . . when you go out there, be careful, please."

"Why the concern? I won't be alone."

"Yes, yes. Just remember—this is a man so cautious that he does not leave a *single hair* behind. I cannot yet guess at his nature, but he may be capable of far worse things than we can yet imagine." She plucked one last mournful chord. "So move slow, and carefully. And bring your sword. You may make use of it."

CHAPTER 21

. . .

I ARRIVED AT THE RIVERFRONT DOCKS EARLY THE NEXT morning. Our boat was a long, narrow thing, with high armored walls on either side, and nine seakips harnessed to its bow. The doughy little creatures rolled over languidly in the brown water as the boat was loaded, their translucent whiskers twitching as they snuffed. I crouched at the edge of the pier and extended a hand to one. It surfaced and sniffed at my fingers, blinking its big, black, soulful eyes at me, before it realized I had no food and dove back down.

"Don't get too attached," said Malo's voice.

I turned to see her walking down the pier to me, an enormous pack tossed over her shoulders.

"If the smugglers ambush us," she said, "they shall kill our steeds first and leave us floating."

"What do we do if that happens?" I asked.

"Then we row, with much complaining." She tossed the bag at my feet and studied my pack hanging from my shoulder. "You seem kitted out well."

"Not my first time in the wilderness," I said. "At least here there will be fewer worms."

"Maybe, but other pests in abundance. Many of them human—the worst kind." A flash of a grin. "Come. I have things for you to move."

I helped load the boat, and as I did she introduced me to the rest of her crew: nine wardens, all green-eyed Pithians, all augmented for scent and sight and hearing; and, for the men, all wildly bearded. Few of them spoke much imperial standard, and instead muttered bits of Pithian at Malo for her to translate for me. One warden stared at me when introduced, and said only, *"Ugasa kavi ki'um livahpam?"*

The other Pithians laughed. Malo shot him a glare but did not reprimand him.

"What was that?" I asked her.

She hesitated and said, "He asked, 'Why we are bringing a big sad poet on a raid?' Do not listen to him. He is an idiot who wipes his ass with the same hand he uses to eat his bread."

I assumed that was a Pithian adage, but still made a note to accept no food from him. "At least I shall have an opportunity to learn more about the Yarrow locals," I said.

She looked me over as if scrutinizing me for a sign of jest. "These are not Yarrows. These are wardens. These are people who spend days in the swamp waiting to shoot smugglers with many arrows. I would no more assume they are an example of Yarrow folk than I would assume a rabid dog is a common pet."

Along with us came a short little Kurmini fellow named Tangis: a medikker princeps with smooth, straight gray hair he combed back around his ears. "I don't speak a word of their language, either," he confided to me. "But we get by with grunts. Besides, you don't have to talk much when patching up a wound. Blood speaks well enough."

Yet it was the last warden to arrive who caught my attention: a tall Yarrow girl who came running down the pier, angrily waving a hand at the jeers of her colleagues, who appeared to scold her for being late. She was about my own age, and sported a wild mane of auburn hair, and green eyes no less wild.

We locked eyes as she grew near, and she slowed in her pace. I recognized her immediately: the girl I'd slept with during my first night in the city.

She nodded stiffly to me. I nodded politely back, and she loaded her kit into the boat.

It was a small moment, I thought, yet it was one Malo spied instantly. She sidled up to me, bumped her shoulder into my arm, and gave a triumphant "Ah!"

"Ah?" I said warily.

"I *thought* I'd smelled something familiar upon you."

"I don't know what you're talking about."

"Don't bother denying it! But by hell, I can't believe you bedded Sabudara, of all my wardens! I am surprised she did not take a bite out of you."

I felt myself coloring. "Her name is Sabudara?"

Malo stared. "You . . . you did not even get *that*, Kol? By the titan's taint, what kind of man are you? Some kind of fricatrat, making your rounds?" She stuck a finger in my chest. "Whatever you have with her, you leave it here now. *No* fucking on a raid, all right?"

I blushed brighter and climbed aboard.

WE EMBARKED JUST after dawn, the seakips hauling us off into the brown tides of the canals. We passed the clearings about New Town and the many junks and barges making their way along the Great Canals; then after a few more hours we came to a narrow little tributary, and turned and headed southwest into the shimmering veil of the jungle.

Soon all civilization was lost, and we saw nothing but forest. The crew fell to silence, watching the trees. Sabudara glanced back at me, then reached into her pack, pulled out a filthy brown cloak, and tossed it to me, saying, *"Tutim baputa vate ake baputa vileh hoi."*

Once more, the other Pithians smiled or chuckled. I looked to Malo.

"She said you are too big and too blue," Malo told me. "And you should cover yourself." She shrugged. "She is right. You are very visible. If you take an arrow to the neck, it will cause me no end of trouble."

I sat low in the boat, tossed the cloak about my shoulders, and studied the trees. "Are we looking for anything in particular?"

"You look for nothing," Malo said. "For you've not got eyes as we do. But the jungle is not trustworthy here, and will get less trustworthy as we go. The smugglers are as ghosts, in many places—yet ghosts that fire a volley of arrows before vanishing."

"Do you expect much combat?"

"Combat is not their nature," she said. "Smugglers wish to stay alive, steal, and make money, not fight wardens. They will run. The tricky thing is approaching unnoticed. So stay quiet." She reached into a satchel on the deck, slid out a small roll of paper, and tossed it to me. "And keep an eye out for this fellow, of course."

I unrolled the paper. Sketched on the inside was an ashpen drawing of a man's face. He looked thin and reedy, with his curly hair pressed flat against his head, and a beaky nose and small eyes set close together: somewhat common features among Rathras folk. Even though the drawing was crude, there was something hurt and sullen to his eyes, as if I had done him a disservice by unrolling the little paper and looking at him.

"That's him?" I asked.

"So the boy at the bank claims," said Malo. "He does not look the sort, no? Yet he may have reshaped his flesh by now. Bones he won't be able to change on his own, but the thickness or thinness of a face, or the shape of his nose . . . that is more mutable. Mark it well, though, and let me know if you spy it among the trees!"

THE HOURS PASSED in a humid torpor. Soon my clothes were soaked with sweat and I was forced to strip down to my white tunic. The other wardens did the same, though Sabudara and I scrupulously avoided looking at each other. Tiny insects flittered about us, taking bites of our flesh, and the wardens showed me how to seal my skin with a dark orange paste that smelled faintly of lemon. I rubbed the paste on my cheeks, musing that this morning I had been a respectable Iyalet officer, yet now I was already as jungle-wild as Malo.

As night fell we moored the boat at a bend in the river, hewing close to a tall cliffside that shielded us from being seen from the south and west. The wardens brought in the seakips for rest and food, and then we set to making our own dinner. We risked no open flame nor light but ate cold rations in the dark, relying on the enhanced vision of the wardens to parse the shadows and spy any threats.

"My least favorite part of going out with you lot," muttered Tangis. "Not just the poor rations, but I got to wait for one of you to tell me where to piss."

"You want your prick gobbled up by a lurking turtle, then feel free to piss where you like," said Malo.

"It's been so long since my prick was gobbled by anything, ma'am," retorted Tangis, "that p'rhaps I'd not turn down a reaper-back's kiss."

Malo was so amused by this that she translated it for her fellow wardens, who whooped and chuckled huskily. It made for a strange sound: they had trained so strenuously as hunters, apparently, that they even knew how to avoid laughing aloud.

The wardens soon fell to playing games, dealing out tiles and dice and whispering near-noiselessly in the dark. There was little light except for the sliver of moon above, and I lay against the edge of the deck, gazing up at it; yet after several games I noticed that the wardens were watching me and muttering to one another, sometimes accompanied by smirks, other times scowls.

"Something wrong?" I asked Malo.

"No," she said.

"Are you sure?"

"They . . . find you curious," she explained reluctantly. "Sublimes never come with us in our work. If we ever see one, it is only to be given orders."

"That's common," I said—for although I'd worked alongside Sublimes for nearly all my career, I knew we were still a rare sight for many in the Iyalets.

"Yes, but especially for we wardens. We stay out in the canals and the jungle, away from where decisions are made. They definitely do not see anyone so well-traveled."

"I'm only well-traveled if you count places no one might wish to see."

Malo translated this to her wardens and was met with another question. "Then where have you been, in the Empire?" she asked me.

"I have served in Daretana, Talagray, Sapirdad, Logirstad, and Qabirga."

Malo looked surprised, translated this, and was met with more surprise.

"You've been to Talagray?" said Tangis softly. "Fucking hell . . ."

Another warden asked a question. Once more, Malo translated: "Have you seen the sea walls there? Do you think they shall hold?"

"I . . . have," I said haltingly. "They are grand works. And they will hold, if there are good folk to work upon them." I added, "And . . . there are, I think. There were some decent men I left behind, when I departed."

Malo translated this. There was much nodding in answer, as if they all saw the wisdom in my awkward words. I wondered if she was actually translating what I said.

Another question, this one from Sabudara. I noticed the wardens all leaning in to look at me, grinning. Again, Malo translated, now smiling as well: "Have you ever met the emperor?"

I smirked. "Afraid I haven't."

Sabudara asked another question, and again Malo translated: "But do you know if he is really a thousand years old? And is he truly a god?"

I paused, discomfited to find myself speaking on behalf of the emperor. "Why does she ask this?"

"Mostly they are fucking with you." Malo shrugged. "But this is not the Empire. They have grown up with a king living in a white city above them, but they know him to be very old and weak. Your emperor is another thing entirely. Stories cling about him like haze on a mountain. And you are the most-traveled person we have ever spent much time with. So . . ." She smirked cruelly. ". . . *is* he a god?"

"Well . . . no. He is over four hundred years old, maintained through arts I do not know. And he is not a god, but Khanum. The only living Khanum now—the last of the first imperial race, the first altered people. He hardly ever comes out of his Sanctum anymore. Some don't even think he's really alive."

Malo, now irritated to still be acting as translator, rendered this into Pithian as well. Then she sighed as another question was voiced and glared at the man who'd asked. "Now they want to know if the old Khanum were actually real," she said.

"If they what?" I said, surprised.

"Many think they are invented," she said, again shrugging. "Stories of some wise, brilliant race that vanished? It is like a spirit's tale."

I looked to Tangis for support, but he gave me a wry smile and a shake of the head—*I'll take no part in this.*

"Well . . . the original Khanum were real," I said reluctantly. "But they did not vanish. Rather, the first imperials changed themselves, until they became something not human, and declined to nothing."

Malo translated this. Her words were met with blank stares.

"They don't understand that shit," she said to me flatly. "No one could. Say more."

"Well, they . . . they became smarter and stronger and wiser than any human being," I said. "So clever they almost became incomprehensible. But they also became like mules—a different species, unable to breed with anyone. They could not reproduce, so they died out. The emperor is the last of them. We Sublimes are like a . . . an imitation of their likeness. We can only do a fragment of what they could do, a piece of what their minds were capable of."

Malo translated this lengthy answer. Now the wardens fell to squabbling, with Sabudara speaking indignantly. She held her hands up about six smallspan apart, as if measuring something invisible. I began to feel a humiliating dread.

"Ahh," I said. "What are they discussing now?"

"This might be an issue in translation . . ." said Malo. "The word for 'mule' in Pithian is the same as 'gelding.' Now they debate if you are an incomplete man." She nodded to Sabudara. "Some testify on your behalf."

Tangis, who had been sipping from a small pot of water, burst into a riotous coughing fit.

"I am complete," I said, stung. "And all functions well. But I do not engender children."

Malo translated again. All the wardens stopped talking. The female ones seemed most intrigued and studied me appraisingly—including Sabudara, who I realized must have been willing to leave all to fate when she bedded me. The men, however, shot me looks both alarmed and resentful.

"I, ah, am no longer sure if I enjoy being an object of curiosity," I said to Malo.

"I know I do not enjoy acting as middleman for it!" she snapped. "Titan's taint! Bring one Iudex along, and they all become as fucking children!"

She rattled off some Pithian to her wardens, and the women nodded derisively—*Yes, yes, we know*. Then she turned to me. "I have told them what I told you: *no* fucking on a raid," she said sternly. "If one of them tries to mount you, shove the idiot off into the water. All right?"

I drew away from the wardens, stuck a pipe into my mouth, and lay back on the boat, watching the stars through the quivering canopy.

CHAPTER 22

⌃⌃⌃

I WAS AWOKEN NOT BY THE LIGHT OF DAWN BUT BY THE tramp of many feet and much whispering. I cracked my eyes, wondering if I dreamed, and saw the wardens stepping around me on the boat to peer out at the river past the cliff's edge.

I sat up. I could barely make out the form of Tangis sitting on the deck across from me. I whispered, "What's going on?"

"Wardens say they smell something dead in the water," Tangis said quietly. "Something floating down to us. Their noses say it's human. They can't see it yet. But it's close."

I clambered to my feet, peering at the trees about me. I thought I could make out slashes of pink light leaking through the leaves, suggesting dawn was near. I hissed Malo's name at the clump of wardens at the prow of the boat until she finally broke away.

"What is it?" Malo demanded.

"Tangis says your people smell a body."

"Yes, Khusabu and Sabudara do. They've the finest noses. But it's not here yet, though it's coming." She sniffed the air. "Ah . . . I think I have it now. About half a league upstream. I wonder why no scavenger has taken it yet . . ." She sniffed again. "Yet it smells . . . strange."

I summoned the map in my mind. "It will be coming . . . downstream from where the camp is, yes? The very one we wish to raid today?"

"It is. But bodies in the water about a camp is not uncommon. Perhaps it is our impostor. Maybe someone got as sick of his shit as I."

I joined her at the prow of the boat, waiting. Dawn light slowly filtered through the trees, and soon I could make out the far bank. Then it came.

The body floated facedown, arms at its sides, its feet low enough in the water that they were lost in the muddy haze. It was not yet bloated, and we could see no marring to the corpse as it approached us. One of the wardens pulled a lance from the stock of arms, reached out, and hooked the body. Then he brought it close and rolled it over.

Instantly the wardens recoiled, crying out; for on the underside, the body was not truly a body at all.

From the chest to the hip bone, the bare torso appeared to bloom into a tangle of silvery, slender skeletons, like the bones of many fish, yet it was difficult to tell where the man's body ended and this twisted storm of glistening fishbones began. It was as if they sprouted from his flesh, or from his pelvis and rib cage, like a school of minnows leaping from his abdomen, and some of the skeletons had eyes that were small, malformed, and peeping.

But worst was his skull, which no longer bore a face. Instead his eyes and cheeks and nose had been replaced by a clutch of coiling, dark tubers, complete with tiny, pale roots. They had apparently erupted from his head with such a violent burst that they had dislocated his jawbone, which hung by a tendon from his skull, and it, too, sprouted tiny dark tubers, some of which had dislodged his teeth.

Malo hissed something at the warden with the lance, and he let it go, then tossed the lance in after it. I watched the body float away and sniffed my vials, carefully engraving the sight I had just beheld, no matter how horrible it had been. The wardens fell to whispering questions, until Malo turned to me.

"Kol," she whispered. "What in *hell* was that? Have you seen anything like that before?"

I tried to calm my heart, and considered it. An idea had already floated to the top of mind, but I fought to ignore it, for it felt too mad to speak aloud. I would not say such things, I decided, not yet.

"I have not seen that, but ... I've seen things like that," I said carefully. "It has the look of serious contagion. Something has altered that man horribly." I looked to Tangis. "Correct, Princeps?"

He nodded, his dark face now white about the lips. "Y-yes . . . I have viewed such things in books, but . . . I've never seen such a sight in Yarrow, or any of Pithia." He swallowed and said to Malo, "We'll have to take precautions, ma'am. For while I've no idea what happened to him, we're going in the same direction—yes?"

"Of course," Malo muttered. She walked to one box in the boat and opened it. Within were two dozen warding helms, and she began passing them out. "Have you worn one of these?" she asked me.

"I wore one in Talagray, for a bit."

"Drink as much water as you can—for I can't say when you'll have your next chance—then get it on. It is a difficult thing to wear in the heat, and my folk shall love them even less, for they'll dull our noses and eyes and ears far more than yours. Yet we must. I don't want us exposed to whatever did that to that man."

I took a great draught of water, stuffed the helm on my face, and strapped it down. Instantly, the world about me turned to dark and acrid oilcloth. I readjusted it until my eyes aligned with the glass eyepieces, and the world coalesced into a blurry, glassy version of itself.

I peered upriver through the eyepieces. "I am ready if you are," I said softly.

Malo laughed dully. "How ready could one ever be for such a task?"

THE JOURNEY UPSTREAM was tense and silent, all of last evening's merriment wiped from our minds. The wardens seemed especially affected. I reckoned that the warding helms disrupted their senses so much that they were bothered a great deal.

"We grow close to the camp," murmured Malo. "To arms, then."

She and the wardens began stringing their bows and fitting them to their slings. The wardens did not wield common bows but ones unusually thick and long. I saw for the first time that many of the wardens had one arm wider and more corded than the other; some had hints of purple to their elbows and hands and forearms, as if the appendages had been grafted for strength.

We followed the little river around one long curve. Then Sabudara flung out a finger, pointing ahead, and whispered one word: "*Ute!*"

"Seen something," said Malo softly. She tugged at the reins, slowing the seakips, and went to Sabudara. Together they huddled and peered off into the trees. Sabudara pointed at some distant part of the canopies, and I stuck a spyglass to the glass bulb of my helm and squinted.

Eventually I found it: the silhouette of a person, crouched on a stand at the top of a tree. The morning sun was just behind them, so I could make out no more than their shoulders and head, but they peered out at the river toward us. They did not move but sat still as stone.

Malo, Sabudara, and another warden knelt behind one of the boat's armored walls, whispering. Then Malo plucked at her cloak, ripped some fibers free, and dropped them, gauging the wind. She whispered something; then, all in unison, the three wardens aimed, drew, and fired, their strings creaking and clacking as the missiles took flight.

All three arrows flew straight and true—incredible shots, so accurate I was awed—and pierced the figure in the tree three times. Yet the figure did not cry out or stagger. They sat still and silent, as if perfectly content to have been shot through three times over.

The wardens frowned, confused. Malo waited for a moment, studying the figure, before tugging at the reins of the seakips again. She nudged the beasts to the shore and gestured to her people. One of the wardens leapt out, slipped into the brush at the bank, and scaled the tree quick as a squirrel.

We watched as he made it to the stand and vanished into the branches. Then we heard a grunt, and a creak above, and something large and dark plummeted into the water before us.

One of the wardens hooked the thing with a spear and hauled it aboard. A few wardens gasped with surprise. It was like a statue of a man in a crouching position, but it was wrought of tightly wound vines, all closely compact and blooming here and there with rosy-pink cups. It had been shot through with the three arrows, two in its wattled chest and one in its neck. I found the figure strikingly lifelike: something in the tilt of its head, like the vine-person had just heard something startling.

"Strange," said Malo softly. "A trick, perhaps, to scare off intruders?"

I spied something glimmering in the depths of the vines. I crouched, drew my knife, and dug at the vines until I freed the thing.

A belt buckle, made of brass. Not just a buckle, though, but also part of a belt, like the vines had grown around it and torn the leather to pieces.

We all stared at it. Then I hacked at the vine-figure, splitting it open like a hunter field-dressing an animal.

I found within the vine-person several talint coins, five buttons—and many bones. Rib bones, two femurs, a handful of vertebrae. Yet far more troubling than any of this was where I found them, for I discovered all these objects in places where I might find them on my own person: the buttons on the shirtfront, the ribs in the figure's side, a femur in its thigh.

"Kol," said Malo softly. "What is this thing? A totem?"

"No . . . I think I know what this is," I said. "As well as what happened to the man in the waters."

"Then what is this devilry?"

The memory of a few words bubbled up in my mind: *The purest of titan's blood—or qudaydin kani, as is the proper name—is powerfully metamorphic. When it comes into contact with a significant concentration of living tissues, it mixes with them, forcing a strange blending. Flesh becomes as leaf, and leaf as bone, and so on. All is warped.*

"I think it . . . it is titan's blood," I said. "That is what has done this. For this was a person once, but no longer."

"By hell," murmured Tangis. "You think . . ."

"Y-yes," said Malo, shaken. "I see. The man in the river—he had tubers growing from his skull, like the hina root I chew. Yet . . . his very face had been transformed into them."

"And now these people, positioned in the brush," I said. "But they have been turned *into* brush, as if they were mixed, warped, or muddled with the world about them."

"Such things have been seen within the Shroud," said Malo quietly. "But—how do we find them here?"

A call from the bank: the warden who'd climbed the tree emerged from the brush and gestured to us. He shouted something to Malo, his voice high and panicked, indifferent to being overheard.

I saw Malo's green eyes grow wide and her helm's glass bulbs grow hazy with hot breath.

"What is it?" I asked.

"There are more of them, he said," she said. "More plant people, standing in the jungle. And . . . something else. Something he saw from the stand." She tugged at the reins until the boat drew closer to the bank. "A growth of plants, so thick he could not see through it." She put her bow on her back and buckled her quiver of arrows tight. "Very strange—and right where the camp should be."

WE MOORED OUR BOAT, leaving two wardens behind to guard it, and slipped ashore, weaving up a narrow trail into the jungle. The trees were close and dark, and after the sights we'd seen and with our warding helms affixed atop our heads, the forest seemed otherworldly.

We found that the warden had been right: standing among the jungle paths were three humanlike statues made of vines and ferns and grass, and even clutches of mushrooms. Yet these were not crouched like the first had been: rather, they seemed frozen in midstride, often with one foot rooted and stuck to the soil. It was like they were running away from something up the path—the very direction in which we now moved.

After a few turns I found Malo and the other wardens stopped ahead, for the way was blocked by a huge, thick wall of interwoven tree branches and vines, all sporting many strange blooms. The wardens were hacking at the wall with their short swords, but they made little progress.

"Here the trail ends," Malo said to me. "We would need axes to go farther."

I studied the strange blooms on the wall of vines. They seemed a mad mixture of flowers: rosy trumpets, spidery cruciforms, and dainty little blue cups, scattered among the dark leaves.

"I've seen blooms of this kind before," I said quietly. "In the Plains of the Path, before Talagray. Where the leviathans of the old days had fallen." I thumbed one of the blue cups. "Malo . . . how does this blood normally function?"

She shuddered. "Titan's blood affects nearly any porous organic matter. If it gets on your skin, or if you breathe it in—or if it lands on leaves, or soaks into the ground to be absorbed by the roots of plants—then it begins changing things, often in unpredictable ways, very quickly. This is why we wear glass and metal and algaeoil when near it, for it does not affect such materials. But there is only so much known of what it can do. Few witness its warpings and survive."

I gazed at the wall of trees before us. "And we've not seen or heard any smugglers about? No sign at all?"

"The helms make it hard, but I have heard nothing," she said. "I think we are alone here. Which should not be so . . ."

I thought for a long while in silence. "If this is titan's blood," I said softly, "how do we still live? Shouldn't we be affected by now? For helms alone can't be enough. We'd need entire suits to protect ourselves."

"I . . . don't know," said Malo after a long while. "I cannot comprehend any of this."

I grasped the handle of my sword and said, "Stand back."

"You think you can cut through?" she said.

My eyes fluttered, and the memories returned to my muscles. I twisted the handle of my sword, unlocking it from its mechanical sheath, and then my glimmering green blade was free.

"The hell kind of sword is that?" asked Tangis.

I turned and hacked at the wall of growth. The green blade cut through the branches like they were simple grass, and soon I had made a narrow portal in the vines and branches; yet the wall was thicker than I'd thought, and I was forced to keep going.

"Follow me," I said to Malo. "But stand clear of my blade."

They did so, filing in behind me as I slashed my way along, cutting a dark path piece by piece and ripping out the tangled branches to clear the way.

Finally the brambles came to an end, yet I did not see daylight filtering through the gap I'd rent, but a shadowy, quivering luminescence.

I pushed through the remains of the wall and staggered into a deeply shaded clearing. I squinted into the shadows about me.

Then I froze.

"Kol?" whispered Malo behind me. "Why do you tarry? Keep going!"

I stood still for a very long time, struggling with the sights before me, my words choking in my throat.

"Kol?" Malo asked.

Not knowing what else to do, I stumbled forward and allowed her and the others to enter and see what awaited us. My mind was so swimming with bewilderment and terror that I hardly registered their gasps and screams, though I wished to scream myself; indeed, I wished to scream until my lungs would break.

CHAPTER 23

∴

IT HAD BEEN A CAMP, ONCE. THAT WAS OBVIOUS FROM the rings of tattered tent shapes, the firepits scattered here and there, and the ramshackle lookout tower on the western side, complete with a quiver of arrows hanging from the tower's top.

Yet everything had been altered, from the blades of grass to the trunks of the trees at the edges. It was as if all life within this place had been instantly transmuted into something else: I saw trees with leaves akin to tongues, creased and pink and dripping; tents whose fabrics appeared to dissolve into dusty moth wings; firepits sprouting not flame or ash but coiling cairns of flowering fats and bones; grasses and weeds whose shoots were weighed down by not blooms but queer bunches of malformed human teeth, or fleshy lobes akin to ears; a flabby trunk of a tree, its bark fleshlike and patchy, and sprouting thick shocks of curling dark hair; yet worst of all were the people.

And they clearly had been people once. You could tell by the shapes: each had a head, and arms, and the arms were always raised, as if to ward off a blow; yet the bodies had somehow unraveled, turning into wild storms of fishbones, or bundles of warped leathers, or boiling, spidery clouds of gossamer threads, with clutches of teeth suspended in their glistening heads.

I stared about in horror. It was dark within the dome of growth, yet shafts of hazy, amber sunlight came stabbing through in places, shivering with the wind and sometimes illuminating some new horror at the edges of the shadow, or giving those close to me the illusion of movement. It was as if this little leafbound bubble of the world had gone utterly insane.

"By hell," said Malo. "By hell ..."

"I ... I am to be sick, I'm sure," gasped Tangis. "I'll be sick in my helm, or ... or I am mad, I am mad, surely."

Some of the wardens were crying out or screaming. Sabudara traced signs in the air, signaling to some god for protection.

I fought to keep control of my thoughts, forcing myself to be calm and contained, to see this sight and engrave it.

"This is where it happened," I whispered. "These people's abdomens bloom fish bones—for their bellies were full of fish. The firepits overflow with fat or bones, and strange plants—for they must have roasted meats over them, and the residue was dusted with pollen, or molds ..."

"By Sanctum," said Tangis. "Then that would mean ..." He counted them silently. "That would mean nigh on forty people met their deaths here, if not more."

"But—again—how in hell did it *happen*?" demanded Malo.

I calmed my mind and looked about the clearing, trying to spy any pattern in the chaos. Unless I was mistaken, the bodies seemed to be raising their arms to protect themselves from some blast, perhaps, and all of them appeared to be fleeing the center of the clearing.

I looked past all the crooked growths and shimmering shadows. There, in the center of the clearing, sat something very curious.

It appeared to be some kind of brewing instrument, resembling a dozen small, interconnected ceramic pots set in a leaning column, stationed over a firepit. The pot on the top featured a chimneyed glass dome, with nearly three dozen brass pipes running from it to the many other pots below. Hanging in the center of the top glass dome was an intricate bit of wiring that looked rather like a tea strainer, as if built to hold some delicate reagent, but now it was empty. It all appeared fabulously complicated to my eye, so much so that I couldn't imagine how anyone could have assembled it here.

I pointed to it. "Have any of you," I asked, "ever seen a thing like that before?"

A shifting as they all moved to look. Then Tangis's voice: "No."

Malo spoke up. "No . . . but it is fermentation stuff, to be sure."

"Fermentation?" I asked. "Like the fermentation works, in the center of Yarrowdale?"

"Yes. The type and amount of piping, the nature of the glass . . . those are all things they make." Malo glanced at me through her helm. "You think that *thing* did this? That, what, it bubbled like a teapot, and then just . . ."

"Perhaps," I said. "Perhaps it is like bombard powder. But instead of showering everything around it with shrapnel, it . . . changes things. Horribly."

I narrowed my eyes at the distant device—it was a good two hundred span away—but I thought I could see something placed upright on the ground before it, facing away from us: a large, heavy sheet of some kind, hanging from two sticks shoved deep into the earth. Like a piece of laundry hung out to dry, or perhaps . . .

"A sign," I murmured.

"What?" said Malo.

I searched the edges of the clearing. My vision was terrible through the glass of my helm, but I spied a small gap in the far western end and pointed at it. "Malo—do you see that?"

She squinted. "Yes. I see . . . a hole in the growth. Another one—one we didn't make." She turned to me. "Someone else has been here?"

"Yes," I said. "And I think they went to that device—*after* all this changed." My eye lingered on the sheet hanging before it. "They left something for us there. Tangis—is it safe to move about in here?"

"Hell no," said Tangis. "*Qudaydin kani* does burn itself out, so the transmutations eventually stop. Then there's a moment of peace, before all the warped organisms begin . . . ah, cross-pollinating, so to speak. Then you can get contagion. A grass that grows on the skin, or a mite that infests the eye, and then the brain . . . Since we don't know when this transmutation took place, I can't say how safe it is now."

"Yes," I said, irritated. "But since we're already *in* here, Princeps, and exposed to this—would walking about be any more or less dangerous?"

A bleak shrug. "Walk if you please, sir."

"Malo," I said. "I'll need your eyes."

Grumbling, Malo followed me as we stalked the edge of the clearing until we could see the sheet placed before the device. Malo's eyes being better, she made sense of it first, and gasped and stopped.

"It's him!" she whispered.

I pulled my spyglass from my pocket, stuck it to the glass bulb of my helm, and squinted at the sign placed in the grass.

It was not a sheet, but a large piece of hide, scraped thin, and it was not covered in writing but rather a grid of bizarre symbols, twenty-five little black circles with many strokes crossing their edges. Though they looked random to my eyes, each one had been so carefully painted onto the board that it was clear they'd been made with great intent.

I studied each symbol, engraving them in my thoughts. A code, surely, just like the tapping. While I did not have the mind to decipher it, perhaps Ana could.

There were words written at the top of the hide, above the symbols. The handwriting was achingly familiar, the same as the note we'd found in the bank. Yet this one read:

And all the world a savage garden, mindless and raging

I stared at the words. They felt unearthly and threatening in this cursed place.

"Malo," I said hoarsely, "does any of that make sense to you?"

"Hell no," Malo said. "But do you have it in that head of yours?"

"I have it."

"Then let us flee this place, and quickly. I will have to send up a flare when we are close to the city. For we must burn all of this, and all that was ever here." She cast one more glance around the clearing. "And good riddance to it, I will say."

CHAPTER 24

▲ ▲ ▲

WE HURRIED TO RETURN TO THE BOAT, THOUGH NOW we panted and staggered, oppressed by the heat of our helms. Malo, Tangis, and I took up the rear position, and for a long while we walked without saying a word. Then Malo dropped back to me, her green eyes sharp and searching behind her helm. "What does this all mean, Kol?"

"We're hardly ten span away from that madness," I said. "You think I should know?"

"Your immunis solved Sujedo's disappearance in hours—and while she is far away, you are close. How did our impostor achieve that horror?"

"I can say little now. But . . . I feel like those smugglers knew him, trusted him, when he did this thing. I think they *let* him do it."

"*Let* him kill them? We found those vine-people frozen as if running away—and within the clearing, they had their arms raised in fear."

"Yes, but if someone had tried to set up that reagent-weapon in a smuggler's camp, and if they *knew* it was a weapon, would they have let him? That device was complex. It took time to assemble. And time to work, for I imagine it had to boil and trigger a reaction. But they didn't expect it, or comprehend it. Some were exposed to it and did not know, I think. They breathed it in, then took up posts in the trees, or . . . or walked down to the river before being affected."

"Like the man we found in the water."

"But then it reached a critical point. Everything around it began to change, very rapidly. Some fled, but they did not get far." My eyes searched the dark trees. "He meant to kill them, I think. All of them, all at once."

"And the sign he left?" said Malo. "What could those markings mean?"

"The likely answer is," I said slowly, "he did not leave it for us."

"Then who?"

My eyes fluttered, and I recalled the anxious face of Immunis Ghrelin.

"Someone with a fondness for codes," I said. "We need Ghrelin and Thelenai to start telling us the truth."

"What do you mean?"

"An Apoth safe is robbed. The thief takes his prize into the jungle—and there he creates a weapon akin to *titan's blood*? One that instantly kills half a hundred people? If that's what is being stored and secretly shipped out of Yarrowdale in common pots, it'll raise no end of hell when people find ou—"

I froze midstep, staring into the brush.

"What is it?" Malo asked.

I stood perfectly still, studying a shock of ferns blooming just off the path. There was a break in the middle, as if someone had trod upon it. But something in my mind told me it should not be so.

My eyes fluttered, and I reviewed my memories of first walking this path. I found my memory of that same fern when last I'd seen it as we'd approached the clearing, but it had been whole and unbroken then. And I had been last in line, so I knew that neither the wardens nor Tangis had touched it.

I began to walk again. "Walk," I said casually to Malo. "And walk free, if you can."

"Why?" she said.

"Don't look around," I said. "Just keep walking with me."

I studied more of the greenery about us as we followed the other wardens. Here and there I spied broken branches or bent leaves where I knew I should not.

"We are not alone here," I said quietly to Malo. "The helms you wear have blinded you to it." I placed my hand on the grip of my sword. "I see leaves broken about us, and bends in the ferns."

Yet Malo turned to look at me, startled. "Like someone walked this path after us?"

"Yes, and they may be watching us sti—"

"No!" she said. Then, roaring: "No, you fool, not us! The boat, *the boat!*"

She cried something in Pithian to her wardens and ran past them, and together they all drew their short swords and bows and charged off toward the river. Tangis shouted some question at me, but I had no mind for it: once again, my hand unlocked the grip of my sword, and I pulled my blade free and chased after them.

Then I heard it: the cries and screams of battle, floating through the trees. I realized Malo feared that the smugglers would attack not us but our boat, which was far more vulnerable, and then we might be stuck here, lost in this warped forest.

I sprinted into the brush, squinting through the foggy eyepieces of my warding helm, all the jungle turned to a smear of leaf and shadow. And then, without warning, there were figures among the trees: men, scrawny and green-eyed and green-mouthed, rising from the undergrowth and wielding short swords and spears. I realized we must have run up on them as we charged. They turned and fell upon us, shrieking like mad things.

Then all dissolved to din and chaos. The wardens broke up, split apart, melting into the jungle to engage our opponents. Somehow in the whirl of screams and leaves, I found myself separated, then saw that I was surrounded by three attackers: one on my right, two on my left.

I took stock of them. They were untrained, weary, dehydrated: I could tell by their movements, by the boniness of their wrists, the cracking skin about their lips. Yet though they were weak, they did not hesitate. One of the men on my left leapt over a clutch of ferns and thrust his short sword at me. I watched the rusty blade shoot toward me, and a voice spoke in my mind, calm and controlled.

These may be the only witnesses we have to what happened. Disable, don't kill.

Instantly my memories of my training poured into my muscles, and I was moving, dancing back, parrying his thrust while shifting away from the man on my right. I waited for the first attacker to thrust again and circled to the left, setting up my play.

He moved in, but his sword arm was weak and his grip feeble. I batted his thrust away easily, exposing his lower body. My blade bit out at the flesh above his right knee, severing the ligaments, then slashed his shoulder—I took a guess that his right was his dominant arm—and he fell to the ground, screaming.

The second attacker paused, intimidated by how quickly I'd felled his comrade, but the man coming behind him did not, hurling a short spear at me before moving in. A common tactic—and one I had trained in—and my body came alive, my memories filling my muscles with the movements of my training, and I batted the spear away with the flat of my blade.

Yet my strike was too slow—likely hampered by the warding helm—and the spear did not tumble to the side, but spun wildly and struck my warding helm, shifting it to the right so I could no longer see.

I staggered about, my environs turned to flickering shadows.

Should have trained in a helm, I thought. *Should have practiced all this under the worst conditions.*

My attacker moved in, trying to take advantage of my vulnerability. I barely glimpsed his stance through the glass of my helm, and saw the angle of his blade. My body responded—speedily, yet blindly.

I felt my green sword lick out and meet his blade at the expected angle; then I pushed, shifting, tilting my leverage against him and trapping his blade in my crossguard, the movement easy, familiar . . .

I could not stop myself. I felt the edge of my blade enter his neck, heard his garbled scream. The glass bulbs of my helm were splashed with blood, and he staggered away, and I could no longer see him.

I stumbled back through the trees, wiping at the bulbs of my helm and shoving the damned thing back into position. As I did I saw my third attacker staring at me, his eyes blinking uncertainly, his sword held limply in his hand.

"Get on the ground!" I shouted at him.

He blinked again, slightly raising the sword. Then he coughed, cried aloud, and fell to his knees.

I stared at him but then saw it: an arrowhead had punched through his left breast, just beside his shoulder. Then he tumbled forward and was still.

I looked up and saw Malo wielding her bow, her green eyes triumphant behind her helm.

"Move," she said. "Now."

I sprinted forward through the trees and rejoined the fray.

IT WAS QUICK work after the first bout. It appeared that some small group of smugglers had been left destitute and stunned after the catastrophe at their camp, and had thought our boat would make an easy means of escape, yet the two wardens onboard had spotted them easily, hidden behind the boat's armored walls, and fired arrows upon them, killing two and pinning down the rest. Then Malo and I and the rest of the wardens had come up behind them. It was such a pitiable spot for any force to be in that I felt quite bad for them.

When it was all done we found we had slain eleven and wounded four, though Tangis testified that most of the wounded would likely perish. The first man I'd felled had the best chances, he said, and together Malo and I helped carry him and a few other survivors back to the boat, where Tangis tended to him with his grafts and tinctures while we checked the rest of the fallen.

"What shall we do for the dead?" I asked Malo.

"Do? Nothing," she said.

"It does not feel right to leave them to rot."

"If we were to dig them graves, the forest would still spoil it," she said. "Better to give them over to the trees and the vines. That is their world, anyway."

I gazed back at the jungle and wiped the blood again from the eyepieces of my helmet. These were not the first people I'd killed, but they were the first I'd left to spoil under the sun. I made a silent prayer for them, picking one of the imperial gods at random—perhaps Davingli, goddess of wilderness and encampments—and boarded the boat.

CHAPTER 25

˄ ˄ ˄

WE DID NOT TALK AS WE SAILED AWAY FROM THE CAMP. We simply sat on the deck, the sun beating on our shoulders, the only sounds the biting flies, the lap of the waves, and the whimperings of our prisoners. No one moved but Malo, who steered, and Tangis, who set to mending the smugglers' wounds.

"Can we question them?" I asked him.

"Not yet, sir," said Tangis. "It will take at least an hour or two for my healing grafts to work."

"You can question them all you like as we sail back to Yarrowdale," said Malo, flicking the reins. "But you may not get to tell anyone. We shall be put under containment the instant we get close."

"Because of what we've been exposed to," I said.

"Indeed. We'll be back to the city soon—easier to go downstream than up—and there we shall be examined and bathed in oils and reagents, and then examined again, and again. If we are lucky, it will not last more than a day or so." She shuddered. "I hope I get a medikker with warm hands this time, and short fingers . . ."

I glanced back at the few survivors, lying prone on the deck of the boat with Tangis's healing grafts foaming over their wounds. "And they'll be taken from us, too, as they could be infected," I said. "So this will be our only chance to question them for some time." I grimaced and tapped at the glass bulbs on my helm again. "When can I take this damned thing off?"

"After you pass your blotley test," Malo said. "Tangis?"

Tangis reached into a cabinet in the side of the boat, slid out a large, heavy metal box, and opened it. Lying within on a bed of white salt were what looked like two dozen insect chrysalises, all brown and withered, each about the size of a finger. Tangis dug in the salt until he found a small wooden tube, and he uncapped it and slid out a little sponge, which he squeezed over each chrysalis, allowing a few drops of fluid to fall on them before repackaging the sponge in the tube.

Quickly the little chrysalises bloomed with a pale red color, and tiny, twitching legs emerged from their undersides. Tangis picked one up with his fingers, approached me, and said, "Roll your sleeve up, please, sir."

I eyed the twitching little chrysalis. Now that it was close, I could see a suckerlike mouth at one end.

"Ahh—what the hell is that?" I asked.

"A blotley larva," he said. "Type of highly altered, parasitic fly. Sucks your blood, yes—but they're *very* sensitive. Even the slightest trace of contagion within you will kill them."

I nodded grimly and extended my arm. "So if this thing dies on me, I don't get to take my helmet off."

"Just so. It's a recent development here in Yarrowdale, sir. We've a lot more contagion to worry about than other places, you see. Especially the kind that sleeps in your blood unnoticed." A sour smile. "It's become one of our most popular exports."

He stuck the little larva to the inside of my arm. There was a slight pinch, then a dull itch. I watched with grotesque fascination as a translucent cavity within the larva turned a deep crimson, yet the thing did not perish, but kept cheerily sucking away at me.

"So Din is clean, and only giving it a meal," said Malo.

"How pleasant," I said. "When will it stop?"

"It won't," said Tangis. "This is an altered, unnatural creature, created for this one purpose. It can't survive in the wild anymore. It can't even eat properly. If I let it go long enough, it'll actually start leaking your own blood back into you." He delicately plucked it off. "But I shall stop it here."

I rubbed my arm, where a painful, winking, red sore was forming. Tangis moved on, doing the same to the rest of the wardens, along with our four prisoners. All of us passed the gruesome little test, and we eagerly removed our warding helmets.

"It's a miracle none of us are contaminated," said Tangis. "I expect that device you spied only dispersed a *tiny* amount of titan's blood, sir, just enough to create the faintest dusting... but it was deadly enough."

There was a dreadful silence at that. I rubbed at the blotley sore on my arm, which was growing steadily more irritated, then drank greedily from a cask of water, desperate to flood my body with moisture.

A cough from one of our prisoners: the man I'd disabled. He moaned and opened his eyes, then gazed around at us, horrified.

"Get him water, and get him up," I told Tangis. "I'll need him talking soon."

IT WAS NOT until early afternoon that our prisoner regained the strength to speak, sipping at Tangis's cures and grafts and cringing every time the boat shifted. I sat with him and Malo in the stern. He was a skinny, pink-skinned thing, malnourished and miserable and dappled with rashes. Like all Yarrow folk, he had a green hue to his eyes and his teeth, which were just as rotten as those of the Yarrow court.

He spoke not a word of imperial standard, but only Pithian, so I leaned on Malo to translate yet again. Yet she warned me as we began: "These are woodfolk. Swamp-dwellers. They have known a grinding poverty and ignorance that you and I can hardly comprehend. They are considered crude even by the basest folk of the Yarrow realm, even lower than *naukari*—servants, I mean. It may be difficult to understand such a person, even if I translate well."

I rubbed at the welt on my arm as I wondered how to start. "What's his name?" I asked.

She asked him, speaking rapidly in Pithian. He frowned at me mistrustfully, then answered. Malo made an irritated face, then said,

"He wants us to call him *Latha*. It means 'corpse.' Because he says he is a dead man."

"Why?"

She spoke to him, but he remained silent, frowning into his lap. "He won't say," she said. "But he did admit he is a member of the Kachu clan—a smuggling gang. One of the larger ones."

I pondered that. I had no idea how to question someone so otherworldly to me. "Tell him who I am," I said, "and tell him I'm from the Imperial Iudex, and no harm shall come to him under my protection."

Malo snorted. "This idiot's not going to understand that shit."

"Tell him anyway. In case he's smarter than he looks."

She did so, speaking rapidly in Pithian. The man looked absolutely dumbfounded.

"Fine. Ask him what happened back there at the camp," I said to Malo.

She translated. He was silent for a good while. Then he bowed his head and began weeping and mumbling. Malo did not lean close to listen, I noticed: her augmented hearing likely meant she didn't have to.

"He says he doesn't know," she explained as he spoke. "Because he wasn't there. That's why he's still alive, along with the others we fought. They went on watch, and came back and found the place . . . changed. Shouted to the people within the wall of trees and . . . and they heard nothing, and guessed all within were dead."

"Does he know why it happened?" I asked. "What we saw back there wasn't a mistake."

She spoke to him; Latha shrugged, but when he responded, his face was full of fear.

"He . . . says he thinks *the king* came," Malo said slowly. "And he found them wanting. Not worthy. A . . . failure? And so he cursed them."

"The . . . king?" I asked. "The Yarrow king?"

Malo shook her head. "Can't be." She spoke to him, more, and the man hesitated a long time before whispering his response.

"He says it was done by the . . . the *pale king*, watcher of the waters, who is different from all other men, for he is blessed with . . . with great foresight?" She shook her head, confused, and asked him something else, insisting he explain. He responded, pointing at the trees, then the skies, then his face. "The pale king has the invisible eye that predicts all," she said. "He thinks the king even predicted his capture, and what he says now, every word."

"You think this man's mad?" I asked her dubiously. "He doesn't look mad."

"Superstitious, yes," Malo said. "Starving, yes. Ignorant, definitely. But, no, not mad."

"What does this king look like?" I asked.

Malo asked, and she listened to his murmured answer. "He says he doesn't know that, either," she said. "Says the king . . . wore a mask all the time." The man jabbed a finger at our warding helms, and he spoke on for a bit. "Like a warding helm. But painted . . . white? It looked as a skull, he says. The king was never seen without it."

"This king wore a warding helm at all times?"

"That's what he says," said Malo.

I considered this. "When did this king first appear?"

She asked, listened to him speak again, and translated. "Over two years ago," she said. "He says the king came to them and . . . hired them? Paid them?"

"Is this pale king working with them, or are they working for him?"

Malo flapped a hand at me impatiently as the man spoke on. "He says . . . the king emerged from the forest like a spirit from the old days, and spoke to the Kachu clan, and proposed a deal. He would pay them a fortune to steal one shipment of reagents."

I raised a hand. "Hold there. This king—he spoke Pithian?"

She spoke to Latha, who nodded.

"How well did he speak the language?" I asked. "Clumsily? Perfectly?"

She asked and translated: "Perfectly. Like a native."

I frowned at this: our quarry this far had seemed an expert in all things imperial. It troubled me to hear me he was also so deft in all things Yarrow. I waved at them to continue.

Latha spoke on, and Malo translated: "The king made the job very simple for them, for he knew everything about the shipment. Where it would be, where it'd be stored, how it'd be guarded. The Kachu clan did this task, and the king was pleased, and . . . and suggested they become allies. The clan had come to see his wisdom and foresight, and agreed. He would tell them where the shipments would come and how to attack them, and they would do the plundering. Every time, they made a fortune, and grew rich."

I studied Latha's fearful face, then glanced at Malo. "Should it be possible for someone to know such things?" I asked.

"No," she said firmly. "Hell no."

"Then how did the king know when and where to attack the boats?" I asked.

"Because . . . the king knew all?" Malo translated uncertainly as Latha spoke. "He knew all things of all people. He could see someone, and look at them, and . . . know things of them, instantly. Their accomplishments. Their histories. Their sins. The king could look at a man's walk, he says, and know every person he'd seen that day. From the quickest glance, he could know all. No secret was safe from him."

I felt a flicker in my heart. The testimony of the guard outside Sujedo's rooms returned to me: *It seemed a clever thing, to know so much from just a glance. I supposed it was just something Sublimes like you could do, sir.*

"Ask him if this king ever tapped on things," I said.

Again, Malo asked for me. The man's face grew grave. He answered, and she translated. "He says the king did tap," she said quietly. "Tapped on everything around him. Stones, trees, everything. He wants to know how we knew this."

I fought a shiver. "How did the king curse them? Does he have any suspicions about what happened?"

Again, Malo asked. "He thinks the king might have gone to . . . bless them," she translated. "Give them the medicines and magics of the emperor. But he thinks the smokes became an evil thing instead. The pale king had blessed them before, made them strong and healthy. He'd made some . . . some tool to suck at? He compares it to a cow's udder, full of smoke?"

"A percolator," I said, surprised. "This king made one for them, I suppose. They must have thought he was making the same thing back there in the camp. Ask him where we can find this pale king now."

She spoke rapidly in Pithian, and Latha hesitated a long while before answering. "He doesn't know," she said. "The king would often appear in the night, then vanish just as suddenly. Such was his skill that they almost thought he was a warden, if not a ghost. But . . . there was a place where they sometimes found him." She narrowed her eyes as she listened. "A . . . shrine? The king would dwell there, among the stones. They would come to seek his counsel. At times he would emerge and speak. Others, he would be absent or stayed hidden."

"Ask him where this shrine is."

She did so and listened keenly as he answered. "The Midlow," she said finally. "A stretch of jungle flooded over from the canals, and very swampy. But also not far from here."

"Then we should go," I said, "and see for ourselves—yes?"

"We can do so. But whatever waits for us there, we cannot stay long. We must report the clearing back to my superiors, so they can dispose of it. It would be a foolish thing to find a place so corroded and leave it to fester."

WE ENTERED THE MIDLOW as late afternoon came on. The sky turned to riotous red with whorls of hazy, peachy pinks. Then the rivers changed to pools, then swamps, and the trees grew heavy with moss, the waters trembling as tiny, black beasts danced in their depths. Finally forms of pale stone emerged from the dark wood, slabs and wedges and huge, curling shelves. I recognized them not as natural rock but the filyra-stone that the Engineers mixed from powder and lime, forming strange, smooth shapes uncommon to the wild.

"They were once dams," Malo explained. "Made while the canals were dug many years ago."

"What happened to them?" I asked.

"When the canals were done and the dams were no longer needed, the Empire pulled them down and let the waters go free again. Now here they sit."

I gazed at the curious, coiling stone sculptures as we passed through the swamp, feeling as if we were not in the wild but some dripping graveyard, piled with fallen monuments. Even the moss-laden trees had the look of grieving widows wandering the tombs in lace gowns. Then Latha pointed ahead with a trembling finger, whispering directions to Malo: a strangely timorous little psychopomp.

A form emerged from the gloom: a broad arch of filyra-stone, rising from a clutch of trees. It had the look of the bow of a giant ship that had run aground on the muddy shores.

Latha whispered a word. "That's it," translated Malo. Sabudara pulled on the seakip reins, and our vessel slowed to a halt. For a great while the wardens simply studied the stone arch and sniffed the air and glanced about: checking for any sign of our quarry, I guessed, or traps.

Then Malo nodded to Sabudara, and the two of them climbed down and entered the muddy waters. They made not for the stone arch but for the network of trees to its east, and there they stepped lightly from root to root, approaching the place silently. I lost them in the gloom, and together we all waited, listening and watching the curling mist.

Then a rough shout: "It is safe. He is not here. Come."

A warden flicked the reins, and we approached slowly. The site I'd glimpsed was not merely an arch of stone, I saw, but a small island, surrounded by a wide bank of mud and many intertangled reeds. The filyra-stone arch lay nestled against a rocky hillock, and this formed a wedge of space between the two, creating a wide, shallow cavern. I was vaguely reminded of the lid of an eye, cracking open to peer out at the world.

Yet it was undoubtedly a place of some significance, for all about the opening of the cavern stood many stone cairns, each carefully created, many rising as high as my shoulder. Some stacks had been connected to form a narrow arch: a fiendishly impressive bit of engineering whose art I could not divine. It all seemed a spectral sight, ruins within ruins in this dismal place.

I leapt down onto the muddy shores, and Malo emerged from the mists. "There is not much here that I see yet," she said. "No reagents, no records, no anything. There is a seat, and many of these eerie stone sculptures, but nothing else."

The cavern yawned open before me. Now that I was close, I saw that most of the gap was veiled with nets of reeds and vines. Positioned in between the two curtains, in the direct center of the cavern, was a set of thick slabs of stones, stacked and arranged in a form that could only have been a chair.

Not a chair, I realized. A throne.

"A pale king," I said softly. "And there he sat and gave his commands to all who listened. Yet we shall still search it all, true?"

"Of course." Malo called to her wardens in Pithian, and they clambered down the boat and vanished into the mists about us.

I wandered the totems and cairns about the cavern, searching all I saw while the wardens did the same. The cairns stood upright from some marvelous manipulation of physics—an Imperial Engineer could have hardly done better—and many were covered with vines, which looped about the stacks in brambly bunches.

Yet the vines were adorned with more than leaves. Some had ribbons tied to their twists. Others had bones or even talints or charms threaded about them. A few sported drawings, done on hide or crude parchment, rolled up and stuffed within their curls.

I plucked one out and studied it in the dim light: it appeared to be a drawing of a man, standing within circles, with arrows and blades bouncing off their edges. A plea for sacred protection, perhaps.

"They worshipped him as a god," said Malo.

"So it seems," I said. I replaced the drawing, unsure why I did so.

Then I saw one tall cairn on the eastern side of the shore that stood naked, unadorned with vines. I confirmed it was the only one like it; in fact, the soil about it was nearly shorn clear of all growth. I had stepped forward to study it when we heard a shout from the other side of the island.

We walked along the shore and found Sabudara and one other warden, pointing at something trapped in the reeds. As I approached, I caught a powerful scent of rot.

"*Lasa mari*," said Sabudara. "Dead things. Many."

I peered at the forms in the reeds. The closer clumps appeared to be the corpses of rats or ground squirrels, yet there were also a few dead fish, pale and swollen, and even the carcass of a snake.

"Not creatures he killed for sustenance," said Malo. "These died from something else."

Sabudara then pointed down, closer to the shore. A small cooking cauldron sat half-submerged in the silt and mud, with some broken clay pots about it.

I stooped to examine it. Lying within the cauldron were the muddy remains of large, shelled nuts. They had a waxy sheen even in the dying light of afternoon. Each one was dark brown and bulbous, and capped with a long, drapelike growth that coiled around their shells. My eyes fluttered as I consulted my memories, but I had never seen their like before.

"He's been boiling these nuts, it seems," I said. "And left them here." My gaze shifted to the dead animals floating in the reeds. "The rats ate the remains of these nuts, perhaps, and died. The fish and the snakes tasted the dead rats and died as well."

"You think he brewed poison?" Malo asked.

"I don't know," I said, standing. "But I do think he left something more here."

"What do you mean?" asked Malo. "We cannot keep searching for hours, not if we need to report the warpings in the clearing."

"It won't take long," I said. I walked to the cairn that bore no vines and shoved it over, sending the stones clattering across the mud. "Provided you have a spade." I stooped, picked up one of the larger flat stones, and began making scores in the mud where the cairn had stood.

"You think there's something buried down there?" asked Malo.

"The one stone sculpture with no vines," I said. "Which means it's new. So—why?" I stabbed at the mud with the slab of stone again. "*Do* you have a spade?"

"Give me a moment," she said. "I did not realize we'd have to pack an entire camp for this!"

She fetched a tiny spade mostly for putting out campfires, and I made quick work of the soil. Within minutes I felt the tip of the spade stop short on something wooden, and the wardens gathered about me as I hastened to pull it free.

It proved to be a small wooden box, no larger than a hand, tied tight with canal rigger's twine. I set it on the muddy shore and sat before it to study it.

"Maybe not a good idea to go about opening this man's shit," muttered Malo. "I mean—we saw trees turned into fucking tongues back there."

"It's been soaking in damp soil for days," I said. "If it held contagion, it would have bled out by now."

I cut the twine away with my knife. Then I stepped back, reached forward with the knife's tip, and flipped the box open.

I stepped back farther, expecting some hiss or pop and a fog of poison to rise up, yet the only thing within the box was a small bundle of cloth, carefully folded.

Again, I stooped and reached out with the knife and parted the folds of cloth. I saw a glittering of silver, then frowned, squatted, and unfolded the rest by hand.

It was a small disc of silver, hard and heavy and cold. It was engraved with the image of a man, grim-faced and sporting a beard in braids, and a narrow circlet set upon his brow.

"Is that a . . ." said Malo.

I gazed at the large coin, and my eyes began to flutter.

I recalled the morning I'd followed Prificto Kardas to the prison on the outskirts of the city. There I'd met two Yarrow nobles, one of them purple-faced Pavitar, and the other the green-faced Darhi, who'd said to me: *It seems a pity for someone with so valiant a task to have come so far, and alone, only to be sent away . . . I am moved to grant him a token of my favor.*

I reached into my pocket and slid out the coin Darhi had given me, for I'd taken care not to discard it. I held it up next to this new coin. The two were exactly alike.

"A Yarrow oathcoin," I said quietly.

"By Sanctum, it is!" said Malo. "What in *hell* was he doing with one of those?"

I turned each coin over in my hands. The one we'd just dug up was more scuffed and muddied, but it was clear they were about the same age, with little difference between the two.

"I suppose it wouldn't be common for a smuggler to snatch up one of these," I said. "Just as so many other stolen valuables come into their hands."

"No, for there are far fewer of these than there are grafts in Yarrow! I'd imagine there are no more than . . . oh, twenty oathcoins in all the realm. That is why I was so surprised when this Darhi gave you one so freely! Yet who could have given our man this?"

"Who would normally give them to a person?"

"Well . . . a Yarrow noble, a member of the court. But they do not consort with smugglers."

"So you say," I said. "And yet, here it is." I stowed the oathcoins away and walked back along the shore.

I RETURNED TO our landing spot to wait for the wardens to finish their search. I gazed upon the empty throne, its stone seat blank and smooth, and I imagined a figure sitting there, dressed in rags, a white, skull-like helm atop his head, peering out at his supplicants as they approached his presence.

"I say we are done here," said Malo. "There is no more to see. But at least we finally found something he did not *intend* for us to find—true?"

I gazed at the throne a minute longer. Then I turned and walked back to the boat.

III

⋯

THE
MARROW

CHAPTER 26

∧ ∧ ∧

IT WAS EVENING WHEN WE MADE IT BACK TO YARROW-
dale. Malo stopped the boat about five leagues from the riverfront
and rummaged about in a cabinet until she found what appeared to
be a large firework. "I hate lighting these fucking things," she grumbled as she stuck it in the prow of the boat. Then she knelt and struck
a flint and steel over the firework's dark wick.

A hiss, a rush of stinking smoke, and a streak of red fire roared up
and crossed the sky. The captured smugglers screamed in terror while
the wardens watched, grim and implacable.

Then all dissolved to hell.

Barges of Apoths came pouring out of the city, and soon we were
surrounded by people bound up in warding suits, not a smallspan of
skin exposed. They bellowed questions at us as they loaded us off
into their barges, waving telltale plants about us like thuribles at a
blessing.

Once on board we were ordered to strip nude for inspection, to
confirm that our bodies carried no visible blot of contamination. The
wardens disrobed with blithe indifference—apparently this was a
common occurrence for them—yet I protested, saying, "I am Iudex.
Not Apoth."

"That I can see," said the Apoth officer inspecting me. "Yet you
were amid all that shit back there, sir?"

"I was."

"Then disrobe, sir. Quickly now!"

I reluctantly removed my clothing and tried to maintain my dignity as best I could. One warden woman turned and studied my naked form with an unabashedly interested eye, then tapped Sabudara on the shoulder and made some remark. Sabudara turned and looked me over, and gave a single satisfied nod, as if to say—*As I said*. I resolutely fixed my gaze on the back of the head of the man before me, and told myself this would all be over soon.

There I was wrong. Once we passed the first inspection, we were given blankets to veil our bodies—most of the wardens, including Malo, just folded them up and sat on them as cushions instead, perhaps out of protest—and we were shipped off to an Apoth holding facility, where we were each put into cells lined with telltale plants. One wall sported a soft moss pallet for sleep, the opposite one a large glass window. Every hour an Apoth arrived at the window to demand that I stand, drop my blanket, and allow him to inspect my naked body, along with my eyes, mouth, teeth, and undercarriage.

After four of these sessions I was instructed to stand in the center of the cell, and then warm, dripping, dark brown oil came pouring down from a pipe in the ceiling. I was told to rub the oil all upon my person, then sat to wait.

My skin began to tingle, then went numb. Then the man returned, told me to stand beneath the pipe again, and this time a hot, acrid fluid came down, cleansing my skin of the oil. When it was done, every rash, cut, bruise, and blemish upon me had vanished, and my gray skin seemed softer and firmer than ever. I half wondered if it was worth exposing myself to contagion to get such treatment.

A team of medikkers came, reviewed my body again—I was beginning to grow as indifferent to these exhibitions as the wardens—and told me I had passed all their tests, though they would need to keep me here for another twelve hours for observation. I asked them to notify Ana of my circumstances, and they agreed and slid a tray with beanbread and water through a slot in the bottom of the door.

I sat, ate, and drank. *Another day in Ana's employ*, I thought, though this one was unusually humiliating. I attempted to calculate how many such days I'd have to tolerate until my father's debts were paid, and quickly gave up.

Through noble vessels such as I, the emperor's justice was made.

I SLEPT FOR so long in my sunless little cell that I lost all track of time. I heard a rapping at my glass, and I cracked an eye to see an Apoth militis smiling hesitantly down at me from the other side of the window.

"I've your clothes, sir," he said. "Would you kindly get dressed?"

I stood, still wrapped in my meager blanket. "Am I free to go?"

"Not quite, sir." He slid my clothes through the slot in the wall. "There's an investigation, you see, sir."

"Has my immunis been notified?"

"I'm not informed of that, sir," said the militis.

"If she isn't included in whatever this is, there'll be hell to pay," I said. "This is not a threat, but just . . . physics. When defied, she breaks things."

"I'm . . . not informed of that, sir," said the militis again.

It was either the wrong thing for me to say, or I was talking to the wrong person. I let it lie.

Once I'd arranged myself, I was led through a hallway and out into the streets of Yarrowdale. I cringed at the daylight—the first sun I'd seen in hours—and climbed into a waiting cart. The militis and I rode together, but I did not bother to ask where we were going; I'd summoned up the map of the city in my mind and knew there was only one possible destination this way.

I eyed the outline of the advanced fermentation works as we pulled up. It looked much the same as the day Ana and I had come here to see Immunis Ghrelin, the fretvine orbs gleaming like fish eggs in the brittle afternoon sun. Yet as we climbed out, I sensed the entire attitude of the place had changed: all felt fraught and anxious, with Apoths darting about like panicked ants whose mound had been trodden on.

I was led through the front gates, then through yet another hallway, winding around until we came to a set of closed doors. The militis knocked, and the doors opened to reveal a meeting room much like the one with the percolator, the vine walls suffused with the watery gray light from the windows above; yet this room was far more crowded.

Malo, Tangis, Sabudara, and the other wardens were seated at one end of the table, properly dressed, their faces either frowning or stoic; on the other end sat Commander-Prificto Thelenai, green-eyed and green-lipped, still arrayed in brilliant robes of red and yellow. Beside her were her three frowning little ducklings, as I'd thought of them last: Commanders Biktas, Nepasiti, and Sizeides. Several other functionaries sat along the wall behind them, captains and signums and princeps I did not know. They mostly busied themselves with notes. I did not see Ghrelin anywhere.

Everyone looked up as I entered. Malo shot me a look as if to say—*Get ready.*

"Ah," said Thelenai quietly. "Signum Kol. Thank you for joining us."

I stepped in, stood at attention, and bowed. "Ma'am."

"I apologize for your treatment, Kol," Thelenai said. "Containment is always necessary after such exposures, however. We cannot risk some contagion taking hold here in the city."

"Understood, ma'am."

"And that, indeed, is why I've asked you here today. Your testimony as an engraver will be most valuable for our safety. Especially given that it shall likely not need extensive translation . . ."

A shadow of a scowl crossed Malo's face.

Thelenai gestured to the far end of the table. "You may take a seat, please."

I did so, sitting beside Malo. Thelenai's green-tinged eyes studied me as I did so. With her bald pate and the light from above, I was reminded of a skull engraved upon a tomb's door.

"Now . . ." Thelenai began. "You are aware that the phenomena you witnessed in the jungle were a symptom of profound transmutation, Kol?"

"I am, ma'am." I considered saying that the cause was surely titan's blood but sensed that this was a meeting where I was to give information that was asked, rather than volunteer my own.

"And you are aware that such phenomena are terrifically dangerous, and uncommon," said Thelenai. "Thus, it is imperative we know everything about it."

"Of course, ma'am."

"Then please review the events you experienced on the canals—starting with the body that floated downstream. Leave nothing out."

I hesitated. "I would, ma'am, but . . ."

A wrinkle emerged in the pale expanse of her brow. "Yes?"

"Being as my head was bound up in a warding helm for most of the events, I could not anchor what I witnessed with a scent. Thus, it may take some time for me to, ah, recount them. And what I recount may not be entirely comprehensible, ma'am."

"We shall take what we can get. Proceed."

I recounted the events exactly as they happened, but because of my lack of a scent, my testimony was stuttered and halting. I felt my eyes fluttering, my face twitching, and I listened to myself awkwardly belching out phrases like "Weather hot, very stilted. Six beads of water on Malo's helmet. Warden beside her, right-handed," regardless of whether this information was of use to anyone.

It took the better part of two hours, but I answered all their questions—especially when it came to the vine-people we discovered. Thelenai questioned me extensively on them, and on all the objects we found within their forms.

Finally we came to the wall of growth about the camp and the clearing.

"And what kinds of plants composed this growth?" Thelenai asked, her voice now faint.

I answered, rattling off all the shapes of the leaves and vines I'd witnessed. The room echoed with the sounds of scribblings as the many Apoths took down notes with their ashpens.

"And when you entered this . . . wall," said Thelenai, "you saw much changed within. Yes?"

"Yes, ma'am," I said.

A long pause.

"But at the center was some ... device," Thelenai said. "An engineered system. That is what the others have told us—is that correct?"

"It is, ma'am. It was a thing of pots and pipes."

Thelenai nodded slowly. I sensed that her next question was of tremendous importance.

"Now ... retrieve that memory for me, please, Kol. Look at this thing carefully, in your mind. Do you have it?"

My eyes shimmered. "Yes, ma'am."

"Good. Now, please ... describe this system to m—"

Then came a sharp, ear-ringing knock at the doors.

Everyone in the room jumped, save Malo and her wardens, who'd apparently heard the person coming.

We all stared at one another, then Thelenai. No one moved.

Another sharp knock came, repeating five times now.

"I ... I told them we weren't to ..." sputtered Thelenai. "Damn it, whoever that is, send them away!"

One of the Apoth militii sprang up, slipped through the doors, shut them behind him, and engaged whoever had knocked. I heard a voice respond, giving a sharp retort that quickly grew to thundering invective.

I quickly cleared my face of all emotion—for I recognized that voice.

"That ..." muttered Malo next to me, "that is your immunis, Kol."

"I am aware," I hissed out the side of my mouth.

Thelenai stewed in her seat as the shouting outside continued, her icy poise melting away. Then the shouting abruptly stopped; there was a silence; and then came a smattering of gasps and chuckles from the wardens seated behind me.

Malo raised a hand, silencing them, and awkwardly cleared her throat. "Ah—Commander-Prificto?"

"Yes?" said Thelenai, irritated. "What is it? What is the matter with your people, Signum?"

"She has ... told me to do something," said Malo.

"She what? Who? Who do you mean?"

"I mean, the person out there . . ." She cleared her throat again. "She must have guessed I am in here, ma'am, and that I can hear her. So. She has told me to ask Din—I mean, Kol here—a question."

Thelenai gaped. "She *what*?"

"She has told me . . ." For a third time, Malo cleared her throat. "She said—*Malo, ask Din if the instruments he saw in the jungle looked like a whole lot of pots stacked on top of one another, and if the one on top had a glass lid with a chimney, and a little wire fiddly bit inside it.*"

Now it was my mouth that fell open. I coughed, recovered, and said, "Ahh. Well. That is rather exactly what the device looked like, ma'am." Then I added: "And, ah, here I am addressing you, Commander-Prificto."

Thelenai stared at me, then Malo, then the closed doors. "How . . . how did she know that?" She looked to the wardens. "You didn't tell anyone, did you? Did you tell *anyone* what you witnessed?"

The wardens shook their heads. Sabudara looked especially truculent.

"Didn't have anyone to tell, ma'am," said Malo. "We were naked in a box. Not the *same* box, mind . . ."

"And you?" said Thelenai, this time to her three commanders and the rest of her functionaries. All of them quickly shook their heads.

A lingering silence.

Then Ana's voice at the door: "*Well? Shall you let me in or not?*"

"Oh, hell!" snapped Thelenai. "Get her in here and let us find out how she knew that!"

WHEN ANA WAS finally admitted, the sheer amount of smugness radiating off her was so tremendous that it drew glares from nearly everyone. She entered blindfolded, bowing as she grasped the forearm of a terrified porter—the very same young man who had fretted over her mounds of oyster shells—and she bore a tremendous sack of papers over one shoulder. The porter led her to a chair, and she fumblingly sat and dismissed him with a flick of her fingers. The boy ran away like the building was on fire.

"Well!" said Ana cheerfully as she slid up to the table. "Good morning, all."

Thelenai struggled to recover her chilly composure. "Is it?" she snapped. "Breaching an investigation of such an incident is a terrible offense, Dolabra. But before we even begin assessing that, I must demand . . . how did you know what Kol saw in that jungle? Who gave you this information?"

"Oh, of course," said Ana. "I have two answers to that, ma'am—one indirect, and one direct. Shall that suffice?"

Thelenai regarded Ana like she was a clump of turd waiting to be scraped off her boot. "If you must."

"For the indirect—I regret to inform you that much of the city is now at least vaguely aware of what has happened. Sending up a big red flare, and then a bunch of folk in warding suits rushing out to set fire to a chunk of the jungle . . . well, that does give one ideas. And it informed my conclusions about what Din might have encountered during his foray." She reached into her satchel and pulled out a huge, messy mound of parchments. "But a more direct answer would be to say that *you* gave me the information, ma'am."

"I?" said Thelenai, affronted. "*I* did?"

"Indeed." Ana hauled out yet another massive stack of parchments and slapped it down with an echoing thud. "I have been studying the records of all the thefts that have taken place on the canals over the past two years, you see," she continued, blindly flipping through the parchments and sliding out a handful of documents. "The very ones *you* gave me, Commander-Prificto. It took me some time to find any pattern, but a pattern there was! For though the smugglers have tended to target the same precursors and shipments—valuable materials for healing grafts, and so on—there were a few *anomalies* spaced out over the months, thefts that made no sense at all . . . until I realized that for these, the smugglers weren't stealing the reagents but rather the *instruments* shipped with them!" Grinning, she arranged the parchments in a sloppy grid before her. "The baker's baskets as opposed to the flour, so to speak."

"Smugglers would have no use for instruments, though," said Thelenai. "Since they lack any knowledge of their construction and use."

"So one might imagine," said Ana. "Yet the facts say otherwise! The more I read about these components, the more I began to comprehend the limited combinations they could be used in. And then I began to realize *what* he was likely making . . ."

"What . . . who was making?" asked Thelenai faintly.

"Oh, our impostor, of course," said Ana mildly. "I am no Apoth, of course, but I guessed he was constructing what is called a *degradation diffuser*, outfitted with a disperser. Looks like a stack of pots with a glass chimney on top and a bunch of pipes. My understanding is that the instrument takes stable reagents and runs them through a series of cycles until they separate into their original, reactive states. For most reagents, this wouldn't be *too* dangerous, but . . ." She slid out yet another piece of parchment. "Some ten months ago, a shipment of highly advanced, altered fertilizer was stolen by smugglers! One intended for an Apoth orchard in the second ring. As such, it contained a high concentration of the base ingredient *qudaydin kani.* Or, in layman's terms, the most potent of leviathan's blood! Run *that* through a degradation diffuser too many times, and then feed it through a disperser so it sends a fine mist floating through the air, and, well . . . one shudders to imagine the consequences! But then, as I said, I am no Apoth. I could be wrong."

There was a stunned silence.

Grinning wider, Ana looked around the room, still blindfolded. "*Am* I wrong?"

Thelenai's side of the room erupted into muttering. One of her commanders snatched the parchments from Ana and gave them to Thelenai, who studied them with a dazed expression.

"A . . . a degradation diffuser is an *immensely* complex instrument,"

Thelenai said haltingly. "We have only three here in all of Yarrowdale. The idea that some smuggler could steal some spare parts and build one out in the jungle is ... is ..."

"Insane!" said Ana. "Utterly mad! I agree. But then, this man is an absolute genius, apparently. We should not underestimate him." She extended a hand to Thelenai: an insufferably magnanimous gesture. "And, indeed, you did not, ma'am. Very wise of you. I commend you for your foresight."

"What do you mean? I did not what?"

"Underestimate him," said Ana smoothly. "That, I assume, is why you assigned him to work within the Shroud."

The entire room seemed to slowly tense: save Ana, who simply slid yet another sheaf of parchment out of her stack and thoughtfully tapped it with one finger.

"Immunis!" said Thelenai sharply. "Are you suggesting that ... that I have *met* this criminal?"

"I am, ma'am," chirruped Ana.

"But ... that would suggest that you *know* who this man is."

"And I rather think I do, ma'am!"

"Then stop playing your goddamn games, woman!" snarled Thelenai. "Tell us your conclusions!"

"Oh, I will," said Ana. "Under two conditions."

Thelenai stared in naked outrage. "You are in no position to make demands! I am the ranking officer here, and this is an emergency!"

Ana shot forward. "And *we* are *not* formally in the Empire!" she said. "That's been quite a useful loophole for you, hasn't it, ma'am? Some rules can be obeyed, others less so. How shall it go when I try the same?" She sat back. "I want to talk to Din, alone. That is the first condition. And the second—I wish to talk to you, Commander-Prificto. *Along* with Immunis Ghrelin. For I feel the two of you shall have much to say to me shortly."

Thelenai's green-tinted eyes widened. I thought I saw a faint crinkle of terror within her gaze. She debated it silently.

Thelenai stood. "Everyone out of this room," she said. "Except for the Iudexii."

"Oh, and Malo, please," said Ana. "I'd like her to stay."

"What!" snapped Thelenai. "The warden? Why?"

Malo raised her hands like someone had pulled a blade on her. "I have no desire to get involved with this shit."

"I suspect Malo's knowledge of the region might be valuable!" said Ana, grinning. "It should take no longer than fifteen minutes, I expect—it'll take that long to summon Ghrelin here, yes?"

Again, the mention of Ghrelin seemed to cow the commander-prificto. Thelenai shut her mouth and swept out of the room. The wardens did the same—Sabudara shot me a quick wink—Thelenai's retinue followed, and then we were alone.

THE SECOND THE DOOR clicked shut, Ana swiveled to Malo. "Signum—keep your ears open," she said, "and you tell me if there's anyone at the door, as well as if someone else is approaching. Do you hear me?"

"*That* is why you asked me to stay?" said Malo, offended. "To act as your guard dog?"

"I also assumed you'd like to be involved in this, too," Ana said, "being as it's *also* your job to catch this fucker!" Her head then turned to me. "Din—I'm going to need you to summarize all you saw out in the jungle there, and damned quickly, too."

"But I have no scent to anchor it with, ma'am," I protested. "I was in a warding helm all that time."

"Given the way all the Apoths were reacting to your return, I'd guessed as much," said Ana. "So I had them brew this up."

She slipped a small vial out of her satchel and passed it to me. I uncorked it, gave it a sniff, and wrinkled my nose.

"Algaeoil," I said. "Saliva. Mucus. And . . . sweat?"

"And also the aroma of the little glue they use for the helms' eyepieces," Ana said, pleased. "Figured you were sniffing that throughout your ordeal. Now you've a scent. So, talk, child! Talk, and talk quick!"

I sniffed at the vial. My eyes fluttered, and I rapidly gave her the full spill of it. Even though we were in the most bizarre of circumstances, it began to feel like every other report I'd ever given her: names, times, words spoken, and the number of the dead. When I finished, there was a tense silence as Ana absorbed it all.

"So," Ana murmured. "Our man is not simply a thief, nor a murderer, but ... something very, very different. A schemer and slaughterer on a level that even I struggle to comprehend. Sanctum knows how many he's killed!"

"What is he doing, ma'am?" asked Malo. "It is all madness and horror to me."

"It is as I told Din," Ana said. "He is sending *messages*. Yet I am not sure who the intended recipient is. I am fairly sure it is not the Iudex, though."

"Ghrelin and Thelenai," I said. "That's got to be who the code is for, yes?"

"Yes," said Ana. "I *think* so. And before you ask, no, I am not familiar with this code, though if given time I might make headway. But it is the words our man left that trouble me greatly. I take it neither of you are familiar with them?"

Malo and I shook our heads.

"Fucking hell," Ana snapped. "I assume you have both shaken your heads? Have you forgotten I am blindfolded? I cannot know *everything*!"

"We don't know it, ma'am," I said.

"Pity ..." Ana said. "Few read the old imperial doctrines these days. The words are from a celebrated quote, from the letters of Emperor Daavir, sent to his captains during his long march to the sea along the Titan's Path. The full passage is famous but rather lengthy. I believe it goes ..." She cleared her throat. "*We fear the elements, and plague, and the wrath of the leviathans. Yet if we are to see clear-eyed, we would admit that the will of men is as unforgiving as these. How many chieftains and champions have wrought just as much sorrow as the wet seasons? We must govern thoughtfully, then, and manage such passions wisely—for if these folk have their way, we shall return to nature primordial, and be as beasts, and all the world a savage garden, mindless and raging.*" She sniffed. "Emperor Daavir really never was one for brevity in his youth."

My skin crawled as I contemplated the quote. "Why would he leave such words for us?" I whispered.

"I am unsure, but a logic begins to emerge," said Ana. "The first quote we found included an inversion of the imperial creed—I *am the Empire*—taken from a quote where the emperor worried his realm would grow selfish and unjust, and fall. And this one is an inversion of the emperor's vision—for Daavir feared the will of cruel men making all the world a savage garden. And yet, what did you two witness out in that jungle?"

Malo and I exchanged a dread-filled glance.

"A piece of the world gone mad," I said. "A savage garden."

"Exactly," Ana said. "My feeling is that this man suggests he has rather unpleasant feelings about the Empire's presence here! He feels the Empire's rule is selfish and unjust, and wishes to unravel it. And yet, if he does feel this way . . . why kill smugglers? Why kill Yarrow folk who are, if anything, *fighting* the Empire, in their own circumspect fashion? I confess, it makes no sense."

"But you know who the killer is," I said, leaning forward. "Or were you lying, ma'am?"

"I was not lying!" Ana said, stung. "Or, not this time, at least."

"Well, surely his identity could reveal his intentions?"

"No," said Ana. "Not yet. For though I have found his likely name, I still know very little about the man himself. I was rather hoping that your testimony could give me some insight into Thelenai and Ghrelin . . . for I am *sure* that this man is tied up with them somehow. They are doing something, something hidden, something they wish to protect . . . perhaps something concerning this marrow our killer mentioned in his first note."

A sour pang of nausea rumbled through me. "The leviathan's marrow," I said quietly. "And the Shroud."

Malo made a gesture, beseeching the aid of some spirit.

"We questioned Thelenai and her people on this the last time we spoke," said Ana, "yet they did not react, because they *expected* us to mention it. That means something, but I do not know what. We have so little damned material to extrapolate from!"

Malo perked up. "I hear footsteps," she said.

Ana's blindfolded face snapped to me. "Din! The code you saw—did you describe it to Thelenai?"

"No, ma'am. We did not get to that."

"So she doesn't know about it yet. Can you copy it down?"

"It's not letters, ma'am, but simple symbols," I said. "So it should be easy for me to write."

Malo frowned. "What would you writing letters have to do with anythi—"

"We don't have time to fucking explain!" snapped Ana, waving frantically at her. "Get an ashpen from over there, boy, and copy it down as quick as you can!"

I snatched up one of her parchments, flipping it over and scrawling out the first twelve symbols I'd seen, carefully completing each stroke. Then Ana took it and stuffed it in her pocket.

"Good," she muttered. "It is not much leverage, but it is better than none."

"Do you understand what it means, ma'am?" I asked.

"I understand fuck-all about it!" she said. "But I suspect Ghrelin and Thelenai will not love that we have it! Perhaps enough to tell us the tru—"

"They are here," said Malo.

The doors swung open.

▲ ▲ ▲

CHAPTER 27

THELENAI AND GHRELIN WALKED TO THE END OF THE table and sat. Both of them appeared terribly shaken, but only Thelenai attempted to conceal it. Ghrelin, however, looked wan and frail, and indeed even more exhausted than last I'd seen him, and his face bore more powders and paints than before: a tragic creature, perhaps, determined to maintain himself even as he fell to pieces. I felt a brief, powerful desire to offer him protection.

"Before we begin . . ." said Thelenai. She stopped to clear her throat. "I would like it observed that I have obeyed your conditions in good faith, Dolabra."

"Oh?" said Ana, puzzled.

"Yes! I have not had you arrested, though that is within my powers. I have granted you time with your signum, and I have brought Immunis Ghrelin, as you requested. But before you begin to badger him with questions, I must now insist you give me the name of this killer. Or the name of this person you *think* is this killer."

"Certainly, ma'am," said Ana. "To prove my case, I shall tell you how I came to it . . . for at first I honestly despaired of finding this man. You gave us a list of officers who had access to the safe that was robbed, and though Din traveled leagues and leagues to talk to them all, none were our fellow. Yet then I remembered . . . you did *not* truly give us a list of *all* officers with access to that safe."

Thelenai blinked. "I did not?"

Ana turned to me. "Din—would you be so kind as to recall the commander-prificto's *exact* words when she gave us that list?"

My eyes fluttered as I summoned up the memory—and then I understood.

"Oh," I said softly. "She said she gave us the list of every *living* officer who had access to that safe . . ."

"Indeed," said Ana. "I realized that the list you gave me did not include *deceased* officers who'd possessed access to that safe—assuming, of course, that the Apoths do not remove the permissions of the dead from the bank? Might that be true?"

Thelenai twitched. Ghrelin turned an unpleasant ashy color.

"Of course," purred Ana. "And why would you? A lot of trouble to go to for a dead person . . . I found there were indeed a few deceased officers who'd possessed access to that safe—but one, I noticed, stood out." She pulled out a single page of parchment. "This particular dead man operated in a position that granted him all the information needed to manage the madness our impostor has wrought thus far. This officer was transferred to Yarrowdale from the Rathras canton in 1124, to work on a very sensitive site—the Shroud. He worked there for just under three years before meeting his untimely end, which is described in his service record as an *accident,* and nothing more." She sat back, fingers threaded over her belly like she'd just consumed a sumptuous feast. "I think our man's name is almost certainly *Sunus Pyktis.* Immunis Sunus Pyktis. I think he is alive, and he is the primary perpetrator of all these horrors. Do you know him?"

THERE WAS A SILENCE. Then, for the first time, Ghrelin spoke. "Pyktis?" he said, astonished. "You think . . . you think this mysterious killer is *Pyktis*?"

"I do," said Ana. "I take it you are familiar with this man?"

The two fell silent. Thelenai glanced at Ghrelin, but Ghrelin stared into the table, lost in his thoughts.

"*Do* you know this Pyktis?" demanded Ana.

"Know . . ." said Ghrelin softly. "That's a complicated word when it concerns any who work within the Shroud." His fingers twitched in his lap; then his hand surfaced at the edge of the table and drummed a little *tap tap—taptap-tap.*

Ana cocked her head, listening carefully. I watched Ghrelin's fingers dance. Just as before, when he talked of the Shroud, his fingers moved of their own accord.

"Why?" asked Ana, impatient.

"We now consider sensitive things, Dolabra," said Thelenai. "Few discuss the workings of the Shroud outside of its veil. I am uncomfortable continuing."

"Must you resist me even now?" sighed Ana. "The sea walls are sensitive things, and these I have seen and toured!"

"But I am still not entirely convinced of your theory," said Thelenai. "You have found a dead officer upon a list who, if alive, might be capable of what you describe. But that is not evidence. That is possibility. I would need more."

Ana thoughtfully sat back. I could see her mentally browsing through all the barbs she could hurl at them next.

"Are *codes* used within the Shroud?" she asked finally.

Ghrelin looked startled; Thelenai, however, remained stony. "Codes are used throughout the Empire," she said.

"Are some of the codes *visual*?" asked Ana.

A slight crease to Thelenai's brow. Perhaps, I wondered, Ana was following the wrong lead. "Visual codes?" asked Thelenai. "As in, an alphabet? Or different characters? Or ..."

"Or something like this," said Ana. She plucked out the parchment of my drawings, slapped it on the table, and shoved it forward.

The effect was immediate: Thelenai flinched, her icy poise dissolving; Ghrelin stood and gasped as if Ana had just pulled another severed head from her bag.

"Oh, by the Harvester," murmured Ghrelin. "Is it really him? But how could he ... how could he be *alive*?"

"Where did you get that?" demanded Thelenai.

"Din found it in the clearing," said Ana. "On a big piece of leather, stuck in front of that instrument that turned fifty fucking people into brush and sedge in mere seconds. Do you know, I rather think our killer left it specifically for you two?"

Thelenai's eyes rose from the parchment to stare at Ana in horror.

"Here," said Ana forcefully, "is what shall now happen. You, Commander-Prificto, are going to start *actually* cooperating with this investigation as if we sat upon true imperial soil. You are going to tell me the truth—even if you do not wish to. And I don't think you do, because I think you know you have done something very wrong. I suspect you believe you have done this wrong thing for all the right reasons—and perhaps you have!—but that is all moot now." All the smugness vanished from Ana's face, replaced by a cold, terrible fury. "It is moot, because someone from *your house* has slipped away into the jungle. He has gone into those trees, and he has reinvented himself, and he has now killed not only *fifty* Yarrow folk, but *Sanctum knows* how many Apoth officers, canal riggers, and imperial servants in the past two years! He may in fact be the most prolific murderer in imperial history, for all I fucking know! And though I don't yet understand him, I know he's not going to stop. This fellow's got a taste for it now. He *likes* it. He's practiced it, for *years*. And he is doing something, making something, playing some game—and I cannot unravel it until you tell me the emperor's honest fucking truth. Am I clear?"

For a long while, nobody moved: Malo sat hunched in her chair, elbows on her knees, watching Thelenai and Ghrelin; Ana was leaning so far forward she was practically standing up, her chin stuck out like a battering ram; Ghrelin's body twitched and shuddered, his fingers beating out a tattoo upon his hip.

Then Thelenai slumped, defeated. "I . . . I can't tell you one piece," she said softly. "For you to . . . to understand one piece, I would have to tell you all. I don't know where to start."

"Why don't you start with the marrow, then?" asked Ana. "For that's what this is about, yes?"

"Y-yes," whispered Thelenai. She shut her eyes. "Come, Ghrelin. Let us tell them."

CHAPTER 28

. . .

"I ... I WAS ASSIGNED HERE NEARLY THIRTY YEARS AGO," Thelenai began quietly. "I was a hypokratos officer in Yarrowdale when the Shroud was originally built, and I contributed designs to nearly all the subsequent expansions. Now it encompasses the whole of my duties. It is my strange child, in a way, and I its mother. And ... to many people, the Shroud is a marvelous achievement. To some, it is almost a holy site." She paused. "But what few see is that everything about the Shroud is so *vulnerable*. It depends on so much for all to go aright."

"I assume you mean," drawled Ana, "it is rather obviously bad for the entire Empire to depend on slaughtering and bleeding these tremendous, horrible beasts once a year ..."

"Yes," said Ghrelin, his voice as quiet as a breeze. "But it's even worse than that. Extracting the *qudaydin kani* is one thing. Storing it is yet another. But it is fragile in other ways, too."

"The location of it all," said Thelenai. "The hostility of the Yarrow king, and the constant smugglers. But the sheer distance is troublesome. The larger shipments cannot be shipped at all during the dry seasons, and so many reagents degrade. Though few Apoths admit it, the conclusion is obvious."

"The Empire has outgrown the Shroud," said Ghrelin. "And Yarrowdale. It cannot function as it has for much longer."

The two Apoths leaned back in their seats, a look of miserable relief on their faces, like they'd both confessed to some horrible sin.

"Yes, yes," said Ana, dismissive. "That is why you sought the marrow. Correct?"

"True," said Thelenai. "The . . . the marrow is a cylinder of spongy bone resting in the inner chambers of their anatomy, you see. When the leviathan is brought to the Shroud, we first bleed it of its most dangerous ichors, and the marrow is saved for last. That is where the *kani* is found. That is what we drain, and extract. *That* is why Yarrowdale exists."

"The Senate of the Sanctum authorized a research project here in Yarrowdale just over a decade ago," said Ghrelin, his voice growing fragile, "to answer one question—what if we could extract not only the blood but the marrow *itself*? What if we could bathe it in nutrients and maintain it so it kept producing the blood well *after* the titan has died?"

"This was your secret task, then?" asked Ana. "To remove an organ from a leviathan and keep it alive, like a child trapping a frog in a pot?"

"Your comparison is crude," said Thelenai, "but apt. We have kept our labors secret, for obvious reasons—if the king of Yarrow were to find out we were laboring in his backyard to render his entire kingdom irrelevant to the Empire, it would be politically destabilizing. But . . . if we achieved this feat, the effects would go well beyond ridding us of the king."

"How so?" asked Ana.

"Many reagents decay during the long journey through the canals," explained Ghrelin. "Which makes many grafts impossible. If we could remove the marrow, stabilize it, and ship it into the inner rings, we could produce *kani* at scale, and onsite! Close to where it would be *used*. We could even duplicate the marrow, perhaps, like taking cuttings from a plant, and grow more specimens. And with this, we could change all the Empire."

"Healing grafts and suffusions you can scarcely imagine," said Thelenai. "We could end the plague of sterility that comes with so many alterations. Bring about an age of abundance like when the first Khanum emerged from the valley in the ancient days and changed all the world before them."

"We could even heal our Sublimes," said Ghrelin. "Many of us are plagued by mental afflictions as we grow old and lead short lives. With an abundance of *kani*, we could change even that."

I had listened to all this with a mix of wonder and horror, but that caught my attention. I had seen engravers grow old and mad well before their natural age, afflicted by hallucinations and dreams; to hear that the Empire could be laboring even now to save me from that fate filled me with wonder.

Ana's cold voice cut in. "Remarkable," she said flatly. "So. Why isn't this wonderful world achieved?"

"Because it is a logistical nightmare," sighed Thelenai. "How could we safely extract, contain, and ship the marrow *itself*, which continually excretes titan's blood in its purest form? It would be like trying to hold a flaming coal without burning your hand, *or* snuffing it out."

"We p-partly solved the problem," stammered Ghrelin. "For we Apoths already possessed arts of preserving pieces of the dead . . ."

Malo spoke up: "Ah! You wish to use ossuary moss, don't you? You're trying to bind it up in ossuary moss, just like we do for our dead."

A fleeting smile from Thelenai. "Indeed. By carefully injecting the organ with an advanced strain of *oli muk*—or ossuary moss, as you refer to it—we could wrap up the marrow like a fly in a spider's web and keep it preserved indefinitely. We had to do it in the right sequence, but . . . but if we could figure that out, then the work could proceed."

Now it was Ana's turn to sit up. She fumbled blindly about on the table and stuck a finger in the parchment of symbols I'd drawn for her minutes ago. "And that's what *this* is, isn't it? This isn't some damned code. This is the process you designed to bind up the marrow."

"Correct," said Thelenai. "The symbols you witnessed, Signums, show when and where to inject the moss to preserve the tissue. Indeed, it is the process we've had the most success with. But it took tremendous effort, years of toil, to get even there."

"Why?" asked Ana impatiently.

"Because as I told you when we last met," said Ghrelin, "each leviathan is always *different*. No two are alike. We suspect that they have evolved to change continuously, adapting to new forms—and that, perhaps, is why their blood is so powerfully transmutational."

"But this means the marrow, too, is always different," said Thelenai. "Biologically different in shape, density, nature . . . so each *extraction* had to be different. We needed a way of reading the randomness. Only then could we succeed."

Thelenai swallowed. Her face looked terrifically aged now, as if saying these words drained the very life from her flesh.

"What we needed," she said finally, "was a different way of looking at it. A different type of *mind*. That is why we produced augury. And that changed everything."

"AUGURY . . ." MURMURED ANA. "What is this augury? I do not know of it."

"It is . . . a type of alteration," continued Thelenai slowly. "It is produced as a black pellet, placed underneath the tongue to dissolve as you slumber. But it alters the human mind, as opposed to flesh."

"A new type of Sublime, ma'am?" I asked. "A suffusion that changes what you are, how you think?"

"No," said Thelenai. "No, not like what was done to you or me, Kol. It is more like a graft, or perhaps a mood graft, bestowing a temporary effect. One that works only upon axioms—and grants those who consume it an unusually heightened mental state."

"Ahh . . ." Ana steepled her fingers beneath her nose. "Let me guess," she whispered. "This graft, this augury . . . did it grant people unusual *pattern-identifying* abilities?"

Thelenai and Ghrelin exchanged a bleak look.

"You have it exactly," muttered Thelenai.

"Under the effects of augury, any normal axiom's cerebral capacities are magnified," said Ghrelin. "They attain a stunning capability to rapidly analyze, dissect, and deduce marvelously accurate predictions, about the most complicated of phenomena, from the *barest shreds* of evidence or data."

"They were instrumental in our progress," said Thelenai. "The physiology of the leviathans is so unpredictable, so dangerous, and so random—only the augurs could make sense of it."

"Then if this augury graft was so successful, ma'am," Ana asked, "why is it not known? Why isn't it used across the Empire, to predict all the ills of the world?"

The two Apoths hesitated.

"I should guess," muttered Malo, "that it had some *unintended* effects ..."

"Yes," said Thelenai quietly. "If an axiom remained in a high state of augury for more than three years, they began to exhibit ... afflictions."

"Apophenia being the worst, and most notable," said Ghrelin. "An uncontrollable, debilitating impulse to spy patterns in *everything*."

I glanced at Ana, but she only smiled and wryly said, "Oh, I'm familiar with *that* one ..."

"But perhaps not to the extent of this," said Thelenai. "Some augurs would sit in their rooms, studying the bricks in the wall, trying to comprehend which spot of earth they came from, and grow so absorbed in the task that they nearly starved to death."

"Others became unreasonable," said Ghrelin. "They believed they had identified some horrible motivation in the behaviors of others. They grew paranoid, mistrustful."

"Enough effects, then," said Ana, "that this augury was never approved for use. Yes?"

"Correct," said Ghrelin slowly. "It ... was not approved for use in the Empire."

The silence lingered. Ghrelin looked to Thelenai, his painted features full of anguish.

"Ohh," said Ana slowly. "Use *in the Empire*. But ... Yarrowdale is *not* technically the Empire. Is that it?"

"True," said Thelenai softly. "It is not."

At that, Ana gave a great, exasperated sigh and said, "Including this Pyktis, then?"

Thelenai's green eyes glimmered like she was close to tears. Then she whispered, "We are a different character of Apoths here. Higher, stronger, nobler. They had to pass many tests. And . . . and they only participated if they wished to. We did not force anyone's consent. They could have stopped any time."

"Oh, for fuck's sakes," snarled Ana. "For *fuck's* sakes! You have damned us all with your high-minded hypocrisy, woman! Do you comprehend that?"

"Wh-what?" I said, startled. "What do you mean?"

"Is it not obvious, Din?" Ana snapped. "Thelenai has been operating her own little trial run of an enormously advanced, unapproved graft that augments axioms until they can predict almost anything. *That's* the secret they've been hiding from us! She's done a very good job of keeping it off the books—until now, because one of her altered axioms has apparently gone stark raving mad! And now we have a preposterously brilliant madman skulking about the jungle—and he is using those powers of prediction for slaughter and sabotage. That is how he's done all this—and *that* is why we cannot catch him!" She sat back, furious and fuming. "Well. *Well!* This is going to be a fucking tricky one, and no mistake!"

CHAPTER 29

⌄ ⌄ ⌄

"TELL ME ABOUT THIS SUNUS PYKTIS," DEMANDED ANA. "Hold nothing back! The more I know, the faster we can respond."

"I can tell you little!" sighed Thelenai. "He was one augur of many. The only significant thing about him to me was his death—for he died in a disaster on the Shroud, or so we thought."

"A mishandling of the blood," said Ghrelin quietly. "Two other augurs died as well. Such were the . . . the warpings that no bodies could be recovered."

"I assume neither of you witnessed this disaster," said Ana acidly, "otherwise you'd both be dead, too?"

"True enough," murmured Thelenai.

Ana crossed her arms. "Hmph! I want all records of this Sunus, and all records of this disaster. *Nothing* omitted, either! There is a time for secrecy, and it is not now."

"I shall make it so," said Thelenai. "You will have them in hours."

"Good," said Ana. "But is there *anything* of use you can give me now? What are these augurs like? What do they desire? This man is an utter mystery to us. Surely you can help describe their nature!"

"What you ask is difficult to provide," said Thelenai, cringing.

"Damn it, *why*?" demanded Ana.

Ghrelin swallowed and said, "Augurs cannot converse like normal people. It is terribly difficult to know any one of them intimately when they are elevated to such a state."

Malo squinted at him. "Eh? What do you mean, they did not *converse* like normal people?"

I glanced at Ana, who was by now practically vibrating with impatience. "Or did they not talk at all?" I asked. "Did they *tap* instead?"

Ghrelin's eyes widened in surprise. Then he nodded. "Y-yes. You already know, then. Of course you do . . ."

"Yes!" snapped Ana. "Of course!"

Malo looked around at us, bewildered. "What is this? What the hell do you mean, they tap?"

Ana extended a hand to the two Apoths—*Go ahead.*

Ghrelin swallowed again. "The . . . the augury affects the mind so greatly that normal conversation is exceedingly difficult, especially when conveying large amounts of information. The augurs read things into the slightest inflection, or word choice, or hesitation. So, on the Shroud . . . they do not speak aloud, but rather *tap* to communicate, in a very old code. This method is much less affected by nuance."

"I go to the Shroud very rarely," said Thelenai quietly. "But when I would visit the augurs, they . . . they'd sit in a circle, their fingers drumming on little boards about their necks. It would seem to make no sense at all, just noise and tapping, but then . . . they would take their ashpens, and all together, they would draw up diagrams and figures and calculations so brilliant and so accurate, they would take your breath away."

"And that is who this Pyktis was," said Ana. "One of these silent, dreamy drummers."

Thelenai nodded. "Yes."

"How long do the effects of this augury last?"

"A decent dose can elevate them for up to three to four months," said Ghrelin. "We cycle the doses up and down throughout the year, to avoid excessive cerebral damage."

"But being as Pyktis has been missing for two years," said Ana sourly, "I'm guessing you have discovered some doses *missing* in the time since?"

Ghrelin's eyes grew very round. "Oh . . . Well. Y-yes. We did notice some . . . some small discrepancies in the dosages . . ."

"I thought those were quite small," said Thelenai, startled. "Rounding errors in dosages, no more."

Ana scoffed. "I'm sure they *appeared* so . . ." She shook her head, disgusted. "And the side effects—if someone were to be maintaining their augury for *five* years, as opposed to the usual three? For Pyktis first went to the Shroud some five years ago, true? How could he manage that?"

Ghrelin contemplated it. "I would guess that he is maintaining a very low level of augury. Not the full, for to do that in the wild would be utterly debilitating. Too much to analyze and predict. Yet even so . . . I would assume Pyktis is now experiencing high levels of paranoia, volatility, and violence. He is likely sleeping little, eating little, and having unstable reactions to . . . well, nearly any human interaction."

A bleak silence.

"Fucker's a damn lunatic, then," said Malo.

"That is one expression," admitted Thelenai. "But even if he *is* maintaining his augury at a low level, eventually it would overcome him—correct, Ghrelin?"

"Yes," said Ghrelin. "The effects should be permanently disabling within . . . well, a few months. Perhaps another year. No more."

"So could we simply wait him out?" said Malo.

Ana chuckled morosely. "Oh, I doubt it. For we should assume Pyktis, being a genius, knows this, too! He is conscious that his time is running out. Thus, this makes him *more* dangerous—which means we must move ever faster."

"SO," SIGHED ANA. "We know almost nothing about this man, except that he is brilliant, mad, he should be dead, and he grows more dangerous by the day. We don't even know why he . . ." Then she went very still. "Hm. The bank, yes . . . Before we go galloping along, I suppose we should go back to the very beginning of this, yes?"

"How might you mean?" asked Thelenai.

"Why, the very crime that brought us all here," said Ana. "The murder to acquire the item that was in that damned safe!"

At this, Ghrelin's and Thelenai's expressions changed yet again: first they looked surprised, like they realized they'd forgotten this, and then, in unison, an expression of utter devastation fell upon them.

"The stolen item obviously wasn't instructions for a healing graft," continued Ana, ignorant of their change. "But I am now troubled . . . for I know it wasn't some component or reagent necessary to help Pyktis kill those smugglers. He'd already stolen everything he needed to do that. Then—*what* was in that safe that Pyktis sought to steal?"

Another pause.

"A . . . a report, from the Shroud," admitted Ghrelin. "One destined for the first ring of the Empire."

"And the nature of this report?" asked Ana.

Thelenai made a face as though to say these words were akin to having a limb lopped off. "It concerned the leviathan marrow. Namely, a . . . a report on how to ship it up the canals . . . and then how to embed it within a nutrient brewery to begin excreting *kani.*"

Ana froze. Then she shivered, the fronds of her snow-white hair trembling like a beetle's antennae. "I . . . see," she said. "And . . . the reason why you were sending this report . . . it was because your efforts here have been *successful,* haven't they? All your augurs, they . . . they actually *managed* it, yes? They successfully excised and stored a titan's marrow."

The Apoths sat still as stone.

"That is so," said Thelenai huskily. "We succeeded last wet season."

"Yes . . ." said Ana. "And this marrow you have bound up in ossuary moss. This tremendously unstable, dangerous chunk of titan flesh . . . it's *here.* In Yarrowdale. It's stored on the Shroud. Isn't it?"

Ghrelin nodded, his face crumpled like he might dissolve into tears at any moment.

"And now a brilliant, murderous madman knows it," said Ana faintly. "And that is what he was telling us, with the sign he left in the warped clearing. He was flaunting that he'd figured it all out." She scratched her head and muttered, "Well, fuck."

"YOU DID *WHAT*?" said Malo, horrified. "It's just . . . over there? Across the *bay*?"

"The marrow is in a very stable state!" said Thelenai defensively. "We have bound and preserved it most securely in moss, and it is hidden behind vaults and walls and armored doors deep within the Shroud!"

"But it would pass through Yarrowdale *eventually*, true?" asked Ana. "It would one day be mere leagues or span from where we sit now?"

"Yes," admitted Ghrelin. "It would. We would have to do so, to deliver it to those who so need it in the inner rings."

"You want to just float that shit *up the canals*?" said Malo.

I shut my eyes, my whole body trembling. "Oh, by the fates," I whispered. "By the Harvester . . ."

"Understand that we have considered every precaution!" said Thelenai. "We know all the risks! But the greatest risks, ironically, are here in Yarrowdale, in this very dangerous land that the Empire does not control at all! And we obviously cannot ship the marrow now. Not if there is some madman lurking in the trees who knows it is coming!"

"The augurs have calculated the chances that they could duplicate their efforts," whispered Ghrelin, "and succeed in extracting the marrow again. The odds are far lower than we'd like. This may be our only chance for years to come. And yet we are forced to sit."

Ana raised a hand, her expression merciless. "Do the inner rings know?" she demanded.

"They know I have succeeded, but not how," said Thelenai miserably. "Of the augurs, they know nothing."

"And Prificto Kardas? Is he aware that he is here pursuing a diplomatic agreement you hope to neuter within mere months?"

"I have had little communication with Kardas at all," said Thele-nai. "My people observe his movements, as they do for all who might bring contagion into Yarrowdale. He comes to and fro from the High City in the west and goes nowhere else. He is there even now, I understand . . ."

Ana impatiently flapped a hand. "And if the marrow *was* successfully attacked? If, say, Pyktis again used his titan's blood weapon and managed to penetrate all your defenses about the marrow, there upon the Shroud?"

A taut silence.

"Then . . . then the marrow would act like . . . a fissure in the earth dripping lava, layer upon layer," whispered Thelenai. "Releasing more blood, and more alterations."

"How much land area would be affected?" asked Ana.

Thelenai shrugged helplessly. "Leagues. Enough to destroy most of the city. Perhaps enough to block up the canals entirely."

"Which would bring the Empire to a shuddering halt," said Ghrelin.

Malo shut her eyes. "By hells . . ."

Ana tapped her chin thoughtfully. "Yes . . . yes, it is a most excellent target for him! We must assume this is exactly what he wants to achieve. And, you know . . . I very much think he could do so!"

"He . . . he could?" asked Ghrelin.

"Well, it depends on how you answer this next question, Ghrelin. The warpings Din and Malo saw in the wood—how much fertilizer would he have needed to do that?"

"Oh, I am not sure, offhand," said Ghrelin. "Perhaps a few small-stone's worth. It was a small effect, really, if Kol and the rest were not affected."

"I see," said Ana. "A bare drop of corruption. Yet from my analysis of the thefts, Pyktis has stolen *six crates* of this fertilizer—with their contents totaling nearly *fifty stone's* worth."

Nobody moved for a long while. Then Malo placed her face in her hands. "Fucking fates alive . . ." she whispered.

"Yes," said Ana. "So he is *very* capable of a far worse attack. Enough to imperil the entire Shroud itself! The question is . . . why has he not done so *yet*? Why did he not strike quickly, before we even knew he was there? Why aren't we all just fucking dead, really? It is most troubling to me."

Ghrelin now looked so horrified I worried he might collapse.

"We . . . we have to find it," said Thelenai weakly. "We must find those reagents before he can use them."

"But the jungle is wide and wild," said Malo. "And one can hide six crates nearly anywhere."

"True," said Ana. "Thus—we find the man, we find the reagents."

"But I still cannot comprehend why he does this at all. Is it all revenge, Dolabra?" begged Thelenai. "Is that why Pyktis plagues us so? Because we put him to a task that nearly killed him?"

"I cannot say for sure," said Ana. "I know nothing at all about the fellow! And how I tire of lists and records and codes! Besides the diseased bastards Din and Malo scooped up in the woods, we have no *real witnesses* of the man." Then she went very still. "So . . . so, so, so. Ghrelin, if you will indulge me . . ."

"Yes?" said Ghrelin warily.

"The only people who *did* know this Pyktis are still inside the Shroud. Is that correct?"

"I . . . I think a few of his colleagues are still there, yes."

"And . . . these colleagues are also augurs," said Ana, "which means they, too, possess hypersensitive abilities of prediction and analysis?"

"Yes?"

"Ones that would be *enormously* useful if they were put to the task of analyzing Pyktis?"

"Well. Ye—"

"Then would it be possible for Din here to *go* to the Shroud," asked Ana, "and simply chat up these augurs of yours to figure out this man's nature?"

Everyone stared at Ana in utter alarm—but none more than I.

Panic rushed into my belly, and up my throat. The idea of traveling to the Shroud—the most dangerous place in the Empire after the sea walls themselves—filled me with horror.

"Ah . . ." I said quietly. "Well, ah, wait, ma'am, I . . ."

"That is not possible," said Ghrelin.

"The Shroud is a clean site," said Thelenai firmly. "Visitors are *tremendously* restricted."

I nearly sighed aloud with relief.

"Can we not get Din here clean?" said Ana. "That can't be so hard, your colleagues just basted him in oil like a fucking pheasant!"

"But it is even more complex than that," said Ghrelin. "The Shroud is a *biological envelope.* It is perhaps even more reactive than the Plains of the Path! Penetrating it is a dangerous procedure. We do so only on regulated schedules!"

"Then when is the next penetration?" demanded Ana.

"Well . . . I believe the next restocking ship shall leave in twenty days . . ." admitted Ghrelin reluctantly.

"That's far longer than I'd like," growled Ana. "So long that the idea is nigh useless . . . yet this bastard is a clever one. It may take just that long to catch him!"

I squirmed in my seat. "Ma'am . . . are we really sure it's a good idea to . . . to send me to the *Shroud*?"

"No, Din," said Ana. "I think it is a *very* good idea to send you to the Shroud! These marvelous bastards apparently see much, and know much—and they're the only people who've known this man. They would be an invaluable resource in hunting him!"

"Yet it is *not* as easy as you think!" said Thelenai. "As we just said, the officers you would send him to interview do not communicate like normal folk anymore. They tap far more than they talk."

"But we have a translator, don't we?" Ana's blindfolded face swiveled to Ghrelin. "Correct, Immunis? Are you *still* an augur? For I notice you tap as well."

Ghrelin blanched. "I . . . I was an augur, during my time within the veil," he admitted. "I often go with the restocking shipments to study the axioms inside. And I must consume augury, very slightly, in order to communicate with them, and to study their works and reports—for they do not make sense to the normal mind. I could translate, yes."

"Good!" said Ana cheerily. "Then this all sounds agreeable to me."

"I . . . I will consent to this," said Thelenai reluctantly, "but *only* as a last resort. It takes tremendous preparation for a person to pass within the Shroud. We should try *everything* else, and only then send in the young signum along with the shipment in twenty days."

"If it takes twenty fucking days to catch this man," said Ana, "then I suspect I'll be resorting to all kinds of preposterously stupid things."

Thelenai nodded gravely. "Then you have my approval."

I looked away. My mouth felt hot and thick, and I felt the unpleasant rumble of vomit at the back of my throat.

That was it, then. I was doomed. We'd have to catch Pyktis in twenty days, or I'd catch some vile blot of contagion while within that unholy veil and be transmuted into something unspeakable. My family would go bankrupt, and all the grand machinations and systems of the Empire would spin on, and I would be ground to dust, and go forgotten.

Thelenai spoke on, ignorant or indifferent to my distress: "Before those twenty days elapse, Dolabra . . . what tactics shall you now pursue to catch this man?"

"Oh," sighed Ana, and she rubbed her face. "Well, for one thing, it would help if I got a full briefing from my investigator in an environment with a little less *pressure*! I've hardly had any time to question poor Din on what he saw. It's all been panicked whispering in your little meeting room here, like a lord and his maid attempting to arrange a furtive fuck."

Malo glanced at me, appalled, but I was still so shaken that Ana's words hardly registered.

"Then how shall we assist?" asked Thelenai. "Do you need simply time?"

"I need time, and to return to my quarters," said Ana, wrinkling her nose. "There are too many vapors and sounds and surfaces here. And—*and!*—I shall need to dine. Great thought, after all, works up a great appetite."

"To . . . dine?" said Thelenai. "Can you not simply sup as you please?"

"Well, I *could*, ma'am. But you are a senior Apoth officer, with access to many reagents, and precursors, and specimens . . ." She grinned. "So, I am sure you could acquire many *exotic* classes of flesh—true?"

CHAPTER 30

⌃ ⌃ ⌃

THE VEGETABLES, SOMEHOW, WERE THE LEAST OBJEC-
tionable part of Ana's feast. I tried not to look at them as I sniffed my
vial and reported to her in her quarters. They were the most undesir-
able vegetation I'd ever seen, being mostly knotted tubers or bulbous
mushrooms or shriveled berries, all in hues either dusky and dark or
unnervingly bright. They seemed to have been cultivated to send one
clear message to any onlooker: *Do not put this in your mouth.*

And yet Ana ate them, carving off slices and stuffing them down
her gullet. She gobbled down the foul things, tasting each sampling,
before then moving on to the eggs. The Apoths had provided us with
dozens of them in many sizes and sporting a spectrum of shells—
"We use their whites to cultivate many reagents," Malo confided in
me, "and some species prove better than others"—and Ana began
sending Malo back and forth from the fire, bringing her hot pans of
sizzling yolks with mustard-colored whorls.

Yet neither the vegetables nor the eggs could possibly compare to
the meats. The Apoths, having been pressured to provide her with the
most exotic edible fleshes they possessed, had apparently taken this
as an opportunity to dispose of their less desired specimens. Most of
these samplings sat suspended in cloudy fluids in jars, and each time
Ana popped one open and fished out a strip of flesh (A leg? Some
animal's face? A clutch of intestines? I dared not guess) I turned away
and stopped up my nose to ensure I caught not a whiff.

And yet she ate these, too. Ana ate, and ate, and ate, carving off curls of meat, slicing the skins of roots and rubbing them in oils, and even once cracking a raw egg and sucking the fluid straight from within. Her appetite was endless and abominable, so much so that Malo—she who had so casually wandered through the reeking ossuary—gagged in disgust. Even when the Apoth courier brought her a pile of reports on Pyktis and his supposed death upon the Shroud, Ana did not stop her feasting: she nibbled, and chewed, and listened to me, a grin often splitting her face as if she could imagine no greater delight than this.

When I finally finished my account, Ana sat crooked in her chair, a dreamy look on her blindfolded face. One hand pawed the pages of the Apoth reports; the other danced along the table, until she dabbed a finger in one of the cloudier jars of fluid—this one an unsettling auburn hue—and sucked at it. I shut my eyes and focused on the scent of the fire in the stove.

"You sound rather pallid, Din," said Ana with a faintly cruel tone. "Are you sure you're well?"

"I will feel far better the second I am far away from this feast of yours, ma'am."

"I second this," muttered Malo. "I am unsure if all on that table is fit for consumption. I do not think you should even dump her chamber pot out nearby . . ."

"Oh, but this is an imperial tradition, children!" said Ana. "Exotic banquets were once a common sight in the ages of the first emperors. This was before the march to the sea, of course, and the conquering of the Titan's Path. In those now-faded years, the ancient Khanum feasted before battles and holy days, and debates, and celebrations, and games. The courts and clearings would fill with dancers and the sacred smokes of thuribles, and they would light their silvered fires. Then came tables laid with many dishes and meats, and all the blessed Khanum sated themselves before they put their minds and bodies to great works." She paused in her dining and said, "Though these works were not great enough to stem their decline and eventual extinction, of course." She speared a lump of pinkish root and gobbled it down. "Such feasts are now unknown in the modern Empire. And perhaps that is a good thing! For those were savage days, for savage folk. And today, we are a far better people—are we not?"

"If folk such as Pyktis still lurk among us," said Malo, "I am unsure."

"A fair point, perhaps," purred Ana. "Let us get to the task of eliminating him from our ranks, then! Malo—I assume your wardens shall search the canals more thoroughly now, yes?"

"Of course. I have my best people combing the jungle now about the warped clearing, since that was apparently where this Pyktis dwelt most."

"And if they find any sign of him?"

"They shall send up a flare right away. But there is nothing yet. All we know is what we've found thus far."

"Mm," Ana said softly, and fell silent.

I hazarded a glance at her and studied the pile of parchments in her lap. "Have you found anything of use in what the Apoths sent us on Pyktis, ma'am?"

"I have found much," sighed Ana. "But of use, I am unsure." She leaned back and recited aloud, "Sunus Pyktis, approximately aged thirty-two, exact birth date unknown! First registered in Ta-Rath, capital city of the Rathras canton. Initial Iyalet scores placed him in the best Rathras Apoth academies, developed his arts working in the ossuaries there. Much information, yes, but little interesting! The only unusual thing I saw was a note from a Rathras registrar stating he thought the boy's birth year was inaccurate, for he seemed far older than the listed birth year of 1097. Yet this tells us nothing about *the man*! Did he prefer sotwine or grain brew? Was the fellow a virgin? Did he know how to fluently speak Pithian? Might he harbor a few mutinous thoughts about the Empire's adoption of Yarrow? We still know terribly little."

"What of his supposed death?" I asked.

"Oh, that is far grislier, and far more interesting!" said Ana eagerly. "Listen to this, children! Our dear Pyktis supposedly perished during an incident in an extraction, trying to tap the titan's marrow with two other officers. It seems there was some contaminant on one of the officers' suits while working the extraction. A light dusting of tree pollen, they think—which should *not* have been there, given all the cleaning and treatments done to their algaeoil suits. The *kani* splashed upon them." She picked up a strip of fat from some grotesque specimen, stuffed it into her lips, and chewed noisily. "The pollen was transmuted, and grew rapidly, penetrating the suit . . ."

Malo shuddered. "So the *kani* found living flesh."

"Correct! This gave way to more transmutations—I imagine a raging storm of bone and ligament—which then killed all three augurs inspecting the carcass. Or so the Apoths thought." Her greasy digits danced over one sheaf of parchment. "The damage was catastrophic. An entire cleansing bay of the Shroud ruined for years. Yet—how did Pyktis escape this end? I cannot say, but . . . I will speculate he may be even more brilliant than we thought."

"Do you think he can be caught?" Malo asked. "Or do his abilities put him beyond our reach?"

"Ah, there you forget one of the foremost rules of the Empire, girl," said Ana. "An augmented person is still a person—even the fabled, lost Khanum!—and thus they are weak in predictable ways. No, this fellow is not all logic, and his mind is not all wheels and gears. Our man is on a *mission*. And he has been for a very long time, I think."

"Two years in the jungle is not that long," said Malo. "Not if you don't mind worms living in bits of you."

"Oh, I mean longer than that. In fact, I think he came *to* the Shroud with these monstrous intentions already in mind, many years ago."

Malo stared at Ana so open-mouthed that I could glimpse the dark clump of hina root balanced on her tongue.

"You think he planned all this before he ever became an augur on the Shroud, ma'am?" I asked. "Why?"

"Well, first there is the missing augury," said Ana. "Ghrelin said they'd found small discrepancies in the dosages over the past few months. This suggests that Pyktis had been stealing them for some time—saving up, then, for a period when he'd no longer have access to it. But then there is the suspicious nature of his death! This man is a genius. So were his colleagues. And yet—someone just *happens* to leave tree pollen upon their warding suit while trudging about in a leviathan's entrails? A horrible coincidence that just *happens* to leave all bodies unrecoverable, and grant Pyktis the cover he needs to fabricate his death? No, his exit was planned, and cleverly planned at that. I believe he has been designing all this for years." She paused. "And I don't think he's doing it alone."

"Eh?" said Malo.

I nodded, grimacing. "The money."

"Indeed," said Ana.

"Money?" asked Malo. "What money?"

"The money that Pyktis apparently used to pay his way into the good graces of the smuggling clans!" said Ana. "Your ragged captive told you Pyktis offered a fortune for the clan's cooperation. But where in hell could he get such a thing, assuming he'd just barely survived some catastrophe on the Shroud? The obvious answer is, someone gave it to him. He is being *financed*. But by whom? And why? We do not know." She sighed deeply. "And then, stranger still, there is the mask... Malo, you said your old fisherman spied Pyktis floating downstream with a bag over his head. And now we hear tales that Pyktis never took his helmet off! Yet why hide his face? He didn't bother to do so when robbing the vaults. What is special about his features that drives him to do such a thing? Again, we have nothing."

An uneasy gloom stole over us, broken only by the sounds of the distant waves.

"It is an awkward moment," Ana said. "We are like a man finding blood upon his feet, trying to discern where he has been stabbed! But at least we know *who* has wounded us so."

Malo scowled. "But it is not just Pyktis who has harmed us. What a thing it is, to have all at risk because of Thelenai's lies! So many dead—and Kol here likely to join their number, when he goes to the Shroud..."

I shot a glare at her. "Thank you for your concern." Then, to Ana: "Do you think the commander-prificto will be charged with high crimes for what she's done, ma'am?"

"Thelenai I shall have to handle in good time," said Ana grudgingly. "I am sure she thinks she did the right thing—that healing so many in the future was worth inflicting pain on a few in the present—but secretly, she did it for the same reason so many regents crumble."

"Which is?" I asked.

"Pride," answered Ana. "She wrote a story in her mind, with herself as hero, clad in the trappings of triumph. It's possible the greatness she has accomplished here could have been done with no deception, and thus less disaster. But a prideful creature can talk themself into believing that every deed they do is legitimate. Thus, they both giddily and greedily spin their own doom."

Unable to bear the stench of Ana's feast anymore, I slid out a shootstraw pipe, knelt before the fire, and lit it on one of the coals. "Will we be so lucky that Pyktis shall do the same?"

"Perhaps," said Ana. "First, I have questions."

ANA STABBED A HOLE in another egg with her fingernail and greedily sucked it back. Then she turned to Malo, her lips gleaming. "First, Malo . . . when shall the Apoths burn the warped clearing?"

"They've already begun, ma'am," Malo said. "Though the work is slow and thorough. I could see the first smokes in the distance as we returned to your quarters."

"Really?" I said. "The skies seemed clear to me."

"Your eyes aren't as mine," Malo said. "But you shall see it soon. The smoke will only grow the more they burn."

Ana tossed the eggshell into the fire, where the whites instantly began to sizzle. "Will the smoke be visible for some leagues?"

"It would . . ." said Malo slowly. "You think Pyktis shall watch the horizon to confirm that we have found his horrid display?"

"I think he watches us most closely, yes," said Ana. "We are in something of a dance with him, though we do not know his steps. And one thing we do not know bothers me most of all—for *how* did Pyktis predict all these Apoth shipments so perfectly? Every time, he knew not only what to steal, but when and where and how to steal it! And that I cannot explain."

"He is a genius at prediction, yes?" I said.

"Yes, but even a genius needs *some* information to extrapolate from!" said Ana. "Which makes me think he had some advance warning. Could it be something as simple as bribing some Apoth in the city to sneak him notice of the shipments?"

Malo shook her head. "Shipment orders are given mere days before the shipment goes out, for that exact reason," she said. "The less time you know something, the less you can sell what you know. We Apoths are not the source."

"Then how was it done, damn it?" fumed Ana.

Malo shrugged. "I cannot say, ma'am."

Ana furiously muttered for a moment. Then she sniffed and said, "Fine! I shall leave it there. But next, Malo—this coin that Din found."

Malo sighed softly. "Shall I be your guide on all things Yarrow? Surely Kardas would be a faster hand at this. He has a gift for words beyond all folk I know."

"Given that Prificto Kardas seems to have achieved absolutely fucking *nothing* during his time here," Ana said poisonously, "I shall take a muddy warden girl over his expertise any day. So! These coins are passed among the Yarrow folk as some kind of . . . blessing? A token of respect?"

"Something like that," Malo grunted. "It is a sign of favor. If a noble does the king of Yarrow a good turn, the king may bless them with a coin. The noble can later give it back to the king to ask a favor, small or large. Or, the noble can grant it to one of the chieftains in service to him, in recognition of their own good works, and they can return it to the noble and make their own request of him—or *they* could pass it on, as well, to their captains or soldiers. And so on, and so on, and down the hill the oaths all tumble . . . yet they always come back up, to the court or the king."

Ana frowned, thinking. "Could a peasant or chieftain skip the man above them, and take their favor directly to someone higher—even the king?"

"They . . . could," she said reluctantly. "But that is a rare thing. Most folk stay within their place. To go higher risks punishment."

"Punishment? Are these not tokens of favoritism?"

"Well . . . the king is obliged to grant any oathcoin boon asked of him, true. But once he has done so, the king may then have the person who asked killed or tortured, if he thinks the demand was too great, or too impertinent."

"He'd . . . he'd have them *executed*?" I asked, shocked.

Malo shrugged. "He is king. There is no law saying he cannot do so. He *is* the law, for he is the crown."

"Ahh." Ana grinned horribly. "The illusion of shared power, as opposed to the real thing . . . yes, that's much more manageable for a tyrant! But would it be safe to assume that such gifts would only circulate among a *select* set of people in the Elder West?"

"Very much so. As I said, the coins always come back to court. I doubt if any oathcoin has ever strayed far from the High City. Before this, I had only seen one once in my life, and it was paid for dearly."

"I see," said Ana quietly. "Thank you, Malo." Then she cocked her head and fell silent once more.

"What about the poison, ma'am?" I ventured. "That's surely what he was making in the cauldron, yes?"

Ana waved at her trunk in the corner. "The green book, wedged in the corner," she said absently. "About two smallspan thick. *Deadly Vegetations of the Third Ring*, I think it's called. Look at page . . . forty-eight? Forty-seven? I forget."

I did as she asked. The book was indeed there, and when I flipped to page forty-seven, I was met with an illustration that exactly matched the nut I'd seen half-submerged in the cauldron, complete with the curious drape affixed to the top.

"That's it," I said aloud, and squinted to read. "It is the . . . the kerel nut?"

"The nut itself is not terribly dangerous, actually," murmured Ana. "In fact, in much of the Kurmini cantons, it is considered a delicacy. Rather, it is the *drape* that contains the toxins. Boil the drape in water long enough, and it shall leak a waxy, shimmering substance that dries into pale flakes. When ingested, it causes a violent inflammation of the throat and lungs, usually resulting in suffocation. The dead often exhibit the common telltale signs of swollen, pinkened lips and a distended throat." A lazy smile. "I take it none of you touched the cauldron and then sucked your fingers, yes?"

"N-no, ma'am?" said Malo nervously.

"Well. That is some good news, at least. It's far worse if it is directly fed into the blood, though. If even the tiniest drop gets into your veins, no amount of medicine or aid can help you."

"So he means to kill again," I said. "But do we know whom he targets?"

"Ah, we must move slower there, Din!" said Ana. "We *think* he plans to poison. But remember, this man is a master of both prediction *and* distraction! Simply because we found the poison does not mean we can trust what we found. For, Malo—how likely do you deem it that your wardens would have found his throne room without the help of your hostage?"

"Very," grunted Malo. "It was not far at all from the warped clearing."

"And he knew we'd find the clearing," I said, "for he left us a note within it."

"True!" said Ana. "And Din—there at his throne room, you found a cairn with no vines upon it! A *very* noticeable thing, yes? So noticeable that you quickly dug below it and found the hidden oathcoin. But recall now that it was left behind by a man who rather infamously does *not* leave things behind that he does not wish to—including a single goddamned hair from his head!"

"You think he left the poison and the oathcoin for us to find," I said, "just as he did the note?"

"I worry it is so," said Ana. "He plays his game—but are we his opponents, or his pieces to move about?"

"Then . . . what shall we do?" asked Malo.

"A very good question," said Ana dryly. "Did he wish us to act on the evidence he left for us, and send us barreling down the wrong path? Or does he signal a crime already done, and wish us to react wrongly to it? I don't know."

"Shall we always subject ourselves to such doubts as we pursue this bastard?" asked Malo, frustrated.

"Oh, probably." Ana smiled. "Infuriating, isn't it?"

"I SUPPOSE," I SIGHED, "that it would be wisest to return to what we *do* know. Correct, ma'am?"

"A wise point, Din," said Ana. "Yet we might find little comfort there. For we know he has stolen many grafts, any of which he could use against us." She turned and rummaged around in a pile of parchments. "Especially those of obfuscation and subterfuge."

Malo nodded. "You worry he changes his appearance."

"I do." She finally fished out a paper and held it out to her. "He could approach us now, wearing a new face, and we'd not know it. Here is what he has. What is your estimation, Malo?"

Malo reviewed the list. "He has some tools, yes, but not enough to grant him an entirely *new* face. He cannot change his bones, for example—so he will be mostly the same size and shape. He could alter his skin color, but it would only last a few weeks, for, being a Sublime, it would eventually revert to gray. But he could thicken himself somewhat or purge himself of fats. Or he could add hair to his flesh or remove it. Small changes, really."

"What about teeth?" proposed Ana.

"He has calcious grafts, true, which can mend bones or regrow teeth," said Malo. "But that is not an unusual treatment." She handed the parchments back. "None of this hides scent, which is our preferred sense."

"I suppose that is a relief, then." Ana flicked a finger at me. "Din— tea, please."

"White, ma'am?" I asked. "Black? Or something more exotic?"

"Something delicate. The white peony, I think. I have had my fill of strong flavors this eve."

I busied myself with the kettle atop the blackwood fire, aware that Malo was watching me with some bemusement. "A swordsman and a tea-maker," she remarked. "Shall I see you in an apron potting plants next?"

"Perhaps I shall borrow the one you wear in the ossuary," I said. "Though I'd rather handle tea leaves than innards."

"Enough jibes," snapped Ana. "I must focus, and it takes too much effort for me to invest any fucking wit in your idiotic banter!" She pressed her hands together, then tapped the gleaming tips of her fingers against her nose. "Din—I believe Thelenai mentioned that Prificto Kardas is no longer in the city, correct?"

"She said he is not, ma'am," I said. My eyes trembled, and I echoed: *"He comes to and fro from the High City in the west and goes nowhere else. He is there even now, I understand . . ."*

"But we must get a message to him, and quickly, too," muttered Ana. "Yet to do so by foot or horse is much too slow." She turned her face to Malo again. "So, Signum—I have a question for you now as an Apoth, not a Yarrow."

"Yes?" said Malo.

"A Treasury prificto on a diplomatic mission is often outfitted with a pheromonic signal, yes? For scribe-hawks?"

"Yes, that is so. If he is following policy, Kardas carries the pheromonic marker with him, so a hawk can find him and bring him communications whenever and wherever he travels. But to my knowledge, he has not used it here yet! Those creatures are highly augmented and very expensive, and the environs of Yarrow are not forgiving."

"Then we shall use it for the first time tonight!" said Ana. She turned, wandered blindly to her table in the corner, pulled out a sheet of parchment, and started writing. She sealed the letter with a dab of tarn-paste and handed it to Malo. "Have this sent to him, by the fastest hawk in the roost. It is a desperate measure, but . . . I must try something."

Malo took it and exchanged a worried glance with me. "I shall do so, ma'am, but . . . what is it I am sending?"

"A warning," said Ana. "Pyktis has targeted the Treasury before and may do so again. But I worry my warning will come far too late to be of use!"

There was a tense pause.

"Do you know what Pyktis plans to do now, ma'am?" I asked.

"You ask me what I *know*?" snapped Ana. "I *know* nothing! I am surrounded by information—data, testimonies, evidence—yet I can draw no firm conclusions at all! I am so vexed by this man's countless fucking plots that I worry I am his puppet, and I should search the airs about my limbs for strings! For now, we can only consent to be pulled. And there is little for either of you to do at all tonight, except what I have already said." She fell silent for a moment, her lips working. Then she opened her mouth, hesitated for a long while, and finally said, "But . . . *but,* I will share one revelation I have had during my days buried in documents . . . for I have found a pattern."

"One you didn't mention to Thelenai, ma'am?" asked Malo.

"Indeed," said Ana. "For it is a very *concerning* revelation. One I cannot trust her with. Yet I feel I can trust you two with it, if no one else." Ana sat forward, her face shining in the light of the fire. "Listen close to me now, children. For during your jaunt upriver, I pored over countless records—many thefts, many murders, many missing materials. I believe I identified nearly all the crimes that were perpetrated by our mysterious Sunus Pyktis. Yet I quickly noticed something *unusual.* For Pyktis and his smugglers only ever raided shipments in the second and third weeks of the month, somewhat rarely in the fourth—but never, ever, *ever* in the first."

The kettle began to burble atop the stove. I watched the flickers of steam from its spout, lost in thought.

"Never, ma'am?" I asked quietly.

"Never!" said Ana. "This rule proved ironclad, across all years, all months, and all thefts. Pyktis *never* emerged from his den in the first week of *any* month. And that I cannot explain. So strange was this pattern that I almost wondered if he was bound by the cycles of the goddamned moon!" Her blindfolded head snapped to face Malo. "Can you think of any explanation for this, girl? Anything related to weather, or tides, or some movement in the wilds?"

Malo thought about it for some time. Then she shook her head. "I cannot, ma'am."

"Mm," Ana said. "And you, Din? Can you think of any timeline or date you have encountered in your days here that could explain it?"

I watched as the flickers of steam grew thick about the kettle's spout, until finally it reached a rolling boil and began to whistle. I grasped the wooden handle of the kettle and poured the water over the leaves, and the room filled with an aromatic fragrance of spice and leaf.

The first week of the month, I thought. My eyes fluttered as I searched my memories for that phrase, for I knew it felt familiar—and then I found it.

"Din?" said Ana.

"Sorry, ma'am," I said. "I was adrift in memories." I lightly shook the strainer, and clouds of rich amber filled the cup. "I cannot think of a date that explains this pattern. But . . . I can think of one that *corresponds* to it."

Ana sighed heavily. "Ah . . . corresponds, you say?"

"Yes."

"Mm," she said. "The Treasury, then?"

"Yes," I said. "You've already noted that, ma'am?"

"I have," Ana said, sighing once more. "But I would prefer it be nearly anything else . . ."

Malo looked back and forth between us. "What? What is this you mention?"

Ana waved to me. "Recount it, boy."

"It was something Prificto Kardas said to us when we first met him," I explained to Malo. "An offhand comment, about when he would meet with the king of Yarrow." My eyes fluttered, and I recounted the prificto's words, helplessly mimicking his Sazi accent as I did so: "*The king is proving to be a master of evasion, if not outright punishment! For a good time we made progress, meeting during the first week of the month for the past two or so years. Yet in the most recent months, it has all stalled out . . .* "

There was a long silence when I finished. Malo had even stopped chewing her hina root.

"So," said Malo finally. "The only time that Pyktis *never* attacked an Apoth barge . . ."

"Was the exact same time when the Treasury was at the High City, meeting with the king of Yarrow," said Ana lowly. "Yes. Quite an odd coincidence, is it not?"

"Well, yes, but . . . but what does it *mean*?" asked Malo, frustrated. "It aligns, but what are we to take from it?"

I studied the teacup, judged the light brown shade as a sign the leaves had fully steeped, and gingerly removed the strainer. "But we have now found an oathcoin in Pyktis's possessions," I said quietly. "Suggesting he either stole it . . . or he has *been* there, in the High City." I placed the cup before Ana and stepped back. "Perhaps as an invitation. Perhaps he was meeting with someone—and many times at that."

Another long silence.

Malo stared at us. "But by hell . . . do you know what you're saying? You are telling me there may be collaboration between Pyktis and . . . and the *court of Yarrow*?"

"Which is where Prificto Kardas is now . . ." I said softly.

"I tell you nothing," said Ana with an indignant sniff. "For we have mere correlation, which is not evidence! But here are my orders. You are to go to the scribe-hawk roost, Malo, and send Kardas my letter. Then—and this is very important!—I want both of you to find and assemble your dress uniforms before tomorrow morning."

"Our . . . dress uniforms, ma'am?" I asked, puzzled. "May I ask why?"

"Perhaps to see if you can follow a single fucking order without comment!" snapped Ana. "Do that, and then rest. Both of you must *rest*. Sleep long, and sleep well. You have had hard days. I think the ones to come shall be harder still. After all . . ." She gestured with a greasy finger. "Why do you think I have dined so, if not to prepare?"

CHAPTER 31

▲ ▲ ▲

MALO AND I EXITED ANA'S QUARTERS AND TARRIED FOR a moment, both of us troubled by her words. So lost was I in my thoughts that I hardly noticed Malo's wardens waiting for her in the street. They approached her uncertainly, seeking news, I guessed.

"Is she mad?" Malo asked me. "For I resent her for pouring such wild suggestions into my mind, and then asking me to sleep!"

"She is mad," I conceded. "But . . . not often wrong."

She shook her head. "My dress uniform . . . by hell, my *dress* uniform? Do you know how unthinkable such a thing is for we wardens? We are accustomed to the wild, and little else!"

"I would get used to it. I suspect we shall soon be taking part in many unthinkable things."

"Fucking hell," said Malo. "I will do your immunis's tasks, and then I shall find company less gloomy than you, Kol!" She stormed over to her wardens and rattled off a few angry lines of Pithian to them. A few of them swept down the street toward the scribe-hawk roosts, while the rest broke up, most of them following Malo toward a nearby sotbar.

"She did say to *rest*!" I called after her.

Malo flapped a hand at me. "I did not ask for your comment!" she snapped.

I smoked my pipe and watched them go, bemused, yet one warden lingered, watching me.

Sabudara approached me slowly, her footsteps careful, her expression somber, her eyes studying me carefully.

I raised my pipe to her. "Good evening," I said.

"Whole?" Sabudara asked. "Healthy?"

"Healthy enough, I suppose."

Her green gaze darted to Ana's door, then back to my face, and she took a step closer. "That was," she said in her stilted standard, "hard talk you had?"

"We have no other kind these days, it seems."

We stared at one another for a moment.

"Much trouble, then," she said.

"Yes," I said. "Much."

She took yet another step forward. I noticed a bright, reckless look in her eye. "Company?" she asked.

I studied her, tempted but uncertain. "Oh. I . . . don't know," I said.

"No?"

"No. I have seen many horrors in the past hours, Sabudara, and many of them cling close to me. And I am weary beyond words."

She rolled her eyes very slightly—*He cannot really imagine I could translate that*—and took another step forward. "Company—yes?" she asked. "Or no?"

I sighed and looked her over once more. Her face was smooth and bright in the blue of the mai-lamps, and much cleaner than I recalled: a likely side effect of all the Apoths' cleansings, I supposed, for my own skin was softer and more fragrant than it'd been in many months.

Ana had told me to rest, true. But, really, a shame to waste such soft, aromatic skin.

I glanced back at my closed door and imagined my empty, silent rooms waiting for me. I did not often yearn for female company in this fashion, but Sabudara was a lovely thing, and far lovelier than what a night of stifling silence offered, especially with all the awful things now boiling in my head.

I opened the door to my rooms and stepped aside. She smirked, cocked an eyebrow, and strode inside without another word.

———

I DREAMED THAT night that I walked the jungles, the canopies high and whispering above me, the starlight cold and shivering. I came to a mirrored pool of black water and saw a fluttering green column arise from its middle, the waters rippling as it climbed into the sky; then it halted, and its emerald skin unfolded like a flower, and I beheld within a figure in pale dress, clad in a white, skull-like helm. They turned to me and beckoned, calling me forward into the waters. I took a step, feeling the cold slosh of the lake against my ankle . . .

Then I heard the bells and awoke.

So deep had my dreaming been, and so abrupt my waking, that it took me a moment to orient myself. I lay naked across my mossbed, which was soaking with sweat; Sabudara lay next to me, her bare back pressed to my belly, my arm cast across her side. I had no idea where my clothes and boots were, nor my bedsheets—and I had no idea where the sound of bells was coming from, or indeed if I was dreaming still.

I raised my head from the bed, listening. The sound was no dream: there truly were bells, their tolling low and deep and rich.

"Eh?" I croaked.

Sabudara awoke beside me, coughed, and cried out something in Pithian—"*Ghati? Ki uha ghati hana?*" Then she sat up, parted from me—there was a wet *click* as I was unmoored from her—and leapt from the bed. Then she went to the window and threw open the shutters, apparently indifferent to her nudity.

"*Nia, nia,*" she said softly.

I rose from the bed. Though I knew little Pithian, I knew *nia* meant no.

"What is that?" I asked. "Are those tocsins?"

She did not answer. I clambered to my feet and realized they were not tocsin bells: not the pure, high, silvery sounds that cried out warning in the imperial cantons. These were much deeper, enormous bells whose tolling was so resonant it shook my bones.

Sabudara cursed under her beath, then swatted angrily at me as I tried to draw a sheet about her and veil her body. *"Murakha!"* she spat. *"Ki tusim suna sakahde ho?"*

"What?" I said.

"Bairana! Bairana mara latha!" she snarled. Such was her agitation that what little imperial standard she knew seemed lost to her.

Yet I paused, for I knew that last word.

"Latha?" I said. "Corpse? Dead?"

She nodded.

"Someone's dead? This *bairana*?"

Another nod. *"Bairana."* She gestured to her head, miming a crown atop her brow. "King. The king!"

I stared at her, then glanced west out the window, though I could not see much of the hills beyond.

"The . . . the *king* is dead?" I said faintly.

"Haim," said Sabudara. "Yes! The king!"

"The *king of Yarrow* is dead? *That's* what those bells mean?"

"Yes! Yes!" cried Sabudara. Then she jumped into her trousers, tossed on her shirt and cloak, and then, without another word, sprinted out the door with her boots hanging from her hand.

I gazed after her, my mind all awhirl, before realizing she had left the door open, and I was still unclothed. With a gasp, I leapt over and slammed it shut.

AFTER I'D STUMBLED into my own shirt and trousers and boots, I darted outside. I intended to knock on Ana's door but saw that the street was filled with folk staring west, murmuring as they watched something in the distance. I joined them, squinting in the morning sun.

Black smoke plumed high from the High City in the west: not the smoke of a wildfire but an intentional smoke, like that of a bonfire or signal.

Or mourning smoke, maybe. Which meant, perhaps, that the king was truly dead.

My mind churned, and images of the oathcoin and the poison burbled up within my memories.

"Oh, hell," I whispered.

I recrossed the street and knocked on Ana's door, heard her customary, singing "Come!" and slipped inside.

"Ma'am!" I said breathlessly. "Ma'am, those bells! I . . . It seems there may be news tha—"

I entered her main room, saw Ana sitting on the bed, and stopped.

Ana had never cared much for grooming or dress. Indeed, she changed garments so rarely that I'd come to believe she often forgot she wore clothes at all. Yet the person sitting on the bed before me was arrayed in a stunningly precise expression of imperial dress uniform code: her blue dress coat was buttoned to her chin, her skirts were smooth and properly arranged, and her pale white hair was pulled back in a taut, severe bun, punctured by a golden-headed hairpin. There was no sign of food or fluid about her lips; indeed, the only signs of her usual madness were the red blindfold about her eyes—of course—and her heralds, which I noticed were arranged in an alternating pattern of small and large, and thus went against Iyalet code.

"Yes?" demanded Ana. "What about these damned bells, Din?"

I attempted to recover. "Ma'am, ah . . . I have been told that those bells possibly signify that—"

"That the king of Yarrow," she snapped, "is dead as a fucking boiled scallop?"

"I . . . How did you—"

"I assume you gleaned this rather insightful bit of cultural information," she hissed, "from the Pithian girl who fucked you halfway across the room and back last night—yes? Despite my very strict and clear orders that you *rest*?"

The tolling bells seemed to dampen somewhat. "Ah," I said. "Well, ma'am . . ."

"I not only heard every thump," growled Ana, "but I am sure everyone up and down the street did as well! Perhaps we should have charged bypassers a half talint for the show! I mean, titan's taint, Din! I don't even know why I bother giving orders anymore, as all the imperial ears about me seem incapable of listening! Have you at least assembled your dress uniform, as I requested?"

I blinked blearily. Though I recalled wearing my dress cap last evening, it had not been related to the preparations of my uniform.

"You . . . you asked us to prepare our uniforms," I said, "because you had already anticipated the next murder."

"I would have thought that fucking obvious!" thundered Ana. "We *knew* Pyktis had produced poison, there in his den! We knew he had an oathcoin, suggesting he'd been to the High City before! And we knew he'd likely seen the smokes in the jungle and would know that we'd found his macabre little display! Thus, he has begun the *next* bit of his game! And though I was not certain *whom* he would choose to attack, I had a reasonable expectation of *where* it might occur, and how we might have to array ourselves to move within that celebrated space!" She sighed. "Though to find now that it may be the king himself slain . . . well, I will say this about Pyktis—the fucker does not lack ambition! Now, damn it, get dressed, boy, and quickly! For I suspect we must go to question some courtly folk, and that damned soon!"

IV

...

DEATH IN THE HIGH CITY

CHAPTER 32

. . .

ALMOST INSTANTLY, THE DAY SEEMED TO UNRAVEL LIKE a cheap fishing net.

To begin with, the bells did not stop tolling for over three hours, which meant all discussions in Yarrowdale had to be bellowed at close distance in order to be heard. But secondly, nobody knew exactly whom to ask about the bells or what could have happened there in the Elder West, for the only people who ever spoke with the high court of Yarrow were Prificto Kardas and his Treasury folk, and they, Malo discovered, were all missing from their quarters.

"They went up to meet with the court yesterday, ma'am," Malo reported to Ana. She groggily dug in her eye with a finger, and continued: "Not a one of them was left behind, and we've heard not a thing from them since."

"And that should *not* be so, I assume?" asked Ana.

"No, ma'am. They were expected to return late last night." She swallowed. "But . . . I did check to see if Kardas had perhaps responded to your letter, ma'am."

"And?"

Malo slipped out a scroll of parchment, darted forward, and handed it to her. "This is the response. I've not yet breached it. But . . . it has an odd look to it."

I looked Malo over while Ana studied the scroll. She had not only hastily rummaged up her own Apoth dress uniform—dark crimson with brown piping and bright brown leather epaulets—but she had also apparently oiled her hair and combed it straight back in a slick, shiny cascade. She looked about as comfortable in her formal clothes as a sallow-cat in a river, and her bearing was not at all improved by the obvious fact that she was frightfully hungover.

Ana cracked the scroll open, then felt it with her preternaturally sensitive fingers, sightlessly reading every scrawl. "Well, well!" she said bitterly. "What luck! This scroll is addressed to *the representatives of the Imperial Iudex*! I believe that's you and me, eh, Din?"

"True, but . . . those do not sound like Kardas's words, ma'am. Who composed it?"

Ana sniffed as her fingers kept probing the slip of parchment. "Why, it is from Prince Camak di Lalaca, heir to the throne of the realm of Yarrow. He requests our prompt presence at court."

There was a stunned silence, broken only by a miserable belch from Malo.

Ana kept reading. "It seems our job may already be done," she said lightly. "For though the king did indeed perish under mysterious circumstances, they have captured a suspect and now hold him captive!"

"They . . . they captured Pyktis?" I said.

"Oh, no. They have captured *Prificto Kardas*. They believe it is *he* who killed their king! And they would like to execute him." She stuffed the note into my hands and said, "Read it yourself!"

I peered at the note and struggled to read it. It was written in a small, outrageously sloppy hand, suggesting the writer was either poorly educated, ignorant of imperial standard, or both.

I haltingly read aloud:

To the representatives of the Imperial Iudex,

I am Prince Camak di Lalaca eh Divaum, tenth of my name. I write to you using this creature at the urging of your Treasury officers. By the time you read this message you will surely be aware of the death of my father, king of the realm of Yarrow.

Prificto Kardas is now held captive here. Many at court believe him to be the killer, and demand he be slain.

Though I still lack the crown, I am now regent. Kardas's
fate falls to me. Yet as I have only just this early morning received
your warning meant for Kardas, I no longer believe he is the
killer, not if you tried to warn him that a killer might be about.
But I must tell you, the circumstances are not kind to his case.
Many who desire his death are of a standing that is difficult
to ignore.

I am told there is among you a person of skill with such
matters. To you I say—riders from my court shall be arriving in
your city midday, to demand your presence at court. Please come,
and come quickly. I cannot comprehend how this act was done, nor
whether my own life may now lie in peril.

I hope this creature finds you speedily. When you arrive, show
no sign that I have warned you, for no one else knows of this
message to you. But bring it to me, so I may know of your
honesty.

A stony silence filled the room when I finished.

"It seems we are now in the business of court intrigue!" said Ana.
She wrinkled her nose. "How trite."

At that, Malo turned about, opened the door, walked to the porch
railing, and vomited into the yard.

THE YARROW RIDERS arrived just before midday, exactly as the
prince's message had said. There were three of them, and they were
grand, glittering things, arrayed in long green capes and steel caps
lined with artful, shimmering bronze. They seemed surprised to find
us waiting for them at the foot of the hills, lined up before our Apoth
carriage with a pilot atop it, yet they regathered themselves and approached.

They began to speak to us in stilted standard, but Malo waved a
hand and said, *"Paravha nahi karade,"* which I took to mean—*Don't*
bother. They discussed the situation for a moment, and then the riders wheeled about. "We are to follow them," said Malo.

"Of course," said Ana.

It was yet another carriage ride, rumbling up and to the west, through teetering jungle paths I did not know. Mud fanned the glass windows as our carriage hit the occasional puddle, and every league or so the tree line would dance back and reveal a yawning gorge or a sprawling set of hills. Then the world would close in again, and there was only the wet leaves, and the mud, and the dark interior of the carriage.

Malo leaned against the wall with her face pressed to the crack in the door, finger ready on the handle should her hungover belly betray her again. Ana's distemper, however, had returned with a vengeful bitterness.

When I asked her what warning she'd sent to Kardas, she spat, "I would think that'd be obvious, Din! I told him I had reason to believe there was a murderous jungle smuggler skulking about the High City with a very advanced poison, and advised he keep himself and everyone around him from sipping or drinking a thing!"

"But . . . you knew this, and let us go to our beds?" I asked. "You did not wish us to try to stop it?"

"No—for I knew you could not! By the time I received your full account, and realized Pyktis's likely intent, it was too late. Recall that this is an *augur* we are dealing with! He'd surely seen the smokes in the jungle and knew now was the time to act! Whatever the manner of his evil, he did it well before we could dream of stopping it. If I told either of you last night exactly where the crime would occur, I thought it probable you'd intervene, or seek some permission to speed up the hill crying alarm and death—yes?"

I grudgingly admitted that would have been so.

"Indeed," said Ana. "And how would the Yarrow court have responded to such a thing, Malo, after their king was laid low?"

"Very poorly," muttered Malo. "They hate the Empire, and would have hated the sight of us riding up uninvited even more—especially if their king had just died of poison, and thought him killed by another imperial."

"Exactly. I have saved us from one error, but avoiding others shall be harder. I know little of the court and Kardas's negotiations. And the task before us is a difficult one, for we must determine *why* Pyktis has made the mad choice of killing the king! Did he simply wish to put the Empire in a compromising situation here? If so, there are far easier ways to accomplish that!"

"And I?" said Malo dully. "Why do you drag a warden to this political meeting?"

"Because it would be quite useful to not only have someone fluent in the Pithian tongue," snapped Ana, "but someone also in possession of a set of ears capable of hearing every whispered word in the room! Not to mention a nose that can sniff out any scent! For remember, children, we not only seek any sign of Pyktis and his plots, but *especially* any sign of where Pyktis might have stored the six crates of reagents he needs to attack the marrow!"

"What, you think we shall find them sitting in a back room of the king's great hall?" asked Malo.

"I've no idea," said Ana. "I only know Pyktis *must* have been there—and thus, we should seek all we can."

I cleared my throat. "And we must also free Kardas and the rest of the Treasury delegation—true, ma'am?"

Ana paused. "Oh, right . . . yes. Yes, that, too, I suppose. It would save me some paperwork if we kept them all alive."

I sighed and turned back to the window.

THE CARRIAGE TURNED again and again through the trees, following the three Yarrow riders. Finally a sight emerged on the hilltops, like a crystal calcifying on the wall of a dark cave. Then we broke free of the forest, and I saw it clearly.

The High City of Yarrow, stone-wrought and solemn and resplendent. It was as if we neared not some regional seat of power but a spirit kingdom from the old stories, one that appeared on the seventh night of the seventh month for seven minutes only. We rumbled on until I spied gates, and walls, and the glints of iron armor, steel caps, and winking mail.

Soldiers. Dozens of them. Perhaps hundreds, all waiting for us atop the battlements. I described it to Ana as we rolled along.

"Remember, children," she said softly. "Remember our story! No one is to know of our forewarning from the prince. We are ignorant visitors here, stunned and surprised by this news, and we know nothing of the circumstances in the High City."

"*Prachina da Sahira,*" muttered Malo.

"What?" I said.

"In our tongue, it is not called 'the High City,'" Malo said, "but *Prachina da Sahira.*"

"What does that mean?" I asked.

She turned her face back to the window so I could not read her expression. "The city of ancients," she said.

We rumbled closer, and the gates opened, and I gasped.

CHAPTER 33

...

OVER THE CENTURIES, THE APOTHS OF THE EMPIRE HAD taught branch and root and vine to form nearly any structure one could imagine. A fretvine house could be planted and shaped within a week or two, for example; a large building, perhaps a month. Other innovations made more complex buildings simple as well: stonewood trees grew planks of unnaturally dense, tough wood, their trunks sloughing off the heavy slates like a lizard shedding scales; mosswalls could be grown to envelop nearly any building façade, giving them a soft skin of effective insulation; and so on and so forth.

While this made housing and construction easy enough, it also meant that the art of stonework quickly became the domain of the wealthy and the powerful; for while resources were plentiful in the Empire, labor was eternally expensive. Only the gentry could afford to hire teams to haul enormous blocks of stone over field and hill, and then construct the complex machinery needed to maneuver each chiseled piece into place, the proof of your wealth and power made manifest in the very bones of the earth.

This, perhaps, was why I was initially so awed at the sight of the High City. For all about me were towers of tall, shining white stone, pearly and opalescent in the late-afternoon sun. The gates and walls and bridges were all wrought of stone as well, and nearly every bit of it was carved to depict the faces of men, or looming figures bearing shield and sword, or great battles between huge forces. One stretch of wall seemed to hold no less than two thousand figures, all falling upon one another with their blades held high, all perfectly articulated with each stroke of the chisel. I'd never seen such an astonishing sight.

I struggled to describe it to Ana, but she seemed far less impressed. "Oh, yes," she said sourly. "I wonder who built it."

I wondered what she meant, and looked to Malo for explanation, but her face told me nothing.

The High City guard was no less impressive. With the exception of the Legion, imperial officers usually had the look of bureaucrats or clerks, and often went unarmed, or with naught but a dagger or short sword. Yet the guards who escorted our carriage to the king's hall wore steel helmets with intricate, patterned face shields, and shining pauldrons, and thick coats of mail. They looked like soldiers from a myth, their blades wide and thick, their armor tinkling as they strutted.

Then our carriage turned a corner in the sprawling stone city, and I beheld the king's hall ahead. If the towers had amazed me, the hall made them look like a child's toys: huge and opulent, the hall made a broad, sloping, shark-tooth form in the center of the city, facing southwest. Its walls were riddled with small cubbies or shelves, and placed within these were totems wrought of stone or wood, each depicting a stern, bearded face with a circlet on their brow. Before each totem sat a lit candle floating in a pool of water, and their flickering luminescence gave the wooden visages the illusion of movement, scowling or grimacing in the shadows.

"What are those?" I asked.

"The faces of the many kings of Yarrow, long dead," muttered Malo. "They watch all who enter here."

I gazed at their blank eyes as we approached. Having never known a line of such antiquity—ancestors meant little to common Tala folk such as I—I found the idea awe-inspiring.

Perhaps that was what drove my astonishment: the sheer sense of age of this place. All the towers felt like they'd been here for centuries, and all the soldiers looked like warriors from some archaic saga. Though much of the Empire was indeed old, few of its structures were, for buildings were constantly being cut down and re-grown whenever needed. And if a structure was old—like the sea walls, or the ring walls—then it was often an unsightly, forbidding spectacle.

This place, however, felt beautiful and eternal. A stunning sight to a person like me, from an improvised Empire that often felt so blandly bureaucratic.

WE RUMBLED UP to the stairs leading to the king's hall. Soldiers stood on every other step, glowering down at us beneath their steel caps. Stationed just down the path from the stairs were three Treasury carriages, though none were reined to horses: the steeds had been removed, I guessed, after it became clear that the Treasury delegation would not be leaving anytime soon.

The three Yarrow riders dismounted and spoke to a little man whom I guessed to be a court messenger, arrayed in gray robes with green paints upon his eyes. He nodded coolly as he listened, then watched our carriage mistrustfully as we came to a stop.

I opened the door and climbed out, then made way for Malo and assisted Ana in exiting. The court messenger called out, asking us something in Pithian—"Tusim hath arabada ho?"—and Ana gestured to Malo, who responded in kind. "He asks if we are armed, and I have confirmed we are not," Malo explained to us.

"What a pleasant greeting," said Ana. "I presume we shall not be served cakes, then."

The messenger gestured, and we followed him up the stairs and through the great doors awaiting us, flanked by armored guards on either side. Then, suddenly, fire was everywhere about us.

Torches blazed and hissed from every wall and corner. The remnants of a huge bonfire glowed in the center of the hall, despite it being late afternoon. At the far end sat a magnificent throne, also wrought of stone, and though it was empty, fireplaces had been built on either side of it, with a blaze crackling in each one.

And with fire came smoke. Though there were chimneys and open windows in the great hall, the air was still heavy with haze, so much so that my eyes and nose burned. It was quite a change from imperial lighting, which used no flame and produced no smoke.

I waved at the haze before my face and surveyed the room. The messenger was approaching the empty throne. I squinted to parse the smokes and spied a figure in white sitting on the steps before it, head bowed. The white figure sat up as the messenger whispered something to him, then rose. The instant he did so, the hall became a flurry of quiet activity, with many servants or officers or attendants rushing about, whispering to one another.

I quietly relayed the scene to Ana.

"Ahh, that would be the prince, I think," Ana said. "For when the regent stands, the world responds, Din!"

I studied the prince through the veil of smoke. He did not speed over to us, as I'd expected of a man who'd pleaded for us to assist; rather, he appeared to be waiting.

Then two men came rushing into the hall, and these two I recognized instantly.

The first was Jari Pavitar, swaggering just like when I'd met him at the prison, his brow still stained dark indigo beneath his black cap, and his fur cape fluttering behind him. His eyes flashed at the sight of me: he remembered me, then, and not fondly.

After him came the green-faced Satrap Darhi. He swayed as he walked, a careful, controlled movement. His locks were still well-coiffed about his thin face, and his cheeks and chin were still lined with green inks, though today he favored soft yellow robes rather than green. His gaze also remained the same: as cold and sharp as a medikker's blade, and the haze of the fires gave me no cover from his scrutiny.

The two men bowed to their prince, who diffidently raised a hand to them. Then they took up spaces behind him and followed in his wake as he began to approach us.

"They near us now, ma'am," I whispered.

"Excellent," said Ana. "Isn't this terribly *exciting*, children?"

Malo shook her head, exasperated.

I watched Prince Camak as he rounded the bonfire. I'd expected someone tall and formidable, but I found him to be a bearded, plump, rather scuttling little man. A silver circlet shone on his brow, a silver necklace twinkled at his collar, and his face was painted in golds and silvers, yet rather than endow him with a commanding look, the paints only highlighted his weakness, for he glanced about the room with a dim, watery gaze.

He did not look at all like a king. I was reminded of a fretful young foal venturing from its paddock for the first time, ready to bolt at the barest flit of a bird's wing. His expression grew only more alarmed as he neared us, his eyes fixed on Ana's blindfold. I could've sworn I saw the color drain from behind his paints, and imagined his thoughts— *This is the person who has come to help me? This is the imperial I've taken into my confidence?*

The three Yarrow men came to a stop before us. There was a long, awkward silence, and we simply looked at one another. I glanced at Malo, who gave the tiniest shrug—*I've no idea, either!*

Finally, Darhi softly cleared his throat and said in careful, precise standard: "You are to bow, and introduce yourselves."

Before I could speak, Ana bowed deeply and said, "Prince Camak! I am Immunis Ana Dolabra, of the Imperial Iudex. How sorrowful I am that we should meet you now! Know that my heart grieves for the loss of your father, whom all in the Empire considered a great king, and a true friend. Words cannot capture the depth of our sympathies, nor our torment, when we learned of these evil tidings this morn."

I looked sidelong at Malo, utterly bewildered by Ana's sudden courtliness. Malo only gaped in response.

"I am here solely to comprehend how such a thing has happened," Ana continued, "for I must regretfully tell you that we are wholly ignorant of nearly every aspect of this tragedy. We do not know how it occurred, nor how Prificto Kardas might be implicated in it. Though we pledge to assist you in any way, at first, unfortunately, I can only offer questions."

Before the prince could respond, Pavitar scoffed. "Oh? Yet why should we answer them?" he demanded. "When it is we who have been so terribly wronged! For you imperials to now burden us with such demands suggests you believe us to be either fools, or lia—"

Prince Camak turned to him. "I have not spoken," he said softly.

Pavitar fell silent, abashed. A tiny, triumphant smile flickered across Darhi's face.

The prince turned back to us. He cleared his throat lengthily—he seemed unaccustomed to stately speech—and said in thickly accented standard, "I appreciate your kind words, Immunis. I have long known that my circlet would one day shift from silver to gold, and my flesh would take up the throne. But I had not ever imagined that the day should arrive so ill-fated. I am thankful that the Empire has so speedily sent assistance." He gestured feebly. "Though, ah, you may already know them, this is my satrap, Danduo Darhi, and my court jari, Thale Pavitar."

The two men nodded to us, though Pavitar did so quite reluctantly.

"Thank you, Your Majesty," said Ana, bowing. "Assisting me is my investigator, Signum Dinios Kol, and Tira Malo, an Apothetikal warden from Yarrowdale."

"Yes . . ." said the prince, uncertainly. His gaze again lingered on Ana's face. Then he frowned, turned, and whispered something to Darhi.

Darhi nodded, his expression the very picture of taciturn servitude. Then he said in his calm, cool voice, "We note you wear a blindfold, Immunis."

"That I do," said Ana.

"Thus, we must ask—are you blind?"

"I am sightless, true," she said. "But my investigator and my warden here see for me. I assure you, we shall have no issue operating within your court, sir."

She then grinned so widely that the prince flinched. Darhi's eyebrows rose fractionally, and Pavitar gazed at her in disgust. I sighed inwardly; I supposed Ana could suppress every sign of madness for only so long.

"I . . . I see," said the prince uncertainly. He made a face like the next words pained him greatly. "It would be best to begin by telling you that your people, though held until we can comprehend what happened, are all safe—to some degree."

Ana cocked her head. "To . . . some degree, sir?"

"Yes." Again, he hesitated. "For I must now tell you that Prificto Kardas has fallen unwell. Indeed, we believe he was stricken by the same poison that affected my father the king."

There was a stony silence as we absorbed this.

"Prificto Kardas was . . . *also* poisoned, sir?" I asked slowly.

"But he lives," said Darhi.

"And yet you still think *he* was the poisoner?"

The prince faltered, then gestured to Pavitar.

"We do," said Pavitar indignantly. "For it was Kardas who gave the poisoned cup to the king! The king drank from it and was instantly stricken. Clearly Kardas handled the poison himself, and was afflicted by it, though much less so than our fallen king." He sniffed. "But then, Kardas was never a competent man."

"Before we delve into these matters, sir," said Ana sharply, "my duty compels me to first visit the delegation and treat Prificto Kardas, if that is possible."

The prince nodded, and now gestured to Darhi.

"That can be done, of course," said Darhi smoothly. "We do not hold them in some pit or dungeon, but in the guest chambers in the southern wing of the hall. It is a most comfortable arrangement."

"Sounds quite pleasant," said Ana dryly. "Very kind of you."

Darhi permitted a trim smile. "But, Immunis, I did wish to ask an unsightly bit of business. For though this tragedy has assuredly brought our negotiations to a standstill, it leaves us in an uncertain position . . . Who shall represent the Empire's interests in this moment? Shall it be you?"

"No, no," said Ana. "I cannot represent my state in any official negotiations. I am here only to understand, and enact justice."

"Then who shall it be?"

"If Kardas proves innocent," said Ana, "it shall be him. If he does not, it shall be someone else from his delegation, acting as his interim replacement."

Another trim smile. "Thank you for the clarification, Immunis. I seek only stability in all things."

Pavitar glowered at him; Darhi ignored his gaze entirely. Indeed, I realized he had yet to look at Pavitar once. It was then that I felt I grasped the nature of the situation: the prince was a young, spoiled man who'd likely never imagined he'd ascend to the throne, given that the Empire was to adopt the territory; yet now his father was murdered, and his two most powerful courtiers were at vicious odds on what to do next. Perhaps he'd reached out to us simply because he'd found his own people utterly unmanageable.

"And if his guilt *is* proven," said Pavitar to Ana indignantly, "will you fight *our* application of justice? Shall you try and steal him away, though he killed our king?"

Ana shrugged. "If I deem he truly is the murderer of your king, then I see no reason why he cannot be killed here! A dead man cannot be greatly bothered by who owns the patch of earth he swings over—true?"

All three Yarrow men appeared utterly astonished. I opened my mouth to protest, then carefully shut it.

"Truly?" asked Pavitar. "If we execute your prificto, you would not protest?"

"I only ask that you hang him rather than behead him," said Ana. "Beheading is considered a sacred death in some of the more ancient parts of the Empire, reserved for high folk. Under imperial common law, all criminals are considered of the same low stock, and thus suited only for hanging." She grinned brightly. "Unless you wish to swing the axe yourself, Pavitar, as a bit of exercise?"

Pavitar gazed at her, torn between bewilderment and outrage.

The prince cleared his throat. "I . . . am glad we have come to an arrangement." He paused, glanced at his advisers, and then gazed very hard at Ana. "Yet before you see to Kardas and his people, Immunis, I . . . I would ask a moment of your time."

Ana bowed deeply. "You may ask for any or all of my time, Your Majesty."

"I must be clearer," said the prince. "I wish you to join me as I keep vigil with my father's body. Alone."

Darhi and Pavitar had obviously not anticipated this: Pavitar's mouth fell open and his face turned a dull pink, while Darhi's green-painted brow wrinkled ever so slightly.

"In the . . . the reliquary, Your Majesty?" said Pavitar.

"Indeed," said the prince.

"But we have never let an imperial enter such a sacred space before. Not in all our—"

"Still, that is my wish," said the prince. "For neither have we had a king fall to poison in this hall. These are strange times. I must have their honesty, and there are many ears at court. In the reliquary, I can have silence."

The prince looked very hard at me. I nodded in response, signaling my comprehension.

"Of course, Your Majesty," said Ana, bowing once more—though I noted that a tremendous grin split her face at the bottom. "I am honored that you would grace us with such intimacy."

"Then come, Immunis," said the prince. He offered Ana his arm. "I shall take you to the reliquary myself." She took it, bowing once more, and he turned and led us across the great hall, leaving the two advisers behind.

Pavitar stormed off to angrily speak with a group of elderly-looking gentlemen in elegant, black coats and caps. Satrap Darhi I lost almost immediately, his movements obscured as the servants and nobles of the smoky hall stirred about us. I assumed he had vanished to join his own supporters, wherever they might be.

It was as I followed the prince through one set of doors that I felt a plucking at my arm, slowing me. I turned to find that Satrap Darhi had silently reappeared beside me, gliding along at a gentle, serene pace.

"How fare you this day, Signum Kol?" he asked softly.

"Ah—well, sir," I said. "But I do recall, the prince did ask us to visit with him alone . . ."

"True," said Darhi. "But it is a long walk to the reliquary, and I wished to inquire about you. These were treacherous times before and are even more treacherous now. Tell me—do you still carry the favor I gave you?"

I slid the oathcoin from my pocket, and his eyes lit up at the sight of it.

"Ah," said Darhi. "Very wise of you to bring it! I shall do all the prince asks to aid you, of course, but . . . if there is any *additional* service I can provide, you need only ask."

"What service might you suggest, sir?"

"Well, both I and the Empire want the same thing, of course— a peaceful transition, with no bloodshed or sorrow. What hazardous days we live in! Keep the coin, Signum. Remember it well. And call on me should you ever need anything."

Then he bowed, and left me to catch up to Ana, Malo, and the prince. When I glanced back at the smoky passageway, he was gone.

CHAPTER 34

∧ ∧ ∧

THE PRINCE LED US THROUGH A NARROW, DARK, WIND-ing passageway. When we finally came to a set of enormous oaken doors, he turned to study us, seeming to debate something. Then he steeled himself, opened the doors, and led us inside.

The chamber within was a tall, circular space, almost akin to a chimney, rising until it opened onto the sky. It featured no other windows, but it did possess three doors, facing west, east, and south. Tiny cubbies were set along the rounded walls, and standing inside them were totems of past kings, wrought of stone. Each one was frowning and bearded, much like those on the exterior of the great hall itself. I was almost reminded of a scribe-hawk's roost, with tiny stone figures in place of birds.

Yet it was the table in the center of the chamber that caught the eye most. It was a long and heavy thing, and upon it was a tremendous mound of flower blossoms of pale white; and there, placed at the mound's peak like a child upon a stack of pillows, was the body of a man.

He was an ancient creature, swaddled in fur robes atop the mound of pale blossoms, with a golden circlet set winking atop his lined brow, and a braided, graying beard cast across his chest. He seemed small to me, and his face was so long and drawn it was nearly fleshless. It had not been death that had shriveled him so, surely: he had been terribly elderly in life, and had lived his last days a withered creature.

The prince shut the doors and walked to block our view of the dead king. "Pavitar spoke truth," he said. "We have never admitted imperials to this chamber before. But I shall permit you to stay here . . . provided you can show your honesty."

I turned to Malo and said, "Three doors here. Anyone eavesdropping behind them?"

Malo cocked her head, listening, then narrowed her eyes at the one we'd just passed through. Then she shook her head. "We are alone."

I reached into my coat, slid out the message the prince had sent to us, and handed it to him.

Prince Camak read it, then took a deep, relieved sigh. "*Asimana da dhanivahda* . . . Thank the fates!" His regal demeanor dissolved before our eyes: he pressed a hand to his chest and sat down on the marble floor, breathing hard as if in a panic. I noticed that his teeth were even worse than Darhi's and Pavitar's, and were as black as tar. "I apologize, I . . . I had no idea if you'd come on my accord or your own! What a relief it is, to be free with someone here. This is the only place in all the High City where I am left truly alone. Now—you must tell me who this murderer is, and where we can find him, and end this nightmare!"

A rare look of discomfort fluttered across Ana's pale features. "Mm. I beg your pardon, Your Majesty?"

The prince stood, noticing her hesitation. "Did I not read your letter correctly? You wrote to Kardas saying you knew of a smuggler operating here in the High City, who intended to kill with poison, true? And that is exactly what happened. And the Treasury folk said you have a genius skill with such things! One that defies belief!" A tone of desperation crept into his voice. "Surely you can just tell my court who he is, and have him fished out, and, I don't know, tortured to confession—true?"

Ana raised a hand. "We go too quick now, sir. I am no sorcerer, able to summon the culprit out of the shadows. Such things take time and caution."

"Then that is ill news! For Pavitar and his supporters expect me to have Kardas slain before this day is done!"

"Before the end of the *day*?" asked Ana.

"Yes, and I was lucky to delay it that long! The very second my father died, this hall filled up with eager counselors. Darhi and Pavitar were but keenest and most powerful among them. They'd never even spoken much to me before! They spoke only to my father, and their own nobles, and the Treasury, but never me. Now I cannot get them to stop!" He moved to bury his face in his hands, but stopped, remembering his paints.

"Then we must move quickly, sir," said Ana. "May my people inspect the body of your father?"

"You . . . you may view my father," said the prince uncertainly, "but you cannot touch him. That I cannot permit, even in these times."

"Certainly, sir," said Ana. Then she waved to Malo and me.

I stepped forward and studied the dead man. I did not need to grow close to see his swollen, red lips and mottled throat: the telltale signs of kerel poisoning, just as Ana had said. It must have been a significant dose, I gauged, so much so that his death had to have been quick.

Malo leaned over the body and sniffed deeply. She shut her eyes, as if savoring the aroma, then opened them and shook her head—*Nothing of note here.*

I returned to Ana and whispered all I saw into her ear. She listened closely, gripping my arm, and when I finished she bowed her head, lost in thought.

The prince gazed down at his dead father. "A strange sight he makes," he said softly. "I come and watch him, sometimes, hoping his chest will twitch. A breath, perhaps, or a heartbeat. But not because I love him and wish him to live—for a king is a difficult thing to love. Rather, if I see he lives, then . . . then I will be saved from this waking nightmare. I can go back to how things were. Isn't that a horrible thing to say?"

Ana said nothing. Her face shivered as she swept through some complex mental calculus. "Prince Camak, were you present for your father's death?"

"I was."

"Then I would like you to provide me with your account of it," she said. "As quickly and carefully as possible—for we cannot sit with you in vigil forever, surely."

"Oh! Of course."

THE MEETING HAD been a diplomatic tea, the prince told us, taking place yesterday evening. It was a somewhat common occurrence in the court of Yarrow: important folk would gather and drink a brew of the saca berry, a bright red, bitter concoction that grants one an unpleasant buzzing feeling—one that the Yarrows believed made people more honest, he said.

"Where did this tea occur?" asked Ana.

"In the eastern hall, just down that passageway," said the prince, pointing to one of the three doors. "It is a passingly good place, with a fine view of the water. My father and I were in attendance, and Darhi and Pavitar, of course. And Prificto Kardas and his . . . girl. The one with the twitching eyes."

Ana gestured to me impatiently.

"Signum Gorthaus, ma'am," I said. "She is his engraver."

Ana's face briefly brightened. An engraver would be a very useful witness. "Please continue," she said.

The meeting had concerned high state business, the prince said, so they'd had no servants present. This meant all six people at the meeting would have to serve their tea themselves, going to a cauldron along the wall and pouring a cup with a ladle. They went back and forth a few times, pouring their cups of saca as they discussed matters. This went on for nearly an hour, with no issue.

"I brought my father two cups of tea, as is my duty," said the prince. "Then Prificto Kardas poured and brought him the third. My father sipped from it several times, but then he . . . he cried out and . . ." His words trailed off.

"It was the *same* cup, every time?" asked Ana. "He was *never* brought a new cup?"

"No," said the prince. "It was always the same cup. I refilled it for him, and later Kardas did the same."

"And the times you served him, sir—when he finished with his tea, what did you do with this cup?"

"I returned the cup to the cauldron, until he asked for more."

"So, there was a moment, then," said Ana, "when this cup sat by the cauldron empty, *before* Prificto Kardas filled it for him?"

"I . . . believe so."

"Do you know if anyone else approached the cauldron then?"

He hesitated. "I do not recall this clearly, I am sad to say."

"Mm. What happened then, sir?"

The king was taken away to his chambers, the prince said, but was pronounced dead before they ever even laid him on his bed. When this news was heard, Jari Pavitar began crying that it was Prificto Kardas who had done it, and that the Empire had killed their king. Swords were drawn, and the hall was instantly clapped shut.

"Pavitar said this the *instant* this news was heard?" asked Ana.

"Very quickly, yes," said the prince. "Then everyone began saying it. Pavitar demanded we kill Prificto Kardas right then and there, and Darhi began shouting as well. It took everyone some time to remember that I was even in the room and had just inherited the kingdom." A weak, miserable smile. "I admit, it took me some time to remember, as well."

The prince had finally declared that they should take the Treasury officers to the guest chambers to be held, he said: a choice that had appeased nobody, including Darhi, who had counseled that they should seek aid from the Empire immediately. The hall guard did so, and then there was much debate among the court about what to do, with many advocating swift execution.

Then there came a screaming from the guest wing. A guard appeared and told them the captives were saying that Kardas had collapsed as well. The prince, Darhi, and Pavitar then went to investigate.

"Prificto Kardas was lying on the floor, wheezing and coughing," the prince told us. "His lips were swollen, and his throat crimson. His people were distraught, yet he did not perish. Pavitar claimed this was yet more sign of his guilt, but . . . even then, I felt the Empire would employ better poisoners than this."

Those calling for execution then began to balk, he said, and Darhi's nobles grew loud in their claims that if Kardas were to perish in their custody, it would be a blow from which the realm of Yarrow might never recover. Yet still no decision was made.

"As morning grew near, I went to visit Kardas again to see if he still lived," continued the prince. "It was then that I saw the bird at the window—a hawk that carried letters, the Treasury people told me. I read your message, and I realized you had tried to warn us of this tragedy before it'd ever happened! Yet I did not think the court would believe me, and . . . truth be told, I . . ." His face crumpled, and I saw a terrific fear in his eyes.

"You've yet to develop sufficient influence, sir?" said Ana politely.

"That is so," he admitted. "So I wrote to you. And here we are."

Ana bowed her head, frowning. Her fingers drummed on my arm as she thought.

"If it is this poisoner," said the prince, "I admit, I can't comprehend how it was done. There was no one in that room save my father, Pavitar, Darhi, and Kardas and his girl. And I do not recall any of them touching my father's cup—save Kardas, who I do not suspect."

Ana remained silent for a long while. "Some other questions, please, Your Majesty. First—are you aware of anyone at court with any dealings with the jungle smugglers to the south?"

Prince Camak shook his head. "No, no! I can't imagine that. Those folk are landless and considered brigands. To consort with them is beyond imagination!"

"I ask, sir, because we found an oathcoin in the possession of this smuggler in the jungle. I understand this is a prized token in the High City. Can you imagine how this man might have gotten it?"

"No!" said the prince, astonished. "That is a precious thing! It must be stolen, I suppose. Or perhaps this villain simply found it."

"Who at court controls or dispenses the most of such favors, sir?"

"Well . . . that would be Darhi, of course. The satrap came into possession of many coins, and gave them out to freely distribute influence, as he manages a great deal of the kingdom. Such things are common for one of his station," he added.

"Thank you, sir," said Ana. "But one final question . . . There is a chance you have seen this smuggler here in the hall, though he is adept at disguising himself. Din—please describe the drawing, if you could."

I described Pyktis to the prince, and he nodded along uncomprehendingly, before finally saying, "No, no. I have not seen a man of this sort."

"In the Empire we would call a man of his kind *Rathras*," I said. "From the Rathras cantons of the Empire. He would stand out quite a bit here, I imagine, sir."

"Why?" said the prince blankly.

I glanced at Malo and saw that she looked as puzzled as I.

"Because . . . I would think Rathras people are quite rare here, sir," I said.

"Oh!" said the prince. "I see. But that is not so—for *I* am one quarter Rathras. As are many in the High City."

There was a stunned silence.

"You . . . you *are*?" said Malo. "I had never heard of this."

"Yes," said Ana quietly. "How is this so, sir?"

"Well, this is old history," said the prince. "But . . . when the Empire came here a century ago, the king moved his court from the old city by the bay, where the towers now lean, to here, which was once the site of our holiest temples. Our court grew much smaller. This meant fewer potential wives for our kings, and their number was already quite few—many of our court are interrelated, you know. So my grandfathers simply, well, looked beyond," he finished vaguely.

"To . . . to *imperial brides*, sir?" Ana said, incredulous.

"Yes," said the prince. "My grandfathers found many imperial visitors who were more than happy to become a wife of the throne, as it meant living in great finery. They came here, Tala, or Kurmini, or Rathras, and gave children to the king and the most esteemed members of his court. It was my grandmother who was Rathras, you see."

I peered closer at him, and though it was dark in the chamber and the prince's bearded face was adorned with gold inks, I began to see what he meant: there was something faintly aquiline and delicate to his looks, features common to those hailing from the Rathras lands.

"It has become an unpleasant bit of history these days," admitted the prince. "My people do not love a prince who has any imperial look to him. But in truth, many here in the High City have the same look. Satrap Darhi, in fact, is also part Rathras."

"I see. So it would be an easy thing for a man of his kind to hide here?" said Ana.

"Perhaps, yes. But could an imperial know such a thing?"

Ana was silent and did not answer him.

"May we review your servants later, sir?" she asked finally. "To see if perhaps this thief and murderer may be among them?"

"Well . . . certainly. But you would need to ask Darhi for that. He runs the household of the king's hall."

Ana allowed a tight smile. "Thank you, Your Majesty, for all your time and answers. I may have further questions for you, eventually . . . but for now, I should like to visit Kardas and his people. Then I will need to speak to Pavitar and Darhi. From there, I do not know where my search shall take us."

"Of course," said the prince. "I shall stay here, as is my duty. Ask the guard in the hall to please take you to the Treasury folk—and let him know if he does not, he shall have to answer to me." The prince swallowed, and he suddenly looked very small next to the mound of white blossoms on the table. "I am still regent of this realm, even if not all know it yet."

CHAPTER 35

⸱ ⸱ ⸱

WE LEFT THE PRINCE WITH THE CORPSE OF HIS FATHER, and were led down yet another passage by the Yarrow guard. I had to remind myself that it was still day. In this windowless, torchlit place, it felt as if we walked not the waking world but Arasinda, the afterlife where betrayers and the disloyal wander sunless caverns filled with reeking fumes. Ten paces from the door, Malo glanced backward and made to speak, but Ana hissed, "No! Not here. There are many ears about this place. And do not speak much before our Treasury comrades, either! I trust them little as well, for now."

The guest wing of the great hall was guarded by no less than a dozen soldiers, and from their bearing I gauged they were fell hands with a sword. They hesitated a great while before reluctantly allowing us to enter. The rooms within were dark, yet as we entered we heard a great rustling as many people shot to their feet. Then we heard voices crying out, "Imperials! They are imperials?"

Then more: "Iudex? They are Iudex? Oh, are we freed? Tell us, are we freed?"

The Treasury officers gathered around us like spirits in the Harvester's kingdom, pawing at us and asking for news. I had to stand before Ana to push them back, and squinted to see in this shadowy place. The chambers would have normally been a grand, stately sight, with four-poster beds and many tapestries, but now it stank of sweat and worse things.

"Calm!" Ana snarled at the delegation. "Calm, now, all of you! Where is Kardas? We must see to him."

The Treasury officers led us to one of the four-posters. Kardas lay upon it, with many pillows propping him upright. His engraver Gorthaus leaned over him, dabbing his forehead with a cloth and water. She looked up at us as we approached, her face gaunt and her eyes sunken. She seemed utterly transformed by her spell in captivity.

Kardas, however, looked far worse: his neck was so swollen that she'd had to unbutton the collar of his shirt, and his lips were distended and thick. His cheeks and eyelids had swelled so greatly that his eyes were now little more than cracks that trickled tears down his face. He was breathing shallowly, and his wheezing was so loud that I could hear it from six paces away.

"We can't move him," Gorthaus warned us hoarsely. "Even if we are freed, and even if you had stretchers and medikkers behind you, I'd not dare to lift him from the bed."

"We are not here to move him, girl," said Ana. She waved to Malo. "Do it."

Malo knelt beside Kardas and took a vial from within her cloak. She held it to the light, peering at it: a tawny liquid swilled within, and a dozen tiny worms coiled about at its bottom, each with a stripe of bright white along its back. Malo uncorked the vial, poked in a bare finger, and withdrew it. Five of the little worms were stuck to her skin, like leeches. She recorked the vial, stowed it back in her cloak, then carefully pulled the worms from her finger and placed them upon Kardas's neck.

"Arvith leeches," murmured Malo. "Altered so their venom reduces even the most potent of inflammations. His breathing should be free soon. In an hour, he should be able to sit up—but he will have a terrible thirst."

"Keep some spare worms, Malo!" said Ana dryly. "Just in case any of us sip from the wrong cask . . ."

Gorthaus leaned back from Kardas's side. Her face crumpled, and she began to weep. "Oh, thank the fates! I . . . I'd resigned myself to watching him die hours ago. Are we freed, ma'am?"

"Not until I've convinced them of his innocence," said Ana. "Tell me, Signum—were you present when the king was stricken?"

"I was."

"And your memories were engraved, I assume?"

She reached down and lifted her engraver's satchel, and all its tiny glittering vials of scent. "They were."

"Then your testimony will be quite valuable. Leave your prificto's side, and come sit by the light of the window, and tell us all you know."

GORTHAUS SLUMPED IN her chair, head bowed, her elbows resting on her knees as the words poured forth. It felt terribly strange to reverse roles, with myself as the interrogator and she the engraver, regurgitating information as her eyes trembled and shimmered.

"It was just a tea," Gorthaus began helplessly. "Like many teas we've had. I thought the events quite dull, and I hate the taste of saca so. There were no *naukari* there that night—do you know this word, *naukari*?"

A soft, contemptuous grunt from Malo.

"No servants, I mean," said Gorthaus. "Just us, for we were to discuss high secrets."

"Please proceed," Ana said.

Gorthaus began, her eyes tremoring. I watched as she tried to navigate her memories. Like many engravers—myself included—she was a fastidiously arranged person, even now: her dark hair was pulled back in a tight bun, her eyebrows were trimmed and smooth, and her uniform was perfectly symmetrical, with every bend of cloth exactly where it ought to be.

This was how most engravers lived: we remembered, perfectly and forever, how all things should look, and if anything was ever askew, it bothered us immensely.

But Gorthaus seemed to take it further than most: even now, her hair remained waxed and carefully fixed; all her heralds still bore a few drops of polish on them, and each was pinned on her coat front in positions perfectly equidistant from the placket of her shirt.

The impression I got was a profound hunger for control. Perhaps that was what running about chasing Yarrow royalty did to a person.

She began to speak, regurgitating her experiences. Her engraved memories matched what the prince had told us: besides herself, there had been five men in the room—the king, the prince, Jari Pavitar, Satrap Darhi, and Prificto Kardas—and no one else. There had been the cauldron of tea, and the cups. Kardas had filled the king's cup, brought it to him, and let him drink. "As he always did for the third cupful," she said, "as a sign of deference." Then the king had simply cried out and collapsed.

"The king's cup," Ana said. "Tell me its movements *exactly.*"

Gorthaus's eyes tremored, her pupils dancing like a beheaded snake. "First the prince served the king. The prince took the cup back when the king was done and placed it next to the cauldron. The prince did the same for the second cup, taking it back and forth, serving his father. Then ... then the cup stayed there for some time, sitting by the cauldron."

"Who else went there?" asked Ana. "Who else served themselves at the cauldron while the king's cup sat in that spot?"

Gorthaus shrugged helplessly. "All of them."

"All?"

"Pavitar, Darhi, Kardas, the prince. They all got up and went there and poured another cup for themselves, then sat back down."

"Did *you* go near the cup, Signum?"

"I did not, ma'am. I did not drink at all, for I don't care for the taste of the tea, and they did not expect me to speak anyway."

I grimaced as I absorbed this. If this was so, then any of the men could have slipped poison into the king's cup. For having now read of kerel poisoning, I knew it acted terribly fast, inflaming the throat within seconds when consumed in high doses.

Gorthaus continued: "They took us to another room. They had us put under guard, with drawn swords. I mean—some of my people haven't ever even *seen* a drawn sword, do you know this? They're axioms, number-readers! They quaked like children awoken by an owl!"

"What happened next?" Ana asked.

"We waited, for what felt like hours. We heard shouting in the distant rooms, fighting. We were terrified, sure we were to be killed. But then the ... the prince came. He was very calm, very lovely. He said we were not under threat tonight, for he would not allow us to be harmed."

"Then what?" asked Ana.

"Then Kardas thanked the prince, and the prince departed, yet ... yet just after that ... the prificto started coughing as well. Then he collapsed, just like the king, and I was sure he was to die ..."

"He showed symptoms *just* after the prince left?" asked Ana.

"Yes."

"Had he drunk or eaten or tasted anything?"

"No. I remember. We even asked for water, and were refused. I ... I truly don't know how it happened. How can a man be poisoned if he's tasted nothing at all?"

Ana frowned and bowed her head, lost in thought. I tried to suppress showing my own discouragement: another mystery, among so many that seemed unsolvable.

"And then?" Ana asked.

Gorthaus continued, and her testimony again matched the prince's: Camak had returned just as Ana's scribe-hawk had come to the window and sent her his response pleading for help.

"We would be dead without the prince," said Gorthaus shakily. "Of that, I'm sure."

Ana pursed her lips. "Are there any at court who might wish the king ill? Any who might benefit?"

"I ... I can't say," Gorthaus said. "The prince springs to mind first, for he'd then inherit the throne, but ... he has never seemed the sort. He is a gentle, somewhat silly person. He goes hunting, but he never actually fires the arrows themselves, do you know? He just likes being around the men who do the hunting for him. Many doubt his appointment as preferred heir, in fact."

I spoke up: "*Preferred* heir? I thought the eldest son inherited. Isn't that how most monarchy works?"

"Well ... no." Gorthaus's eyes shimmered in her head as she consulted her memories. "King Lalaca has—had?—seventy-six wives in his harem, and two hundred and sixteen acknowledged children. This means he has rather a lot of heirs to choose from."

Stunned, I looked to Malo, who shrugged.

"Wherever did the fellow find the time?" I asked.

"Shut up, Din!" snapped Ana. "Now—what of Pavitar? Could he have any reason to do it?"

"No, no," said Gorthaus. "Pavitar is the jari. He practically worships the monarchy. I can no more imagine Pavitar killing the king than I can the emperor burning down his Sanctum."

"Darhi, then? The satrap?"

"I can't imagine him doing it, either, honestly. He is a shrewd man, but he works to make friends, to ensure everyone views him favorably, and that all are in his debt. He is in a powerful place here, just as he likes it, and is too clever for such a mad move."

"Did any of them behave suspiciously during the time before this tea?"

"No. Not that I could think of. Except that . . ."

"Except?"

"Well, the king *had* been eluding us for months. We hadn't been able to meet with him at all. Then yesterday morn, we received the summons for the tea. My prificto said it was the work of Darhi, for he was laboring to continue our work."

"It was Darhi who had arranged this tea?"

"Yes, ma'am. We thought it a good sign at the time. But . . ." She trailed off, concerned.

Ana was silent for a long while. Then she asked: "Tell me more of the room where the tea took place."

"It was in the eastern hall, with glassless windows that look out onto the bay, and the Shroud. We have had meetings there before. The king always complained much of the view, and how the Shroud tainted it."

"How many doors or chambers or passageways did it have about it?"

"Two, ma'am, but I did not see anyone come in or ou—"

"I did not ask you what you saw, Signum," snapped Ana. "How many doors, and where did they lead?"

Her eyes flickered. "There is a door to the south, which takes one back to the great hall. Then there is one facing west, which takes one to the reliquary. From that chamber you can return south to the great hall, or go west to the king's private chambers, though his bedchambers are upstairs. But these passages are highly guarded, and again—I saw no one come in or out of any door while we drank."

Ana turned her face away and was silent for a great while. Then she raised a hand. "Thank you, Signum. We are done, I think. I have what I need—though it is not what I sought. Kol—take me and Malo to a safe space here. I have something to discuss."

I LED ANA to the far corner where the Treasury folk could not hear, and Malo followed. It was after I passed by one open window that I saw that Ana's blindfolded face looked terribly strained.

"Ma'am," I said, startled. "Are you all right? You lo—"

"Of course I am not!" Ana snapped. "I rarely leave my settled environs for a *reason*, Din! To venture so far and expose myself to so many new people taxes me greatly. But we have many knots to unravel, and so I push myself."

A long moment passed. A muscle twitched in her cheek, then her neck. When she spoke again, her voice was unusually deep and hoarse, as if she'd just awoken from a long sleep.

"I feel Gorthaus speaks the truth," she said, "yet it comforts me little. We are left with the same questions—*how* did Pyktis kill the king, if there were only those six people in that room? And what did he mean to gain from it?" She sucked her teeth. "It confounds me! How can we speak to so many, and still learn nothing?"

Malo turned to me. "Want to tell her what Darhi asked of you when he pulled you aside? For I heard his murmuring down the hallway."

I relayed Darhi's brief meeting with me, and how he had pressed upon me to remember his oathcoin. "It seems he controls much of this place, ma'am," I said. "I almost feel he was the true ruler here, even while the king lived. Perhaps he intends to control even us."

"Perhaps," said Ana. "But is he a villain, or simple political swine? It is often hard to tell those two apart." She turned her blindfolded face to the ceiling. "We are out of friendly witnesses. Now we must delve into liars and schemers. Tell the prince that we need to speak to Pavitar next."

"Pavitar?" said Malo. "You are sure? The man nurses a great hate for us."

"And that is why he shall speak truth when he does not wish to!" said Ana. "There is no one more forward with the unpleasant truth than a powerful, prideful man with a grudge. That is why you shall conduct this interview, Din, for I feel he dislikes you strongly. But I would like you to ask Pavitar about the king's *health*. For you say his body appeared very old?"

"To my eye, yes, ma'am," I said.

"But then, living in a monarchy ages a body," said Malo, "even when you are the monarch."

"True! Still, you will ask, Din. But before I forget, Malo—I have heard it said that a warden can hear the flicker of a lie in a man's heart. Is this so?"

"A tremendous overstatement," said Malo reluctantly. "I can hear some things, ma'am, if I sit very close to the subject. The smell of sweat divulges far more. But it is not a precise thing. The lie must be most emotional, and emotions do not always speak truth."

"It shall have to do. It won't be too hard a task to sit close to the jari, yes?"

Malo pulled a face and turned away.

CHAPTER 36

. . .

THE THREE OF US WERE LED TO A SIDE ROOM WITH TOW-
ering walls bristling with horns, wings, and occasionally hooves from
countless preserved creatures: hunting trophies of birds and beasts,
and many creatures I could not name. They shivered and danced in
the light from the blaze in the fireplace, casting wicked shadows on
the dark stone.

Jari Pavitar strode in, his broad feet stamping on the stone floor.
We stood as if he were of royal stock himself, but he simply waved at
the smoke with one hand, then walked to the far wall and opened the
shutters of a window. He paused, peered out at something, then
shook his head in disgust, walked back, and sat down in a huge
wooden chair.

"You may sit," he said brusquely.

We did so, with Malo sitting directly across from the jari, and myself right beside her, watching his every move. Ana sat behind me,
bent in her chair, head cocked. Pavitar watched Malo very closely, his
pale, green-tinged eyes shining under his indigo-stained brow.

"So. How may I be of service to your Empire?" he asked curtly.

"To begin with, sir," I said, "I would like to hear you recount what
happened last night, from the beginning."

He scratched his tremendous, green-tinged beard. "If you wish,"
he grunted, and then launched into his tale.

His story matched those offered by the prince and Gorthaus almost exactly. There had been the six of them there, and the cauldron,

and the cups; they had drunk many cups of tea as they talked; yet then, just after Kardas had served the king tea, he'd choked, cried out, and fallen over, never to breathe again.

"It was after the king collapsed, sir," I said, "that you accused Prificto Kardas of being the poisoner—true?"

"I did."

"Why was that?"

"I know well of your magics, your thaumaturgy. For it was imperial magics that contorted the swampfolk in the forest to the south and turned the very land into an abomination. Is that not so?"

"The tools used to accomplish that were stolen, sir, and no imperial authorities were involved, bu—"

"Yes, yes. But it was your arts, your skills, that killed a hundred or more of Yarrow folk without the unsheathing of a single sword. If any state had the power to achieve such a thing, then a poisoning would be even simpler—and, again, it was Kardas who touched the cup last."

"Do you consort much with swampfolk, sir?" asked Malo innocently.

An affronted pause. "I do not. They are low folk, akin to vermin."

"Then if they are such low folk, why does their passing concern you?" she asked.

He glared at her. "Because they were still Yarrow! They fell under the domain of the king. Any curtailment of the king's power is a harm against him, and the realm of Yarrow."

A trace of a smile played at the corners of Malo's mouth. She had rattled him, and took great delight in it.

"Could anyone else at the meeting wished to have harmed the king?" I asked.

Pavitar smirked as if I'd said something foolish. "No. Only an imperial could do this. We Yarrows worship our ancestors, the kin of before. The king is ancestry made *flesh*. All of his judgments are the judgments of the ancients." He shot me a glare. "Nor will I have it suggested that it was the prince."

"I didn't make such a suggestion, sir," I said.

"But you did," he said. "You asked me to consider if anyone else at the meeting meant harm to the king, and the prince was present. I know how your minds work, pulled to this idea that the prince might kill his father to inherit. But this is *apavitari,* a terrible sacrilege, an offense to the ancestors. He would do no such thing."

I watched him carefully. His eyes and movements were full of conviction. Either this was truth, or he was a very convincing actor.

I recalled Ana's orders then, and asked, "How was the king's health in the days before his poisoning?"

"You think his death natural?" demanded Pavitar. "Are you so foolish?"

"Not at all, sir. But it is procedure to ask."

"His health was very good," he said forcefully. "My king was strong in flesh, spirit, and mind. Never have I beheld a man so strong, in fact."

At that, Malo reached over and gently tapped my thigh, without ever taking her eyes off Pavitar. A lie, then.

"Are you sure of this, sir?" I asked.

"Very!" he said angrily. "Or do you suggest I did not know my own king?"

I paused, worried he would storm out if I pressed him on this.

Suddenly Ana spoke from behind me: "Thank you for that, sir! I would like to know—who is it that conducts most of the negotiations with the Imperial Treasury?"

Pavitar could not keep his words from dripping with disdain: "That is Darhi."

"And how do you feel the negotiations are going?" she asked politely.

"I think having them at all is an offense to our holy ancestors. The contract with the Empire should never have been signed."

"And yet, by saying this," said Malo, "you doubt the ancestors—for was it not King Yodhi di Lalaca eh Cautha, fourth of his name, who made this pact with the Empire?"

A vein slowly began to calcify at the edge of Pavitar's thick, purple head. "He was deceived in doing so. Lalaca eh Cautha did not know what the Empire planned to do with his lands."

"Do you think Darhi feels the same way, in his negotiations?" Ana asked.

"Darhi . . . Feh!" spat Pavitar. "No. He has always been the Empire's thing. He seeks trade, and wealth. As we say—*Ika aḍakohsa la'i ika siki da parasi.* He has a purse for a scrotum, and coins instead of balls."

"What a colorful colloquialism. Does Darhi ever hold any meetings with Treasury folk in the *reliquary,* sir?" asked Ana.

"The reliquary? Of course not," said Pavitar. "We never allowed an imperial foot to fall in that sacred place before today, and that was only because the prince insisted." He glowered for a moment: this plainly still displeased him. "But he should be given some grace, I suppose, given the darkness of today."

Ana nodded and gestured to me, indicating I should continue.

"Did Satrap Darhi ever meet with smugglers?" I asked. "Or swampfolk?"

"What? No. Not that I knew."

"I ask because we found an oathcoin in a smuggler's den, hidden in a box and buried in the earth. And I have only ever seen Darhi give one out."

"That would be akin to giving a dog the first night with your daughter," he said. "I cannot imagine Darhi being such a fool, nor any other noble." He stood. "Enough! These questions grow foolish. I am loyal to the prince, and the prince wishes to give the Empire all they need, it seems, but . . . even my loyalties have their limits."

We hastily rose and bowed to him.

"One more thing, sir . . ." I said.

His beard shivered as he gritted his teeth. "What now?"

"This time a very broad question . . . Have you seen *anything* strange here recently? Anything even remotely out of place? For the man we seek tampers with the world in strange ways. Anything of note would be valuable to us."

That gave him pause.

"Yes," he said quietly. "My . . . my dogs have perished."

"I beg your pardon?"

"My dogs, my fine hounds. Keen of nose and eye, and fierce of tooth. They were my pride, and I took them to court often, though Darhi protested. He disliked how they sniffed so at all who came and went. But six days ago . . . I took the prince hunting, in the west of here. When I returned, I found them dead or dying. Poisoned, my people suspected, or sickened."

I narrowed my eyes. Another poisoning, perhaps. Yet I struggled to imagine how dogs might be connected to Sujedo, or Pyktis, or even the king's murder.

"Do you have any idea how it happened?" I asked.

"At first I thought it sabotage by the boy-keeper, or perhaps stupidity. I debated having him beaten or taking a finger from him for it. But he is not so clever. Yet I know the cause."

He pointed to the open window. I sat forward to see.

From this angle I could see into the Bay of Yarrow, the moonlight glittering on the dark seas, and there, rising above them, a shaft of shimmering green: the Shroud.

"Ever since that arose in the waters," said Pavitar, "our lands have failed. Our cattle and lands blacken. And we have forgotten the ways of our fathers. It is a blight upon this world, an unnatural thing, compared to the natural, ancient rights of crown and throne. I pray each night to my fathers and forefathers that it shall fall. One day, perhaps, my wishes shall be heard."

"What makes you say that, sir?" I asked quietly.

"It is merely a prayer. Is it a crime in your Empire, to beseech the fates for justice?" He made to leave, yet paused to look Malo over. "*Tusim naim dikhadi ki uham neh tuhadi?*" he whispered.

"The Empire can't take away what the realm of Yarrow never gave me," she responded coolly.

He glared at her for a moment, then swept out.

"WHY THE HELL did you ask to see that man first?" Malo asked Ana once he was gone. "You knew he would fight us most! He practically swaggered up with a belly full of bile!"

"Did he lie, girl?" snapped Ana. "Did he ever once speak false to you?"

"His heartbeat was high, as was his sweat, but it rarely wavered," she said reluctantly. "He spoke a lie but once—when he claimed his king was healthy in his later days. But nothing else."

"Then that was why I asked for him first. He is stupid, and hostile, but he is mostly truthful. He lies only to give dignity to the dead— that, or he is so skilled an actor that even you could not see it, Malo."

"But am I right in thinking that he directly threatened the Shroud, just now?" I asked. "Could he truly be so audacious?"

"Not so audacious as foolish," said Malo. "But I am unsure if hating the Shroud is unique. Many Yarrow nobles curse and decry it every day."

"Nor are his claims novel, really," said Ana. "The Empire's influence grows strong here, and as it does, less and less of the common folk of Yarrow wish to toil on farmlands under the watch of chiefs and nobles. They are all too happy to work for the Empire, which offers food and medicine in abundance. This means less folk to work their farms. Fields go fallow and yields dwindle—but it is easier to claim mystical imperial poison than upend the rule of the king." She sighed. "But I still catch no hint of Pyktis about the jari—or not yet, at least. Let us speak to the trickiest one. Send in Darhi. We shall have much to ask him."

THE DOOR OPENED and Satrap Darhi entered, his face cool and contained. He tossed his long locks to the side before sitting in the chair before the fire. Then he smiled at us—a practiced expression, I felt instantly—and extended a hand, asking us to sit. Again, Malo sat just across from him; again, I watched his face and hers, while Ana sat behind us.

"I hope our testimonials have been helpful to you," Darhi said calmly. "I wish to find this killer, Signum Kol, for many reasons. Justice, diplomacy, the safety of the realm—but many personal, of course."

"Certainly, sir," I said. "But . . . what personal reasons might you mean?"

"Well, I do not think Kardas is the killer. Instead, I believe the poisoner wishes to harm the Empire and disrupt our relationship. As I have been the primary court member pushing for a beneficial close to our negotiations, then I assume I'd also be targeted. In fact . . ." He reached into his robes and produced a slender slip of paper. "I have recorded the names of all in attendance at the hall in the days preceding the tea. I have also added the names of all the *naukari* who were present—the servants. Or, at least, all I can confirm. The king's great hall is a busy place."

I took the list and glanced at the names. The writing was thin and neat, but the letters danced before my eyes, as always. I handed them back to Ana, who greedily snatched them from my grasp.

I then asked Darhi to recount his memories of the event. His testimony was quite detailed, but it matched what Signum Gorthaus, the prince, and the jari had seen.

"I admit, I can't comprehend how it happened," Darhi said at the end of it. "Or even that it *had* happened. I play the events back in my mind again and again, but I can see no moment when I might have spied poison in the cup of the king *or* Prificto Kardas."

"Can you think of any in the hall who might wish the king ill, sir?" I asked.

"The *naukari*, possibly," he admitted. "There have been times when they have broken out in fighting and insurrection in the past, but we have always quelled it quickly. Though I cannot yet see how they could have managed the poisoning, since only Kardas and the king were affected."

"What about the prince?" I asked. "Or Pavitar?"

"Oh, no, no, not at all," Darhi said. "The prince is a good man, but he is young and soft at heart. And Pavitar, well . . ." He smiled a very careful, steady sort of smile. "Never has there been a jari more devoted than he!"

"How has the king's health been of late?" I asked.

"Very good, for a man of his advanced years," said Darhi.

"Truly? For Pavitar said the king had been ailing in his last days."

Darhi hesitated. "Pavitar said this?"

"Can you describe the nature of the king's health, sir?"

"I . . . am reluctant to. I do not wish to break his privacy, even in death. And we mourn him now, of course." His face tightened. "But . . . I will admit he forgot things."

"Things?"

"Yes."

"Did he forget who *you* were, sir?"

"Sometimes, yes," he said, now very reluctant. "Sometimes he forgot more. Yet he was still ancestry incarnate," he added quickly. "The spirits of his line still governed his mind and soul. Thus, this sacred wisdom was with him when it was needed."

A soft, derisive exhale from Malo.

"We are worried there might be a connection here with another imperial criminal, sir," I said. "A rather infamous thief—a Rathras man."

Again, Darhi's face tightened. "A . . . *Rathras* man, you say?"

"Yes. In fact, when we spoke to the prince about this, he . . . had some rather fascinating history to tell us, sir."

His eyes danced in his serene features, calculating how to respond. Finally, he took a quick breath in and said, "So! It seems it is the business of the court to air all our foul winds the second they meet so charming a stranger. I assume the prince told you he *and* I are one quarter Rathras?"

"He did, sir," I said.

A nod of grim resignation. "Then I also assume he told you how the kings of the past had a predilection for imperial brides, both for generational issues as well as . . . personal interest?"

Another soft, scornful snort from Malo.

"He, ah, did not mention personal interest, but yes," I said.

"Thankfully, the king aged out of such passions. And like any member of the king's harem, his imperial wives have received every comfort. We are no brutes here."

"That is a reassurance, sir," I said. "But . . . some do die in child-birth, correct?"

I'd thought this would irritate him further, but Darhi merely shrugged. "Yes? It is a common threat. No pregnancy is without dan-ger, especially for the royal Yarrow line."

"Why is that?"

"Because so many give birth to twins, or triplets, or more. Did you not see it, Signum Kol? Look closer at our guards and *naukari*, and you will find some faces repeat themselves."

I paused, and summoned up a memory of Ana speaking to me: *Did you know that the lyre duet is one of the ancient arts of Yarrow, Din? Yes. Some say it reflects the dominance of twins and triplets in the royal lineage here—a rather fascinating biological quirk. Led to some very inter-esting issues with inheritance, and many brothers killing brothers, some-times at ages as young as six. Horrible shit, really!*

I looked back at the satrap and saw him watching me with a calm look. He was quite accustomed to the sight of an engraver's eyes flut-tering, perhaps. Curious.

"Does the king have a twin, sir?" I asked.

"He did," said the satrap with a shrug. "But the child died at a very young age. I myself am a sole survivor of three. Pavitar's twin was born dead. So it goes."

I paused, quietly horrified by his indifference to the death of so many young. Yet this new piece of information made me think.

"Are you related to the king, sir?" I asked.

He smiled, a rather chilly expression. "I am his second nephew. That is why I wear the green paints, you see."

"Is that ever a point of conflict?"

"Mm. You imperials find it interesting to have so many of royal line living so close to the throne, yes? You have watched many dramas in your odeons, read many tales of prince killing prince, and king kill-ing king, seeking power. But that is not how it is done here—or, not anymore." He reached into his pocket and produced a small, wooden token hanging upon a leather loop: a bearded man's face, scowling and stoic, with a circlet upon his head. "This is my ancestor, King Yodhi di Lalaca eh Cautha, fourth of his name. I keep this with me, for we Yarrow labor under the watch of our ancestors. All we do must honor their name. Yet the king is ancestry manifest, and the king picks his inheritor."

"And that is simply that?" I asked.

"It is. Did you see the silver circlet on the prince's brow? And the silver chain about his neck?"

"I did, sir."

"Those are the signifiers of the king's chosen heir. The silvers go to him—and *only* to him, and we accept this. The children and relations of the king are mere tools to his ancestry. If the king asked us to throw down our lives, we would do so." He stowed the little totem away. "That is the nature of the will of the king, and thus the will of Yarrow."

Ana spoke up behind me: "I would like to know, sir, a bit more about your negotiations with the Treasury."

"Oh? Certainly."

"What is it you and Prificto Kardas discuss in these negotiations?"

"Do you not know this yourself?"

"I *think* I do," said Ana. "But I would like to hear you confirm it."

He blinked and shifted in his chair. I glanced at Malo and saw that her eyes had gone wide, like a cat stalking its prey in the night.

"Why, taxes, of course," he said. "Who owns which lands, the revenue of each, how all of them shall be accorded management when the realm is adopted by the Empire. Is this truly not known to you?"

Malo gently tapped my thigh with her finger again: a lie.

"Of course, of course," said Ana softly. "But thank you for confirming it."

THE DOOR CLOSED behind Darhi. I looked to Malo, who sat with her head tilted toward the door and the hall beyond. Finally she nodded and said, "We may speak—but quietly. Guards remain, and they are not far."

"Din," said Ana softly. "Summon a memory for me, and quickly now!"

"Which one, ma'am?"

"That first day here, when you and Malo went to the Treasury tower and Sujedo's rooms. You peered out the window at the top of the tower—but what did you see?"

My eyes shimmered, and I recounted that moment as I'd taken in the Yarrow coast, with Yarrowdale and Old Town sprawling below.

Ana interrupted: "When you gazed southeast, though—did you see New Town?"

"Well. Yes?"

"And the waterfront, and the canals?"

"Yes, some."

"The Apoth works? Could you see what ships come and go from their manufactuaries?"

I frowned, bewildered, but realized I had. "Yes?" I said.

"Thank you. Good. Very good . . ." Then she bowed her head and was still for a long time before finally saying, "Please tell Darhi to send in Signum Gorthaus."

I stood, but paused. "Would it be better if we went to where the Treasury officers are held, ma'am? We could simply talk to her the—"

"No," snapped Ana. "I do not *wish* to speak to her there! I want her separate, and I want to make sure no one else hears a thing we discuss! For though I think Pavitar and Darhi both lied to us, I am now *sure* our comrade Signum Gorthaus did the same." A fearsome, mirthless grin split her face. "And I think I know what about."

SOON WE HEARD footsteps in the passageway beyond. The door opened and Signum Gorthaus entered, still quite gaunt and frail-looking, accompanied by a grim-faced Yarrow guard. She nervously blinked in the light of the fire as the guard shut the door behind her, then sighed with relief when she saw us. "Oh, thank Sanctum. I . . . I wasn't sure . . ."

"Wasn't sure what, dear girl?" asked Ana.

"Well. This was the first time I've been out of that room, ma'am. I wasn't sure if I . . ."

"If you were bound for execution?"

A meek nod. "I suppose so, ma'am. But I'm not sure why they'd do so for me, when . . . Well. I think it's Kardas whom they hate so."

Ana gestured to the same chair Pavitar and Darhi had recently occupied. "Sit! Sit and relax, for a moment at least, child. This ordeal must have been terribly unpleasant for you, true?" She smiled as if they were having a quaint afternoon discussion on her porch.

"I've not had it as hard as some, ma'am," said Gorthaus, though she cringed as she sat, and rubbed her left arm. "But I feel so *stiff.* I'm not sure if it's the stress, or if it's how I sat over the prificto for so long . . . Have you made any headway in proving his innocence, ma'am?"

"In proving?" said Ana. "No, for proof is in short supply here. But I know he's innocent—for I know how *he* was poisoned, at least."

Gorthaus paused. "You do, ma'am?"

I glanced at Malo, frowning. She raised a dubious eyebrow, but we stayed silent.

"Oh, it is quite simple, really," said Ana. "Prificto Kardas had often made a point of allowing the prince to carry the first two cups of tea to his father, and then carrying the third himself as a show of respect—true?"

"Yes?"

"Well, the killer, knowing this, had poisoned the king's cup just before, to make it appear as if Kardas was the poisoner. Yet as Kardas poured the cup and carried it to the king, he unknowingly *touched* some residue of the poison. Ordinarily, this would be harmless—yet can you, as an engraver, recall a particular nervous mannerism of your prificto's?"

Gorthaus's eyes shimmered in her head, and mine did the same. I summoned an image of Kardas waiting before the bank vault, and again as he left the meeting at the Yarrow prison: his face tense, shoulders hunched . . . and his thumb placed between his teeth as he bit at the nail and pad at once.

"Oh," I said softly.

"Ah," said Gorthaus at the same time. "He . . . he bites his thumb when agitated."

"Indeed," said Ana. "And Kardas had a *great deal* to be agitated about after you all were locked up and threatened with execution, yes? I am sure he bit his thumb then—unaware it bore a trace of the poison that had just killed the king! It was just a trace, however. Enough to lay him low, but not quite enough to kill him."

"Oh," said Gorthaus. "Then . . . it is solved, is it not? Can't you simply tell the prince, and—"

"No," said Ana. "I cannot, for I still cannot prove anything. And I have not yet found the culprit, this traitorous poisoner. But we have made some headway there, for I believe I know someone who *knows* this poisoner."

"Do you?" said Gorthaus. "Who?"

"Isn't it obvious by now, girl?" said Ana. "It's you." Her grin was fearsome and mirthless. "For you've been betraying both the Empire *and* Yarrow for the past two years, haven't you?"

CHAPTER 37

. . .

GORTHAUS STARED AT ANA, HER EYES WIDE IN HER
gaunt face. In this smoky, gloomy chamber, she had the look of a wandering eidolon in a crypt. Finally she moved, her right hand creeping
back to her left arm, where she anxiously massaged the flesh above
her elbow. "I don't . . . I'm not sure I quite understand you, ma'am,"
she said. "Surely you—"

"Perhaps you need simply listen, then," said Ana. "For I find myself in a storytelling mood, and I think I've a *fascinating* tale to tell. It
is a story of corruption, betrayal, and murder. It is most hideous,
really! Are you ready for it?"

Gorthaus gazed at her, incredulous, then looked to me as if seeking support. I simply watched her, engraving her movements, carefully recording how she responded.

"I shall begin thusly," said Ana. "The Imperial Treasury delegation has been meeting with the court of Yarrow for *many* years now.
Over a decade, at least! And off and on, there have always been
petty smugglers and pirates marauding about in the swamps. But in
the last two years, things changed rather drastically. A few of these
smugglers got very organized. They got *coordinated*. And they got a
lot deadlier. The reason for their success was that the person running them was simply a genius at prediction. This fellow could
comprehend so much with just a *tiny portion* of observations! Give
him the right details, and he'd know which barge to rob, and when,
and how."

She sat back in her chair, adjusted her blindfold, and continued: "Yet before he could do any of that, he needed someone to first *get* him at least some of these tiny observations. He needed a contact within the Empire, in other words. The Apoths, of course, wouldn't do—they were guarded against such plots, and only doled out information at the last minute—so he needed someone else. It was then that he had a very clever idea, as he was so wont to do. What if he corrupted someone at the *Treasury*? The Treasury, of course, has very limited insight into the Apoth works . . . but what if the Treasury delegation was stuck up at the top floor of that very high tower back in Old Town? Because you can see quite a bit of the bay from the top floor, can't you?"

Gorthaus's face was still as stone. Her fingers continued working on her left arm, squeezing the triceps and deltoid, her face occasionally cringing as if pained.

"So!" said Ana, grinning. "Everyone might *think* the Treasury delegation had been put in that shitty old tower because the king of Yarrow wished to punish them, but . . . why, if you looked out the right window in the tower, you'd see all the movements of the Apoths, night and day, wouldn't you? If our genius smuggler got these *tiny* observations—which ship went to which brewery, which dock, and when—well, he could predict so much, and steal all he wanted! And the perfect candidate to do this task, of course? Well, an engraver. Someone who could remember everything they saw *perfectly*."

Gorthaus did nothing. Her face remained perfectly stoic.

"Yet the tricky thing was then *getting* all these observations to this genius smuggler," said Ana. "For the swamps and the canals and the jungles are quite a long ways from Old Town! So he needed a *third* actor—a liaison, in essence. Someone to take these observations and smuggle them out to the swamps. He found just such a person, a very useful one who had frequent contact with the Treasury folk—yet this liaison left a very distinct pattern. For I noticed . . . in all their months of raiding and piracy, the smugglers *never* conducted a raid in the first week of the month. And, most strangely, that was *exactly* when the Treasury delegation met with the court of Yarrow in the High City."

She grinned. "Because that's when the *exchange* took place, didn't it? The liaison for these smugglers is someone here at court."

Gorthaus's eyes danced about: calculating, perhaps, what she could do now to affect her fate.

Ana readjusted the folds of her dress. "I wasn't sure it was you, at first, actually. Originally, I thought it was Kardas, for he's seemed so useless here in Yarrow! But then, just earlier today, I asked you a question about all the passageways connected to the room where the king was poisoned." She snapped her fingers. "Din—what was her answer?"

My eyes shook, and I recited it: *"There is a door to the south, which takes one back to the great hall. Then there is one facing west, which takes one to the reliquary. From that chamber you can return south to the great hall, or go west to the king's private chambers, though his bedchambers are upstairs."*

"And yet," said Ana, grinning, "both the prince and Pavitar told us that no imperial before us has *ever* stepped foot in the reliquary! So how could you have such a familiarity with the passageways of the king's hall ... unless the smuggler's liaison here has, perhaps, held secret meetings with you in many sacred places?"

Gorthaus whimpered softly, now rubbing her left arm from wrist to shoulder.

Ana leaned forward, her face bright with a strange hunger. "Here is the crux of it, girl," she said. "You can tell us all you know now, right *now*. Then I can be lenient on you. But if you withhold, we will return to the city, and search all your vaults and chambers and what have you, and find all the rotten money that has tumbled your way, and prove your guilt. And then I'll give you nothing—save the noose, and a thief's death."

"But ..." stammered Gorthaus. "But I ... I don't know anything about who killed the king!"

"I didn't think you did," said Ana. "My concerns lie elsewhere, for now. Because this smuggler has stolen six crates of reagents that are *tremendously* dangerous. So much so that they threaten the whole of the Empire. We have searched the swamps but have found only corpses. I think these six crates are now in the possession of his contact here at court—his liaison, who slipped him all your observations about which barge to rob, and when."

Gorthaus's face gleamed with sweat in the firelight.

"All I need is a name," said Ana. "Give me the name of your contact here, girl, and I can save you."

"I . . . I didn't want anyone to die," Gorthaus said, panting. "They didn't say anyone would die. But then after the first attacks, they . . ."

"They blackmailed you, I am sure," said Ana. "Threatened you with death or worse. But that is in the past. I need that name now, child, and then all can be set aright."

"I . . . I want to *know* I'll live," said Gorthaus. Tears began to run down her cheeks. "I don't want to get hanged for this. I want a . . . a contract, a deal, or I . . ."

"Just tell me, damn it!" hissed Ana.

Gorthaus choked for a moment, her mouth making curious shapes as she struggled to speak.

Then the sounds from her throat changed. She was not just stammering anymore. This was something else.

I stepped closer, alarmed: Gorthaus's face was quite red, and her eyes were beginning to bulge. "Ma'am . . ." I said.

"Speak, girl!" whispered Ana furiously. "Tell me the *name*!"

Then Malo swooped forward. "Her hand. Fucking hell, look at her hand!"

"Her hand?" cried Ana. "What of her damned hand?"

I glanced down. Though Gorthaus's right hand was fine, the fingers of the left were a dusky purple and were as swollen as fish sausage, so much so that the ring on her middle finger bit into the flesh. Gorthaus gazed down at her own hand, as if mystified. Then she gasped, choked, and slid from the chair until she lay upon the flagstone floor, quivering and trembling.

"What is this?" demanded Ana. She gazed around blindly. "What's happening?"

Malo stooped over Gorthaus's body and slid her knife from its sheath. With deft movements, she parted Gorthaus's left sleeve and ripped it free from her arm.

I gasped. The flesh below had been transformed: her forearm and bicep were horribly swollen, bulging about the elbow until the joint resembled that of a well-fed infant. Yet one spot seemed worst of all: a bright, puckered little volcano sitting atop her triceps, surrounded by whorls of horrid, purpled flesh.

"She's been poisoned," said Malo.

"What?" cried Ana. "How?"

"A tiny stab, or a sting. But it's kerel poisoning, ma'am, by the look of it. A very small dose. That's why it took so long. But it's surely worked its way back to her heart by now . . ."

I gazed down on Gorthaus's pink, bulging face and listened to her breathing, which seemed to be growing shallower by the second. I recalled what Ana had said: *It's far worse if it is directly fed into the blood, though. If even the tiniest drop gets into your veins, no amount of medicine or aid can help you.*

Ana shot to her feet and thundered: "Then he's still here!"

"What?" I said, startled.

"He's *here*, he's in the *goddamned building*!" She blindly stumbled to the door, flung it open, and bellowed, "*Darhi! Darhi, get in here, damn it!*"

A flurry of footfalls, and Darhi arrived. His usual expression of frigid serenity dissolved when he saw Gorthaus lying on the floor. "*Savariga* . . ." he murmured. "What happen—"

"Lock down the castle!" thundered Ana. "Lock down the building! Search everyone, *everyone*! Our poisoner has struck again, right before our very eyes!"

⌃ ⌃ ⌃

CHAPTER 38

THE GUARDS OF THE KING'S HALL REFUSED TO LET MALO or me partake in the search for the poisoner. Whether the prince or anyone else had been attacked, we were not told: the guards kept us confined to our chamber, and all we could do was sit and listen to the shouts and cries in the halls beyond, and Gorthaus's dwindling breath.

Malo tended to Gorthaus, cursing and swearing as she applied her tiny worms to her throat and arm. I assisted her in doing so, pulling Gorthaus's uniform away to free the swelling, and eventually moving her body into a better position, though I had handled the fresh dead before in my service, and knew from the feel of her that Gorthaus was likely among them now.

Ana callously told us not to bother—"Surely you can hear that fucking girl's breathing stopped long ago!"—but Malo was resolute: "I am a warden, true, but an Apoth first. If there is a chance I can breathe life into this flesh, I will try." Yet after an hour of ministrations, Malo sat back from the body, sighed, and drew a symbol in the air beseeching the attention of Kesir, the deity of forgiveness. Then she began to pluck her worms from Gorthaus's body and return them to her vial. "We may have need of them yet," she muttered, "given how black this night feels."

Finally a captain of the guard came to our chamber. He brought with him one of his subordinates: a sweaty and terrified-looking fellow whom I identified as the guard who'd escorted Gorthaus to our chambers. Stammering, he told Malo his story, and she translated his words for us.

"He says he was sent to fetch her from the guest chambers," said Malo.

"By whom?" demanded Ana.

"Satrap Darhi," said Malo. "He did as he was ordered, and got her and walked her across the great hall, then down the passageway to this chamber. But . . . then another guard came walking toward them, wearing a steel cap and a cloak. This second guard bumped into Gorthaus as she walked, and she cried out. The man mumbled an apology before hurrying down the hallway. Then Gorthaus and this fellow here came the rest of the way to this chamber, and . . . Well. We saw what happened."

Ana snarled, "And what did he look like, this guard who simply *bumped into* Gorthaus?"

Malo listened as the man rambled on, then translated: "He doesn't know, for it was dark and smoky in the passageway. He saw the cap, the cloak, the beard, and little else. He does think the beard was rather light colored. He has given this description to the satrap, and they search for this man now."

"A light-colored beard!" said Ana. "Fucking hell. Get these damned fools out of my sight, so I can think!"

I escorted the guards from the room. Then we stood in the smoky chamber, too dismayed to speak.

"He has already slipped away as quickly as he came, I'm sure," said Ana. "But he *was* here. He was watching. And he did not love it when I called for Gorthaus to come to me, after speaking with Pavitar and Darhi."

"He realized you'd figured it out," I said. "That you'd seen Gorthaus was the traitor, and she'd tell us all she knew."

"Of course. He needed just a tiny bit of poison, and a needle, or a thorn. Something that would cause only a slight bit of pain, but not enough to cause alarm."

Malo glowered into the coals of the fire. "I should have noticed how she kept rubbing her arm."

"Yet even if you had, it would have done no good," said Ana. "Even a drop of kerel in the blood is fatal. Once the heart swells, all is lost." She shook her head. "The opportunity to catch him is gone as quickly as it came. I doubt if even your nose could find his scent, Malo, if it's been trod upon by so many other guards—true?"

"True enough, ma'am," she admitted. "If I'd been freed at the start, I might have found him. But he has muddied his trails before. Even if I'd leapt after him, I might have been led astray."

"That is so," muttered Ana. "We are helpless once again and can only wait for news." She waved a hand at the window. "Please shut that, Din. The aroma of the nenuphar blossoms in the waters beyond distracts me terribly."

I did so. The only light in the room now was the glow of the fire. I took down a tapestry and cast it over Gorthaus's body, then stood by the door and waited.

EVENTUALLY WE WERE escorted by guard back to the main hall. There we found the prince, Darhi, and Pavitar waiting for us, all looking quite shaken, and accompanied by guards in a wide array of dress and armors. Some even appeared to be wearing sleeping clothes beneath their jerkins. I guessed that the emergency had pulled many off their duties, no matter where or when.

Darhi said, "To my sorrow, we have found no hint of this mysterious guard. All our guards and soldiers and staff have been accounted for, and we have confirmed that at least two people can identify each man as himself. There are no unknown faces here. This poisoner, whoever he was, is now gone."

Ana fumed for a moment. "And the servants?" she demanded.

"We now do the same for them," said Pavitar. "But there are so many more that it shall take some time."

"Naturally, your delegation shall no longer be held," said Prince Camak, "since we know that Kardas, being still bedridden, could not have been the one to poison your signum."

Pavitar stuck his nose in the air, unrepentant despite having been proven so terribly wrong. "Yet I must ask," he said brusquely, "why would someone poison the girl at all? She seemed of no importance to me. The deaths this poisoner has brought about here make no sense."

"Is he a madman, perhaps?" proposed Darhi. "Poisoning at random?"

There was a taut silence. I studied their faces, keenly aware that any of these men might be Pyktis's partner, and thus might know of Gorthaus's treachery, yet their expressions gave me nothing.

"I cannot yet say," said Ana. "But I would like to have all your accounts. For you were all in the castle at the same time as this poisoner, correct? Did you see any sign of anyone unusual?"

"I was alone in the reliquary, sitting vigil with my father," said the prince. "No one passed through that chamber—but then, he would have had no need to. Few come there."

"I was in the great hall, working to convince the nobles to grant your delegation freedom," said Darhi. "I saw no one strange, though I was engaged in deep conversation."

"I spoke to the nobles as well," said Pavitar gruffly, "but I argued to keep them, of course."

"Was that in the great hall, sir?" I asked.

"No. I was in the clerestory, in the floor above. But those rooms are small, and I am sure I saw nothing."

Ana nodded, then sighed. "Then we shall review the guards and servants. Then we must escort our people home, before another falls dead here."

The servants and guards trickled in one by one for Malo and me to review. Their health was shocking, being gaunt and sickened creatures, and their teeth were in a horrid state, if they had them at all. I engraved the faces of each, sniffing at my vial. Darhi had been right: nearly two out of every fifteen was a twin, or even a triplet, with many faces repeating almost exactly, or echoes of their features found in others. I guessed that, given that childbirth was so difficult here in Yarrow, the number would have been even higher if more infants had survived. I also saw what he'd meant about the kings' imperial brides: here and there I spied a hint of Kurmini features, or Rathras, or even Tala, like myself. The experience was quite surreal, to see so much familiar in this strange place.

Yet none resembled Pyktis, or at least the Pyktis I knew from the drawing. None seemed the right height, nor the proper build, nor did any of them obsessively tap their fingers. They were an anxious lot, wary of so much attention, but they seemed innocent.

I watched Malo's face as each one came before her. She sniffed and shook her head each time—*Nothing of note.*

We thanked them for their time, then let them go.

By now it was near morning. The prince, Darhi, and Pavitar escorted us outside, accompanied by some three dozen guards. "What shall we do now?" the prince asked Ana. "Is there nothing you can give us to help us find this man? For he might still be lurking here, somewhere."

"We could give you wardens, Your Majesty, and Apoths," said Ana, "and many practitioners of our arts to crawl throughout your hills and halls and attempt to track him down. Yet I feel you would not take this, sir—true?"

The prince solemnly shook his head. "Would that I could. But many doubt my reign now. If I were to permit the Empire to flood the valley with your people, the outcry would be so great that I would hardly have a kingdom at all at the end of it."

"Of course," sighed Ana. "Even if I could give you his exact description, Your Majesty, even one so precise that it would make identifying him a simple thing . . . well, it may do little good. It seems he is so adept at changing his likeness that he could always appear as someone else entirely. I can give you no more advice than to step with caution, have your food and wine tasted, and do not sleep unguarded. In the meantime, I shall pursue my own inquiries in the city."

"And you shall share what you know?" asked the prince. "You will tell me what you find of this man?"

"Of course, Your Majesty."

"Then I thank you," he said gravely. "If you can give me anything precise, I can call my people to action. But until then, I can do no more than pray for luck and the kind attentions of the fates."

MALO AND I spoke little as we worked with the Yarrows to harness the Treasury horses and lead the shaken axioms from their captivity. Prificto Kardas was now somewhat conscious but still had to be carried out in a sheet, his face dappled with broken blood vessels. Once the Treasury carriages had departed, we loaded into our own and followed.

Still we did not speak. The death of Gorthaus hung over us like a cursed blanket from a folktale, bewitched to bring sickness: both because of the awfulness of her murder and the awareness of how it had robbed us of so many answers.

"Din," said Ana finally. "Tell me all you saw of Darhi's interview. We've not had time to discuss that yet."

I did so as quickly as I could, sniffing at my vials. When I finished, Ana asked, "So Darhi had a very *strong* reaction, Malo, when he was asked about the Treasury negotiations?"

"He did, ma'am," said Malo. "The scent of his sweat changed, and I swear I felt his pulse leap within him. Very strange, I think, to have the negotiator react so when asked a simple question about his negotiations."

"Because, I assume," said Ana softly, "his negotiations are not simple at all. There are secrets there as well, I feel. The question is . . . are they known to Pyktis? Do they matter? Or are they mere ephemera, in this most complex of places? I shall have to think on it."

We rumbled along in silence, with Ana's face turned to the window. For a long while, she did nothing but sit there, hardly breathing. She only shifted once, when she emitted a discomfiting, glottal click from her throat; then another. I wondered if she was so dismayed by our investigation that it quite literally choked her, but I did not think so: this clicking seemed a very different thing.

Then she began to tremble, yet it was strange. The entirety of her

body did not quake, but rather she shook in distinct, isolated seg-
ments: the twitch of a muscle in her shoulder, then the flutter of a
cheek; a quaking in some ligament of her neck, then a quiver in her
thigh. I studied her, this pale, skeletal, shivering figure sitting bent
upon the carriage seat, and for some reason I began to feel distinctly
uneasy. While Ana often did many queer things, I had never seen her
behave like this. Perhaps she truly was unwell from so much exposure
to the wider world.

She finally spoke, yet her voice was again strangely deep and resonant: a different voice entirely, almost. "Did I ever tell you, Din," she
said softly, "of the case of the cooper in Branilin?"

"I don't believe so, ma'am."

"It was an investigation I consulted on, some years ago," Ana
continued, still in that queer, deep voice. "Three young boys murdered in the countryside there, over the course of six months. They
were found lying in open fields, spoiled and sullied. They were from
different homes, found in different places, taken at different times.
No one could make any sense of it—until a *fourth* boy was found,
bricked up in the wall of an old house, his body dashed with lye.
And so we wondered—why was this one treated differently? Why
would the killer work so hard to hide him? But then, the answer was
obvious . . ."

The rumble of the wheels. The shiver of the trees against the
dark sky.

"Because the killer was familiar with him," I said.

"Exactly," said Ana. "The killer had a *personal connection* to that
one, so he felt compelled to hide him deeper. Once we knew this, we
found the killer quickly—the dead child's uncle, a lowly cooper, whose
mind was corrupted beyond description." She leaned back in her carriage seat. "I do not know why Pyktis has chosen to kill the king.
But . . . he has worked very *hard* to obscure his movements about this
deed, has he not? No one knows how the poison got in that cup. No
one has seen any hint of the man in those halls. He even made himself vulnerable, emerging from the shadows to poison Gorthaus. So
much effort! Which makes me wonder, for this one . . ."

"If Sunus Pyktis has a personal connection . . . to the king of Yarrow?" asked Malo.

"It may be so," whispered Ana. "It may indeed be so."

The mai-lamps shuddered outside as we made a turn, and then the beryl-tinted lights of Yarrowdale congealed in the distant darkness.

"When we return to the city," said Ana, "I want you both to go through every possession Gorthaus ever touched, be it in a vault or in her chambers. Perhaps there is some clue as to where our six crates of poisonous reagents now lie."

"What shall you do in the meantime, ma'am?" I asked. "Is there any report or meal or aid I can give you?"

A gleam of her smile in the dark. "A kind thought, Din. But no. I will wait for Kardas to awake. Then I will summon you both . . . and Thelenai. For I shall have much to discuss with all of you about the path ahead—which only narrows, I feel, toward most unpleasant places."

CHAPTER 39

∧ ∧ ∧

IT WAS BARELY MORNING BY NOW, BUT THE TREASURY bank was already open and serving its many customers. Malo and I discovered that Gorthaus had kept only the one vault in her personal name—Signum Tufwa, the engraver there, sniffily told us that all imperial clients were restricted in this manner to avoid fraud—yet all we found within was some rather mundane jewelry, documents and sigils of transport, and letters from her family. No matter how Malo sniffed or squinted at any of it, none of it seemed of import.

Abandoning this, we returned to the leaning tower in Old Town and searched her quarters. Like those of most engravers, her room was spare, neat, and tidy: there was her pikis on the windowsill full of tinctures, her trunk of clothing in the corner, a poche hanging from the door containing a handful of talints, and a bottle of kir-mite eggs for the cleaning of clothes.

For a moment we just gazed about, taking in the space. Then my eye fell upon a handful of scratches in the stone floor, just before the corners of a small bookcase beside her bed.

I pointed to it. Malo cocked an eye and said, "It can't be that easy."

We pulled the bookcase away and found a loose stone in the base of the floor just behind it; then, below that, a small parchment package tied up with twine. Malo's knife was out in a flash, and she plucked out the package and slit it open, sending dozens of small gold coins spilling upon the floor.

"Perhaps it is," I said. "An amateurish choice, really."

Malo sighed. "She was no hard thing," she said. "Perhaps we should not be so surprised."

I quickly counted up the coins. "This comes to . . . three hundred talints? She betrayed the Empire and risked the noose for the price of a fine horse, and no more?"

Malo picked up a coin and eyed it. "That, or your immunis was right—once she'd made one deal, they had enough to blackmail her into more service. Which makes sense. They often favor threats above gifts."

"They? Criminals, you mean?"

"No." She handed the coin back to me. "Kings, and those who rule with them. But perhaps there is little difference between the natures of such men and criminals."

We continued our search but found nothing to indicate who Pyktis's agent at the High Court might be, nor where Pyktis himself was now, nor where the six crates of reagents might be stored. Perhaps it was the fatigue, but my heart grew heavier the more we searched, still finding nothing.

Finally an Apoth militis came to us with a message that Prificto Kardas was now awake, and he, Thelenai, and Ana awaited us in the medikker's ward. Malo and I trooped back downstairs, both of us yawning and desperately tired, and wound our way back through the muddy streets of Yarrowdale.

WHEN WE ARRIVED at Kardas's chambers we found that the prificto was, thankfully, no longer in the milky tides of a healing bath but was instead lying in his medikker's cradle, chatting amiably with Ana, who sat beside him. Thelenai stood behind her own chair, apparently too anxious to sit. With her queenly bearing and long, red robes, she had in this place the look of a priestess of a flagellamer's shrine, waiting to take confession before the penitent submitted to their pains.

Kardas looked up when we entered—his face still bore a few broken blood vessels, but other than that he seemed quite recovered—

and, smiling, said, "Ah! Here are the brave signums! I suppose I owe you my life for rescuing me from the debacle in the High City, true?"

I looked to Ana, surprised by his good spirits. "He doesn't know?"

"He does not," said Ana. "I wished to wait for you."

"Know?" said Kardas, puzzled. "Know . . . what?"

"Apparently anything," muttered Malo as she sat along the edge of the wall.

"I take it from the melancholy timbre of your voices, children," said Ana, "that you've found nothing?"

"No, ma'am," I said. "Nothing of use."

"Hm. As expected."

"What do you mean, found nothing?" said Kardas. "What are you talking about?"

Ana then gave him the full report of the night in the High City, including Gorthaus's death, of which he'd heard no news. Kardas reacted so violently that I worried for his health: the man's face went perilously white, and his entire body began to tremble. When Ana finally revealed Gorthaus's full betrayal, I feared he might collapse again.

"By hell . . ." said Kardas weakly at the end of it. "Oh, by Sanctum, my signum did *all that*?"

"If it's any consolation, sir, she'd begun this evil service well before you were assigned here," said Ana. "But yes, it is so. I grieve for her death—chiefly, I admit, because I wished to get more answers from her. And now, as Din here says, she left none behind."

"This is horrifying news," said Thelenai softly. "Another attack, another loss. How now can we stop Pyktis?"

"We still have options," said Ana. "Before we explore some of the most radical choices, I wish to ask something of you, Prificto. I am convinced there is an agent at the court who was aiding Pyktis in all his evil—either one we know, or one still unseen. Is there anyone or any strangeness you can recall in all your exchanges with the Yarrow court that might suggest who this traitor is?"

Kardas shook his head, his long mustaches swishing about. "No, no. I cannot think of any such thing. My emitias abilities read much, but in such heightened, difficult circumstances, where many are filled with anger and distrust, it is a hard thing to spy any one moment worthy of suspicion."

"And there is no person who spent an *unusual* amount of time with Gorthaus?"

"Not that I saw. Pavitar was ever present, for he distrusted all we did, and forced his way in to all our meetings. Darhi, of course, managed most of those same meetings for us. The king and his people and the prince were often about. But none of them stand out to me as a conspirator who could be aiding this creature."

"Mm," said Ana softly. "And you cannot conceive of how Pyktis was able to move about the court unseen, unnoticed, and kill not only Gorthaus but also the king, and nearly yourself?"

"That horrifies me most of all, for I cannot imagine how it was done."

"I see," said Ana. She bowed her head. "So we've nothing, for the moment. Nothing save a dead girl, who has left not a trace of a trail to her killer."

There was a long, uncomfortable silence. Then Ana sat up and brightly said, "Well! What about your negotiations with the Yarrow court, Prificto?"

"What of them?" said Kardas.

"Well, I worry they might be influencing Pyktis's actions. Is it possible he knows of them?"

"I can't imagine there is much to know. We have been stalled for weeks now. Though we continue to advocate for the adoption of Yarrow, and the fulfillment of our ancient contracts, there is little progress to spy upon. I thought this situation was known to you, Dolabra."

"Hm!" said Ana. She smiled politely. "But I must admit, sir . . . I no longer think what you say is true."

Kardas narrowed his eyes at her. "What do you mean?"

"I mean that while you and the court have been all too content to tell everyone you've done *nothing* here," said Ana, "in secret, I believe there has been another set of negotiations going on. One even Signum Gorthaus did not know of."

Kardas's features remained fixed in an expression of charismatic confusion, yet he stayed silent.

"What do you mean, Dolabra?" asked Thelenai softly.

"I propose, ma'am, that the Treasury knows much more than they let on," said Ana. "For example—you *knew* about this project to extract the titan's marrow, didn't you, sir?"

Kardas said nothing.

"I think you also knew that Thelenai's people had succeeded in this feat," continued Ana. "And if that was so, well . . . obviously, the Empire doesn't really *need* to be in Yarrow at all anymore, do we? With the marrow secured, we could develop many methods of creating all the titan's blood we need, deep in the safety of the inner rings. No more Shroud, no more canals, no more barges." She scratched her chin. "So . . . you weren't negotiating the final imperial *adoption* of the realm of Yarrow, were you? You were secretly negotiating our *withdrawal* from this place."

There was a stunned silence.

"Wh-what?" said Malo. She gazed at Kardas in outrage. "You were *what*?"

"Is this so, Prificto?" demanded Thelenai.

Kardas glanced around the room at us, then sighed so deeply he seemed to deflate. "Yes. Fine! Yes, I confess, it is so."

"You pursued this *without* informing we Apoths?" Thelenai asked.

"Again, yes," said Kardas heavily.

"But you'd . . . you'd truly leave?" asked Malo. "The Empire would just *leave* us here? Why?"

"Oh, for a very simple reason!" said Kardas bitterly. "It is because the folk of Yarrow do not *want* us here! They do not *want* to be part of the Empire. And if that is so, then there is no cause for us to stay!"

For a moment we all reeled in shock; save, of course, for Ana, who patiently waited for us to catch up.

"We're *giving up,* sir?" I said, astounded, for never had I heard of such an imperial retreat. "We're abandoning the adoption of this realm?"

"We are, Signum Kol," said Kardas. "There are many throughout the Empire who assumed we'd simply take the realm, if negotiations stalled. But that is . . . well, it's simply not what we *do* anymore!"

"Why not?" demanded Malo. "Does the Empire no longer behave as an empire?"

"No!" said Kardas. "We don't! We *can't*! Because while the Empire is prosperous, it is also *brittle*. We hold back the leviathans, yet our populations decline. And our dwindling people are satisfied and stationary. They do not *want* to seize other lands, for there is hardly a need for such a thing! It is not like we'd derive much wealth or security from the mere act of conquering! Our people know this and are unwilling to devote money and lives to dabble in such vanities. Even if we didn't have the marrow, we were always going to delay the adoption!"

"How so?" asked Ana, suddenly interested.

Kardas shrugged feebly. "Extend the deadline for a decade. Maybe two. Dump another trove of gold on the High City. Buy time, quite literally. It would be a fraction of the cost of sending the Legion here and trying to hold it! Yet better still would be to simply walk away— which we could do, if we had the marrow. For then we'd no longer need the Shroud, or Yarrowdale itself, or any of these delicate things that cost so much to defend."

"And the *naukari*?" asked Malo, her voice deadly soft. "What of them? Would you leave them to their fates, after promising to end such an evil practice?"

The prificto shifted uncomfortably. "If I could banish all the evils of the world, child, know I would do it. But it is not our purpose to wade into the affairs of other cultures and scold them into decency."

Malo bowed her head until her red cloak hid her face.

"Who was the primary negotiator for the court of Yarrow?" asked Ana.

"Satrap Darhi, of course," sighed Kardas. "He has been managing these secret talks this entire time. He does not know we plan to leave, however! He thinks we merely wish to delay the adoption and pay a fortune for the privilege of doing so. Darhi kept this a secret from the rest of the Yarrow court, for many nobles don't want the contract extended at all! Yet I was *also* to insert a clause stating that if we ceased our payments, we would be forced to begin withdrawals immediately. Darhi believed this was a punitive arrangement—yet for us, it was always a *goal*. We stop paying, and then we go."

"Only if the marrow is secured, however," said Thelenai, her voice quiet and cold.

"True," said Kardas.

She shut her eyes and shouted, "But . . . but by hell, Kardas . . . *By hell!*"

It was a rare emotional outburst from the commander-prificto, so much so that all eyes turned to her.

"You thought you worked toward protecting the Empire, perhaps," Thelenai cried, "but so focused were you that you've weakened it even *more*! Your damned signum is the one who helped Pyktis get those reagents and put the marrow in such danger! And now it is in no way secure, and we grow desperate!"

She stood there, hands pressed to her sides, eyes shut and her face trembling.

"What might you mean by that?" asked Ana. "How desperate?"

Thelenai grabbed a small stool and sat, legs quaking. "I have my own ill news to share," she said hoarsely. "For we mean to move the marrow, to get it out of this dangerous place. And damned soon at that."

"*MOVE* THE MARROW?" asked Ana, aghast. "Move it how? You don't mean up the canals? Not with Pyktis still lurking about?"

Thelenai laughed, a deep, melancholy sound. "No! Yarrowdale is not safe, and we will not wait and let it grow even less so. Instead, we have been laboring to secure the marrow for *another* voyage, one that is far more treacherous—not upriver, but east, across the ocean to the mouth of the Great River Asigis, and thence into the inner rings. We shall skip the canals altogether and float the marrow to safety that way."

"Is such an ocean voyage even possible, ma'am?" I asked.

A bleak smile. "We hope it is so. The marrow is far smaller than a leviathan's carcass, and easier to transport. It is safer than staying at the Shroud, which Pyktis could attack at any moment, and far safer than the canals! But it will take all the wit and art of my people to move it, and countless valuable resources. And even then, it is no certain thing." She shook her head. "How I lament now all the Treasury's maneuverings! I can hardly think of a blacker time in all my career."

Kardas looked away, ashamed.

"But let us recall, ma'am," said Ana, quietly yet curtly, "that it wasn't the Treasury who created Pyktis, who is the source of all this peril."

Thelenai closed her eyes. "So I remember. None of us are free of guilt here."

"Yes," said Ana. She cast her head back, her sightless face turned to the ceiling. "But we must consider what to do now."

"We move the marrow," said Thelenai. "With all due haste. That is all we can do, surely."

"Perhaps. But I would like to see if you and I could retreat to a private place, ma'am, to discuss something else. An even more unpleasant matter on this most unpleasant of nights. Though the murders of the High City are but hours old, many paths there now seem closed to us. So . . . we must resort to the radical options I mentioned, and hope to win wisdom there."

Thelenai nodded. "I see. We should withdraw to my offices, then. For though I am no augur, I feel I know what you are about to ask of me, Dolabra. Come."

I stood to guide Ana but glanced at Malo, confused, as Ana had not mentioned any such revelation; yet Malo's face was still hidden behind her cloak, and it remained so throughout our winding journey through the Apoth works.

CHAPTER 40

∧∧∧

ANA HAD ONCE REMARKED TO ME THAT AN APOTH OFFI-
cer gathers specimens like a hog might collect burs in the forest, and
indeed, Commander-Prificto Thelenai's office was no exception:
though hers was a stately chamber, with a high fretvine ceiling and
teardrop mai-lamps hanging about the oval windows, much of the
walls were consumed by hanging pots and trellises, each containing a
flower, vine, or shrub. Though it was too dark by now for me to make
much out beyond the riot of stem and leaf, the room was so redolent
with aromas and fragrances that I could tell each little plant received
a great deal of care.

"I apologize for the state of things," Thelenai said absently as she
fetched pillows for us to sit on the floor: the traditional Rathras
method of seating. "This place mostly acts as a nursery for my courtyard garden, where I nudge the little ones along before being
planted . . ."

I guided Ana to her pillow, and then Malo and I sat on our own.
Thelenai gracefully rearranged her robes: again, the Rathras method
of swooping the skirts forward, sitting with one's arms out, and then
folding the fabric of the arms in the lap. It was quite a production,
especially on a person so tall as she. "How shall we begin, Immunis?"

"With where our story begins, I think," purred Ana. "With Sunus
Pyktis. I would like to tell you all we have collected of him—and I
hope these comments shall spark some memory in your mind,
Commander-Prificto."

Thelenai nodded, her bald pate gleaming blue like a new moon. I touched Ana gently, indicating she could proceed.

"We know, of course, of the tragedy that occurred on the Shroud in 1127," Ana began. "The one that supposedly killed Pyktis to begin with. Your augurs were to enter and explore the carcass of a leviathan, and though their warding suits had been cleaned and prepared most thoroughly, somehow a dusting of pollen came to be on one of them. The pollen met the *kani,* the titan's blood, and reacted. The *kani* then found the flesh of the augur within. And thus, all was lost."

"The greatest catastrophe in the history of the Shroud," said Thelenai softly. "It might have consumed the structure itself, had not the envelope of the Shroud itself sensed the contagion and contained it."

"Yes," said Ana. "How Pyktis survived this, we do not know—but I now believe I know where he went immediately after his survival. I believe he went to the High City of Yarrow."

"You have evidence for this?" asked Thelenai.

"I have testimony," said Ana. "And guesswork. One of the smugglers told us that during their first meetings, Pyktis brought a great deal of money to his clan, seeking to buy their favor. But how could he get such a thing, unless he'd fetched it from the High City first? Which meant he'd met with his agent there before ever becoming the pale king of the swamps, as he later became known. But it is quite a leap from catastrophe to castle, is it not? In fact, it brings up all manner of *practical* questions—namely, how in hell did Pyktis even manage such a maneuvering? Imagine this figure, staggering ashore after his escape from the Shroud. How could he—stranded, with no resources—get to the High City? Most imperials do not even know such a place exists! And even if he *could* get to the High City, how could he secure an audience with a court official who had access to such funds, and convince this person to lend them to him? I mean, this man is a Rathras axiom! Could he even *speak* the Pithian tongue? Perhaps with his augmented mind, Pyktis could do such a thing. But it still leaves much unanswered."

Thelenai blinked her large, dark eyes. "I agree," she said softly. "But I have no answers to give you here."

"Unfortunate!" said Ana. "But expected. Yet a deeper question awaits—why do *any of it*?"

"Why?" echoed Thelenai.

"Yes. Why leap to consort with smugglers and Yarrow nobles? Why become the murderer among the canals? Why did he so steadfastly set himself against us?"

"I . . . I assumed he hated us," said Thelenai. "For what I had put him through. His brush with death, and the many burdens of his duty."

Ana grinned madly. "I think otherwise, ma'am. He has moved too quickly for that. Indeed, I do not think the disaster upon the Shroud in 1127 was an accident. Nor was it solely intended to fabricate Pyktis's death—rather, I believe it was an attempt to destroy *the entire Shroud*—yet he failed in doing so. And when he washed ashore in the realm of Yarrow, I believe he immediately began plotting how to attempt this *again*. To complete this attack, he needed *kani*, the titan's blood. To attain that, he needed reagents. To get those, he needed smugglers. To secure their allegiance, he needed money and allies— one agent in the High City, and another in Yarrowdale." She waved a hand. "A simple enough chain. And it has worked perfectly thus far, I must admit! But now, he is executing his final stages . . . and to ensure that all goes as he plans, I think he is eliminating all his allies, one by one, so they cannot betray him."

"You mean . . . the smugglers in the jungle," said Thelenai. "And . . . and the king of Yarrow . . . ?"

"The smugglers I am sure of," said Ana. "The king, less so, for I have many questions there. I do not even know how he managed it, to be frank!" She sighed. "I think most on what Malo once told us . . . Din, kindly recount her words regarding how Pyktis may fashion a new face for himself!"

My eyes shimmered, and I spoke: "*He has some tools, yes, but not enough to grant him an entirely* new *face. He cannot change his bones, for example—so he will be mostly the same size and shape. He could alter his skin color, but it would only last a few weeks, for, being a Sublime, it would eventually revert to gray. But he could thicken himself somewhat or purge himself of fats. Or he could add hair to his flesh or remove it. Small changes, really."*

Malo scowled at me. "How I dislike your impression of my words."

"Thus, we come to it," said Ana. "We know much of Pyktis and his movements. And yet we still know nothing! We do not know what form he has woven about himself. We do not even know *why* he so wishes to destroy the Shroud." Her head twitched toward Thelenai. "Thus . . . we must speak to those who know *more*. Do you understand, ma'am?"

A cold needle stabbed into my heart at that. I suddenly felt my flesh crawling with sweat. "Pardon?" I asked, softly.

"Yes," said Thelenai. "You wish for your signum here to go to the Shroud now and consult with the augurs."

"Indeed," said Ana.

"Oh, shit," said Malo.

"AHH—PARDON?" I said again.

"It is the only way, Din," said Ana gently. "We know now that Pyktis has been planning all this for years. He has controlled his own story at every step, with lie after lie. A masterful performance, truly! But the truth comes out in moments of extreme stress—and the Shroud is a *terribly* stressful place, is it not?"

"True," said Thelenai heavily. "And we do have many ships breaking the containment there now, for we must bring many resources there to prepare the marrow for its journey. One of them could ferry the boy across the bay."

"As I hoped," said Ana. "But I wish for Din to do more than simply speak to the augurs—I wish him to inspect the marrow itself, and all you prepare for it."

"I'm sorry—*pardon*?" I said, my voice now hardly more than a whisper.

"That is a heavy ask, Dolabra," said Thelenai. "The marrow is our greatest prize. The odds of us securing one again are so small it plagues my dreams."

"I sympathize," said Ana. "But I am plagued as well—namely by a question ... Why hasn't Pyktis attacked *yet*? He has possessed these poisonous reagents and known of the marrow's location for some time now. Why delay so long that we become aware of him? Unless his attack has *already been made*, and we do not know it."

"That is not possible," said Thelenai lowly. "We inspect all we receive."

"But this is Pyktis," said Ana. "And thus, I worry."

Thelenai meditated on this, her face wan. Then she whispered, "All right. I shall make it so. Yet we have never let an engraver within the Shroud, and certainly never allowed one to glimpse our greatest treasures. It is against policy. Policy can be waived in an emergency, but engravers may still be fragile in such a place. Such memories lie differently within the mind. It will require a different formula of soothings and grafts to calibrate him."

"You're going to ... to alter my moods, ma'am?" I asked.

She laughed lightly. "Of course! Almost all who go there receive such treatments. Yet I have never done so for an engraver ..."

"May I assist, ma'am?" asked Ana. "For I must have all of his memories to do my work."

"Certainly," said Thelenai wearily. "I would welcome such help ..."

She offered Ana an arm, and together they went to her desk on the far side of the room to plot my fate.

I SAT ON MY PILLOW, dazed and horrified. It was not the first time my duties had required me to go to unholy places, yet the Shroud was another thing entirely. The sea walls of the East were dangerous once a season; the Shroud was a dangerous thing at every hour of every day of the year, like a dreadful chrysalis always threatening to hatch. And here I was, set to go traipsing within the guts of the thing, the marrow perhaps sleeping just beneath each footfall.

"Feeling doomed, Kol?" asked Malo beside me.

"Yes," I said faintly. "You know, I rather am."

A bitter laugh. "At least if the Shroud kills you, your death will be quick. Others will have to wait and dread ours before it finally falls."

I frowned a bit, then realized what she meant. "I'm sorry," I said. "I didn't know what the Treasury planned for . . . for Yarrow."

She grunted but said nothing.

"Surely they won't abandon you here?" I asked. "You're an Apoth signum, after all."

"Will they? I do not know. I am not a citizen of the Empire. And even if they did get me out, where would I go? I've never been beyond the borders of these fetid swamps. But this pain feels small, knowing how many others will be damned to useless toil on the land of some noble or another, for all their miserable lives."

"I can't imagine what it's like, to have this glimmer of hope, and then have it so quickly smothered."

"I can," muttered Malo.

I glanced at her. "Were you one of them once?" I asked. "A *naukari*?"

She debated answering, then shrugged. "As were many."

"Did you run away?"

"Do you really want to know?"

"Only if you wish to tell me."

She was silent for a long moment. "I did not flee. I was freed. But . . . such an act came at a cost." She looked back at the window and the slice of the moon shining through. "I have seen only three oathcoins in all my life, Kol. The second was the one you have now in your pocket. The third was the one we discovered in Pyktis's den. But the first . . . it was when a boy I toiled alongside saved the life of our lord. Lord Prabhu di Gudia was the nobleman's name. A lover of horses but a terrible horseman. He was thrown from his steed and broke his arm in a ditch. The bone cut through a vein, and he could have bled out—had not young Dokha leapt into the ditch, tied off the wound with his belt, thrown the lord over his shoulders, and run him back to his ancestral house. He saved his lord's life, and for this act, Dokha was granted an oathcoin, passed down from the king through many lords.

"But there is a silent agreement of how oathcoins work. You return it to the man who gave it to you for a favor. You *could* go above him, to a higher lord or even the king—but only if the need is great, and the favor does not bring insult. Otherwise, you would be in tremendous peril. But Dokha . . . he was a very good boy. Very selfless, you see."

"He asked for your freedom?" I guessed.

"He did," said Malo. "The freedom of all the *naukari* who were below the age of ten. And they made us watch as they killed him for it. Struck his head from his shoulders as if it were a piece of clay, then sank his corpse to the bottom of one of our holy lakes."

"That's horrible," I said softly.

"Yes. But that is what it takes to break so much tradition, so much old power. Yet do you know what saddens my heart most, Kol? It is not that Dokha died so, though I grant that is a horror. It is how my folk so eagerly cling to the poisoned relics of throne and chain. They would gladly die clinging to them and proclaim it salvation." She plucked a leaf off a plant and kneaded it between her fingers. "So. You will leave, as any wise people would. We will stay here, ruled by the king and the nobles. Those who once served the Empire will be hunted, I expect. And things shall stay the same—or grow even worse. Maybe I will go into the swamp and live as one of those people. I could find a use for my nose and eyes there, at least."

I gazed at Ana and Thelenai, murmuring at her desk on the other side of her chambers. "What if . . . what if I could get you out?" I asked.

"Out? To where?"

"To somewhere else in the Empire."

Malo grunted. "Are such powers available to a signum?"

"I have no control over the Apoths, but . . . I could ask Ana. You could transfer, perhaps, to the Iudex, who could then assign you to other duties deeper in the Empire. The Empire makes it easy to be-come a citizen, for so many cantons decline in population—but you must be on its soil to do so."

"Do you know of what you speak?" she demanded. "Have you done this before?"

"No," I confessed. "But . . . it could be tried, yes?"

She thought it over. "Would I have to serve under Ana, to do this?"

"Oh, no. She is . . . not easy to serve, and she only ever has one assistant. Why do you ask?"

"Well. She is brilliant, I suppose, but . . ." She shuddered. "I con-fess, there is a strange scent to that woman sometimes. One I don't quite know. It troubles me. You can ask her, if you like. But to me, your plans taste like the fantasies of a young man, attempting to invent a way out. We are small things, Kol. We are given no charity in this world." She gave me a sad smile. "But I thank you for thinking of me, even when your own fate takes such a black turn."

CHAPTER 41

...

ONCE ANA AND THELENAI HAD DECIDED ON HOW TO maintain me during my trip to the Shroud, I bade farewell to Malo and was herded downstairs, then through the many winding passageways of the Apoth manufactuaries, until we returned to the fermentation works. Thelenai brought us to an unusual chamber, wrought of rippling gray wood that formed a curving, rib-cage-like ceiling above us. Set in the middle of the room were many tables, bedecked with vials and pots and casks with little copper spigots.

Yet I recognized the structures at the back of the room: tiny cells with a large glass wall and a slot for food; within each one, a cot and a floor with a drain in the middle; and above these, many pipes, for showering the occupant with solutions.

"We will have to keep Kol here under observation until the time of departure," said Thelenai. She swooped to one table and rapidly began assembling many cups and pots. She slid out six little copper flasks, all tightly secured with screwed tops. Then she produced a pair of tweezers and began plucking out tiny pellets and pills from the flasks and placing them in six bronze cups on the table. "But I do not wish to give you the impression that I have not prepared for this day at all," she continued. "For I *have* identified two individuals now serving on the Shroud who worked with Pyktis."

I led Ana to a chair set to the side. "Two augurs?" said Ana. "Only two?"

"We were lucky to get those," said Thelenai. "Augurs usually serve in three-year shifts, at most. Any more than that, and they begin to experience debilitating apophenia and paranoia. As it has been two years since he left, almost all of Pyktis's former colleagues are now gone, save these. But there will be more restrictions here . . . for you shall only get two hours to speak to them."

"Why?" asked Ana. "We often interview for much longer."

"Because the Shroud is a clean site in many manners," said Thelenai, dropping another pellet into a cup with her tweezers, "but it is also *intellectually* clean. The augurs are by nature driven to ingest information and relentlessly analyze it. When we give them too much stimulation, it distracts them—often to disastrous effects, given their work. Thus, the Shroud is as bare of incitement as we can manage."

I cleared my throat—I had not spoken in what felt like hours—and said, "You want them focused on the leviathans, ma'am, and not on me."

"Correct," said Thelenai. "But they *will* be focused on you, Kol. They are starved for information, so you shall be rather like a mouse dropped within a den of cats. That is why your interview must only last two hours. And that is why I am preparing you this draught." She muddled the contents of one cup, then took it to one of the casks, turned the spigot, and filled it with a creamy substance. "It is of tinis, katapra, and dosi."

The names lit up memories in my mind. "Mood stabilizers," I said. "Far more powerful than what they give the Legionnaires at the walls."

"Yes, and for many reasons." Thelenai stirred the creamy cup with a long spoon. "For the augurs see much, and they are skilled at enticing people to reveal what they would prefer to hide." She tapped the spoon on the edge of the cup, shaking off a few milky drops. Then she advanced on me, cup balanced in her fingertips like a priestess administering a holy balm. "This graft will suppress your ability to emotionally react—to anything. I am hopeful it will not only aid you in the Shroud but keep you from saying too much before the augurs.

Still, I must be clear ... do *not* answer any of their questions. You are only to *ask* questions. Is that clear?"

"It is, ma'am," I said.

"Good," said Thelenai. "They will doubtlessly tell you this at the Shroud, but another thing you must also avoid is doing *any* tapping, or making any music in any way. If you create any kind of rhythm, their minds will try to analyze it, even if there is nothing to be found. It often irritates them to the point of fury. Is that understood?"

"Yes, ma'am."

"Immunis Ghrelin will have to consume some augury himself to interpret their tapping for you. That is the exact procedure I have him going through now, for this is no easy thing. He will *change* as he enters the veil, Kol. He may be less reliable than you expect. Is this clear as well?"

I nodded.

She handed me the cup. "Then drink this, please. It will take some time for it to affect you. I wished to avoid the sudden, thundering high, followed by the crash after ..."

A soft "Mm" from Ana, as if revisiting a favored memory.

Thelenai watched me swallow. The grafts bubbled away in me until I felt my legs growing wobbly, and I sat on the floor.

"An easy start, I hope," said Thelenai. Her eyes grew slightly sad. "But is it still salvageable, I wonder?" she asked aloud softly.

"Pardon, ma'am?" said Ana.

"We take great risks now, but ... I worry you shall not find him in time, Dolabra. Perhaps I shall be forever stained as the imperial servant who came so close to securing a better future for our people, only to lose it all at the last moment."

The lamps of the chamber seemed to grow brighter to me, and the darks darker, until it seemed like Thelenai was a bright, burning, crimson icon, standing over me as if to grant a benediction; and there behind her, a hunched, shadowy figure, black and watchful, teeth glinting in the shadows.

"I cannot yet say," said Ana's voice. "But in some ways, you are already stained, ma'am—are you not?"

"What?" said Thelenai.

"Gorthaus did betray us, true. But again, it was your works that created the devil that tempted her. Even if I were to perform some miracle and save all you treasure, the deaths of those Apoths—members of your own Iyalet!—would still hang upon your name. Is that not so?"

The tall, crimson form of Thelenai bent very slightly. Then she poured a cup and said in a high, quavering voice, "Another dose for you, Kol."

CHAPTER 42

▲ ▲ ▲

ONCE I'D CONSUMED THE GRAFTS, I WAS STRIPPED YET again, taken to one of their observation chambers, and washed. Then we waited, I sitting there on the floor of the chamber, no more than a blanket to veil my form, and Ana hunched and blindfolded on the other side of the glass.

"Fourteen hours until your departure," she muttered. "Unless my math has gone awry . . . Are you still well, Din?"

I gave a vaguely affirmative grunt.

"Not feeling a great gust of high spirits yet?" she asked, grinning. "Perhaps once this is done, I'll let you try katapra pure. It can make for a very giggly day."

I gave another grunt, this one far more hostile as the potions in my belly began to affect me. There was the abrupt hypersensitivity of various body parts: a nipple suddenly flaring hot, then the back of one thigh tingly and cold; and, inevitably, the pounding headache, though this one felt chilled and foggy, like a stone from the bottom of a mountain river. The only thing I could feel with any great awareness was the powerful itch of the blotley welt upon the flesh of my arm, which irritated me so much that I couldn't stop scratching it.

Ana sat up. "Boy—what are you doing there? I can hear you fuss with something. What is it?"

"The blotley sting, ma'am," I said resentfully.

"What about it?"

"It pains me still."

She cocked her head. "*Does* it? Despite all the healing treatments you've received since the creature was applied to you?"

I grunted vaguely.

Ana paused for a very long while, her head crooked on her shoulders. Then she asked, "Tell me, child—how large is this welt? Is it about . . . about the size of a talint coin, say?"

"I would suppose so. Perhaps smaller, ma'am."

"How fascinating," she whispered. "How *fascinating*. Sometimes the smallest thing can sometimes prove to be of greatest importance . . ."

I grunted again.

"Hm! You seem rather bitter about this whole thing, Din," she said. "Usually you're very prim and proper in your speech."

"Perhaps it's on account of that you're on that side of the glass, ma'am, fully clothed," I muttered, "and I am here on the other, and am not."

"Maybe so! But I feel there is something else on your mind. Speak, boy! Speak at will."

I glowered at her, pulled my blanket tight about me, and said, "It's the wardens, ma'am. I find it hard to tolerate the idea of abandoning them here, after they've served us so. I proposed to Malo the thought of transferring them to the Iudex to reassign them elsewhere . . ."

"Did you?" Ana said, bemused. "I did not think you such a deft bureaucratic navigator, boy."

"But Malo doubted if this would work," I said. "And I understand why. For . . . the Empire has not always proven willing to allow its people to serve it, or serve it to the best of their powers—even if they may fervently wish to."

Ana arched her eyebrows at that. "Ohh? Am I to believe, Din, that you now compare your own struggles with those wardens and *naukari* of Yarrow? That your own stymied hopes of transferring to the Legion make you akin to abandoned warriors and entrapped slaves? That's really rather rich, isn't it?"

"I made no such comparison," I said, blushing.

"No, but the sketch of it is there, under the paint." She rested her chin in the palm of her hand. "Regarding the wardens and the *naukari*, I personally find the situation reprehensible. But good governance is about choosing the *least bad* option. Invading and holding Yarrow, well . . . is not that. Yet do not despair! There may be options less foul than the ones now presented to us. But as to your own predicament . . ." She sighed. "You still yearn for the blacks of the Legion, and the sea walls—don't you? That is where you plan to be, at the end of all this."

I said nothing.

"Was where we left it not agreeable to you?" she asked. "I told you I'd recommend you to the Legion myself, when the time came."

I wondered what to say. Yet she had asked me to speak, and speak I would.

"But . . . I won't be able to do so," I said softly. "My father left too many debts, ma'am. And the Legion is far too perilous, you see."

"Ahh. So—your creditors will call in your debts if they think you risk your life too cavalierly?"

"Yes."

"Hm." She sniffed and drummed her knees. "Hm. Would the people who possess all your debts be the Usini Lending Group, Din?"

"Yes," I said, startled. "How did y—"

"I am aware of them," she said archly. "Another question, Din—have you been approached here by a representative of the Usini Lending Group? Perhaps one intending to use your stationing to this dangerous canton as an excuse to alter your loans to a ruinous arrangement?"

I hesitated.

"A yes, then. Hmm!" she said. "Fascinating. Now, one final question." One long finger tapped her cheek. "Back in Talagray . . . was it a girl? Or a boy, perhaps? I am merely curious, you see."

I watched her guardedly. "What do you mean?"

"I mean the person you left behind there, of course. For I know you are a sentimental sort, Din. Someone made an impression on you, so much so that you are drawn back to that place. True?"

I swallowed, stung. "There . . . was a man, yes. But that is not why I wish to serve there and be counted among the Legion."

"Oh? Then why?"

I sighed and spread my hands. "How can I live knowing that he and thousands like him expose themselves to such danger each day? Why should I be one of the folk they save each year? I wish to save lives in my service, ma'am, and be put to tasks that are much ..." I trailed off, unsure what to say.

"More important?" she suggested.

I stayed silent.

She chuckled lowly. "Oh, child ... are you not aware you are about to be sent to perhaps the *second* most dangerous site in the Empire? All because some wretched villain threatens the very foundations of our civilization? Do you *truly* claim these tasks are so insignificant?"

My face grew hot, and I turned away.

"Oh, no," she said, sighing. "I do not mean to mock you, Din. For I understand. Justice is not a terribly *satisfying* task, is it? The Engineer can see a bridge span a river, and marvel at what they made. The Legionnaire can look upon the carcass of a leviathan, and know they've saved countless lives. And the Apoth can watch a body mend and heal and change, and smile. But the Iudex ... we are not granted such favors."

She leaned closer to the glass. "This work can never satisfy, Din, for it can never finish. The dead cannot be restored. Vice and bribery will never be totally banished from the cantons. And the drop of corruption that lies within every society shall always persist. The duty of the Iudex is not to boldly vanquish it but to *manage* it. We keep the stain from spreading, yes, but it is never gone. Yet this job is perhaps the most important in all the Iyalets, for without it, well ... the Empire would come to look much like Yarrow, where the powerful and the cruel prevail without check. And tell me—does *that* realm look capable of fighting off a leviathan?"

"No," I said softly. "But we have the gentry, and many powerful folk in the inner rings. We have our own lords and nobles and kings, don't we?"

Her pale face shot closer to the glass. "Perhaps! But recall, boy," she hissed, grinning savagely, "that I traveled to your tiny canton specifically to entrap the *most* powerful, *most* corrupt gentryclan in all the Empire—and we did it! We broke their backs, and they *stayed* broken! And oh, how that deed warms my heart still!"

I fell silent, abashed.

Ana withdrew. All warmth and sympathy was gone from her face now, and when she spoke again, her voice was taut and joyless: "Do you know, Din, that when I first considered you for this job, there was only one manner in which you were deficient. And it was that you weren't *hurt* enough."

"Hurt?"

"Yes. For the most passionate Iudex officers are the ones who've been harmed, you see. Those who have been wounded once and watched the wicked go unpunished. It puts a fire in them. Doesn't make them *good* at what they do, necessarily, but it does make them . . . enthusiastic, let us say. Willing to suffer, and bear burdens others could not." She licked her teeth. "You are not like this, Dinios Kol. You serve to support your family—a decent, dutiful cause, certainly, but one born of desperation, not pain."

There was the click and roan of a door in the room beyond, then footsteps, many of them.

"For this reason, some in the Iudex doubted my selection of you as assistant," Ana continued. "They did not feel that you possessed this conviction, and could not succeed. Thus far, they have been proven wrong. We shall see if that trend continues! Personally, I believe that at the end of this, you will still gladly don the blues of the Iudex, rather than the blacks of the Legion."

"Do you expect me to be harmed, and filled with this vindictive passion you describe?"

"Oh, no, no, no," she said. "I think no such thing. Rather, I think you are clever and decent, more than most. You shall learn it all in the end."

"Learn what, precisely?"

She sighed. "Do you wish me to make a prophecy, like a fortune-teller in a canton fair? Fine. If that will please you, I shall do so." She thought about it for a moment, and a sly, rather evil grin crossed her face. Then she pressed her thumb to her forehead, assumed a theatrical pose, and said, "You shall soon receive two revelations, Dinios Kol! One very obvious, and one very secret. Together, they shall change the course of your life."

"Even now, ma'am," I said, "you make a joke of everything."

"Oh? Was I joking?" She stood and turned to the approaching gaggle of Apoths. "Ah! Good afternoon. Would one of you be able to assist this poor woman to see Thelenai?"

One officer helped her away. Another placed a small pot within the slot at the bottom of the glass wall and murmured, "For sleep, sir. You shall need it."

I drank, lay back, and slept.

V

...

THE
PALE KING
ASCENDANT

CHAPTER 43

∧ ∧ ∧

I WOKE IN THE DARK, AND THE DAY PROCEEDED LIKE A dream.

The Apoths came and dressed me, sliding an algaeoil suit over my limbs. I felt none of it, but simply watched my own flesh being maneuvered about like it belonged to someone else. Then they placed the warding helm upon me, fastened it tight, and spoke to me, murmuring commands. Some core of my mind must have understood their words, for I followed them.

There was no word for my existence: the grafts within me were bubbling brightly, and in their froth, time and location lost meaning. Events continued, unrolled, unraveled. I was moving; I heard my own breath hissing in my helm, then the rattle of carriage wheels; I slept; then someone shook me, and I awoke once again.

I was at the shore. The sky was slate-gray and mutinous, the dawning sun a narrow blade of riotous red in the east. I clambered out of the carriage and stumbled along the jetty to the waiting cargo ship, trying to coordinate my arms and legs to move aright. I was lost inside my body, which was lost inside the suit, and the whole of me was lost on this wandering stripe of rocky coast.

There were figures toiling ahead of me, also bound in algaecloth and helms, loading goods and crates onto the cargo ship. I spied one person standing alone and identified him as Immunis Ghrelin by the bars and circle at his shoulder: even in such mad circumstances, the Empire scrupulously maintained rank.

Ghrelin did a double take as I stiffly approached. I saw that his face was unpainted behind his warding helm, yet his eyes crinkled in a smile. Then I heard his voice, faint and wispy through the barriers of our helms: "Good morning, Kol. How goes it? Are you managing it all well?"

"I . . . am standing, sir," I heard myself say.

"Are you." He held up four fingers. "How many fingers do you see here now, Kol?"

"F-four, sir," I said numbly.

"Oh, good. That was a reasonably fast response, given the katapra in you. And at least you got the answer right."

I stood limply beside him, watching the workers load their goods. There seemed to be a great number of folk, but I no longer had the faculties to count them.

"So . . . you are truly no closer to catching him, then?" asked Ghrelin suddenly. There was a desperate note to his voice. "He evades you still?"

"We are closer, sir," I stammered. "But not close enough."

"I see . . ." he said faintly. "Well. I hope this shall help. We will be embarking shortly, and will sail for the northeastern portion of the Shroud, pass through the veil, and dock. You must follow me carefully then, Kol. Do not deviate from my path—is that clear? Some wished to blindfold you for this, but . . . given that so many preparations for the marrow now take place there, the Shroud is very busy, and the wrong stumble would be disastrous. Is this all clear?"

"Yes, sir."

"I am told you also wished to review our preparations for transporting the marrow to the inner Empire. We shall do this first, then proceed to the . . . interview."

"Yes, sir."

There was an awkward silence. He turned to face inland. "If you wish to see something of import, however, this pier is most certainly such a place!"

I turned about, woozily staring at the pier, which appeared to be little more than a long strip of wood and stone dangling out into the gray waters, and many fretvine warehouses clumped up together at the shore. "Is it, sir?"

"Oh, yes. You were told of the commander-prificto's plan to move the marrow, yes? Here is where the ship shall first come to restock, before continuing on to the Shroud. We get so few vessels that sail abroad that this is the only place that can handle a ship of that size—yet it's hardly ever used, Kol. No reagents have passed through those warehouses in months, and what few wardens we've spared to search this place have found not a whiff. Hopefully the Shroud will offer more guidance for you ... Regardless, let us board, so we can get comfortable, and wait."

We did so, I walking wobbily as the cargo boat rocked beneath me. Then we sat and waited. My bones felt heavy where they rested within my flesh. It was something of a struggle just to sit upright.

"Thelenai told you how the interview should proceed, yes?" Ghrelin asked. "I will accompany you to the augurs, and then ... I will change. I will be someone different, as the grafts within me take hold."

Again, I nodded. "You were an augur yourself, sir, weren't you?" I asked. "What was it like? What should I expect?"

"That's a little like asking about a half-remembered dream, Signum," he said. "And more so, former augurs are strictly instructed not to discuss their work within the Shroud. But I suppose I can break policy for this ..." His eyes narrowed in a reflective half smile. "In a large group, it is wonderful. So much sharing of information, so much work, so much worth ... In smaller groups it is powerfully, curiously intimate. Relationships there are ... very different." A pause, lost in a memory. "Which is all to say, I do not know what to expect. I was an augur long ago, and it is different for each one."

I gazed at him for a moment, my thoughts lumbering through the channels of my mind. "Has your memory perhaps been altered, sir?" I slurred.

His helmeted head snapped to face me. "What?"

"Y-your memory, sir. My immunis said the Empire can alter some folk, so that they cannot discuss certain subjects, and speculated if it might have been done to you. I have not heard of such a thing truly done, but I wondered if yo—"

"No!" Ghrelin said vehemently. "No, no! No, my memories have not been altered." He shuddered. "Such a practice exists, certainly, but I can't comprehend why Dolabra brought it up regarding myself! I personally have never heard of it being implemented, but I can only imagine . . ."

"Imagine what, sir?"

"Well. That if it were ever truly used, it would be done for secrets far more dreadful than any found here."

"Than . . . the *Shroud*? There are secrets in the Empire more dangerous than even that, sir?"

Ghrelin was silent. Then I heard a tremendous fluttering, and I looked up and saw the billowing sails unfurling above us. They rippled, caught wind, and snapped into sharp white blades set against the slate-gray sky. A great, curious swimming feeling came over me, like the sky and sea were spinning about the ship.

Ghrelin's voice echoed from deep within his helm: "We're leaving."

I fought to find the shore and saw that he was right: Yarrowdale was receding, the cheery tips of the fretvine cottages growing smaller before my eyes.

THE CARGO SHIP tumbled out into the gray waters, and soon all of civilization fell to a tiny, rambling thread of black in the distance. Despite the grafts within me, I felt my pulse quicken as the expanse of water between myself and civilization grew. I had never truly grasped the enormity of the sea, this great, swilling, surging blankness. I tried to imagine its depths, to wonder how deep it reached, and then, inevitably, came the question of what might be lying down there on the sea floor, gazing up at me—a drifting giant in repose, perhaps?

We drifted on, and on. Then I heard shouts from the crew, calling to one another to be careful, be ready.

"We come to it," said Ghrelin quietly. "If you wish to see it, now would be a good moment."

I turned and looked ahead.

To call it tall, or big, or immense did not come close to capturing the nature of the thing rising from the sea. It was unimaginably colossal, a towering sheath of shimmering green that seemed to fill all the horizon ahead of us. I had glimpsed the distant sea walls in the East, yes, and witnessed the landfall of a leviathan from leagues away, but never had I in all my life been so close to something so enormous. The only thing that could contest its size, I thought, would be the sea itself.

We sailed nearer. The Shroud was not a tent, I realized, nor a structure of gauze or moss, as I'd previously imagined; rather, it was thicker, fleshier, more gelatinous, less akin to fabric or vines and more like some colossal growth of seaweed rising from the waters. Nor was it all one piece, but layered like a flower's petals, each roll of its husk coiled about the next, its viridine flesh shot through with veins of dark green bubbles.

And it moved. It rippled and shifted, billowing in one long, undulating flex from end to end, over and over. It was so strange, and beautiful, and artful; yet there was a subtle terror to it, and to look upon it set something crawling behind my eyes.

Ghrelin pointed up at its peak. "Do you see that bit there?" he asked. "That arch? I made that. It grew weak after a storm, and they raised me and a few others up on scaffolds, and I planted the grafts and nurtured them over the weeks, and . . . now look at it. I rather think I did a good job . . ."

I kept watching as the Shroud rippled, studying the gentle, silent curling of the massive construct.

Then I frowned, my muddy brain struck with a thought.

I glanced at the sails above me and saw that they were tight and firm. The wind was constant, then, and very strong.

I looked back at the Shroud. Its strange billowing, I realized, was not caused by the wind.

"It . . . it moves, sir," I said quietly. "It moves on its own."

Ghrelin said nothing.

"Does it, sir? Am I right?"

"You are," he said. "I take it you, like many on the shore, have as-sumed it was shifting in the breeze, like a flag or a standard?"

I was speechless for a moment, transfixed by the thing's undula-tions. "I knew it was a living thing," I said. "But not . . . quite so alive as this."

"Yes," he said. "The Shroud is one organism, Kol, one being. It is one we have created. There is no other like it in this world. We had to make it so, to stem back the bloods of the leviathans."

"Why didn't you tell us this, sir?" I asked.

"I believe I did," he said, bemused. "I told you the Shroud was based upon the tissues of a leviathan. But perhaps I did not make the ramifications of this clear."

We pounded on. The world tipped and turned again, and the prow of the cargo ship leaned to the right, making a large curve, then back to the left, toward the Shroud.

From this angle I could see that the green sheath was not perfectly symmetrical: the northeastern side of it stretched out, making me think of a gentrywoman's elaborate gown, fitted with a trailing veil. I thought I could spy enormous chains reaching down from some high, hidden mechanism, linked to the corners of the sweeping portion of the sheath. I imagined the chains retracting, lifting this edge of the Shroud high like the hem of a dress, so that ships could tow in . . . something.

Something enormous, surely. Something that would lie in the wa-ters there like the spirit maiden from the old tales, floating in her pool, awaiting a kiss to return her to the waking world; yet this maiden, I knew, would be something very different. Something mon-strous beyond mention.

"People worshipped them as gods once," said Ghrelin quietly. "I think of that whenever I make this voyage."

The great, glimmering skin of the Shroud loomed ahead. My body was slick with sweat, my mouth thick and heavy.

"And I cannot blame them," Ghrelin continued. "These giant, in-explicable things, thundering ashore, bringing so much death and strangeness with them. That's what faith and the divine is, isn't it? A line stretching from little beings like us, to the ineffable, the incomprehensible."

The wall of the Shroud ahead trembled, like the skin of a drum. Then it split and, shuddering tremendously, it began to draw back. The foamy sea came rushing in to fill it, and I was struck with terror, imagining it to be a mouth. Suddenly I was sure that the Shroud was no imperial creation but rather a leviathan in hiding, this monstrous thing that now opened its maw to consume us.

But then I saw chains at the end of the corners of the split wall of skin, and I realized there was some mechanism inside, shifting back the curtain of Shroud like one might a drawbridge, allowing us within: a smaller version of the massive sheath intended for the titans, perhaps.

"But then we found a way to kill them," whispered Ghrelin beside me. "Slaughter them and haul their flesh and bones so far from where they once wandered, to . . . here."

We passed through the veil, and I beheld the structure within.

It was not a conventional building or a fortress, and though I spied many braids of tissues and tendons about it, neither was it an organism, precisely. Rather, it was a mixing of both, an uncanny, churning, shuddering flower of brick and flesh, bronze and ligament, bone and stone and coiling wood. A bright, tremulous wall of pale flesh would subside into a wall of dull, brown brick, only to then be followed by a hull of plated steel, with tiny, glassy windows stubbling its surface; and all about it were looping pipes and vessels, some wrought of bronze, others of flesh, like tracts of ropy intestine, carrying fluids up and down the hide of the tremendous thing.

And toiling on every layer were tiny, glimmering dots: people, I realized, bound up in crimson algaeoil suits. There were hundreds of them, and I was reminded not of Engineers or officers as much as I was of ants, frantically attempting to strip a chunk of carcass; yet the people did not break or tear the construct, but rather built, and healed. They appeared to be feeding the citadel, mending it, suffusing it with grafts, patching up its wounded flesh, stitching shut any rents or tears, or sealing the hulls where they had rusted or split.

We built this, I thought. *We have built this unnatural thing, and it has built us in turn.*

The ship sloshed on through the waters, the green veil now behind us, a small pier awaiting ahead.

I heard Ghrelin's voice continue beside me, whispering, "So I wonder now. I wonder—what does that make us?"

"I . . . I beg pardon, sir?" I asked.

I turned and saw him smiling sadly at me through the glass of his helm. "What does it mean," he said, "when the line that once connected us to the inscrutable and ineffable instead coils about, forms a great loop—and then comes back to us?"

The veil of the Shroud closed with a gentle sigh, and all the world turned to green.

CHAPTER 44

. . .

I KEPT STARING UP AT THE GIANT, FLOWERING CITADEL above as we approached; so much so that it was quite the surprise when the entire ship was hosed down with reagents so acrid they made the air shiver, and I could hardly see three span in front of my face.

All fell to movement and chaos as the dripping workers unloaded the cargo. Ghrelin and I worked our way around them until we climbed a set of steps. I glanced back only once to see that the world beyond was a shimmering, green smear, as if I saw the horizon through the thickest of tinted glass.

Four guards awaited us at the top of the stairs, each bound in algaecloth and wearing warding helms. "Immunis Ghrelin?" asked one—a militis, judging by the markings on their suit. "And Signum Kol?"

We nodded, and the four guards saluted.

"I am Militis Torgay," said the one who'd spoken, who bowed. Though sex was difficult to determine given our suits, I believed her to be female. "I will be accompanying you on your journey today and shall first escort you to the western transport bays, where the preparations for transport are taking place. Are you ready to depart, sir?"

A dribbling sound echoed from above. I glanced up to see a bulging, pale white wall of flesh suddenly flex and retract within a crevice of brick.

"Ahh—yes," I said. "Yes, I . . . think I am?"

"Excellent," she said brightly. "Follow me, please, sir."

We entered a tall steel door set in the side of the citadel, and from there the comparison to an ant mound became even stronger: though the flooring within was mostly level, the passageways resembled bowel-like chambers or tunnels more than an orderly hall of an imperial fortress. Teams of workers in Apoth red algaeoil suits poured about us, rushing down a twist of tunnel or emerging from hidden doors to go about their duties. I could see no faces, just warding helms, and steam-fogged glass, and the occasional glimpse of a panicked eye.

"Very busy here, sir," said Torgay. "Though I'm sure you understand." A sidelong glance. "You have been fully briefed, I assume?"

Ghrelin's voice, soft and hushed: "He has been, Militis."

Torgay shook her helmeted head. "Still a bit stunned that word is being shared shoreside. Even here, that shipment is a deadly secret."

"And I will keep it." I wished to add—*If I manage to leave here alive*—but did not say this.

"So I hope," said Torgay. "The shipment reagents are just ahead. It is not far!"

We wound through one intestinal passageway and came to a great door wrought of iron and stonewood. Torgay undid its heavy latches, pushed it open, then bowed, bidding us enter.

The chamber within was akin to a massive, rippling orb, made of a strain of fretvine whose fibers more resembled stone than bark. Watery green light filtered down from above, where open windows looked up on the shimmering envelope of the Shroud. Stacked all about us were reagent crates. Nearly a dozen Apoths were clambering over the boxes like goats on a rocky cliff. Each one carried a caged set of plants like a priest might a thurible, waving the clutches of ferns and mosses over each crate and carefully inspecting their leaves and curls.

Ghrelin's voice was a whisper in the dark: "We check them now, to confirm that our enemy has not sabotaged them, for these shall all accompany our gift on its travels. It's rather like the funeral rites of the emperors of old, perhaps, transported up the Asigis on barges painted purest white and attended by their greatest possessions ..."

I swallowed, unnerved both by this place and by the tenor of his voice. Perhaps the grafts he'd consumed accounted for his strangeness. "What are these reagents?"

"Many things. Nutrients. Stimulants for the unique strain of *oli muk*, the ossuary moss that binds the marrow. And contingency germinations should the excised sample grow unstable."

"How likely is that?"

A wry, weak chuckle. "Greater than I prefer. But that would always be my answer, Kol."

I turned about, gazing at the Apoths doing their work. "They've found no sign of tampering on any of the crates in here?"

"No, sir," said Militis Torgay. "But there are four other chambers just like this one, of course."

"There are *four* others? How large will this vessel be?"

"It shall be borne within an imperial hydricyst," said Ghrelin, "the second largest of our seagoing ships, two hundred span long and seventy-five span wide. It shall dock in Yarrowdale briefly to stock up on simple goods—rope, water, food for the crew—and then it shall come to the Shroud to be adjusted. From thence it shall be less like a ship and more like a floating manufactuary, with all these reagents and precursors and compounds flowing within. All shall be part of a system designed to do one thing—to keep our gift sleeping soundly in its bed of bone, until it comes to the port city of Qapqa, on the River Asigis. There it shall be transferred again to barges of a similar type, but more suited to riverwork—for we control the whole of the Asigis." His words grew soft and sad. "Strange that we control that long river but not the canals of our own making."

We continued to the next chamber, and the next, each stocked with cargo crates and crawling with Apoths and their telltale plants.

"How much will this all cost, sir?" I asked.

"Cost?" said Ghrelin. "The cost is so great it's nigh beyond thought. You look now upon the product of thousands of hours of labor, which are themselves the product of thousands of grafts and suffusions and augmentations to make the people capable of making them. And this hardly speaks at all to the cost of *life*—how many people have we lost on the Shroud this year alone, Torgay?"

"Eleven," she said softly. "Two augurs and nine reagent mesinomies, sir."

"And I myself know the full number of folk who perished to pursue the marrow," said Ghrelin. "We sing their names even now in the annals of the Apoths, and here on the Shroud, on the days of remembrance. Their families shall be endowed with dispensations and lands, but . . . in many ways we have yet to compensate them enough. For each of them perished in the pursuit of this great goal—to control that which is uncontrollable and bring safety and healing to thousands. A future so much better than this present it is like a foreign country to me." He stopped, his shoulders anointed with rippling green. "Would you like to see it now, Signum?" he whispered.

"See what, sir?"

"The dark miracle we have trapped, the fruit of all our sorrowful labors."

I looked to Torgay, but she did not meet my eyes.

"Come," said Ghrelin. "Come, Kol, and see!"

GHRELIN TOOK ME to a long stone passageway. "It sleeps, you see," he whispered as we walked it. "Like a baby. Silent yet fitful, always threatening to wake."

The hallway ended in a stonewood door that had been reinforced many times over, with a viewing hatch positioned in the center. I gazed at it, my skin crawling and my suit boiling with heat.

Ghrelin nodded to the hatch. "There it lies. Look! Look upon it and know that it is real."

I walked up to the hatch, opened it, and peered through.

Within lay another curving, rippling spherical chamber wrought of stony fretvine, again lit by the swirling green light of the Shroud above. To my confusion, it appeared to be sleeting within the room:

thick, white flakes danced about in the darkness, churning and swirling as they rippled through the green light.

"Sir," I said. "What is . . ."

"Petals," said Ghrelin. "Petals of the kyap tree blossom. They are light and plentiful—and shall be the first to warp, should the marrow's containment fail. How many times I have looked within a chamber like this, and seen them change color, or grow heavy and fail to dance on the air. Then our prize's bony cradle would bloom with curious growths, and sprout teeth and ribs, and then we were forced to burn the entire creation and await the next wet season. But look past the flowers now! See past their drifts, Kol!"

I narrowed my eyes, peering through the snowstorm of flower petals. Standing in the center of the chamber was a tall frame of stonewood, fifteen span wide and long. Hanging within it was a web-like array of thick, ropy, coiling shoots of a material that resembled ossuary moss, yet it had a metallic sheen to it. And there, in the middle of the spiderweb of shining moss, sat a growth: a lump, a curious, misshapen tumor, five span tall and wide, shaped almost like a calf's kidney. It sat suspended in the web, entombed in the metallic moss, yet unless I was mistaken, very occasionally, the lump would . . .

Shake. Vibrate. Quiver. Like an egg just before its hatching.

"Do you see the moss?" whispered Ghrelin beside me. "How it shimmers? It is a breed we created specifically for this purpose, fed with iron deposits to line its bark, which already had the nature of stone. Only this can form the sheath that resists the *kani* and the many alterations and mutations of the titan's blood. And yet even still, it stirs. Do you see?"

The gleaming lump trembled again, like a lyre string gently plucked. A bulge emerged in the silvery carapace, like a bubble about to burst, but then it froze, and shrank, yet did not vanish.

"I do," I said softly.

"In that shell lies the future, Kol. Some are so bold as to call it the Fifth Empire—a nigh sacrilegious thing, as new eras are only anointed at the death of an emperor! And yet, if he were here, I feel Emperor Daavir might agree . . ."

I pulled my eye away from the hatch and shut it, my blood buzzing in my veins.

"Thirty-two," said Ghrelin to me.

"Sir?"

"Thirty-two augurs died to bring us that treasure," he said. "And how I weep for each of them. But once the count was thirty-*three* . . . for we thought Pyktis dead, didn't we, Kol? Yet now we know otherwise."

I said nothing, haunted by the sight of the marrow suspended in the dark among the dancing flowers.

"Strange, that he intends to make a weapon of the thing he once fought to procure," said Ghrelin somberly. "Our deliverance, but his armament. Now—are you ready to speak to those beings who secured that prize?"

CHAPTER 45

▲ ▲ ▲

WE FOLLOWED TORGAY DOWN YET ANOTHER WINDING passageway, my suit now so hot it felt like I was being braised within a bladder. I struggled to collect my thoughts and prepare myself for how this interview would go.

"Will the augurs I speak to be in algaecloth suits and helms as well?" I asked.

"Oh, no, sir," said Torgay. "The citadel of the Shroud is built in two layers. There is the outer layer, which is an operation section where personnel are required to wear warding garments at all times. Mostly only service personnel labor here. Then there is the inner. That is where all the most dangerous work occurs."

"I'm not being brought into the inner layer, I assume."

"No, sir. You cannot pass through without days of testing and ob-servation. I am taking you to a review chamber on the north side of the inner layer of the citadel. There you will be able to speak to the designated personnel through the chamber's glass wall, much like how you viewed the . . . ah, shipment."

We turned again. By now I had lost all concept of direction and had no idea where we were.

"I do ask that you follow the policy for such an interaction, sir," said Torgay. "Do not touch the glass wall. Do not remove your helmet or any component of your algaecloth suit."

We took a flight of wooden stairs down, then a flight of metal stairs back up.

"Do not discuss anything personal with the designated person-nel. Do not show them any personal items of your own. Do not shout, speak loudly, or move quickly before them. Do not mention the shore-side world or its developments."

A door, then a short passageway; then another door, and another short passageway.

"But most of all, do not tap, or beat out any rhythm before them. Nor should you hum, sing, or whistle any tune. That will agitate the augurs greatly, for they shall seek meaning and pattern in it. And when your two hours are done, they are done. No negotiations on that. Is that understood, sir?"

"Yes, Militis."

"Very good, sir."

Torgay took out a ring of keys, unlocked one last door, and ges-tured to me to enter. We passed into a small, dull, white stone pas-sageway, lit by a string of blue mai-lamps. Three bronze doors were set on the left-hand side ahead. Besides these, the passageway was barren.

Torgay walked to the closest bronze door and unlocked and opened it. "You can enter, sir," she said.

Bracing myself, I walked inside.

THE LITTLE ROOM was much like the observation cell I'd been placed in back in Yarrowdale, but larger: a thick, rippled glass wall split the space in two, with three plain wooden chairs on either side. Placed on each chair on our half were curious instruments: two plain wooden boards, set inside a small frame so there was a shred of a smallspan's gap between them. Besides these, and the two mai-lamps glowing up above, the room was completely bare.

"Please take a seat, sirs," said Torgay. "The officers will be with you shortly."

We sat. The guards retreated and shut the door behind them, though I could tell by the shadows at the bottom that one stood out-side, observing us through a slit in the door.

I eyed the glass wall. It looked to be at least two smallspan thick. "Will we, ah, be able to hear the augurs through that, sir?" I asked.

"We will," said Ghrelin. There was a quaver to his voice now. "There are gaps in the ceiling to allow sound through. They are packed with moss to absorb contagions, so it will be faint—but we shall hear."

"I see, sir."

A silence passed.

"The Apothetikal Iyalet is actually the greatest consumer of glass in the Empire," Ghrelin said suddenly. "Did you know that, Kol?"

"Ah—no, sir. But that makes sense."

"Yes . . . the neutral, nonpermeable qualities of glass make it ideal for storing reagents. Though a tempered pane of this size is extremely difficult to create and ship." He extended a hand to the glass, like he was imagining the caress of its surface. "A glass of this thickness, some two smallspan, perhaps more . . . I would estimate that this was tempered in Basiria, some hundreds of leagues to the south. Very fine sand there, of a most agreeable quality, and a proud and sprawling glassworks nearby."

"I see, sir," I said, puzzled by his enthusiasm.

"They heat the sand with blackwood until it is white-hot, then left to fine out, the bubbles weaving through its boiling puddles . . . Then it is layered and cooled, and bundled up in packings of moss from Qabirga, and shipped across the vast Lake of Khanum to Mycel—probably in spring, for that's the period of calmest weather—and then down the Great River Asigis to here. I wonder if I see flaws in the glass . . . Some speck of seashell or earth that was lost in that sand, and then boiled into the tempered glass. What a miracle it is, to sit and stare through soil made transparent. What lake beach or valley in Basiria is it from? Kesy? Beik Enis? Layli? I wonder if I could smell it on the glass itself . . ."

I glanced sidelong at him. Though he'd acted strange before, now there was a feverish look to his eyes, and the words tumbled from his mouth so quickly they were nearly unintelligible through his helm.

The augury, I guessed. It had been working on him all this time,

I'd suspected, but now it was at its zenith. I wondered what he was now, somewhere inside that suit.

Then there was a click of a door: not from our side but the other.

I looked up, and they entered the room.

THE FIRST STRIKING thing about them was their clothing, if it was clothing at all. From their necks to their knees they wore not shirts nor jerkin nor hose, but rather what first appeared to be a shapeless, formless tangle of papers and parchments. I squinted and saw that the papers were attached to a set of underlying robes by string, or pins, or adhesives, and were not of uniform size or type: there were many colors and shades of paper, with some large and neat and others crumpled, and some no more than torn-off corners. All the papers were covered in scribblings and text and numbers, equations and calculations and paragraphs, all rendered in smeary ashpen.

They were notes, I realized. The two augurs made so many notes and had secured so many of them to their bodies that they had almost come to resemble sheep, their figures white and plump and rustling.

I studied the augurs' faces as they entered. They were gray-skinned, like myself; yet they were not simply bald, but totally hairless, their heads completely depilated, like Ghrelin and Thelenai. Their faces were smudged with ash and ink, which made it difficult for me to determine their sex; but one was a woman, I thought, and the other a man. Though perhaps these terms meant nothing to beings such as they. Perhaps the augurs, like some folk of the innermost cantons, had dispensed with such concepts altogether.

The two augurs walked to the barrier and looked at me, their faces so close to the glass that twin flowers of steam bloomed below their nostrils. There was something inaccessible to their gaze, as if they did not truly have eyes but rather the images of eyes painted on stones sitting within their sockets.

The augurs stared at me for a long while before fumbling about in their coats of parchments. They produced a set of boards that hung from their necks by ribbons. Then they sat down before the glass, placed the boards in their laps, and then . . .

Tap-tap. Tap tap-tap-tap.

I watched as their fingers danced over the boards, their fingertips so dark with ashpen that they left smears of black behind.

There was a silence. Then, slowly, Ghrelin picked up one of the boards from our half of the room. He took a deep breath and tapped out a response. The design and framing of the boards made the taps quite loud.

For the first time, the augurs looked at him. Then they began tapping again, their fingers rapidly flying on the wood. Ghrelin responded, tapping back, and they drummed out another response. This went on for some time, and as it did, the moods of all three began to change, growing relaxed yet also excited.

They were adjusting themselves to one another, I thought. Like dancers moving with a new partner, trying to adjust to this person's height and weight and speed, yet enticed by the newness of it all.

Finally the tapping ceased, and Ghrelin turned to look at me. His pupils were wide and dilated, and when he spoke, there was something misty to his voice.

"I will speak for them now," he said. "As best I can. I will no longer speak for myself. Is this known?" The last three words were sharp and cold.

"Yes, sir."

Ghrelin stood, walked closer to the glass, turned to face me, and sat on the floor. The male augur sat in a position over his right shoulder, and the female on his left. Ghrelin's eyes closed within his helm, and all seemed to go dark within, like the man himself had vanished and only shadow remained.

The augurs studied me, their eyes wide and earnest, yet unknowable. Then the male one tapped out a message on his board.

Ghrelin dipped his head toward the male and said in a dreamy voice: "Iudex. They said an Iudex was coming to talk to us. But there's a narrow shaping to your eyes, and an undercolor of pale brown to your dermis. Are you Tala?"

I looked at Ghrelin, confused. It took me a moment to adjust to the absurdity of the situation: the augur's words coming out of Ghrelin's mouth, like the man's body was being used as his voice box.

Then the female began tapping. Ghrelin's head dipped toward her, and when he spoke again his voice was slightly different: tauter, wryer, and without a trace of warmth. "Tala he is," said the woman. "Fluctuations in the pupil. Slightest widening, the shift in the shoulders. He heard truth. This is a Tala man—and a young one, at that. He moves too quick."

The male augur tapped again, and Ghrelin dipped his head back the other way and spoke: "Tala is far from here." The augur rummaged in his paper suit and pulled out a single note tied to a string, held it high, and tapped again on his board. "Less than seven percent of all serving imperial officers in Yarrowdale are of Tala stock. This is known. Though these numbers are from some time ago . . ."

Then the woman, cold and harsh: "Mostly Rathras, and Kurmini, and Pithian here. Peoples who grew up by rivers, by the Apoth works. Old Empire folk whose tribes knew the domain of the emperors long before the march to the sea. Familiar with the smell of reagents and the scents of the smokes."

The man: "You are unusual here. And an Iudex officer has *never* entered the Shroud before. This is known, here on the inner layer. We share. We remember."

The woman, digging in her own suit, salvaged some measly scrap of smudged parchment and proudly held it high. Then she tapped, one-handed: "I have predicted the arrival of an Iudex conzulate soon. I have predicted this. The transition from Yarrow to Empire will come with pain. The presence of such a being is inevitable."

"But even so," tapped the man, "such a personage would not send one young Tala man to the Shroud, all alone. No, no. You are not part of that entourage."

The woman dropped her note and cocked her head. "So why now? And why a Tala man, of all folk?"

Then the man: "But then . . . Tala lies so close to those hallowed grounds. The Titan's Path, and the sea walls, and Talagray."

The woman dipped forward, eyes wide and keen: "Have you served in Talagray, Iudex? Have you walked in the shadow of the sea walls, and the Path of the Plains, with its ancient cenotaphs and strange blooms?"

My suit suddenly felt very hot.

The ghost of a smile crossed the woman's face. She tapped out: "He has. See the stillness to his gaze, the measured movements as he breathes within his suit? This boy is full of grafts—but he is not broken. There is steel in his eye and sand in his spine."

"And his visit here was not planned," tapped the man. "For the suit is not arranged well. Baggy at the knees and hips, tight at the shoulders. It was not grown for you—even though it takes but ten days to grow an algaecloth suit for a person . . ."

"So—why?" tapped the woman. "Why is such an accomplished Iudex officer coming here, so quickly, and so unplanned? Unless . . . something very wrong has happened on the shore."

"Murder. Death."

"Disaster. Catastrophe. Tell us. Which is it?"

"Tell us, please, Iudex, tell us."

I watched as Ghrelin twitched where he sat, like he was possessed by the figures on the other side of the glass. No less unnerving was the experience of listening to these two, my eyes flicking back and forth as one spoke, then the other, an alternating volley of taps and words.

"I am here," I said very carefully, "to ask about a man who served with you as augur some time ago."

The two augurs slowly turned to look at each other. The meaning of their gaze was unreadable to me, but they held it for a long moment. Then they turned back, and the woman tapped out a short, simple message.

Ghrelin spoke for her: "Are you here to ask of Sunus Pyktis?"

My blood flushed hot. I tried not to let my eyes react too much.

"Yes," I said evenly. "How do you know this?"

Another long silence. The augurs sat there, inscrutable. Then the woman dug in her suit and held up a tiny scrap of paper covered in scribblings before tapping again on her board.

Ghrelin spoke for her: "This was *known,* Iudex. This was *predicted.* We have *projected* that these events may come to pass."

"How did you predict this?" I asked.

The woman shook her head and replaced the note within her suit. Then she tapped again: "He lives. He *lives.* Yet how is this so?"

"I cannot tell you," I said. "I am here only to ask about his service in this place."

More tapping from the woman: "We will tell you about his service here, if you tell us of his acts in the world beyond."

Then the man: "For his service here was strange, and troubled. Though most could not see it, we did."

"When he perished," tapped the woman, "we thought it wrong, even then. Such a clumsy mistake, such a blundering—from Sunus Pyktis? The golden child who could do no wrong?"

Then the man: "The augur whom all marveled at? Brightest among the bright, most brilliant among the brilliant?"

The woman said: "No."

The man said: "No."

"It was wrong. All of it, wrong."

"This we knew. This was known."

The woman leaned close, her nose nearly touching the glass. "And when we were told the Iudex was coming to talk to us, and only us . . ."

The man then: "Yes. He has been found. He lives."

The woman: "We have been *ready* for you, Iudex. We can say much. Just—tell us. What has he done out there? Is he safe, and whole?"

I watched as their fingers fluttered out these final messages. Then they went totally cold and still, as if refusing to grant me any hint of information.

Yet I noted: they were concerned with Pyktis's safety. They did not think him a murderer or a criminal, and had not yet contemplated that I was here because of some act he had done.

I wondered what to do. Then I realized: all this felt rather familiar, didn't it? Didn't I know very well how to deal with a person so ravenous for information?

I said, "Aren't you wise enough to determine the answers by what I cannot say, as opposed to what I can?"

Their faces flickered: I caught a flash of anger, perhaps. Then the woman tapped, and when Ghrelin spoke, his voice was cold and resentful: "Flirtatious. A tease. I dislike this."

More tapping from the man, and Ghrelin said, "He has been told the rules, yes. Swallowed them up, swilled them about. How foul."

"Thelenai has gotten to him," said the woman. "Told him not to tell us a thing. Cruel, cruel Thelenai."

"Cruel, cruel Thelenai," said the man. "No more, nothing new. Instead we shall read only innards, and nerve clusters, and no more."

The woman: "Bones and sinew, veins and viscera."

The man: "Blots of blood and strings of membranes."

The woman: "Why do you condemn us to such a fate? You ask of us and we shall ask of you. It is only fair."

I stayed silent, wondering if I should ask another question or wait it out. In many ways, this was rather like how I often dealt with Ana, though the augurs seemed more alien than erratic.

Then the woman cocked her head and tapped out: "Oh . . . do you see that?"

I waited and did not move.

The woman tapped again: "I do not like how he blinks so little. Such a paucity of eye movement. Does this Tala man seem . . . *accustomed* to us?"

The man grew excited: "Does he? I think so, yes. We startle him not at all, and he moves so little."

"Has he *met* augurs before?" said the woman. "Has he dallied in their company so? How could that be, if augurs are only here, and no Iudex has ever come to this place?"

The man: "Has he met an augur, or . . ." He cocked his head. ". . . or something *like* an augur?"

The woman: "Tell us, boy—have you? Have you held parley with a being akin to us?"

I swallowed, disliking this shift in the conversation. I did not wish for them to ask me about Ana, who suddenly—startlingly, in fact—did seem very similar to them. If they grew too interested in her, I felt sure they would eat up the whole of our time asking about her.

I remembered the rules Thelenai had said: I was not to answer any of their questions or listen to their predictions.

But I needed to say something, now. Something startling that would send their augmented minds barreling down another path entirely.

Time enough to dispense with the rules, then.

I said, "Pyktis lives. He means great harm. I must know more of him to stop it."

The augurs blinked in unison at that. Again, they shared a cryptic glance. Then they began tapping, and Ghrelin shuddered as he spoke for them.

The man, now worried: "Great harm . . . this cannot be. Not Pyktis."

The woman: "Sunus Pyktis was a troubled thing, a tortured man, but . . . he was not a villain. This was not predicted. I cannot fathom this."

I said nothing.

The woman, tapping slower, quieter: "He means truth. His eyes do not waver. He thinks Pyktis a criminal thing."

The man: "I cannot comprehend this. Not from our Pyktis. Not from the man I once called friend and brother."

The woman, her tone sharp: "Called him such we may have—but he never called us so. Not in his heart."

Another silence. I sensed consternation now.

They began tapping again. Ghrelin, shuddering, shivering, spoke once more.

"We will tell you of Pyktis," said the woman. "For though he was a puzzle to us, a thing lovely yet unknowable, we . . . we worry now."

The man, soft and tremulous: "If we were wrong about him, then all our predictions, all our calculations . . . they now sit askew."

The woman shook her head and tapped out: "It cannot be. We are his last defense, then. He was difficult to know, but we knew him best—and we *know* he must be innocent of whatever you imagine."

The man: "What do you wish to know, Iudex?"

"All you saw of him," I said. "Start at the beginning, please."

CHAPTER 46

∧ ∧ ∧

THE MALE AUGUR BEGAN TO TAP, AND AS HE DID, Ghrelin chanted in his dreamy, misty cadence, his head lolling back and forth as the words coursed through him.

"Small and secretive and strange, our order is," said the man. "But if it were to have saints, surely Sunus Pyktis would sit among them, so wisely did he serve."

"The stories were told to us when we first passed through the veil to serve," said the woman. "For he was best and brightest of us. A man without peer."

"Quiet and modest," said the man. "Humble to the point of effacement."

"Yet the stories were loud and grand, even if he was not," said the woman. "It was Pyktis who pioneered the use of *oli muk* to bind the titan's marrow. Winding it up in ossuary moss and smuggling the secrets of their flesh away for us to study."

"He did not invent it," the man corrected her gently. "But he made the most advances with it."

"He guided it through their tissue like a needle through cloth," the woman said.

The man's wide, shallow eyes danced up and down my figure, and he tapped: "You know of the marrow. I feel you may have even laid eyes upon our prize. You know that when the wet seasons are high, and the Legion fells a titan, we augurs wend through the depths of these great, rotting entities, passing through chambers and veins and hollows like the deepest of mines."

"It is we who read their bodies, their flesh," tapped the woman. "Like dowsers in the steppes, sensing sleeping water beneath a curl of clay. This is no easy task. It takes many minds, and powerful minds at that, to read the flesh of the leviathans."

"We work in groups," said the man. "*Polytia* is the word—groups of three, who live together, labor together, learn together."

"In a polytia we become one," said the woman. "One mind, one stream of thought, one entity."

"And Pyktis was a member of your polytia?" I asked.

The woman's hands tapped out a message, and Ghrelin breathlessly translated: "He was our eldest, our prificto-polytia. We were his juniors, serving with him during his third, final year. He was to drum the beat of our lives. It was an honor to serve with him."

Then the man, cautious, anxious: "Yet . . . we augurs are skilled at learning the natures of folk. This is most important in a polytia. To doubt your colleagues while wandering a titan's breast . . . that is certain death. But when it came to Pyktis . . ."

"Pyktis was bright, brilliant—but also unreachable, *unknowable*," said the woman. "He would give us truths, offer us data—but it was only data. Information. Facts."

The man: "Where he was born—in Ta-Rath, in Rathras, far to the southeast."

The woman again: "His mother, beloved and beautiful, who had perished when he was a young man."

"His desire, endless and passionate, to bring betterment to the Empire—healing and growth and restoration."

"His perfect marks, perfect scores, perfect service record. It was data. Records. It was not knowledge. Not *comprehension*."

The man, wistfully, dreamily: "To serve with him was akin to loving a person made of glass. So difficult to perceive. So still, so cold, so hard to the touch."

They lapsed into a meditative silence.

Yet I noted: love? They had loved him?

I recalled what Ghrelin had told me: *Relationships there are . . . very different.*

"He lived a story, then," I said. "And hid his true self—is that it?"

The augurs frowned. The woman riffled through her coat of notes and produced yet another smeary piece of parchment, which she studied like it was sacred script. Then she absently tapped on her board with one hand, and Ghrelin translated: "No . . . not entirely. For sometimes he *did* show one side of himself so hidden. During the days of remembrance."

I recalled Ghrelin mentioning these as we toured the reagent crates. "The days of remembrance . . . What are those?"

"It is a holy day upon the Shroud, every six months," explained the man. "It is on these days that we memorialize the ones we have lost. Augurs and officers killed in our duties, laboring away on the carcasses of these great mysteries."

"Devoured by contagion," tapped the woman. "Sickness. Madness. Plague."

The woman: "During these holy days, we read the names of those who have perished in the past months. We thank them for their service, and pledge our love, to remember them always. And it was on these days, only these two days that I saw, that Pyktis . . . wept."

"Wept?" I said.

The man tapped rapidly: "Yes. He *wept*. Wept with anguish, wept with agony. I have never seen a person weep so."

"It pained him," said the woman. "So great was his pain that I asked him of it. He said to me—*Does your family think you shall die in this place?* I said I did not know, but I assumed they had accepted my fate, whatever it was to be. I had chosen to serve, after all. He thought on this, and then said—*My father expects me to die here.* I said that could not be so, no father could truly expect such a thing. But then he . . ." A pause in her tapping. Then: "He grew angry. He grew so *angry* at this comment, and he withdrew, and we could not find him."

"He disappeared?" I asked.

The woman issued a single set of taps: "Yes."

"But the Shroud is a contained place, yes?" I asked.

The man tapped in response: "Contained, yes, but also enormous, especially here on the inner layer. When we two searched for him, we found nothing. He returned to us, eventually. Yet he was cold and aloof, and we feared to ask of it."

The woman: "After that, this behavior became more frequent. He would disappear to some place within the Shroud, some place we could not find. When he returned, he would be moody and distant. We could not comprehend it."

The man limply tapped upon his board, and Ghrelin slowly translated: "We thought the culprit was the end of his term. Too much augury. Too much time on the Shroud. The mind breaks down."

The woman: "It is why we serve only three years. The personality undergoes shifts. Often dangerous ones. It is like the Khanum of old, or so they say."

I frowned at that, for in all I'd ever been taught, the Khanum had been depicted as wise and blessed.

"How is it like the Khanum?" I asked. "They were the first imperials. Why do you say they were as dangerous as Pyktis?"

The augurs again exchanged an inscrutable look.

The woman tapped, and Ghrelin, now panting with exhaustion, translated: "Do you know of how Sublimes such as you were made in mimicry of the grand and ancient Khanum? Possessing a portion of their cognitive powers—memory, calculation, spatial conceptualization, and so on—but no more than that *one* portion? For we can duplicate little of what the first imperials were."

"I do," I said.

The man said: "But this is not the whole of it. The Khanum of old could enter a . . . a *fugue*. An elevation of their minds to the highest levels, calling upon all their faculties. This made them capable of incomprehensible brilliance, feats of intellect even we cannot decipher."

The woman: "*This* is what augury is. It is an attempt to replicate this powerful elevation. We have only found a way for it to work with axioms, however, and no other Sublime. And it is limited in the same ways."

The man then: "For the Khanum of old grew incomprehensible as they aged. The more brilliant they became, the more mad they grew, and inarticulate. They spoke languages no one knew—if they spoke at all."

The woman: "Augury does this *same thing*, but over a much shorter period—only three years, and the third year can be treacherous. It is tempestuous and wild. That is when those of our order exhibit the most paranoias, the most erraticism."

The man smiled weakly and tapped out: "But it could be far worse. There are whispers of other attempts to replicate the Khanum, to re-make the emperor's bloodline anew. These efforts produced beings wild and savage, and full of strange passions and alien appetites. None of them lived past a year, we are told."

I shuddered in my suit and tried to focus on the investigation. "And you think Pyktis was suffering a madness like this?"

The woman slowly tapped out a response: "We did, yes."

"Why?" I asked.

The man's response was quick. Swallowing, Ghrelin translated: "Because we came to believe he was contemplating self-termination."

"You mean . . ."

The woman: "Suicide. Yes."

THE MAN BEGAN TAPPING, and Ghrelin—very weak now—translated: "We smelled it in the wind. And in sensing this, perhaps we . . . we hastened his choices."

"We tried to follow him during the last of these vanishings," said the woman. "We used all of our arts to decipher the pattern of his movements, the possible places he could slip away to."

"And . . . then we found him," said the man. "We came upon him standing in a tall, open window on one of the upper floors, facing one of the high courtyards of the inner layer."

The woman, head bowed: "As if to jump. To send himself plummeting to his death."

The man: "A desperate thing, as if to escape."

"He heard us coming," said the woman. "Tried to step back in and pretend all was aright."

The man: "But he tried to hide something. Something he held in his hand, which he placed in his pocket."

"A flash of metal," said the woman. "Small and delicate, and bright. A knife, or so I thought."

"We did not ask upon it," said the man. "For he seemed on the border of a rage. We averted our eyes, apologized, and returned to our works."

"The days after this were frozen and fraught," tapped the woman. "To him, it had been a secret thing. And to have it known was a great harm."

"And then," tapped the man.

"And then . . ." The female augur's eyes trailed up the walls to stare at the ceiling. "The accident. And the nature of this accident, it . . . it . . ."

They fell silent: the first time they had been inarticulate, I noticed.

The male augur leaned forward, peering into my eyes, his fingers tapping frantically on his board as Ghrelin spoke: "We thought it was an *intentional* mistake. Like a man setting a trap for himself, a noose hanging just so, and then allowing himself to proceed through his day, claiming to be unaware that he walked through his last moments of his own devising."

The woman, harshly: "No! An accident. That was what it *was*. He was degrading. Decaying. It is *our* fault that it happened. We should have done more to stop it."

The man: "But we did. We did warn our superiors. They spoke to Pyktis. And he convinced them that nothing was wrong."

The woman: "Yet he could be convincing! This we know! Even as he was filled with despair, he . . ."

The man glanced at her, then looked to me and tapped out: "A man can be many things. Despairing yet confident. Mad yet persuasive. And he could have loved us, while . . . while still planning his death."

The woman tapped out a sharp *"No."*

A tormented silence fell over them.

I sat forward, sensing something lurking in his comments. I asked, "Why do you say he loved you in doing such a thing?"

The man, hesitantly: "Because it should have been *us* who approached the marrow with him that day. We who tried to help bind it with him, to bathe it in nutrients so it could sleep and persist, for we were of his polytia. Yet he asked to be accompanied by others that day. At the time, we thought it a slight, but . . ." He trailed off.

I said, "But now you think he was sparing you death."

The man bowed his head and tapped: "Could that be love? Could a thing capable of that also love? I do not know. And now, here you are, Iudex, with a coldness to your eye, and I wonder . . ."

I studied them both, taking in the mournful looks on their faces. Yet my mind strayed back to what they'd said of Pyktis's supposed thoughts of suicide, when they'd found him standing in the window of the tower, and I recalled their first statements to me, bold and proud: *This we knew. This was known.*

They have already found the truth, I thought.

I imagined Pyktis, a figure standing in the window in this strange place, and then I recalled a moment with Malo, from the very start of this investigation.

Plucking a man from such a high room, she'd said, *with the windows locked and all, and no one saw nor heard a thing . . . I cannot ken it.*

Another window, another vanishing.

I said, "But you returned to the window, in the tower. And you found out that he hadn't been planning to jump. You found he'd been climbing *out* of it, didn't you?"

The sorrow vanished from the augurs' faces. They gazed at me, fascinated and slightly outraged.

The woman's fingers turned into a blur, and she tapped: "How was this known? How did you come to know this?"

Then the man: "Yes. How?"

I said nothing.

The woman shuddered, her lips tight. "How awful you are. We are like wanderers in a desert, begging for water, and you give us only sand."

"What did you find?" I asked.

After a resentful silence, the man tapped out: "We realized he had not been contemplating a jump from the window. Rather, he had been about to climb *down*."

"There was a chamber just below the window," tapped the woman. "Leading to a section of building that had been sealed off. The consequences of an old contamination. Walled off and forgotten."

"This was where he'd been vanishing to," tapped the man. "Through holes and crawl spaces, to halls forgotten and dark."

"We did not know this," tapped the woman. "Until weeks after he died. Until we solved his puzzle ourselves."

The man: "For we finally followed in his footsteps. Climbed down to this secret place. And then . . ."

Another silence. The augurs exchanged a tense look. Then the man tapped out: "We found a *shrine*."

"A . . . a shrine?" I asked. "To a spirit? A pantheon?"

"We did not know," said the woman. "Do not know. It was no cult that I recognized, but a shrine it was. Decorated and secret, with oil lamps and delicate bowls."

"With ribbons, and cloths," said the man. "Wreathed with facsimiles of flowers and herbs, wrought of paper. We do not know how he made it all. But then, he was most brilliant."

"Describe this shrine, please," I said. "What did it look like?"

"Why describe it," said the woman, "when we can show you?"

THE TWO AUGURS dug in their robes again, as if seeking to find yet another prediction, but they took out not parchments but rather three small wooden figures, carefully carved, still tied to their robes with string. Then with slow, thoughtful movements, they untied them and placed them before the glass for me to see.

They were figures of men, robed and bearded and stern, with their stubby arms extended. Circlets sat upon the brows of each one, the very image of kings of ancient days, high and tall and proud.

The man's fingers tapped upon his board: "These formed the heart of his shrine. We took them from it. Kept them. Puzzled over them. As we puzzle over Pyktis to this day."

The woman watched me closely and tapped: "Can you see reason in this? Can you see truth in this carven wood?"

The man: "For we cannot. We think it is incomplete. The figures seem to be made to hold something. A stick, or rod, or wand. We do not know."

I stared at the figures for a great while. An idea began to calcify within my mind, like ice forming at the top of a pool of water, and as it grew, my spine went cold.

I had seen such figures before, arranged on the king's hall in the High City of Yarrow, their carven figures illuminated by oil lamps floating before them. And I'd seen smaller versions of them, as well, had I not?

My eyes fluttered, and I recalled what Satrap Darhi had told me, a wooden totem much like these held in his hand: *We Yarrow labor under the watch of our ancestors. All we do must honor their name.*

Our ancestors.

"No," I whispered. "It is impossible."

The woman, tapping harshly: "What do you mean?"

My mind raced on, hurtling toward thoughts that seemed senseless. Pyktis had been a great augur, a Rathras Apoth, prized among the Shroud. He could be no other thing.

The prince's words: *This is old history. But . . . my grandfathers found many imperial visitors who were more than happy to become a wife of the throne, as it meant living in great finery. They came here, Tala, or Kurmini, or Rathras, and gave children to the king and the most esteemed members of his court . . .*

But it could be so. Perhaps it could be so.

Trembling, I cleared my throat and said, "The metal you saw in

Pyktis's hands, the day you found him in the window. What color was it?"

"It was silver," said the man. "This I saw. Why?"

I ignored them and kept staring at the totems, studying their crude faces. Their stubby arms, extended as if to hold something: perhaps a stick, or a string.

My eyes fluttered again, and I recalled more of Darhi's words: *Did you see the silver circlet on the prince's brow? And the silver chain about his neck? . . . Those are the signifiers of the king's chosen heir. The silvers go to him—and only to him.*

No, I thought. *No, no, it is insane.*

Yet it would fit. A necklace might have once draped here, in the hands of these crude totems, as if to keep the signifiers of one's birthright safe in the hands of the ancestors.

My father expects me to die here.

To die here. Of course.

A tapping filled the air. Then Ghrelin's voice, speaking for the male augur: "He knows. He has seen a truth. One invisible even to our eyes."

The woman, pleading: "Tell us. Please, tell us."

"Is there more?" I demanded.

"Tell us," tapped the man. "Please, please, tell us what you know. We starve for it."

"Is there more?" I asked again. "More to show me, or more to tell?"

The woman's fingers danced on her board: "We know no more. This is all we have, and it is not enough."

I stood up, quaking. I had to leave, to return to Ana, to spill all I'd seen here as quickly as I could, for I could not carry this dreadful secret for long.

"Please," said the man, standing and tapping. "Please, please, we beg you, tell us."

"I can't," I said. "You know that."

Then the woman: "No, no. Do you know what it is like for we augurs to possess too small a piece of information? Enough to tantalize, but not enough to comprehend?"

The man: "And to have it for this man of all men, this one of all we augurs? Can you imagine how this torments us?"

I studied them. I'd thought them inhuman and alien when I'd first seen them, yet the plaintive, pained looks in their eyes were ones I knew very well. I'd seen such sights often in my work, among those who grieved the dead and the missing: still human, and helpless, and still so full of hurt.

"I can say no more than you already know," I said. "Sunus Pyktis lived a story while he was among you. In doing this I believe he harmed not only you but himself as well. If you find me when your term is over, I shall tell you all I know."

They stared at me, despondent. The woman's fingers tapped: "When we leave this place, we shall no longer be these things."

The man: "This will be as a dream. Sunus will be as a dream."

"I'm sorry," I said to them. "But I can say no more."

I stooped to rouse Ghrelin from his trance. Yet the female augur shot to her feet, her fingers flickering on her board.

"And if you are wrong?" Ghrelin said, still mumbling her words. "If you are wrong about all this, about Pyktis, about everything? What then? For this was not projected. It was *not* foreseen. It was not!"

I helped Ghrelin to stand and gently guided him away.

Still she tapped, and still he spoke, whispering beside me: "You are wrong, you are wrong, you are wrong! This was not predicted! You are wrong, wrong, you *must* be wrong!"

CHAPTER 47

. . .

THE JOURNEY BACK TO YARROWDALE WAS STRANGE AND uneasy. All I'd seen of the Shroud had been like a nightmare: the rippling green husk of the veil; the sight of the trembling marrow, bound within the shining moss; and then the augurs themselves, who had at first seemed so inhuman, yet in the end had proven so vulnerable and despairing.

And then there was the truth I'd spied in that awful place, which boiled in my mind like a hot ball of iron dropped into a cooling bucket. I had to be rid of it, for otherwise it might burn me up.

Once ashore, Ghrelin and I were led to yet another Apoth observation chamber, and washed and cleaned again, and then plied with many blotley larvae of different colors. I grimaced as they pulled the horrid things from me; I still had not healed from my first blotley, and Sanctum only knew how long the new ones would persist.

It took some hours for me to pass my tests, but pass them I did, while Ghrelin was rushed away to recuperate from the effects of the augury. I asked one of the Apoths to thank him for his service and wish him well, then hurried to dress as they processed my release. The door opened before me, and I rushed outside.

Then I stopped. Malo stood across the street from me, bound in her red cloak, arms crossed.

"You alive?" she called.

"I am," I said.

"You're not sprouting horns, or growing grass out your ears, or dripping fluid from any bits of you?"

"I am not."

"Good." She crossed the lane to me. "Then I shall risk the airs about you to tell you ill tidings—for the prince has sent us a message." She looked me in the eye, her face as grim as I'd ever seen it. "Darhi is gone."

"Gone? Pyktis has killed him as well?"

"No," said Malo slowly. "Not that. Rather, he has fled in the night. *After* grabbing a sizable chunk of the Yarrow treasury from the king's vaults, too."

I gaped at her, trying to make sense of this. "Darhi . . . So. He was . . ."

"Pyktis's contact within the court," said Malo. "Yes. So we think."

"*Darhi* was the one coordinating with him and Gorthaus . . . and now he's run?"

"So it seems!" said Malo. She grinned cheerlessly. "Makes sense, as he was the fucker managing all the diplomatic meetings! And he, of course, was already willing to betray his realm by indulging in Kardas's double dealings. Perhaps we should have seen it sooner."

"But Gorthaus's murder rattled him."

"As it should have! If Pyktis really is killing off all his old allies, and if he's so clever that a citadel full of armed guards can't stop him, I'd wish to flee in the night, too."

I sighed and pinched the bridge of my nose. "And do we have a guess where he might have gone?"

"The prince's folk have no fucking idea. We are told Darhi has fled so quickly and thoroughly that it is clear he planned his flight for some time, and ensured he is difficult to track. The amount of money he stole is apparently so great that the prince is now nothing short of despondent. The dolt has even pledged permission to let us pursue him deep into the realm! Ana thinks on how best to do this but wished to wait for you. I hope you have better news for us?"

"No," I said huskily. "No, I do not."

"Then let us go to her. She waits in Thelenai's office. Perhaps she has a miracle in her pocket and can stab a hole in these black clouds for us."

I SAT AMONG the blooms of Thelenai's office, hunched and shivering as I clutched a cup of tea, recounting to them all I'd seen within the Shroud. Thelenai stood at the windows, facing away, while Malo lurked behind a clutch of coiled vines like a predator stalking its prey. Only Ana moved, sitting hunched before the wall of flowers, rocking back and forth, yet even in such a colorful place, the sight of her made my blood cold: she seemed thinner and gaunter than ever, as if she was so burdened with thought that her body burned up its sustenance faster than she could replenish it.

When I finished, there was a silence. Then Malo said, "By gods . . . they let you *see* it? They truly let you *see* the marrow?"

"Yes," murmured Thelenai. "What a privilege that must have been. One even I myself have not experienced . . ."

I glanced at Ana, who had stopped moving. It seemed Malo and Thelenai had not grasped my revelation. I wondered if I had been mad for thinking it.

There was another disturbing, glottal click from Ana's throat, and she shifted on her pillow. "I am most fixated by the Shroud itself . . . a thing so terribly unnatural, bred and formed to survive all the cruelties nature throws at us. It is most grotesquely imperial, in a way!" Her pale fingers crawled over her knees. "Yet I am even less surprised now to find that my theories of Pyktis prove true. Even he was broken by dwelling in that strange place—enough to reveal a great secret of himself." She turned her blindfolded face to Malo. "For you recognize the descriptions of those totems, do you not, Signum?"

"I do," said Malo. "They almost sound like ancestor totems of Yarrow. But I can't fathom why an augur would ever wish to—"

Ana's blindfolded face swiveled to me. "Din!"

"Y-yes, ma'am?"

"You've already put it together, haven't you? Just as the augurs said."

"I ... somewhat think so, ma'am."

"Then out with it. Speak, child."

Again, I balked, feeling like the words swilling in my mouth were howlingly mad. "I ... I think Pyktis—or the man who came to the Shroud claiming to be Pyktis, ma'am ..."

"Yes?" purred Ana.

"I think he is not Rathras at all," I said. "I think he is *Yarrow*. And not just Yarrow—I think he is a child of the Yarrow court. Perhaps a child of King Lalaca himself. That, or ... or he believes himself to be these things."

There was a silence, broken only by the afternoon breeze sweeping across the shore outside. Thelenai turned to stare at me, her mouth hanging open in shock.

"*What?*" said Malo, astonished.

"That is not possible," said Thelenai.

"Oh, I surmise the same," said Ana mildly. "And I, for one, am tempted to conclude that it is more than belief! I think Sunus Pyktis *is* the child of the dead king of Yarrow. And I think he has known this for all his life."

"But ... no!" said Malo. "That's the maddest thing I've ever heard! Surely he just ... just happened to ..."

"*Happened* to keep these ancestral totems of the Yarrow regent?" asked Ana. "*Happened* to build a shrine to their kings in secret? *Happened* to perpetrate an attack on the Shroud? *Happened* to assist the High City in undermining the Empire for the past two years? No. No, no, that is all too much coincidence for me."

"No," said Thelenai faintly. "Still, I ... I cannot ..."

"Think, all of you," said Ana. "Long have we wondered how Pyktis seemed to possess such a mastery over Yarrow culture. How does he know the language, and the court? How does he know about the High City at *all*, when most imperials are utterly ignorant of it? The answer, though improbable, is simple. Pyktis is part of the culture, because he is the *child* of the king. For the thing he cherished most was a piece of jewelry, yes? A silver necklace, just like those given to countless princes before him."

"That just can't be so!" cried Malo. "There already *is* a prince of Yarrow! Though we know he is a weak fool, Prince Camak is the one and only prince of the realm!"

"True, but it is what *Pyktis* believes that matters!" said Ana. "And I think he believed he was heir—the true prince, living in secret."

"I still cannot accept this!" said Thelenai. "It is sheer insanity!"

"Is it?" said Ana coyly. "The king has over two hundred children. Chance alone suggests it's possible for some of them to wind up in very unusual places, yes?"

"But we check all of our Apoths most rigorously!" cried Thelenai. "How could we not have learned this man was Yarrow? He is not just of Rathras folk, he is *from* Rathras! How could he have fabricated his entire history, and performed well enough in his duties to get placed on the Shroud?"

"I think the answer there is that much of his history was *not* fabricated!" Ana answered. "Din—when I reviewed the files on Pyktis, I mentioned a note about his birth year. Kindly recount it for me!"

My eyes quivered, and I quoted in her own accent: *"The only unusual thing I saw was a note from a Rathras registrar stating he thought the boy's birth year was inaccurate, for he seemed far older than the listed birth year . . ."*

Malo shuddered. "How strange it is to hear her speech come from your lips . . ."

"But you both see what it suggests, do you not?" asked Ana. "For I believe when he was born to his Rathras mother in the High City, Pyktis was taken away—probably by his mother, or the king's servants—and formally registered in the Rathras canton. That accounts for the confusion over his birth year! And I think there, in that distant place, he was raised to be *two things at once*. A hardworking, brilliant student in the school of Apoths who could pass as a Rathras native . . . and then, when he was with his intimate family, he was a secret prince of a faraway, wondrous realm, whose kingly father awaited his return. Each night they poured enchanting stories in his

ears, and he forged the whole of his being for one purpose." She tutted her tongue. "I did say at the start of our search that he seemed like
a man on a mission . . . yet even I did not expect this."

"But what mission could this have been?" asked Thelenai. "Why
make one's entire life into this story?"

Though I did not mean to, I found myself reciting something
Darhi had said to me, muttering: "*The children and relations of the king
are mere tools to his ancestry. If the king asked us to throw down our lives,
we would do so . . .*"

Ana tipped her head to me. "Thank you, Din—for there it is! I
believe his father the king plotted this long ago—a plot to place a Yarrow loyalist deep within the Empire's workings here, with the eventual
goal of *sabotaging* the Shroud itself! He would use one of his own children to stab at its heart, like marring the heartwood of a great tree.
With this act, he would damage the Empire most terribly, and unravel
its influence over his kingdom." She raised her blindfolded eyes to the
ceiling. "It was, I think, a suicidal mission. Pyktis himself said his father expected him to die on the Shroud, after all. Yet perhaps his will
failed him, for he saved not only those he loved but his own life. Perhaps that sentimental impulse is what saved the Shroud, as well."

"Yet I wonder, ma'am . . . why did Darhi appear ignorant of this,
ma'am?" I asked. "We know now he was Pyktis's agent, and we also
know he was practically running the realm. Surely he would have discovered this plot?"

"But you forget that the king was terribly aged and addled by
Darhi's time, Din!" said Ana. "So much so that I think the king *forgot*
he'd ever put such a secret plan in place to begin with, thirty-some
years ago! Thus Sunus Pyktis washed ashore, a prince who'd not only
failed in his one and only duty, but a prince *completely forgotten* by the
realm he'd lived to serve! A rather tragic thing, is it not? He returned
to his country as a man with no nation and no identity to call his
own. So he invented a new one—the pale king, lord of the canals."

A dreadful silence fell over us as we absorbed this.

"Though all my reason fights this," said Malo reluctantly, "I must
admit, it hangs, though horribly."

"But even if we know this mad truth," said Thelenai, "how shall it help us now? We do not know where Pyktis is, nor where we can find those stolen reagents that can bring down the Shroud!"

"Yet there is one person remaining who might," said Ana. "Satrap Darhi. He knows much that I wish to know."

"But do you have any clue where he might be?" cried Thelenai.

"Ah, no," said Ana, smiling. "But . . . can anyone *truly* flee from the wardens of the Empire, who are so famed in powers of nose and eye?"

There was a silence. We all slowly turned to look at Malo.

Malo blinked for a moment, surprised. Then she considered it.

"I presume he has flown far, through dense woods," said Malo. "That will be no easy thing for us. So . . . it will take a lot of wardens. A lot of noses. And a method of scent distillation that is most . . . unpleasant."

"But you can do it?" asked Ana.

"Probably," she said grudgingly. "But it will depend mightily on whether someone in the Yarrow court still has some of his undergarments."

Ana's smile turned into a grin. "Let us have hope in the lethargy of Yarrow maids, then—and move quickly to follow him!"

WHILE MALO AND the wardens mustered and prepared, I kitted myself out in the Apoth works with all the supplies I might need for such a pursuit. The last time I had followed such a killer had been across open plains on horseback, yet I would have no such advantages in the hills of Yarrow. Thus, I packed as lightly as I could: rope, healing grafts, water, augmentations to aid my thirst or energy, and last, a standard-issue imperial knife and my sword. I also shed myself of my traditional blue cloak and garbed myself in blacks and grays, and tied down every metal buckle and clasp to ensure that it made no sound and would catch no moonlight in the trees. It was a queer thing to transform myself in such a fashion: no longer an instrument of justice but rather stealth and violence.

"I have one other gift for you, boy," said Ana's voice as I finished.

I glanced up and saw Thelenai leading her toward me, one pale hand trailing on the wall. Again, I tried to ignore how worn Ana looked; Pyktis seemed a parasite within her innards, feasting upon her from the inside.

"Yes, ma'am?" I asked.

"Not a reagent, nor arm, but advice," she said. She managed a weary grin. "For I think the commander-prificto and I have found a way to *identify Pyktis*. One that cannot mislead you!"

"Truly?" I said, surprised. "If so, that is tremendous luck, ma'am."

"Luck has no damned part of it, child!" Ana snapped. "This prize took great work and much reading. Bare your right arm, Din, and show it to Thelenai here."

I did so, though I cringed as I raised the sleeve, as my arm was now pained with several more blotley welts.

"Do they persist?" demanded Ana. "Are the blotley wounds there upon him, Thelenai?"

"They are," said Thelenai. "I admit you . . . you may be right, Dolabra."

"What's this about, ma'am?" I asked.

Thelenai cleared her throat and looked at me hard. "When blotleys were first created by we Apoths, Kol, they were not intended as a mechanism for testing blood for contagion. Rather, we planned them as a method of *transfusion*. For the blotley fly does not actually *digest* blood. They do not break it down like you or I would our sustenance. That is why they are so useful as contagion tests to begin with. Rather, their systems first alter the blood with a venom so that it can be directly integrated into their own bodies. They *convert* it, in other words, which is why we hoped we could make them useful transfusion mechanisms—for not all folk have the same kind of blood within them. We theorized that if we could drain the blotley of its altered blood, and place this blood within a new body, then the venom still within the sample would help convert it again, so it could reside within a new host. However, this never worked, for very obvious reasons . . ."

"Because blotleys are an accursed pain in the ass," said Ana, grinning.

"Again, true," sighed Thelenai. "Blotleys could only transfer mi-
nuscule amounts of blood, and the welts they leave behind were too
painful—and worse, they are most resistant to healing grafts. Thus,
we abandoned it."

"But recall now, Din!" said Ana. "Recall what the medikker Tangis
said would happen if you left a blotley attached to you for too long!"

My eyes fluttered, and I summoned the comment: *"This is an altered, unnatural creature, created for this one purpose. It can't survive in the
wild anymore. It can't even eat properly. If I let it go long enough, it'll actually start leaking your own blood back into you."* I paused as the memory
left me, and murmured, "Back into you . . . ma'am, are . . ."

"Yes?" said Ana, giddy.

"Are you suggesting that *this* is how Pyktis got into the Treasury
vault, and used so many blood rights he could not possibly have possessed?"

"Correct!" she sang. "It's quite simple, is it not? Pyktis, being both
a genius and an Apoth, saw a way to cleverly misuse the horrid little
things. He stole a crate of them from an Apoth barge, stuck countless
larvae on Sujedo, let them drink their fill, then stuck them on his *own
body*! He left them there long enough so that they leaked *Sujedo's*
blood into him—and that allowed him to just walk into the vault like
he belonged there!"

"And that is why Sujedo's body was so queerly marred!" I whispered, eyes fluttering. I recalled the sight of the curious wound: a circular section of skin, excised from the flesh on the back of the torso,
about the size of a talint coin. "He . . . he had a patch of skin removed,
shorn away on the back shoulder. You think he was . . ."

"Yes!" said Ana. "I think he, so cautious and ever-wary, had done
this to the body because he did not want us to know how he'd taken
the blood rights from Sujedo! Because the little bastards leave a stubborn visible trace behind!"

"So if you, Signum Kol, in your pursuit of Darhi, happen to find a
soul you suspect to be Pyktis," said Thelenai, "then the way to confirm
it is to see if this man has *blotley welts* upon his body, in many hidden
places."

"Dozens of them," said Ana. "Forty or fifty or more. He is quite literally a marked man, in other words!" One scrawny hand reached out and grasped me firmly by the shoulder. "Here is your path now, child. First, you pursue Darhi. Question him, for we must find either Pyktis *or* the stolen reagents! By achieving either, all our threats shall be ended."

"Of course, ma'am."

"Good. Next, Pyktis may be close to Darhi. But if you do not find him on your search, you must return to the High City and seek a man with many blotley welts upon his flesh. For no matter what face that man wears, he is surely Sunus Pyktis himself! Do not tarry—go immediately, for you cannot give him time to scry our movements and slip away! Do you comprehend this?"

I bowed. "I do, ma'am."

"Then go, and make haste. And do not be slow to strike him down if you think you must! For he has proven a wily thing." Her fingers released me, and again a glottal click emanated from the base of her throat. "Perhaps too wily to take alive."

CHAPTER 48

∆ ∆ ∆

THE KING'S HALL OF YARROW WAS A GHOST OF A PLACE compared to when I'd seen it last. All its torches and bonfires were dark, and its many passageways seemed far emptier. As I walked the palace, I consulted my memories and gauged that nearly half the guards had fled. Had so many of the king's guard truly been under Darhi's influence? I found the idea unsettling, but I still seemed more composed than Malo and Sabudara: Sabudara appeared especially unnerved to dwell in the palace of her realm's autocrat and clutched tight the large leather box she carried, while Malo whispered comments to calm her as they walked behind me.

"I've . . . I've no idea what to do now," said Prince Camak as he wandered before us. "I have nothing now. No crown, nor throne, for I've not yet been formally declared regent. But neither do I have much of my treasury, nor many of the High City guards! Dozens followed Darhi to wherever he has gone, and the others fled in fear. And such is the amount that Darhi stole that I cannot afford to purchase more!"

"You've no word of where he's fled to, sir?" I asked him. "You've done no searches, heard no news?"

"Jari Pavitar advises silence," sighed the prince. "If word were to get out that I'd been so taken by Darhi, I'd never regain a steady hand upon the throne. Instead, he has insisted he go to his own allies in the kingdom and seek the traitor secretly. But . . . that will take time. Time I do not have. But I . . . I received your notice about what you require to find Darhi. I hope what we gathered may suffice." He shot me an uncertain glance. "But you're sure this will work, Signum?"

"I am told it will, sir," I said. "But I've not a nose like my peers here."

His gaze lingered on Malo and Sabudara. He made a disdainful pout, as if the sight offended him, and turned away.

We came to the same trophy room where Gorthaus had perished not more than two days ago. Now it contained a large table, and there upon it were the personal belongings that Satrap Darhi had left behind: scarves, robes, belts, jewelry, soaps, trousers, leggings, and other attire of a kind I did not know but guessed were Yarrow undergarments.

"Which piece would you, ah, prefer, Signum Kol?" the prince asked me.

I stepped back and gestured to Malo and Sabudara.

The two wardens sauntered up to the table and reviewed the garments like a carpenter might study planks of wood, estimating their grain and quality. Sabudara placed her leather box on the ground, and then the two of them went to work, plucking a few garments from the table and tossing them aside—rejects, I supposed. Then the prince and I were treated to an unusual sight: the two wardens began stooping and rigorously sniffing each remaining garment, swallowing occasionally as if they could taste the aromas on their tongues.

"Is such an act . . . common in the Empire, Signum?" the prince asked.

I watched as Malo came close to burying her face in a pair of leggings. "I do not know, sir," I said. "But it is quite uncommon to me."

Malo and Sabudara then stood and made hand signals to one another: speaking in a silent language of gestures, I reckoned, for they knew the folk about them spoke Pithian. It appeared to be a debate of ferocious belligerence, but finally Malo yielded and gathered five of the remaining garments from the table.

While she did this, Sabudara opened the leather box. Within lay a strange contraption, consisting of a small bronze barrel, lined with glass on the interior, with a crank jutting out from one side. Sabudara took the barrel out and opened it at one end, and Malo dropped the garments inside. Malo then rummaged about within the box and produced a small vial of reagents, uncorked it, and dribbled it over the clothing. Then she corked it again, closed the barrel, replaced it, and began vigorously turning the contraption's crank. The barrel spun within the box, whirling like a top. She spun it until her arm was exhausted, then let Sabudara take over.

When the two wardens had cranked the apparatus for nearly ten minutes, they removed the barrel from the box, popped the crank from one end, and placed it into a new notch on the box's side. Malo turned the crank once more, but now the top lid of the barrel descended on a little track, squeezing the fluid-covered garments tight. When Malo could crank it no more, Sabudara produced four empty glass vials and held them out. Malo opened the contraption and, like a vintner doling out a precious liquor, tipped the barrel over. A tiny thread of umber fluid came dribbling out, which Sabudara quickly collected in the vials. Sabudara corked three of the vials, then held up the final fourth, shot Malo a loathing look, and took a sniff.

Sabudara then exploded into an attack of sneezes and coughing, but then she recovered and gestured to Malo—*Yes, yes.*

"It works," sighed Malo. "We have distilled Darhi's scent, unpleasant as it is. It is a horrid thing, to sniff at such a distillation, but it is our best hope. We shall disperse this to our wardens and be off."

"Then you can track him?" said the prince. "And return all he stole?"

"We shall follow the scent as far as it goes, sir," she said. "Beyond that, I can say no more, besides that the longer we wait, the more the scent shall fade."

"Then by my father's blood, go!" said the prince. "Find this traitor, and return my kingdom to me, I beg of you!" Then he sat down in a chair, buried his face in his hands, and began to weep.

AS WE LEFT the king's hall we were joined by six of Malo's wardens. Eleven more watched from the wood, I knew, silently moving with us.

I was unsure what kind of resistance we'd be met with, but given how I'd seen them perform in the jungles, I felt that seventeen wardens would be enough to overcome nearly any Yarrow force; or so I hoped.

When we left the High City, both Malo and Sabudara took another great sniff of the vial of Darhi's scent. Muttering discontentedly, they then put pads upon their knees and thick gloves upon their hands, and then fell to all fours and crawled upon the earth, sniffing the wet grass as if they were hounds. Then Malo rose, pointed, and said, "That way. I catch it bright now!"

"Are you going to crawl the entire way?" I asked.

"You'd catch more scents, too, if you put your nose to the earth," she snapped. "Try it sometime!"

We went west, slipping down the carriage paths of the rolling hills and off into the trees as the sun met the horizon. The rest of the wardens rejoined us, silently emerging from the jungle like spirits. The vials of Darhi's scent were shared among them, and they prowled through the leaves, occasionally dropping to the ground to sniff the soil or the base of a tree.

At one fork, Sabudara paused, sniffing a patch of clay quite hard, and arose and said, "*Gora.*"

"Horses," explained Malo. "She catches their scent here."

"He fled on horseback?" I asked. "Not with all that gold, surely."

"Let us assume, then, he fled in a litter," said Malo, "moving as quickly as horses can pull such a load over poor roads. I gauge they must have moved some ten or fifteen leagues since last night. We shall have to hurry. Are you ready for a dose of kinephage?"

I pulled a face. "How I detest that stuff. Not just the taste, but I shall be hungry for days after . . ."

"Yes, but we will feast and be merry if it helps us catch our prey!" She gestured to her wardens and hissed, "*Sapida posana!*"

Then we stopped, pulled tiny black bottles from our packs, uncorked them, and took a great draught.

I shuddered as the acrid, black substance dripped down my throat. Yet the second it struck my stomach, I felt a brightness in my arms and legs as if my veins had flooded through with fresh mountain water, and the world grew still and clear about me. I had the sudden, flighty urge to laugh and jump and twirl.

"Let us move," said Malo. "And stay close, Kol! We shall cut across country, and it may be hard to spy my folk in the trees as the sky grows darker."

THE EMPIRE HAD long struggled to produce unnaturally fast forces that could live tolerable lives, and the effort had eventually proven so difficult they'd abandoned it. Instead, they either opted for imbuing some soldiers with unnaturally powerful stamina or, preferably, dispensing a graft like kinephage, which granted folk a temporary aptitude for speed and endurance. A soldier with a belly of kinephage brewing about in them could run all day and night and never tire.

Run we now did, the wardens and I, sprinting through the darkening forests of the Elder West, dodging between towering trees and dancing through the ferns. Our passage was speedy, shadowy, and nigh silent; and though our mission was fraught, the graft made my heart glad and sprightly, and I bounded along like a hind romping on a dewy morning.

Hours passed, and I lost all concept of how far we'd traveled. I occasionally caught a glimpse of torchlight amid the darkening hills: perhaps a noble's distant estate, or maybe the lanterns of Darhi's litter. I did not know.

Our trail led us along a babbling stream, and there Malo raised a hand, and we slowed. It was deep night now, the stars glimmering greedily above. She whispered with her wardens, then said to me, "Few of us know this part of the Elder West well, but we know we are now on the River Kanda, which runs parallel to the Bunti Road to the north."

I wiped a rainstorm of sweat from my brow. "All right?"

"It used to be an estate road, where many noblemen once lived. But as the Elder West has declined, many of these estates are now abandoned. Or so we thought."

"You think Darhi has gone to one of these abandoned estates?" I said.

"Yes. His escape has been well-prepared, so I assume he prepared this place for his flight. He has been wise enough to take this back path rather than the main road, as well. We must catch him before he gets to where he is going, for he shall surely get fresher horses, and perhaps more troops. We will have a fight ahead of us, regardless! Prepare yourself."

WE SANK LOW and continued our run along the river. After another three leagues, Sabudara raised a hand and pointed off into the ferns north of us. We slowed and studied the hills before us, and Malo spoke so quietly that only her wardens could hear her, and many began creeping off into the foliage, vanishing like eidolons into the night mist.

"You will stay with me," she whispered to me. "We find many ill signs about us now—torch smoke on the wind, many boot prints in the soil, and more. We are close to Darhi, we think."

I followed her up through the ferns as more of her wardens left us, melting into the night. Then I spied torchlight and lamplight filtering through the trees, and occasionally heard the call of a man's voice.

Finally Malo and I stopped behind the trunk of a large tree and peered out. A low, sprawling clutch of buildings was arrayed before us, all built of wood, and most rather crudely. Many of them had been intended for the sheltering of animals or harvests, though at the center of their constellation was a large house, sporting two stories and a wide, sloping roof: the house of the master, I assumed.

Positioned before the house was a long litter of soldiers and horses and carts, bedecked with many boxes and crates and trunks. I squinted at them but could not make out much besides the glint of armor and iron about them.

"Nigh thirty soldiers," Malo whispered. "Well-armored, and all of strong make. Darhi bribed the best of the lot."

"A wise choice, if so much Yarrow treasure is on that litter," I said.

"True. We shall kill the soldiers but take Darhi alive, if he lets us."

"I assume we cannot attack to disable," I said.

"This is no arrest, Kol. An injured Yarrow soldier will still struggle to strike us down. When we attack, we mean to kill. My folk will surround this place and signal when they are ready—a soft frog's call. Then I will give another signal and launch the attack."

I gazed at the troops gathering about the master's house. "The soldiers are well-clad, though, in mail and helm."

A soft snort. "That will not be an issue. When enough have fallen, go and secure the litter. I will not have some bastard filching a chest and cause Pavitar to bellow that we stole his kingdom's filthy money."

We watched the Yarrow soldiers milling about, some going to and fro to fetch new horses, or water, or other materials. The wait was nothing short of agonizing, and I fought not to jump at every sound or movement, for the woods were alive with the cheeping of frogs and the fluttering of errant moths.

Then Malo hissed beside me. I glanced at her and saw that her eyes were locked on something ahead.

One of the soldiers was ambling along the estate houses with a low form at his side: a hound, large and well-muscled, its pink tongue dangling cheerfully from its mouth. Both of us sank lower as the soldier and hound walked the tree line. For a moment I felt sure we had not been spotted, and my belly flooded with relief.

Then the hound stopped. Its ears pricked up, and its pink tongue retracted. It gazed at the tree line where we crouched and took a cautious step forward.

There was a long, frozen moment as neither we nor the hound moved; then it erupted, baying at the trees, leaping back and forth, its nose pointed in our direction.

Another hiss from Malo. Then a soft click as she nocked an arrow.

The beast's master approached and chided the hound in Pithian, as if to say *Enough! Calm your noise.* Yet though he tried to restrain it with a lead, the hound resisted violently, baying at where we lay.

Finally the soldier paused and peered into the trees. His body tensed, and one hand slowly moved to the hilt of his sword. The hound continued howling at his side, and two more soldiers emerged from the houses. One called a question, and though I knew little Pithian, I knew he said, *What's wrong?*

The guard with the hound responded uncertainly, *I'm not sure.* Then he drew his blade and began to advance toward the trees.

I swallowed, and gripped my sword. Then I peered through the leaves and counted our foes: three soldiers, one hound. Yet the soldier at the back was of most danger: he bore a shortbow with him, and from his handling of it, he was well-familiar with the weapon.

Stay low, I told myself. *Defend Malo. Low strikes. Make yourself obscured in the dark.*

I steeled myself as I heard the crunch of the soldier's footsteps in the leaves.

Then several things happened at once.

First, there was a series of curious clicking calls from the forest about us. Then Malo pressed her hand to her mouth and made another sound, this one higher and warbling, like that of a dove.

Then she sat up very slightly, drew her bow, and fired.

The soldier with the shortbow made a low, gurgling cry, and he fell to the ground, thrashing wildly. The hound ceased its baying and whined. The two remaining soldiers jumped and turned to stare at their fallen comrade: Malo's arrow was now protruding from the base of his throat, and he pawed at it uselessly before going still.

Then the night lit up with screams as the many wardens in the trees loosed their arrows. I drew my blade and leapt forth, my muscles filling with memories, my blood hot with violence, my bones like ice within my flesh.

The two soldiers fell easily to me. The first was still gazing at his fallen comrade when I struck him down; the next was struggling to unsheathe his sword when I fell upon him. The hound proved a coward, thankfully—I had never fought a dog before and did not know the nature of it—for it barked twice before whining and slinking away. The screams in the night grew louder and wilder, and I darted back to the cover of the trees and knelt beside Malo.

"Shall we stay or move in?" I panted.

"We move in!" she snapped. "But I could have killed them faster had you not leapt before my aim! Do not be so eager in the next fight, or I might accidentally shoot you in the fucking back!"

I rolled my eyes and helped her to her feet. Then we joined the battle, I leading with my sword, she firing arrows over my shoulder.

I had drawn my blade several times in my service for the Iudex and felled a fair few foes who'd been a deathly hand with a sword, but this was my first time taking part in a battle of such scale, with over a dozen allies fighting with me and the enemy emerging from all about us. It was a mad, wild, confusing thing, all the night screaming and surging. I had no time for clarity or conscience: my body thrummed with all the memories of so many movements, the way I'd trained my flesh to respond to threats, and I felt myself pulled through the night, hacking and feinting and dodging, while Malo hissed, "Calm your blood! You shall get us both killed with your frenzy!"

I tried to do as she bade, and as I did, I realized I now saw unfamiliar faces among the fray: not Yarrow soldiers, nor wardens, but skinny, starved Pithian folk, wielding clubs and knives and ropes, and farm tools and cooking blades. They did not attack me but instead fell upon the Yarrow soldiers, beating them or choking them or stabbing between their armor with what appeared to be kitchen knives, screaming howls of unbridled hate.

Naukari, I realized. This estate had housed servants, and now that they had an opportunity, they rose up against their masters.

"This sight cheers me!" Malo shouted. "But it is not what I wished! They could spoil all if this goes awry!"

"You seek out Darhi," I said. "I shall secure the litter—that clear?"

She nodded and cried out to the *naukari* in Pithian. I raised my sword and dashed off into the night.

THE FIGHT WENT quickly after that, but to my battle-crazed mind every second was an hour. I raced to the litter and found one soldier standing at the back, unsure whether to fight or flee. When he realized I was running at him, he raised his sword and cried out, but I cut him down easily, wounding him in the thigh, then the arm. He lay on the ground, screaming in pain, but I ignored him and focused on securing the litter.

The train of carts stretched before me. To my eye, most of its burden was the treasure of Yarrow, yet as I walked the litter, I spied a few boxes that looked unusual.

They were crates of an imperial make, for only imperial shipments used fretvine in such a way. I stepped closer, squinting in the dim light, and saw a symbol imprinted on the sides of them: the sigil of the Apoths, the drop of blood set in a hexagon.

I stared, nigh overcome. Then I stepped closer and took a mighty sniff. A powerful, acrid scent hit my nostrils: the unmistakable aroma of reagents.

These were reagent crates, almost assuredly robbed from the Apoth barges on the canals. I'd never expected to find them here among Darhi's stolen treasure, but it did make a crude sense: reagents were some of the most valuable things in all the Empire, and a greedy soul like Darhi would ensure he got a price for them, wherever he might flee.

Yet were these the reagents Pyktis needed to make his weapon? Had Darhi been hiding them the entire time, here at his secret estate? I was no Apoth and could not tell. I returned to the front of the litter, to guard it and wait for the battle to end.

After what felt like an eternity, Sabudara emerged from the night and gave me the report: twenty-six Yarrow soldiers dead, with three wounded, unlikely to survive, including the one I had just cut down. All the wardens had survived, but four *naukari* had fallen as they'd fought against those who had enslaved them.

"And Darhi?" I asked.

Sabudara shook her head. "Of him, nothing."

I cursed. "Tell Malo I need her!" I said. "Tell her I have found something important among the litter here, and to come when she can!"

Sabudara nodded, then vanished back into the darkness.

———

AN HOUR LATER I heard Malo calling my name. I ventured into the clutch of buildings and found her standing with her wardens over five bodies that had apparently been dragged from the houses.

She pointed at one. "Take a look."

I did so and moaned in dismay. I did not need to consult my memories to recognize that green-painted face or those cold, cutting eyes, indifferent even in death. Satrap Darhi's throat had been viciously slashed open, it seemed, and his chin and chest were soaked in blood.

"How did this happen?" I asked.

"One of the *naukari* cut his throat," said Malo. "And she got run through for trying. Poor girl is dead, and didn't even see the age of fifteen, I wager. A cruel thing. I wish they had all waited. We would have gladly freed them!"

I fell to my knees, struggling with the weight of it. "So," I said softly. "The one man who knew Pyktis most is now dead, and we shall get no help from him."

Malo spat, and bitterly said, "So it seems. He cannot tell us where our foe hides now. A black fate, this is, and I curse it gladly. But... what is this important thing you wished me to see?"

I shot back up, remembering. "The reagents!"

"Reagents?"

"Yes! Darhi had many crates of stolen reagents on his litter— perhaps *the* stolen reagents!"

She stared. "Then not all is lost?"

"Perhaps! Let us go see!"

I HELPED MALO'S wardens sort the reagents crates from all the chests of Yarrow treasure. Rather than open them one by one, Malo and Sabudara sniffed them, claiming that they knew well the aroma of the fertilizer they sought. "We have sniffed the jungle for it for weeks on end!" said Malo. "I smell it even in my sleep."

At first, they frowned and grimaced as they crawled over the crates. Then their expressions brightened, and they became overcome with excitement.

"It's here!" cried Malo. "By the titan's taint, it's here!"

I hauled the crates away from the litter, whispering "Thank Sanctum, thank Sanctum," again and again, for I myself had never quite believed that Darhi had possessed it all.

First we found four, then five, and then after some searching, we found the sixth crate of reagents, hidden in the back of one of the barns.

"That's all of them, yes?" said Malo. "Your immunis said there were *six* crates missing of this fertilizer, true?"

"Six, yes," I sighed, wiping my brow. "But let's open them to confirm it."

We did so, prying off the lids with spears taken from the dead Yarrow guards. Each of the six boxes contained wax-wrapped bundles of a deeply black, soil-like substance that smelled powerfully of rotten eggs.

"That's it," said Malo. She almost began to weep. "That's it! That's the damned stuff, it's all here! Darhi surely didn't know what he had, but he's kept it out of Pyktis's hands and brought us to it!"

My legs began to quake, and with a deep sigh, I sat down in the wet grass.

AS THE RUSH of combat drained out of me, the rest of the night passed in a torpid stupor. The wardens tended to the *naukari*, sharing water and food and applying healing grafts. One warden went to a high hill to fire off a rocket for Yarrowdale to see; the rest of us went about opening the remainder of the crates to take inventory, yet we did so lazily, and without panic.

"You are decent with a sword, Kol," said Malo. She grunted as she cracked open another crate. "Almost as good as I am with a bow."

"Thank you," I said politely.

"If only all fights were so courtly as to allow you to get so close," she said, "and engage in single combat! Then you might actually be useful."

I smirked, happy to hear her jibes again. "That was not single combat," I said. "There were two of them, at least at the start."

"Well, yes, after I shot one in the neck. You'd have had none at all if you'd just stayed low. But . . ." Then she trailed off, her face troubled.

"What is it?" I asked.

She glanced about. "I smell something . . . rotting."

"So? There are over thirty corpses just a few span away."

"Yes, but those corpses are freshly killed, and not yet rotting! I smell flesh that has been putrefying for some time. I could not smell it at first, because of the aromas of these reagents, but . . . something is dead here, Kol."

Malo began to dart about the crates upon the litter, sniffing the air. Then she pointed to one—this one a large chest of Yarrow treasure—and a warden hurried over and pried the lid open. They peered down into the crate, and their expressions changed to utter shock.

I staggered to my feet, leaning on my own stolen spear. "What?" I said wearily. "What is it now?"

"Kol," said Malo slowly. "Come and see this."

"If it is ill news, can you at least give me a hint?"

"No! Just come and see!"

I limped over to them. The smell of rot was indeed terrible, and I covered my nose with my sweat-soaked shirt and peered inside the Yarrow chest.

A body lay within: the body of a man, lying on his side and bunched up like an infant in slumber. He was rather small and dressed in rags, but most notable was what was placed beside him.

A warding helm, painted white. In the faint light of the fading moon, it almost resembled a skull.

I gazed at the body of the little man, and the white-painted helm beside him, my pulse thudding in my ears.

"No," I whispered.

"I know," said Malo.

"It can't be . . ."

"I know! Let's get him out and look him over."

We pulled the body out of the chest and placed him on the road. He had perished of a stab wound, I saw, just under his heart and placed between the ribs: an expertly given wound if ever I'd seen one. His face was distinctly Rathras, with a thin nose and rather small eyes, though his eyes were faintly green, and he had a rather starved look to him, much like one might expect from a man who'd been surviving in the wilderness for months on end.

But more, he looked exactly like the drawing Malo and I had studied: the sketch of the man who had come to the Treasury bank and opened the Apoth's box.

Malo sniffed the air. "Been dead about two days," she pronounced. "Perhaps more."

I stayed silent, my mind whirling.

"Could . . . could it truly be him?" asked Malo.

I knelt and pulled his shirt up to his collar. There, in ghostly imprints all across his belly and chest, were dozens of rounded, puckered welts, the imprints of tiny insects that had once fed upon his flesh—or, perhaps, leaked stolen blood into his veins.

"Blotley welts," I said quietly.

"Fucking hell," said Malo. "Exactly as your immunis said. He set many blotleys to Sujedo, then to himself, to draw the proper bloods into his flesh. By the bloody eyes of the fates . . . it looks like Darhi finally got hold of our friend Sunus Pyktis and killed him before this devil betrayed him in turn! What a shameful way for his miserable life to end. At least it is done—true?"

I gazed at the corpse and said nothing.

CHAPTER 49

AN IMPERIAL BARGE AND SEVERAL DOZEN APOTH MILITII awaited us at the bend of the River Tarif, at the edge of the Elder West, having come when they'd seen the rocket in the sky. They escorted us and all we'd secured into the city, and as we traveled I gave them my report, which they quickly recorded and sent to Prificto Kardas by scribe-hawk. "He speaks with the prince now at the High City," said a militis to me. "Yet his talks shall soon change! I wager we have all his realm's fortune aboard our vessel."

Once we returned to Yarrowdale we brought the entire hoard into one of the preparation rooms of the fermentation works: the very chamber where I'd been so thoroughly dosed before my trip to the Shroud, in fact. There Thelenai and Ana both awaited us, and Thelenai watched fretfully as the wardens laid out each crate, listening as I breathlessly recounted all we'd experienced.

When I finished, there was a long silence. Pyktis's corpse lay in the open Yarrow chest before Ana. The wardens sat beside the long-sought six crates of fertilizer, weary but triumphant. I stood at the edge of the room, feeling far less victorious, for as I'd spoken, Ana's blindfolded face had twisted in a way I found distinctly unsettling.

Thelenai stared down on Pyktis's body. "How strange it is, to feel sorrow at the sight of this man," she whispered. "He is a creature I made, in a way. Yet all this time he'd been secretly made by another, and bent wholly toward my destruction. How we would have loved and adored him if he'd come to us honestly! For his genius was great, and we would not have cared from whence it came. All fruits of flesh are equal in the eyes of the Empire." She turned to Ana, who still sat in silence, a deep glower on her face. "What do you proclaim, Dolabra? It seems a great triumph, to find all we sought and all our enemies dead, and all at once."

I winced; for that, I knew, was precisely what troubled her now.

Finally Ana spoke: "Why keep the body?"

"Pardon?" said Thelenai.

"Why would Darhi keep Pyktis's body?" Ana demanded. "Why package it up so?"

We all looked at the corpse and thought on that.

"I do not know," said Thelenai. "Perhaps his hatred of the man was that great."

"You think he was going to . . . *do* something to it, ma'am?" said Malo.

"Again, I do not know," said Thelenai, affronted.

"Or," I said, "perhaps . . . Pyktis was killed by another, ma'am?"

Ana's head snapped up to gaze sightlessly upon me. "Oh? Say more, Din."

"W-well," I said. "Someone might have killed Pyktis and stored his body in the chest in the Yarrow vaults, packaged as if it were a pile of gold. If Darhi's aim was to steal all he could and flee, he might not have known he'd just stolen a body as well, just like he might not have comprehended the value of the grafts he'd stolen."

"So . . . you suggest yet *another* killer?" said Thelenai uncertainly. "A killer of Pyktis, who stored his body in this chest? I cannot comprehend that . . . but I confess, I have little appetite to pursue it. The clear conclusion is that the man in possession of the body is the one who killed him. Indeed, the same man who had a tremendous *reason* to kill him—Satrap Darhi. For you believed Pyktis was killing his old allies one by one, true?"

Ana was silent.

"And even if someone else killed him," said Thelenai, "how troubled are we that Pyktis is slain, given that we have secured the reagents he so needed?"

Ana's next words were like the snapping of a steel blade: "Have we?"

The wardens fell to muttering and drew symbols in the air.

"You said six crates had been stolen, ma'am," said Malo slowly. "And six crates is what we've found."

"Yes," said Ana tersely. "We have crates. But I would like their contents tested, for merely having the crates makes me less than content! Specifically, I want to test their *concentration*."

"You worry it has been diluted?" asked Thelenai. "Cut with another substance?"

"Oh, I worry about all things, with this investigation," said Ana. "Please test it. And hurry."

The wardens and Thelenai quickly produced tools and instruments to take samples from the fertilizer. I felt myself nearly toppling over from exhaustion, yet Sabudara pressed a small vial in my hand. "Clariphage," she said. "To keep your eyes open, pretty one."

Mumbling about being grafted so often, I tossed the vial back. It was sickly sweet, but the instant I consumed it, I felt energy return to my limbs and watched the Apoths work.

The first four boxes, they pronounced, were the proper concentration of reagents, exactly as they'd been shipped from Yarrowdale. The fifth, however, was somewhat diluted, but only slightly. "Yet this," Thelenai said, "could be from decay, or improper storage."

But as they tested the contents of the sixth crate, their faces changed. Thelenai peered at the cloudiness of the reagents in her instruments, then went pale and announced, "It is . . . forty percent of its expected concentration."

Malo shut her eyes, dismayed. Again, the wardens fell to muttering and made more strange gestures to beseech the aid of the fates. Such was my despair that I had half a mind to join them.

"Meaning over half of its contents have been removed," said Ana, "and replaced with another substance?"

"Yes," said Thelenai, her voice hardly a whisper. "A much more common fertilizer. One with far less *qudaydin kani* in its production."

"How much has been removed, in weight?"

"Just over four stone," said Thelenai. She pressed a hand to her brow. "So. Enough . . . enough to achieve a warping much, much greater than what was seen in that jungle clearing."

A miserable silence filled the chamber.

Thelenai turned to Ana. "He . . . he already took all he needs, didn't he? He did it long ago."

"Yes," said Ana softly. "I rather think he has."

"So . . . so another weapon lies sleeping somewhere." A tremor of panic rang in Thelenai's voice now. "Doesn't it, Dolabra?"

Ana's response was light and unbothered: "Yes. I think it does. For he is just the sort to manufacture an attack that would succeed even if he himself perished."

"But . . . but where is it?" begged Thelenai. "Where has he hidden the weapon? What does he mean to strike at now, from beyond even the barrier of death?"

Ana pursed her lips and cocked her head, her fingers flitting in the folds of her dress as they so often did. Then she said, "I don't know."

"AFTER ALL WE'VE DONE," whispered Malo. "After everything . . ."

The wardens began chattering to each other in panicked Pithian, and Thelenai paced the room, her crimson robes fluttering. "It must be somewhere," she said. "Yet we have checked all the tools and shipments upon the Shroud, and have found not a thing! How could he still intend to attack it? What methods does he devise now?"

I could see Ana's face twitching. I stood and, feeling bold, said, "Calm, please, Commander-Prificto. My immunis will need some quiet to think upon this."

Again, a silence filled the dismal chamber, and we all watched as Ana sat before the crates of reagents and the chest containing the corpse, her pale face twisted in thought. Minutes passed, and we did nothing but smell the reek of the fertilizers, the rot of Pyktis's body, and the musk and sweat of the wardens and myself.

Finally Ana whispered, "Apophenia."

I leaned close. "Pardon, ma'am?"

"Apophenia," she said again. "The affliction of spying meaning and patterns in randomness. The augurs struggle with it, yet . . . I feel it is this state he aimed to induce in me. He bombards me with so much evidence and motives and mysteries that my mind cannot function! It is as if he knows my very nature." Then she shook her head. "There is no more to it. I must do something now that I have long since avoided."

"What's that, ma'am?" I asked.

She sighed deeply. "I shall need to *dine.*"

A stupefied pause. Sabudara sat forward, peering at Malo for confirmation, mouthing *Dine?*

Malo ignored her, crying, "You *what?*"

"Ahh—beg pardon, ma'am?" I said. "Dine again?"

Ana waved a hand like our bewilderment was beneath acknowledgment. "Yes, I shall need to *dine!* But it will be very different from every meal you've seen me consume before."

Everyone looked to me, as if to confirm that her words were true. I shrugged, feeling quite as confused as they.

"Dolabra . . ." said Thelenai. "So grateful I am for the works you have done for us that I am nearly moved to grant you anything you wish without thought. But—this is an emergency, surely. Is it wisdom to stop now to sate your hungers?"

"It is!" said Ana. "As I said, this meal will be different. For I must *think* differently to evaluate this problem. Tell me, Commander-Prificto—do the Apoths here possess any stock of kizkil mushrooms?"

Thelenai blinked, startled. "We do. That is a highly regulated substance, as it is very psychoactive and dangerous."

I covered my face as I realized what she was asking. "Ma'am," I said. "You can't seriously be asking us to acquire you psychedelics *now?*"

Yet Ana's bearing was utterly grim. "Oh, I am *deadly* serious, Din," she said. "As you should be if you wish me to divine where this weapon now lies! Can you get me this, Thelenai?"

"I . . . Yes. But why would you need them?"

"I have been quite clear," said Ana. "Just as the augurs need their augury, I have my own hungers I must sate to prod my thinking. I shall only need three smallstone worth or so."

Thelenai stared. "That is enough to sicken or even kill a person, Dolabra."

"Not all people. Can you fetch them before dark falls?"

"Well . . . yes, I can do so."

"Good." Ana's head turned to me. "And you, Din—you will need to hurry to the Yarrowdale butchery. I will need two calf livers for my meal, as rare as possible."

"Livers," I echoed faintly.

"Yes—*calf* livers, specifically. Bring them to me wrapped in paper, please. Then I shall sup, and reflect on the situation, and decide how we shall proceed. Go now, and hurry! For while we have some time to prepare, we do not have days' worth!"

I COMPLETED MY strange errand and returned to the testing chamber just as evening came on, feeling like an occultist practicing some rite of witchcraft with this dark, bloodied parchment package under my arm. Thelenai had already provided the kizkil mushrooms, and the small, shrunken lumps sat in a bowl atop a table the Apoths had provided. Next to the bowl sat a fork and a knife and a napkin. Besides this and two chairs positioned on either side, the table was clear.

"Your two calf livers," I said, laying the parchment next to the bowl. "Fresh enough to soak through the paper and stain my coat. How would you like me to cook this for you, ma'am?"

"Oh, not at all, Din," Ana said. "For this meal, I need only what has been provided. However . . . I would like you all to leave, if you could."

"You desire privacy?" said Thelenai.

"This seems hardly a fine place for a private meal," muttered Malo, "given the corpse in the box just over there, and the stink of that altered soil."

"And yet privacy is what I ask!" said Ana. "Save for Din, of course. He is my engraver, and I shall need someone to witness my revelations, should I be blessed with any. Now, I can eat here, or I may remove to my chambers, where I can then eat in peace. Which do we all prefer?"

"Say no more," said Thelenai, sighing. "We shall leave you to this rite, Dolabra. I hope it yields heady dividends!" She gestured, and they all began to troop out.

As she followed at the end of the line, Malo stepped close and whispered, "You remember how I said your immunis sometimes has a strange smell to her? Well, she smells very queer to me now! So much so that I am glad to leave this room."

She walked out, and the door swung shut, and I was alone in the room save for the corpse of Pyktis, and Ana, still sitting sprawled on the floor.

CHAPTER 50

. . .

ANA GESTURED TO ME, CALLING, "COME! COME NOW, Din. Help me to my meal."

I walked to her, took her by the arm, and guided her to her seat at the little table.

"Now, please—veil the lights in here a little," she said. "It is too bright! I can see the luminescence through my blindfold."

I did so, casting cloths over the mai-lanterns. Soon the chamber was quite dark, the corners swimming with deep shadows.

With a slight clearing of her throat, Ana squared up to the table, unwrapped the livers, and placed the black, gleaming nuggets of flesh in the bowl. Then she began violently cutting them to ribbons with her knife and fork. "Now sit," she said as she worked. "Sit across from me, child, and give me a moment."

I did so, repulsed by her mangling of the innards. Then she uncer-emoniously dumped all the kizkil mushrooms on top of the raw livers and began to mix them.

"Isn't that dosage dangerous for you, ma'am?" I asked.

"You need not speak, Din," she said archly. "For I shall be unable to respond soon."

"Because . . ."

A wry smile. "Because my mouth will be quite full, of course." She then gobbled down the awful dish, bite by bite. The sight was so hor-rid I had to turn away. She even lifted the bowl to her lips and feverishly scooped the dregs into her mouth. Finally she lowered the bowl and sat back with a satisfied sigh, her chin and lips now dark and bloodied.

"Another meal," I said softly, "like the Empire of old."

Her blindfolded head snapped to attention. "What?" she said.

"The last time you ate, ma'am. You said such banquets were a common sight in the ages of the first and second emperors."

She remained totally silent, appearing to wait for more. A drop of blood gathered at her chin and dropped into her lap.

"And you made many proper deductions then," I said nervously. "So . . . perhaps the same shall happen now?"

"Hm. That is true, Din," she murmured. "And I thank you for your indulgence. Now . . . I shall reflect on our quarry's nature, and desires. Then, perhaps, I can spy his last, most hidden works, and decide how we will proceed this black night."

Ana fell silent once more. She sat back in the darkness, her pale form dappled with blood, her blindfold still tight about her eyes. I worried that the mood reagents might sicken her, and she'd topple over at any moment.

"Are you all right, ma'am?" I ventured.

"Be still, child!" she answered softly. "I am thinking."

I waited. Minute after minute passed in the stinking dark of that place.

And then Ana seemed to undergo a change.

It was one of the strangest things I'd ever seen; though *seen* was not the right word, for it was so dark in the chamber that I sensed it more than anything. Ana's body remained still, her blindfolded head bowed at an angle, yet I became aware of ligaments tensing at the edge of her face, or about her neck, a curious coiling that somehow reshaped the whole of her visage.

Then I smelled it: a strange, acrid, shivering musk, slowly suffusing the air. It leaked into my nostrils and tickled the backs of my eyes, as if I'd accidentally punctured some chamber of fume in the earth. My heart raced, and my pulse quickened. I began to feel a deep, unnatural sense of threat, like I was not sitting with my commanding officer at her table, but rather trapped in this place with a predator, stalking me in the dark.

I stared at her then and saw not the Ana I knew, but a skeletal thing, draped in shadow, with bloodied cheeks like corded leather and her snowy scalp pulled far back from her brow. Her neck appeared elongated, and her long, pale fingers twitched in her lap. Her grin no longer seemed to have any trace of humor in it but was enormous and savage, and though I felt it had to be my imagination, her smile suddenly seemed to have far more teeth than I'd recalled before.

Then Ana spoke, yet her voice was once more queerly deep and resonant, like it emanated from some glottal chamber in her chest: "Why has he not yet attacked the Shroud? Why not strike when we are vulnerable? Still I think upon this . . . Why not yet?" A wet click from the back of her throat. She cocked her head, and I saw the glint of bloodied teeth in a wide grin. "What does his heart desire, this man who has no nation, no kingdom . . . nor even a face?"

She shivered and sat back, moving past the penumbra of the lantern light. More minutes passed, and when she spoke again her voice was even deeper than before; not the voice of a man, but a voice distorted and warped, so much so it was difficult for me to parse her words.

"How was he there that night?" she murmured.

"P-pardon, ma'am?"

"How did he poison that cup without anyone ever noticing it?" she whispered. "Did he do it before it ever touched the king's hands? And how did he fell Gorthaus without anyone spying him and seeing he was a stranger to this court? Or . . . was he *always* there?" Her pale fingers reached forward, as if grasping an invisible arm. "Tell me . . . the king had a twin, did he not?"

My eyes fluttered as I recovered the memory. "So Darhi said, yes."

"And Pavitar had a twin, born dead. And Darhi was a survivor of three."

"Yes, ma'am."

She meditated on this, then turned her face to the west. Then she twitched in her chair and turned yet again, now facing where Pyktis's corpse lay in the shadows. She pulled her blindfold away—a normally mad thing for her to do, given her dislike of new environs—and gazed at the body, as if enraptured.

"Din," she said. "Your knife."

"What, ma'am? You—"

"Your knife. Give me your knife, boy—*now!*"

I did so, dismayed by the request. She took it, then flew to the corpse's side. For a moment I feared she intended to mar the body, butchering it in her madness, yet a voice in my mind told me this was not so.

She will not savage it, the voice said quietly and calmly. *She plans to eat it, to feast upon it—for this is the feast she has so long hungered for, true?*

Ana raised the knife; but my horror was entirely wrong, for rather than slashing at the flesh, she wedged the blade between the corpse's teeth and wiggled it back and forth, until a tooth came free with an awful crunch. Then she dropped my knife and turned the tooth over and over in her fingers, like a witch reading her scrying stone.

"A fine tooth," she whispered. "A fine imperial tooth, healthy and strong from many calcious grafts . . ." She tapped it against the floor. "And *recent* grafts at that. This has no staining or weakness from months in the jungle. Why would Pyktis bother to modify his teeth? Except . . ."

She froze, and dropped the tooth. Then she stood and turned to the northwest. She walked to the chamber walls as if she could see through them and behold some distant movement in the High City on the hills above.

"His dogs," she whispered. "Of *course* . . . of course he killed the dogs first."

"His . . . dogs?" I asked. "Jari Pavitar's dogs? Do they matter in this, ma'am?"

"Do they matter?" Then she shook her head, laughed, and turned to face me. "Do they *matter*, Din? I . . . I see it now! A hidden piece! One kept off the board entirely, while all our eyes were fixed on something else . . ." Then she cried out: "Oh, how I see it! I see all of it now, *I see it now!*"

Still shaking her head, Ana dreamily walked toward me, and when she entered the light of the lamps, I gasped.

Her wide yellow eyes were quivering and dancing, shaking in her skull just as my own shook when I summoned my memories. In the blue mai-light, and with the blood still fresh on her chin and her features so strangely distended, the sight struck me cold.

"I see his game, his mind!" cried Ana. "I see all the warp and weft he spins about us, even now! What a fine, clever officer he was, and what a finer one he would have made, had his heart not been so poisoned by the puerile dreams of petty men!"

Her devilish smile lingered on her face for a moment; then she seemed to suddenly remember my gaze, and she turned away into the shadows, like she'd committed some indiscretion. She wiped her mouth of blood and replaced her blindfold. When she returned to the dim lamplight, she seemed returned to her ordinary self, though there remained something strange and stretched to her face.

"I have made my decision," she whispered. "I know where the other weapon lies."

"D-do you, ma'am?" I said softly.

"Oh, yes. I know all the threads within his design now! Fetch my lyre!"

"Your *lyre*, ma'am?"

"Yes, for that shall be most critical! Fetch that and bring Thelenai and the others back in! For I've a task for her, and much scheming to do. And then, Dinios, you shall lead myself and the wardens back to the High City, to return the wealth of that kingdom." She grinned horribly. "And there I shall lay the entire plot bare."

WE THREW OURSELVES to it then, hurtling about in the dark, following Ana's cries and exhortations, building her grand plan beneath the darkening skies. When our work took us outside she stayed within her carriage, whispering or crying instructions through a crack in the door, sightlessly predicting our movements. I was reminded of the tale of the eidolon trapped in its mausoleum, whispering tales of how all its neighboring dead had come to lie in their shelves.

With each horrible revelation, our pace grew faster. Thelenai nearly screamed in rage, and Malo gasped and cursed; but still we worked, breathlessly and thoughtlessly, seizing weapons and tools to secure our path ahead.

"A red rocket," Ana said to Thelenai as our preparations ended. "We *must* see a red rocket when your work is done. Only then can I proceed with confidence. Is that clear?"

"Very," said Thelenai weakly, now stripped of all her pride and dignity. "I shall send it into the skies at the very moment."

"Excellent. Now, Din—how long has it been since the scribe-hawk departed with news for Kardas?"

"Nearly three hours by now, ma'am," I said.

"Good," purred Ana's voice through the crack in the carriage. "Then I believe we are ready to proceed."

I assisted in loading the last of the Yarrow treasure onto the litter, and we began our long trek up to the High City. Yet my thoughts lingered on the sound of Ana's voice just now.

Was that tenor still present? That queer, sepulchral timbre? What did we make here in the deep dark, in service for this strange being?

I thought of the Shroud, and how I'd once imagined it to be a chrysalis, holding some brewing horror within its flesh. As we hastened our steeds up the slopes in the depths of night, I wondered if this hidden threat still remained true, but perhaps I had been looking in the wrong direction entirely.

CHAPTER 51

⌄ ⌄ ⌄

WE WERE NOT MORE THAN THREE LEAGUES FROM THE
High City when one of the wardens hurried back to our carriage and
whispered: *"Thauta!* Blood! And human blood, at that."

Ana gestured, and I exited to review the way ahead with Malo.
There we found many corpses lying about in the trees or in the road,
cut down by sword or shot with arrows. They were all Yarrow men, to
my eye, but they had the look of soldiers, clad in armor and well-
armed.

"They are Darhi's men, I imagine," Ana told us when we reported
the scene to her. "Or men suspected of being loyal to the former satrap. I believe Jari Pavitar and his allies have now won out."

Malo spat into the night. "That purple-faced bastard truly runs
the whole of the Yarrow court now?"

"That, or thereabout. The young prince found himself deserted,
but Darhi is now slain, and news of his death is known to all. Pavitar
rushes in to fill the gap. I suspect this will not be the last corpse
we see tonight. Steel yourselves, children—but do not forget our
purpose!"

Her words proved true. When we approached the gates and reported to them our purpose—Prificto Kardas, it seemed, had notified
them of our arrival—we were led through and saw the bodies of slain
Yarrow men hanging from the gates within, as if stuck there by a
srika-bird.

"An ugly thing, when the crown changes heads," said Ana when I told her of this awful sight. "For it is often paid for only with savagery. But tell me now, Din—have you seen a red rocket in the distance?"

"I've seen none, ma'am."

"Hum. And Malo—you've heard no signal from your wardens?"

Malo shook her head. "None yet. So they have not seen the rocket, either."

"Then Thelenai has not yet succeeded. You're sure you'll be able to hear the signal from your wardens once we're inside, Malo?"

"I could hear that call," said Malo, insulted, "from half a league away."

"Good. But I may have to slow my step a little. Let us have hope!"

The Yarrow soldiers escorted our train of carriages toward the king's hall. We were met at the base of the stairs by several dozen guards; and there, striding at their head, was Jari Pavitar, himself arrayed in a cuirass, a short sword at his side, and his head bare but his brow stained indigo as always. I climbed out to meet him.

"Do you finally bear our treasure, *phansi vala*?" Pavitar demanded as he approached. "You've tarried for too many hours, when it should have been brought back swiftly!"

"We have it, sir," I told him, bowing. "All royal treasure shall be accounted for."

Malo helped Ana exit the carriage, and she turned her blindfolded face upon him and grinned. "Specifically, Jari Pavitar," she said, "we shall do so before the eyes of ourselves, the prince, *and* Prificto Kardas. I believe Kardas communicated that to you?"

Pavitar stuck his nose in the air. "Do you think us thieves?"

"We suggest nothing," she said. "But we know the court has been upended recently by treachery. We'd prefer our counting done in the sight of all, to ensure that no other treachery occurs. Is that not a safe choice?"

His glare lingered on us for a moment before he waved a hand. "Fine, then! Bring it in. But know now I've little patience for you this night." He grinned his broken, misshapen smile and gestured at one of the hanging corpses, which twisted in the night breeze. "Darhi and his greedy folk are gone, and our tolerance for the Empire is gone with them. If we discover Darhi did indeed kill the king, and at your request, the hall may prove a dangerous place for you."

I listened to the creak of the dead man's rope. "Noted, sir."

The soldiers hoisted the trunks of treasure and bore them up the great stairs to the king's hall. Pavitar watched, pleased, yet his grin vanished when two Yarrow wardens removed the final chest from the litter and bore it inside. "Why does that box stink so?" he demanded.

"Why, it contains the body of the man who did so much harm to you!" said Ana cheerily. "Surely one more corpse will make no difference here, given that you appear to be using them as ornament."

"But . . . you wish to bring it inside?" asked Pavitar.

"Indeed! Do you not wish to look upon the face of the man who wounded you?" asked Ana. "Come, follow our dead man with us, Jari! For I shall have many merry tales about him once we are settled."

WE ENTERED THE KING'S HALL, smoky and bright with firelight once more. Many Yarrow women were stationed about it, all small and meager and seated before lambskins stretched out upon the floor. The soldiers lowered the chests of treasure before them, and the women opened the chests and began taking heaps of coins and placing them upon the skins, quietly but rapidly counting them out one by one. They only slowed in their counting when the wardens bore Pyktis's corpse within the hall, and the reek of his rot filled the room.

At the far end of the hall was Prince Camak, seated atop the throne. He appeared exhausted but relieved, his silver crown on his head and his chain about his neck, his gold-painted face smiling sadly at us as we entered. As always, there was a dimness to his look that suggested he did not entirely comprehend what he was seeing. Beside him stood Prificto Kardas, clad in his bright white Treasury dress, and at the sight of us he bowed to the prince and paced over to me.

"Is all well?" Kardas murmured to me. "For the prince is ecstatic to hear that Darhi is slain and the treasure recovered—though it does mean Pavitar's influence here is now strongest. I daresay you saw the horrors outside? I suppose we must accept these, Kol, for the sake of stabili—" He trailed off as he spied Ana, who stood next to the body of Pyktis. "I say—is that a *corpse*?"

"It is, sir."

Kardas's face had already been quite grave, but it grew graver still as he absorbed this. "I . . . I knew Dolabra was coming, yes," he said, "to explain all that had happened, but . . . why in hell have you brought a damned body with you?"

"To explain all that happened, sir," I said—for that was the answer I'd been told to give.

Kardas peered at me, mystified, then leaned to Ana and said, "What scheme are you playing, Dolabra?"

"The winning one, as always, sir," said Ana, grinning.

Kardas shook his head but said nothing.

Pavitar swept into the room behind us, his brow bristling, and bent low to whisper into the prince's ear. The prince listened, his rather vapid features fixed in concentration, then nodded and cried, "Immunis Dolabra! How pleased I am to find your work done so quickly! You found not only Darhi, but this smuggler-killer, at last?"

"I have indeed, Your Majesty!" said Ana, grinning. "I have finally found him, at the end of all things."

We slowly began to take up positions in the chamber. Malo, Kardas, and I stood along the wall to the prince's right, while Pavitar and his soldiers stood along the wall on his left. Before the prince stood Ana, bent and blindfolded, and the crate containing Pyktis's corpse; behind her were the trunks of treasures and the many counting women, quietly doing their work.

The scene was quite orderly, but I could feel nothing but overwhelming tension. I glanced at Malo and saw that she was watching Ana fixedly, a bead of sweat trapped in her greenish eyebrow. I took a breath and recalled what Ana had told us before we began: *Be still, and move little. Simply let me lay the trap, and we shall see how things proceed.*

To which Malo had responded: *And if the trap goes poorly, ma'am?*

Then we shall have to improvise, she'd said with a shrug. *With sword and bow, perhaps! Be ready.*

Ready I tried to be, but I could hardly imagine how this night might go.

The prince leaned forward, peering at the corpse in the crate. "This is the man who killed my father? How odd it is to finally look upon him now. For he is quite small, and all the evils he wrought so large . . ."

"And we still do not know *how* he killed our king," said Pavitar. "For all we know this might be the corpse of some unnamed *naukari*, or imperial indigent, and the Empire simply wishes to claim the deed is done. I still think it was Darhi who slipped that poison in."

"Ah!" said Ana. "A fair point. It is a worthy story! And it is the exact one I wished to tell you, to explain how all this was done to your realm."

"Yet why would we listen?" demanded Pavitar. His voice grew loud, like a canton councilman lecturing before a crowd. "It was Darhi who planned the most with the Empire, and it was he who stole our fortunes and fled! To any wise eye it would seem that you imperials are friends of schemers and knaves."

Then Malo twitched and grasped my arm. She pulled me close—perhaps too quickly, for I nearly stumbled to the ground—and whispered into my ear: "I hear a whistling outside! Many of them, very soft!"

"Your wardens?" I asked.

"Yes. They have seen the red rocket from Yarrowdale. All proceeds as planned!"

I let out a sigh and softly muttered, "Praise Sanctum!" I stepped closer to Ana and laid a hand on her shoulder. "Thelenai has succeeded, ma'am," I whispered in her ear. "The red rocket has taken flight."

"Ah!" whispered Ana. "Most excellent, Din. Thank you."

I withdrew, my whole body thrumming, and stood beside Malo to watch the meeting proceed, my hand now much closer to my sword.

Kardas bowed to the prince. "Majesty, I must protest! Satrap Darhi was no friend of the Empire, for he harmed us as well! We know now it was his wickedness that caused the harassment of our shipments and murders of our bargefolk—for many imperial treasures were found among the litter, too."

Prince Camak turned to Ana, surprised. "Is this so?"

"It is indeed!" Ana said brightly. "This dead fellow aided Darhi in many things, yet he was repaid with only sorrow. Allow me to regale you with his journey—and then grant you a gift that I have prepared for you."

"Oh?" said the prince. "What gift?"

"A song. For I have practiced greatly upon the Pithian lyres, as you may soon see, and would much enjoy providing you with music! That should make a fitting end to these sad days, yes? To play a Pithian song before a Yarrow king, in celebration of his coronation?"

She waved to me. I reached into one of the many crates and produced her twinned lyres, bound up in cloth, and brought them to her. She unwrapped them and played a tune so melodious that some of the guards gasped in surprise.

"We have minstrels enough," said Pavitar sourly.

"Ah, but this song shall accomplish something quite startling, Your Majesty," said Ana. "One that will astonish even one of your high breeding!" A wide grin bloomed on her face. "It is going to achieve a *miracle*."

"A miracle?" said the prince.

"Yes," proclaimed Ana. "For with this song, I shall make this dead man talk!"

There was a shocked silence. The soldiers in the back of the chamber muttered as a few of them translated what Ana had just said. Kardas stared at me, his gray face coloring, but I studiously avoided reacting.

Malo hissed to me: "What in fuck is she doing?"

"I've no idea," I whispered through clenched teeth, for this mad flourish had not been part of the careful instructions Ana had given us.

Pavitar scoffed. "What is this foul jest? Do you mock us at such a time?"

"Did you not once declare us thaumaturges and magicians, Jari?"

said Ana. "I swear to you that it is so. Or would it be acceptable if I asked a *favor* of you, Your Majesty?" She reached into her pocket and, with an artful twist, produced an oathcoin: the very one that Darhi had given me so many days ago.

The prince gazed upon the oathcoin. "Ah. Yes. An unusual request, to ask for something so simple in exchange for so valuable a token. But . . . I shall take your coin, Immunis Dolabra, and hear your tale and your music . . . no matter how odd it may seem." He plucked the oathcoin from her fingers and placed it in his pocket. Then he sat upon the throne, with Pavitar sitting on a small stool behind him.

"Excellent," said Ana, grinning. "Fetch me a chair, please, Din, and I shall begin."

"FIRST OF ALL, YOUR MAJESTY," said Ana, sitting, "I shall tell you the most startling thing I discovered—for the dead man in the box is actually not imperial at all!" She sat back in her chair, pausing dramatically. "Can you guess which land he hailed from, so long ago?"

The prince blinked when he realized Ana would not continue until he guessed. "Ahh . . . I've no idea. I am little traveled, other than in my own lands."

"Ah—but he *is* from your own lands, Your Majesty!" said Ana. "This man is *Yarrow*, through and through."

"Is he?" said the prince, interested.

"It's true!" said Ana. "Yet he comes from broods closer than you may know! For despite his imperial look, this man is actually a child of your dead father, Your Majesty—royal issue of the now-fallen king of Yarrow *himself*!"

Pavitar, Kardas, and the prince stared at her, open-mouthed.

"Pavitar," said the prince, shaken. "Pavitar, surely . . . surely that isn't . . ."

Pavitar swept forward, knelt beside the reeking corpse, and opened the dead man's eyes with a thumb. "This cannot be so! This man's eyes are white, and bear only a hint of green. And his teeth are unnaturally white from your accursed magics! And besides, his features are clearly that of the Empire!"

"True!" sang Ana. "I will grant that the masquerade was quite masterful. Why, the dead man even bore an imperial name—that of *Sunus Pyktis*! Yet he *was* your father's child, Prince Camak, though he left this realm long ago, before his eyes ever greened. As for his race, this Pyktis, like many true Yarrow souls here—including Darhi and yourself, Your Majesty—had *Rathras* blood in him. For many children of the court bear imperial bloods, do they not?"

Neither the prince nor Pavitar answered, though I sensed this question was deeply distasteful to both of them.

"Yet his fate sent this fellow on a journey far from here!" said Ana. "For long ago, your father had this Pyktis sent abroad to hide among the Empire. There he was to pass as a common Rathras child, gamely pretend to be an imperial boy, and join the Empire's ranks, in the hope of achieving one thing only, something your father had desired for years untold—he was to return to Yarrow and destroy the Shroud."

The prince now looked so stunned he nearly slipped out of his throne.

"These are lies!" snarled Pavitar, standing. "You admit this villain was an imperial, then invent far-fetched tales to deny it!"

"I regret to say, Your Majesty, that it is true!" said Ana. "So secret was Pyktis's identity that even Darhi knew nothing of his existence— nor did he know of the king's plot to place one of his own trusted children upon the Shroud, with the hopes of destroying it! Indeed, he could *not* know, for the king by then had sadly lost a great deal of his wits and had forgotten it entirely."

Now Pavitar was positively apoplectic, and he gestured so violently that he leapt off the stone floor. "Now you impugn the dead!" he bellowed. "I demand you cease this, or I shall strike the head from you, witch!"

I tensed at that. Ana seemed to sense my movement and waved a hand at me. "You may try, but I do ask that you wait until I'm done! Besides, I don't think you're *allowed* to demand I stop, given that your prince took my coin, yes?" She turned back to the prince. "And don't you wish to hear this, Your Majesty? For these are the once-hidden works of your father—and that man in that box was your half brother."

The prince gaped at her for a moment, then gazed upon the dead body. "Yes . . . please continue."

"Thank you, Your Majesty," said Ana, bowing. "This Pyktis once attempted to destroy the Shroud from within. To do so, he rose in the ranks of the folk there to become an *augur*, one of the most esteemed of imperial ranks—a fantastic genius whose cognitive powers match nearly any in the Empire. Yet even with these abilities, he failed in his final task, and the Shroud survived. But he did not abandon his efforts! Pyktis escaped that site and became the partner of your former Satrap Darhi, some two years ago now. From thence he worked as a smuggler, stealing riches from the imperial barges, with the intent of fashioning a weapon capable of attacking the Shroud yet again. But his choice of partner was unwise—for Darhi betrayed him just like he betrayed you. Now here he is, dead in this box, and all that he and Darhi wished to accomplish is but dust and ashes. A tragic tale of waste, is it not?"

The prince raised a hand. "What evidence do you have for this tale, Immunis?"

"I have the testimonies of many imperial officers," said Ana, "and soon I shall have another witness with more testimony." She laid her hands on her lyres, grinning devilishly.

Pavitar scoffed. "Your dead man shall now speak for you?"

"Oh, yes!" said Ana. "Let me pluck my strings, and we shall listen to his words!"

Then she bowed, sat up straight, placed her hands upon the strings of her lyres, and began to play.

But the song did not at all resemble any tune she'd yet strummed upon her lyres. Those songs had been beautiful, and sad, and woodsy, yet this song was harsh, lacking all melody, and grated upon the ears, a syncopated, peripatetic song that seemed to alter and shift every second. The very sound of it bothered me immensely, and judging

from the faces in the crowd in the hall, I was not alone. Pavitar especially was growing more furious by the second.

Ana played on and on, her snowy head tilting back and forth as
she plucked out this tremendously irritating rhythm that almost
seemed to fight itself.

Then came a loud, unearthly moan.

Everyone stared about, seeking its source. Quite a few stared at
the corpse, awestruck. Yet the corpse remained still, and because of
the shaping of sound in the hall, it was difficult to tell where it had
come from.

"How . . . how is this done?" said Pavitar.

Ana ignored him and played on, strumming out her horrid tune.

Another moan split the chamber, this one far longer and stranger
than the first, warbling madly at the end. Then, slowly, everyone
realized.

The moaning was coming from Prince Camak. Yet his moaning
was a terribly strange thing: he sat in his throne in a position of
utter calmness, hands in his lap, his gold-painted face fixed in an
expression of benign disinterest; but as Ana's plunking continued,
his mouth opened very slightly, and another low, uncanny groan
escaped him. It was as if he was trying his hardest not to cry out but
could not help himself, and all his anguish came leaking through
his lips.

Yet this time, the moaning did not stop. It grew and grew, rising
into a wild scream. His entire body began to quake, every bit of him
trembling horribly, until at last his fingers flew to the arms of the
throne and he began tapping arrhythmically, his fingers beating out a
strange, awful rhythm.

Pavitar gazed at him, horrified. "What have you done to the prince,
woman?"

Ana quit playing, an infuriatingly smug smile now on her face.
"Oh, nothing!" she said cheerily.

Again, the prince screamed, his body trembling, his eyes now rolling up into his head.

Ana stuck a finger out at me. "Din! Kindly recite the firmest instruction you are given when visiting augurs on the Shroud!"

My eyes trembled in my head, and I said: *"But most of all, do not tap, or beat out any rhythm before them. Nor should you hum, sing, or whistle any tune. That will agitate the augurs greatly, for they shall seek meaning and pattern in it."*

Prificto Kardas stared at the prince, then at Ana, his eyes wide. "What are you suggesting, Dolabra?"

"Don't you see?" said Ana. "The augurs of the Shroud are unusually vulnerable to *music.* And I just happen to have composed a percussive song that is *uniquely* irritating to an augur—always suggesting order yet dissolving before it coheres! A song to drive an augur *mad,* in other words, no matter how iron their will. And so it has." She grinned. "For that man in that throne is not the prince. He is an *augur.* He is, in fact, none other than Sunus Pyktis himself!"

CHAPTER 52

. . .

EVERYONE TURNED TO STARE AT THE PRINCE, WHO SAT limply in the throne, occasionally twitching like a mouse freshly stung by a spider. So agitated did he seem that he didn't voice any protest at this.

"Wh-what?" said Pavitar.

"*What?*" said Kardas. "Dolabra—what . . . what plot is this?"

"It is no plot at all, sir," said Ana. "That man in that throne is *not* the prince. He is Sunus Pyktis, augur of the Shroud, plague of the Apoths of Yarrowdale, and killer of the king of Yarrow! He is, just as I said, the dead man brought to life—for he was never *truly* dead at all! Yet again, he has so expertly faked his death!"

"A ridiculous assertion!" shouted Pavitar. "The stupidest of—"

"Is it?" said Ana. "Let us see how he responds if I play again."

Once more she plucked out the bizarre, syncopated song. Prince Camak looked up and tried his hardest to keep a firm face. A twitch emerged in his cheek; then he began to quake and tremble, until finally he lost all control of himself, and he screamed at the top of his lungs, a long, unearthly, disturbing cry. He fell back upon the throne, hands pressed to his ears, thrashing his legs.

"*Stop it!*" he shrieked. "*Make it stop, make it stop! Please, stop, stop, stop!*"

Pavitar stared at him, astonished. "Prince . . . Prince Camak," he said. "Your Majesty, why do you—"

Ana ceased her playing. "Is it not obvious, Pavitar? I told you that

Sunus Pyktis is the son of the king—but in truth, the relation goes far further than that! For Pyktis is actually the prince's brother, his *perfect twin*! The two shared a womb, and indeed look almost exactly alike!"

Again, the soldiers about the hall began muttering, though now there was an anxious tone to it.

"No!" said Pavitar. "No, I will not listen to this!"

"Are not twins and triplets *unusually* dominant in the royal bloodline, Pavitar?" demanded Ana. "And have you ever seen the prince respond in such a fashion to music? I suspect you haven't, true?"

Pavitar's face was troubled, but he shook his head. "It is a mad suggestion! I have known the prince since childhood, and I would know if another had taken his place!"

"*Do* you know him so well?" asked Ana. "For I once theorized that the true Sunus Pyktis would be marked by blotley welts. This corpse before me bears their stings, true—but perhaps check the prince's arms and chest, and see if you can find any there!"

"Then that shall be an easy thing!" said Pavitar. He turned to the prince. "Raise your sleeve, Your Majesty, and put these people in their place!"

Yet the prince did not move. He hesitated, swallowed, and said, "I . . . I will not."

Pavitar blinked. "Your Majesty?" he asked.

"I will not do so," said the prince stolidly. "I will not give any credit to . . . to these wild accusations."

"You see?" said Ana. "He refuses."

Pavitar took a step toward the throne. "Prince Camak, I . . . You need only raise your sleeve, Your Majesty. With that, all can be finished here."

The prince blinked. He opened his mouth, thought for a moment, and said, "I want them thrown from the hall. I want them thrown from the hall for these claims, because they . . . they . . ."

All the pride and indignation began to leak from Pavitar's bearing. "Why do you hesitate, my prince?" he asked. "Why would you not show me?"

"He can't, Pavitar," said Ana slyly. "Because if he did, you would see . . . and then you would know whose body *really* lies in that box."

Pavitar stared at the man in the throne. Then he turned to gaze at the chest containing the corpse, and a dreadful horror filled his face.

The prince saw this and froze.

Then he changed.

First the prince's entire body seemed to go limp, and he collapsed in his throne, his head falling to the side. It was as if his flesh and bones were the stuff of a puppet, mere matter to be tugged about by invisible strings, yet all the strings had been suddenly severed; but not his eyes. His eyes filled with a flat, cold, brutal intelligence, and they swiveled in his slack face to stare at Ana. So stark was the change that some in the chamber gasped at the sight of it.

I understood then: he had ended his performance, ceased sending out all the signals and gestures and motions that suggested Prince Camak inhabited that body. Now he was something very different: Sunus Pyktis, augur of the Shroud.

His mouth shut with a click. He slowly sat up, again like he was being pulled by an invisible string. Then he whistled, a low, curious note.

Then blades were drawn and the entire hall fell into chaos.

I SAW THE SWORDS glinting in the firelight. In an instant, the green blade was in my hand, and I leapt forward.

Half of the royal guard of Yarrow—some dozen men in total— now sprang forward and attacked, all at once. Their targets were many: they leapt for their fellow guards, who were quickly struck down, astonished; they attacked Jari Pavitar, who barely managed to unsheathe his own sword; and they moved for Ana, who sat calmly before the throne and Pyktis.

Yet the wardens and I were moving as well; for Ana, of course, had predicted this. *He will have seeded traitors and brigands among the court,* she'd told us. *Only when he is sure all is lost shall he call upon their aid.*

The first soldier to leap for Ana was met with an arrow to the mouth, and he stumbled to the ground, choking; somewhere behind me I heard Malo let loose a wicked, triumphant cry. The second soldier I met with my green blade and struck down quickly and easily. Yet as I readied to face the third and raised my sword, he was struck down by not another arrow but by the short sword of Jari Pavitar, who was screaming in rage.

Between Pavitar, myself, the wardens, and the few loyal Yarrow guards who had managed to respond, the battle was over quickly. Soon the hall was silent, broken only by our labored breathing, the moans of the wounded, the trickle of blood, and the gentle crackle of the fireplaces.

Yet Sunus Pyktis had not moved at all. He slouched on the throne and stared at Ana. Much like the augurs I'd seen on the Shroud, his eyes simply sat in his skull like little wet stones, brimming with an alien intelligence.

Ana grinned, completely unperturbed. "I am guessing," she said to Pyktis, "that you made a calculation, and decided it would be better to try to save some, than wait and lose all."

Pyktis said nothing. He just stared at Ana with that flat, cold gaze.

"How . . . how has this been done to us?" whispered Pavitar.

"Well, my guess, Pavitar, is that Sunus Pyktis made the swap with the prince some time ago," said Ana. "He likely did it when you took the prince on that hunting trip in the west. For it was after this when you returned to the High City and found all your dogs slain, of course."

"My dogs?" murmured Pavitar.

"Yes! Killed by Pyktis, of course!" said Ana. "For if he planned to switch places with Prince Camak, your dogs would have recognized the different scents! They were a liability, and thus had to be removed. Having killed them, he then pursued you into the west and ambushed Prince Camak, perhaps sedating him—and then he applied the handful of alterations necessary to himself *become* him. A little extra fat, a little extra hair. I suspect he had already used the waters of your region here to stain his eyes the proper shade of green. The teeth were tricky; he had to color and stain his own to match the prince's. And, of course, he applied the gold paint upon his cheeks, and the circlet atop it all ... Really, it must have been his easiest performance yet, given that he already had the prince's face! Except, of course, he had to refrain from his obsessive finger-tapping ..." She smiled at the prince. "... but a creature of iron will like yourself can resist that, eh, Sunus?"

Pyktis's flat gaze danced around the chamber, as if checking to see if any ally survived in any state.

"Once the transformation was complete, he then killed Prince Camak," said Ana. "A quick, simple stab to the man's heart. But before doing this, he altered the prince's body just as he had his own— applying grafts now to *remove* fat and hair, not to mention wiping the face of gold and clearing the eyes of green stain. He even gave the man better teeth—fresh, pearly, imperial teeth! And that was the giveaway, you know," she said sweetly to Pyktis. "For why in hell would Sunus Pyktis wish to grow himself a nice set of teeth while out in the jungle?"

Again, she was met with Pyktis's stony stare.

"He was then left with a body possessing the same bone structure," continued Ana, "the same skin tone, similar teeth, the same slight Rathras features ... In other words, he made the prince look like *himself*, altered to become the jungle-dwelling creature of the canals! For he planned to *use* him, you see. He intended to use his twin brother's corpse for this very night—for Sunus Pyktis always thinks thirty steps ahead! And *how* did he preserve the dead body, Din?"

"With ossuary moss, ma'am," I said quietly. "For Pyktis was a master with its use, when he served with the Apoths upon the Shroud."

"Of course!" said Ana. "He bound the dead Prince Camak up in moss and stored his brother's body away, waiting for the perfect time to fake his death *again*. For if the trick worked once, it could certainly do so a second time! And he did just that, extracting the body from the moss at the right moment, then placing it in a chest in the royal vault. For that was when he put the *second* piece of his plan into play— Satrap Darhi, whom he'd been preparing to be his patsy for *years*.

"You fed Darhi's greed, and his avarice," Ana said to Pyktis. "An easy thing, for a snake like him! You even knew he'd eventually betray you. But then you arranged the trail just *so*. It was you who hid the oathcoin in your den, knowing that Darhi was so free with them! And you knew we'd eventually identify Gorthaus as the traitor, and she would name Darhi as the architect of all of this. Honestly, what fools we'd be if we thought it was anyone *but* Darhi behind it all!" She stuck a finger out at him. "But it was you, of course, and *not* Darhi, who killed the king."

"Wh-what?" said Pavitar weakly.

Pyktis's glare grew slightly icier.

"It was Pyktis, you see, now pretending to be the prince," said Ana, "who dropped the poison in the king's cup. He did it as he carried it back to the cauldron of tea, knowing that Kardas would soon refill it. We never suspected the prince as the killer, of course, for the true prince would never do such a thing." She turned back to Pyktis. "All that went swimmingly for you . . . until *I* arrived and identified Gorthaus as a traitor far faster than you'd anticipated. That made you a little desperate, but you'd already arranged things. You were alone in the reliquary, true, sitting vigil for your father as Yarrow tradition demands. None of the guards said you left that chamber while Gorthaus perished—but I am guessing they *did* see a *guard* exit. For you've become quite handy at disguising yourself, haven't you? After all, what is a disguise but signals, and patterns, and gestures? All very easy things for an augur's mind to unwind. You disguised yourself, slipped off into the halls, pricked Gorthaus with your poison blade before she could give too much of the game away too early, and returned swiftly, becoming the prince once more. And now that this was done, the throne was yours, and soon you would be king."

Ana paused, tapping her chin, and grinned horribly. "But you never wanted to *just* be king. It would do you no good to inherit a realm destined to be annexed by the Empire. Yet nor would it do to destroy the Shroud and unravel the Empire itself, as Thelenai and I so feared—for what would so much chaos win you? No, no. Your thoughts were much more practical. You were dreaming of a way to destroy the *marrow,* and the marrow alone."

Kardas stared at her, open-mouthed.

"If the marrow was destroyed," said Ana, "then you knew the Empire would *have* to stay in Yarrow for years longer. The Empire lacked the will to fully adopt the region—you'd already put that together ages ago—but they'd be more than happy to keep paying the court to keep things *just* as they were. And oh, you'd make sure the Empire would pay you a *fortune.*"

My eyes fluttered in my skull, and I recalled what Kardas had said to us: *Extend the deadline for a decade. Maybe two. Dump another trove of gold on the High City. Buy time, quite literally.*

"Oh, fucking hell," whispered Kardas.

"Only that could explain why you waited to attack the Shroud," said Ana. "And, of course, it also explained your macabre campaign of terror—you *wanted* to terrify Thelenai into taking a desperate measure. All this business of heads and warped smugglers . . . all of it was a story you fed us, to make Thelenai panic and move the marrow by ship, far away from here. A most vulnerable choice, really . . ." She sat back, idly plucking a string of her lyres. "Because that's where your titan's blood weapon *truly* is, isn't it? It's hidden in the mundane, forgettable, overlooked docks where that ship will stop *first.*"

Pyktis twitched slightly, but his dead, cold eyes never deviated from Ana's face.

My eyes fluttered as I recalled that day when I'd sailed for the Shroud, after first meeting Ghrelin on the pier: *We get so few vessels that sail abroad that this is the only place that can handle a ship of that size—yet it's hardly ever used, Kol. No reagents have passed through those warehouses in months, and what few wardens we've spared to search this place have found not a whiff.*

"Your weapon's not on the Shroud," said Ana. "It never has been! It's hidden in the *docks of Yarrowdale,* at the very pier where the hydricyst shall first make anchor. It's probably been hidden there for *weeks,* perhaps before you even kidnapped Sujedo! I am guessing you crept to Darhi's secret little estate and stole the reagents before even that. Very brilliant! Yet Thelenai went searching there this very night, and I told her to be *thorough*. She fired a red rocket high into the sky just minutes ago, alerting us that she'd found your waiting weapon." She grinned lazily. "My guess is that it's disguised as some common resource they'll load onto the boat . . . never realizing they carry death with them. Tell me—am I right?"

It might have been my imagination, but I thought Pyktis's eyes narrowed very slightly.

Ana *tutted.* "It was a very brilliant game, I admit. And it very nearly worked! You put your brother's body in a Yarrow treasure chest, having predicted long ago that Darhi would grab all he could, when rattled enough. You also knew we'd easily track him. You probably realized that the first time you met Malo and saw her altered senses."

Malo gave a quiet, indignant sniff.

"You didn't expect that Darhi would die, of course," said Ana, "though that was a rather lucky break. But even if he'd lived, the goal would have been achieved anyway—for how could we believe such a liar when he claimed he was *not* the killer of the body found in his litter? You'd win either way. We would think all the villains captured or killed, and all was safe—and we would relax, and relent. The hydricyst would dock in Yarrowdale and unknowingly load your weapon aboard. Then it would go to the Shroud, take the marrow, sail for the River Asigis . . . but then, somewhere out at sea, your weapon would finally unravel and destroy it all—yes? The marrow would be forever lost. The Empire would be dependent on the Shroud for *years* to come . . . and thus on Yarrow, and your rule."

Still Pyktis said nothing.

"How small-minded it all was . . ." Ana shook her head. "You'd deny the imperial people so much healing, so much advancement. You'd rule over a nation of slaves and slavers. All for gold. For a golden crown, and a throne, and a little bit of money."

"No," said Pyktis. His voice was a cold and icy whisper.

"Then why?" Ana asked.

He was silent for a moment. Then he whispered, "It was . . . the sight of him. To lay eyes on him."

"The prince?" said Ana. She cocked her head. "Or . . . your father?"

"I . . . I had never even seen him before," whispered Pyktis. "I had asked once, before I went to the Shroud, to meet my father, my king, but was rebuffed. But after I deceived you all into thinking I was dead, I . . . I came here. Crept in like a thief in the night. Gazed upon him sleeping. He woke and asked me to fetch him his chamber pot. He thought I was my brother. But he was . . . he was so *old*, and so *weak*. Just a man. Just a doddering old fool. It had all been a . . . a story."

"What had?" asked Ana.

"Kings." Pyktis shuddered. "For so long I was told they were wondrous fathers, farsighted rulers touched by the divine. The natural rule of strength, of crown, of throne—a noble thing, unlike the Empire, so unnatural and invented. But when I looked upon my father, I saw they are just . . . men. Little men with muddy, ugly little minds, who fall to common corruptions just like anyone." His face twisted. "Just like everyone in the Empire. Just like Thelenai."

"Is that so?" said Ana.

"She is just like him, do you know that?" he asked. "She made tools of us, asking us to sacrifice ourselves, to risk our lives and minds for her own little treasure. You *all* do. The Empire weeps so grandly, and bedecks the dead with gold and lands, but . . . it is still the same as my father. You call it serving. But you are slaves, and your masters shall never know any consequence."

"Are you so sure of that? For Thelenai shall see many consequences, and soon."

"She will wriggle out of them," said Pyktis bitterly. "It is the same in all nations of the earth. You are either a slave or a master. I had my chance. I made my choice."

Ana nodded slowly, then tsked. "I see . . . Simple nihilism, then. How terribly unimaginative. With you being so brilliant, Pyktis, I thought your motivations might wind up being a bit more interesting! But now the game is done, and your fate is sealed. And it's to be quite horrid, isn't it?"

For the first time, Pyktis blinked. "What?"

"Oh—did you think we were going to arrest you?" said Ana, feigning surprise. "Haul you before your taxiarkhe? After the scene of slaughter in this throne room? That would not be a very diplomatic choice!"

Pyktis gazed about and seemed to realize for the first time that every green eye in the room was staring at him with a look of profound hatred; save for Pavitar, who stood beside the open chest, staring down on the corpse within.

"I . . . I am an imperial citizen," Pyktis said. "I demand my rights to imperial justi—"

"No! No, sir," said Ana. Her grin contorted into something monstrous. "Don't you see? You are an *abomination*, Pyktis, and abominations must be dealt with. But even if we tried to arrest you, I doubt Yarrows here would let us—true, Pavitar?"

Pavitar swallowed very slowly, his eyes still fixed on the true prince's corpse. "No," he said hoarsely. "No, I would not."

"No . . . for you have committed *apavitari*, sir. The murder of a king and a prince, done by their own blood to gain the throne." She stood. "Thus, I shall excuse myself and leave justice to those who have been wronged."

Pyktis stared at her, speechless. Pavitar took a deep breath, his short sword held tight in his hands, and began to walk toward the throne.

"No," said Pyktis. "No, you can't . . . you . . ." Then his face twisted, and his voice rose to a shriek. "You call me an abomination, but I know what you are! I have read it in your body, in your very movements! You disdain kings, but *I know what you are!*"

Pavitar drew closer to him, eyes still averted, short sword low at his side.

Ana yawned. "Hum," she said. "How you bore me, child."

The sword struck but once, at the base of Pyktis's neck, the blade biting deep into his throat, then retracting: a swift, practical blow. As always with such wounds, the rush of blood was tremendous. Pyktis fell back into the throne and gazed up at the ceiling, choking once, a look of utter incredulity on his face, as if he simply could not believe this was happening to him. Then his neck grew limp, and his head lolled to the side, and he was still.

There was a long silence. Pavitar dropped his sword and dazedly stared about the bloodied room. "Get out," he said quietly. Then, louder: "All of you, get out. *Get out, now, now!*"

"Prificto Kardas?" said Ana. "I believe now is a good time to make our exit."

"Y-yes," said Kardas, shaken. "I agree, Dolabra."

We began to make ourselves ready to leave, and Pavitar walked to the open crate. Then he sat at its side, lifted out the body, and began to cradle it in his arms. "What did they do to you?" he whispered.

I looked back as we filed out, studying the soldiers and the money-counters and the servants, who all stared at Pavitar sitting among the piles of gold, rocking the dead body in his arms as he wept.

CHAPTER 53

⸪

ANOTHER RIDE BACK DOWN THE HILL PATHS TO YARROW-
dale, this one conducted in near silence. All of us were still in some
state of shock, and exhausted yet again by the dwindling excitement
in our blood. Even Ana sat leaning in the corner of the carriage, her
head lolling as we bounced down.

"He cried at the end," said Malo quietly. "I cannot ken that."

Ana's voice was raspy and deep: "Pavitar? Yes . . . Fascinating, isn't
it?" She took a rattling breath. "Both the kings and the thieves, the
angels and the utter bastards, are all inevitably quite human. Though
that should not let our hand be any softer when justice is delivered!"

"Yet Pavitar shall not see justice," said Malo.

"Are you so sure?" She coughed. "The man cherishes his kingdom
and ancestry above all. Yet what kingdom could survive this? The days
of Yarrow shall dwindle ever faster now, I think . . . and he shall have
to watch it, like a neutered steer watching all the cows run free."

Ana gasped and sat back against her wooden seat. It was not until
the carriage lantern swung about just so that I saw the pained expression on her face.

"Are you all right, ma'am?" I asked.

"No," she snapped, "I am not! I . . . I have pushed myself too far,
visited too many different environs. I must soon get to a medikker's
bay, and rest."

"Shall we go there now?" I asked. "Or would yo—"

"I would rather have my guts pulled from my ass!" she hissed. "I have toiled and gnashed my teeth far too much to retreat to the comfort of a pillow now! *No.* I shall see this done." Her blindfolded face turned to me. "And I wish to see you doing it."

"Doing what, ma'am?"

She turned back to the window. "We must proceed to the Yarrowdale docks and see what headway Thelenai has made. By talon and chitin, I mean to bury this one, and bury it deep."

WE FINALLY CAME to the last pier of the docks, all creaking wood and lapping waters. Ana waved us on, coughing, and Malo and I exited and raced along down the pier toward a clutch of lights at the end of it.

The lights proved to be a circle of lanterns arranged on the wooden platform. The officers within the circle were all bound in warding suits and were gathered about an open box upon the dock. The scene seemed akin to a midnight ritual, rather than the work of Apoths.

I stopped one of the officers and asked, "How goes it?"

The officer waved a hand forward and said, "See for yourself." Perhaps it was because of his helmet, but I could not tell if the comment came from relief or despair.

We pushed our way through until we came to the open box. A figure knelt before it, also bound in a warding suit, but their suit glimmered with the heralds of a commander-prificto. As I approached them, they turned their helmed head, and I saw green eyes within widen at the sight of me.

"Ah, Kol," said Thelenai softly. "Excellent. Tell me . . . was it all as Dolabra foresaw? Was he there, upon the throne?"

"He was, ma'am," I said.

"And?"

"He is dead, ma'am. Slain by another of the court."

"Ah." She paused. "How odd it is that this neither saddens nor gladdens me. Perhaps it is because I have already grieved him once this day. Or . . ."

She turned back to the open box. I saw hints of a familiar device within it—the chimneyed glass dome, the intricate bit of wiring suspended in it that looked rather like a tea strainer, the brass tubes snaking about it—yet the thing was cocooned in moss, and vines, and flowering fungi I'd never seen before, a queer riot of textures and colors.

"By the titan's taint," muttered Malo. "What manner of madness is this?"

"We found it suspended perfectly in a cask of water, you know," murmured Thelenai. "One of twenty that would be loaded into the hydricyst. It's a very common procedure. Something simple, even thoughtless. And because of its suspension in water, the wardens could never catch a whiff of it! We'd never have found it at all, had Dolabra not told us to open up everything we found here. I cannot comprehend how Pyktis or his people managed it. Perhaps he put it here weeks ago, even before he kidnapped and killed Sujedo—the very first move he ever made."

I gazed down at the tangle of growth within the box. "What has he done to it?"

"Graft trips," said Malo. "Organic traps, all wound together, each dependent on the next."

"Correct," said Thelenai. "It's quite clever, do you know? There is a time element to it. After several days, certain aspects of it should decay, and then . . ." She laughed lightly. "How amazing! He was able to predict not only what I would do but also the *precise* amount of time to build into this contraption, to ensure its evil purpose." Her smile faded. "What a thing I did, in granting such powers to that man. And yet . . . even he could not predict Dolabra."

I cast my eye along the pier to our carriage, waiting in the darkness.

"Can you stop it, ma'am?" asked Malo.

"Mm?" said Thelenai. "Why, of course, Signum! I've already done so." She reached behind the crate and produced a long bronze cylinder. "Without the very fertilizer that would make the *kani*, the diffuser is quite useless."

Malo and I stared at her, frozen in disbelief.

"It's . . . it's safe, then?" asked Malo in a strangled voice.

"This is the Empire, children," said Thelenai, "and no reagent is truly safe. But once this is burned and disposed of, yes, all will be safe."

We both breathed a deep sigh of relief. "Oh, thank Sanctum," said Malo. "Thank fucking Sanctum, it's done? It's truly, finally *done?*"

Thelenai smiled sadly. "Done? Not quite. There is one more thing to do." She removed her helmet, baring her bald, sweat-dappled brow to the night. Then she shut her eyes, taking in a deep breath of the sea air, and said, "Kol—would you walk with me for a moment?"

I FOLLOWED THE COMMANDER-PRIFICTO to the very end of the pier, where she stood gazing out at the bay. I joined her in staring at the tremendous, shivering green construct of the Shroud, glowing in the fading moonlight.

"What a sight it is, eh?" said Thelenai.

"It is, ma'am," I said. "First I feared it, but . . . now I find something beautiful in it."

"How kind of you to say! I once thought it beautiful, but . . . now I find it strange to look upon. First, all my life was bent on making it. Then all my life was bent on making it irrelevant. But now, perhaps, I shall succeed . . . and the Fifth Empire—as some call it—shall unfold." She sighed. "A pity that I shall not see it."

"You won't, ma'am?"

Another high, light laugh. "No. No, of course not." She turned to me. "So. How do these things commonly go now, Signum Kol?"

"I'm . . . afraid I don't comprehend your meaning, ma'am."

"My arrest, Signum Kol," she said gently.

I stared at her blankly.

"I now turn myself in," she said, "you see, for all the wrongs I did in bringing these threats about."

The waves lapped about us. There, in the distant belly of the horizon, a lance of gray dawn light stabbed through the clouds.

"You mean, ma'am," I said, "that you wish me to—"

"Did your immunis not tell you?" she asked.

"N-no?"

"I see ... She asked me to make my choice days ago, and make it I did. The marrow is now safe. My plans shall succeed. I will win an era of peace and prosperity for the Empire ... but I committed great crimes in doing so. I kept the augury a secret and worked mightily to hide it from the Senate of the Sanctum. Because of this choice, dozens are dead, and the entire Empire might have unraveled. I would not wish for any other Apothetikal to follow in my steps, or grow so prideful and careless as I. And ... I feel I do not deserve to see the bright future I have made." She gazed west, toward the High City. "I, perhaps, am more like Pyktis and his father than a true imperial servant. And I should not taint the world to come with my touch."

She turned back to me, smiling sadly. I stood there, struggling to imagine how to respond. I had never arrested someone of such high office before. The idea felt slightly surreal, especially since all the suffering she'd brought about had been for a very noble purpose.

"But you did so in service to your people," I said. "You thought tha—"

"No, Kol," Thelenai said. "I was *not* thinking of my people. My eyes are clear now. I was thinking of myself. To serve is a tremendously humbling thing. How easy it is to mistake glory and fame for duty! But duty is thankless, invisible, forgettable—but oh, so very necessary." She smiled at me again. "You know that, of course. Long have I heard it said that the Iudex is the most thankless of all imperial services—yet without it, all my labors here would have come to naught." She stood up straight, sniffed, and smoothed down her robes. "What is one more life to give, for this great pursuit? I have asked it of others. Now I shall do so myself. So. Let us go, Kol. Finish my story for me, so the next one can begin unblemished."

I listened to the waves crashing about me and watched the shimmering form of the veil in the distance. How great the world seemed in that moment, and yet so small.

"Kol?" she said.

I took out my engraver's bonds and said, "Commander-Prificto Kulaq Thelenai of the Imperial Apothetikal Iyalet, I am now placing you under bonds for the imperial crimes of extreme disregard of duty, negligence for the lives of imperial servants, and the hindrance of an Iudex investigation. You shall henceforth be detained and placed within confines until you are submitted before the authorities of the Imperial Taxiarkhe. I warn you now that all actions and speech shall be submitted as testimony, and suggest you consider how you respond."

Another sad smile, and she nodded. "Yes. Yes, of course." She extended her wrists to me, and I placed my bonds upon her, and I led her away into the night.

WHEN IT WAS OVER—when she'd been formally charged, and transferred to confines, and locked away in the Apoth holding cells—I exited to find Ana's carriage waiting outside for me. The pilot had climbed down from her perch and looked quite alarmed.

"She told me to follow you, sir," said the pilot. "Though she is quite unwell . . ."

I dashed to the door of the carriage and threw it open. Ana lay upon the wooden seat, her head at an angle, her breath rattling.

"Is it done?" she gasped. "Did you do it?"

I moved to lift her up. "Ma'am! Ma'am, I . . ."

Her white hand flashed out and gripped my wrist with shocking strength. "Is it *finished*, Din?"

"I . . . It is. Thelenai is in confines. She turned herself in."

Ana nodded weakly, murmured, "Good," and slumped back against her seat. "All justice duly done, be the culprits Yarrow or imperial. Good job, boy . . . Now. The medikkers, please?"

Her eyes closed, and I shouted to the carriage pilot to take us away.

CHAPTER 54

∧∧∧

THE MEDIKKERS SWEPT ANA TO A CRADLE WHERE THEY began to examine her, all their augmented eyes and noses and ears poring over her like beetles seeking a bruise upon a gourd. Ana whispered to them as they worked, and though I could not hear her words, the medikkers seemed quite surprised, consulted their various tomes, then approached me.

"She asks us to put her in an *uyumak*, sir," said the medikker. "A profound sleep. One that could last for days."

"She said she needed *rest*," I said, shocked. "That seems much too far."

"It is her orders. And it is a possible solution for her issues, but it is a very rare balm, one only done when the brain has suffered immense trauma. Has this happened to her?"

"Not that I saw."

"Then perhaps you can convince her otherwise."

I approached Ana, who lay on her side like a child—the position reminded me strongly of Pyktis's false body in the box—her spindly ribs rising and falling with each rattling breath.

"Ma'am," I said hesitantly, "they say—"

"Don't bother trying to persuade me, child," she said, her voice soft yet surprisingly strong. "This is not my first experience with such exhaustion. Five days of sleep should do it."

"You wish to sleep for *five days*?"

"I do! For you have things under control, do you not? You remember all I said and did. You may speak for me as things . . . settle."

"It may be a very violent settling, ma'am."

"Then you should be aptly placed. For though your wits are merely sufficient, you are wicked with a sword! I shall trust you as I rest."

I watched as she took another deep, labored breath. "Are you in pain, ma'am?"

"Pain? Feh? That is but nerves reporting discomfort, and can be ignored." She raised her blindfolded head and whispered, "But . . . do you know what hurts worst, Din?"

"What, ma'am?"

"Why, it's the . . . the crushing disappointment of it all. The investigation ends. It's all over now. No more riddles, no more need for imagination. And all was so small, at the end. It was for money, and land, and brutal, petty nihilism. Honestly, how . . . how tremendously *disappointing*."

I studied her, curled upon the cradle. I suddenly realized for the first time that Ana might feel much as I did at the end of an investigation: the loneliness, the alienation. Yet hers was different, perhaps: a hunger unsated, and hopes dashed.

A person, just like everyone else. It made me think on Pyktis's last true words, before he died.

"You think of him now," said Ana faintly. "Don't you?"

"Can you read minds as well?" I asked.

"Despite all my wishes, no! But a frustrated imperial servant might see a little of themself in the man who was killed tonight—true?"

"Some . . . some words he said had the semblance of truth," I admitted.

She laughed bitterly. "And which words are those?"

"That we are but tools. I make my body and mind an instrument for others and have no say in its use."

"You are a junior officer, Din," said Ana, bemused, "a hypokratos. All such officers feel so. Indeed, many senior ones feel the same—as do many civilians, I suspect! What are we, if not instruments in service to one another? But . . ." She sighed deeply. "I do owe you something, boy. I owe you a conversation about your future, and which path you shall choose."

"Even you cannot change my debts, ma'am."

Another bitter laugh. "How certain you seem! But we shall soon have more to discuss than debts, dear Din." She paused for a moment, panting. Then she said offhandedly, "I . . . I need for you to recall a segment of conversation we had, boy. Just after we first met Ghrelin and Thelenai—I mentioned an art the Empire occasionally uses to keep secrets safe. Recite what I said now, please."

My eyes fluttered in my skull as I summoned up that evening. "But . . . what would it pertain to no—"

"Just do it, please," she said, but her voice was oddly strangled.

I took a breath, and her words spilled from my mouth: "*Did you know, boy, that the Empire has methods of rendering certain secrets unmentionable? Grafts and arts that, when suffused into the body and mind, alter a person in such a way that they are* physically incapable *of divulging a specific piece of information?*" I blinked as I finished. "But then, you told me you *didn't* think this had been done to Ghrelin."

"True," she said weakly. "I did."

Slowly, my skin began to crawl, and something went cold in my belly.

"Why do you mention this now, ma'am?" I asked softly.

Ana swallowed, then said in a carefree manner, "I have a gift for you, Din! Listen carefully now. I wish to give you a . . . a blue scarf."

"A scarf?"

"Yes. One that I enclosed in a book, to keep my place. The book is under my bed." Again, she swallowed. "Please open it and get the scarf for me. I believe it would look quite lovely on you, with your uniform. Again—open the book and get it for me." She rolled over and hid her face from me. "Do that, Din, and let me sleep. And in five days, we shall talk again."

———

I RETURNED TO my quarters, my mind awash in blood, betrayals, and the sight of Thelenai so pristine and despairing before the Shroud. I knew that the cause of this was fatigue, at least in part, but before I slept, I went to Ana's chambers to fulfill her request, no matter how strange it might be.

I got down on all fours before her bed and found many books waiting there, but only one had been marked with a blue scarf. I pulled the book out and squinted to read its spine: *The Letters and Conversations of Ataska Daavir, Fourth and Final Emperor of the Great and Holy Empire of Khanum.*

I grunted in surprise: this was the very book that Pyktis had quoted so often when taunting us. It was a slender volume, a bare slip of a thing compared to the usual ponderous tomes Ana so frequently preferred. She'd marked her spot with a blue scarf, just as she'd said, yet this too was strange, as she often read so quickly that I could scarcely recall her needing to mark a page at all.

Hints and suggestions, but nothing ever said outright.

"Because," I said softly, "she *cannot* say it outright?"

I flipped to the marked page, and slowly read:

"And so we have wrought edifices and structures and entities to replace the brilliance of my lost kin," the emperor said to them. "For while one common man is no equal to a Khanum, a great host of them working in agreement, and describing all they see and know, may not only match my kin, but exceed them in their deeds. Thus, with laws and strictures, and offices and election, and the changing of coin and the scribblings of many ledgers, shall a new Empire be fashioned. And should all proceed as I have foreseen, I shall watch these fruits ripen from within my Sanctum, and smile as the years slide over me, and stay silent." And at this, the Senate of the Sanctum made great acclamation.

And Portniz Minor approached the throne, and bowed sixteen times, and said, "So shall it be, Your Grace, and very justly so. Yet eagerly shall we await the day when the titan's blood spills forth new life, and the great and venerable line of Khanum can be remade again, and your holy kin can walk among us once more." But at this, the emperor was silent.

I looked at the book in my hand. My fingers gripped it so tight they had turned white.

Remade again.

The fretvine house creaked about me in the breeze. I reopened the book to the marked page and read the words again.

Pyktis's last words emerged in my mind, and his desperate scream to Ana: *You call me an abomination, but I know what you are! I have read it in your body, in your very movements! You disdain kings, but I know what you are!*

I whispered aloud, "What you are."

Memories came bubbling up within my mind, one after another.

I recalled what the augurs had told me in the Shroud: *There are whispers of other attempts to replicate the Khanum, to remake the emperor's bloodline anew. These efforts produced beings wild and savage, and full of strange passions and alien appetites. None of them lived past a year, we are told.*

Legs quaking, I slowly sat down on the floor.

Strange passions, I thought, *and alien appetites.*

My eyes shimmered, and I pictured Ana, sitting within a mound of oyster shells, her chin gleaming with their liquor as she said: *You can taste in each one which reef they came from, which side they grew upon, which waters they flourished within. They are like melodies of the ocean itself rendered in flesh . . .*

The augurs again, whispering: *The Khanum of old could enter a . . . a fugue. An elevation of their minds to the highest levels, calling upon all their faculties. This made them capable of incomprehensible brilliance, feats of intellect even we cannot decipher.*

Her face, twisted and stretched and bloodied in the shadows, her yellow eyes dancing in her skull: *I see his game, his mind! I see all the warp and weft he spins about us, even now!*

And then what Malo had said to me: *I confess, there is a strange scent to that woman sometimes. One I don't quite know . . .*

Another memory. I had watched her play her lyres, here in this very room, and asked: *When are you going to tell me what augmentations you have, Ana? And how it is you can do all you can do?*

To which she'd cheerily responded: *When I need to, you little shit, and no earlier!*

I projected the memory on the empty floor before me. How she'd sat, how she'd lovingly held the lyres, how she'd cocked her head. Her pale skin, and snowy hair, and her familiar, predatory grin: too many teeth, and all too white.

"The day when the great Khanum can be remade again," I said to myself quietly. And yet—what if that day had already come?

I RACED BACK to the medikker's bays. I was unsure what my goal was in doing so—for if her hints had all been true, she herself was incapable of telling me anything—but I knew I had to see her, to signal to her that I had understood, that I'd comprehended all her suggestions.

Yet when I returned, the medikkers shook their heads. "She sleeps now. You may look upon her, but she will not wake."

I tottered into her rooms and gazed upon her lying in her cradle. They had removed her blindfold from her. For some reason it made her seem small and shrunken, this pale little thing wrapped up in gray blankets, like a seashell emerging from the dark sands of a beach.

I wished to ask her many things then. I wished to know what she was; how she had come to be this thing; why she toiled here, in the hinterlands of the Empire, applying justice in such broken places. But I dared not speak any of it aloud, for fear of being overheard.

She coughed in her sleep, a short, pained sound. I recalled more of her words then: *The most passionate Iudex officers are the ones who've been harmed, you see . . . It puts a fire in them. Doesn't make them good at what they do, necessarily, but it does make them . . . enthusiastic, let us say. Willing to suffer, and bear burdens others could not . . .*

Willing to suffer, and bear burdens. She had been hinting at it even then, though I could not have comprehended then the nature of her suffering; nor could I even now, truth be told. Though she slept before me like a child, this frail white thing remained beyond me.

I gently lifted her blindfold from her nightstand and tucked it about her eyes again.

"For when you wake, ma'am," I said softly.

Then I left.

EPILOGUE

⋯

THE
WATCHMAN

CHAPTER 55

∴

I VISITED THE MEDIKKER'S BAY EACH MORNING TO check on Ana. Each day, the medikkers told me she slept. Each day, I collected her post, and compiled it in her quarters. And each day, I began the long chain of answering endless questions: questions asked of me from high Apoth officers, and Treasury officers, and then—inevitably—a commander from the Legion.

They asked me again and again to recount all I'd experienced here in Yarrowdale: all the people I'd interviewed, every scrap of evidence, and every drop of blood I'd seen spilled. All seemed frustrated and furious by what I'd found; though, to my relief, none had much criticism for me, or Ana.

Though I myself did not venture west, I came to gather that the entire realm of Yarrow had splintered and dissolved after Pyktis's death, with some heirs claiming the throne, and others fleeing the realm outright. I did not know what Pavitar attempted, but the stream of *naukari* flooding into Yarrowdale suggested he was not successful.

One afternoon I happened upon Prificto Kardas, sitting slumped in a sotbar, deep into his third pot. "We've no idea what to do with them all!" he sighed to me. "Perhaps not a full adoption of this nation, then, but a mass migration, with many wardens shepherding them out from their estates! It seems hardly better. The barges of the Apoths may soon be carrying families, as opposed to reagents." He tossed back another sip of sot. "But I shall not touch it, no! That has little to do with the coin of the Empire. I shall not dip my toe back into these beshatted waters!"

I sought Malo in the city but could not find her. I guessed she had to be one of the shepherds Kardas had mentioned, leading the *naukari* to freedom in the night as the realm crumbled. I invoked the blessing of Zynjir, deity of the free, and wished her well.

On the fourth day of Ana's long sleep, I fetched her post and found one parchment for me. I squinted at it and saw to my horror that it was from the Usini Lending Group. Yet when I opened it, the notice did not concern my loans but rather read: *NOTICE OF TEMPORARY SUSPENSION OF THE USINI LENDING GROUP DUE TO ONGOING IUDEX INVESTIGATION.*

I read the letter carefully and felt an audacious hope flutter within me. It seemed that there had been accusations of corruption within the Usini Lending Group, and after an investigation had been announced, much of the company had collapsed, as the value of their debts had suddenly become very uncertain.

I looked back at the medikker's bay and recalled my discussion with Ana: *Even you cannot change my debts, ma'am.*

To which she'd responded: *How certain you seem!*

I folded the parchment and put it in my pocket, thinking. It was her work behind this, surely, but why had she arranged this? Why impart to me her deadly secret, and then make it simpler and more enticing for me to leave her?

The answer was obvious, once I thought about it.

"Am I so simple to read?" I asked softly.

ON THE MORNING of the sixth day I found Malo waiting for me before the medikker's bays, idly watching as one of the attendants swept the front porch. She looked thin and exhausted, and bore many scratches—perhaps injuries from delving deep into the woods of the Elder West—but there was an air of quiet triumph about her.

"I was told that the crazy Iudex woman was here," Malo said, and then asked, "Is she well? Or have they shipped us a second one for our sins?"

"She has slept for a great while but is to wake today, I've been told." I smiled at her. "But tell me, Malo . . . how many did you save?"

An innocent shrug. "I don't know what you mean! I have been on leave and have not meddled in the affairs of the Elder West, which I have been strictly forbidden from doing. This order," she said somberly, "I have carefully obeyed." Then she grinned, popped a chunk of hina root into her mouth, and spat on the floor of the porch.

The attendant paused in her sweeping and looked up. "Please don't do that."

Malo narrowed her eyes at her. The woman scoffed, quietly shook her head, and continued sweeping.

I smiled wider. "And they have confirmed you've *stayed* here, on leave? You, who are so talented at disappearing?"

"They have had their eyes elsewhere, let us say. Who can say what they know? Nobody knows anything here, anymore."

"But now your leave is over, yes? What shall you do?"

Her glow of triumph faded. "That is a good question, for it is another thing nobody knows. The *naukari* are flooding into the Empire, either by official means or otherwise. We wardens are kept here to keep the peace, but we know we cannot stay. Some seek another role in the Empire. But even if they take me, I am unsure what awaits me within the rings. I do not have a medikker's eyes or nose, nor that of a reagent-brewer, an ascolytic. And I am most uncouth, I think, for even the Outer Rim and the third ring."

"Having been to those places, I'm not so sure," I said. "But things are changing, surely, and shall change yet more. They still plan to move the marrow by sea, true?"

"Yes, and sooner than you think!" Again, she spat a gob of black spittle onto the porch.

"*Please* do not do that!" cried the attendant.

"Shut up!" snapped Malo.

The attendant, scandalized, shook her head, huffed, and continued sweeping.

Malo turned back to me. "That was what I came to tell you. The hydricyst is scheduled to sail into the bay *today*. It shall be quite a sight! The fucking thing is practically the size of an island, they say! Will you watch it arrive with me?"

"That may offer little fun, since with your eyes, you'll see it well before I do. But—certainly. Let me check on Ana first."

I slipped inside. I heard the attendant say behind me, "No. *No!* No more!" followed by a string of swears in Pithian.

I WALKED TO Ana's cradle, as I had for the past mornings, but this time I found it empty and neatly made up. When I stopped a medikker to ask what had happened, he seemed confused.

"Why, she asked to be taken away!" he told me. "She practically forced one of our attendants to do so, saying she had something to witness this morning. She did say you would know someone who could find her. Especially, ah—well, since she refused to partake in our final bathing, she said . . ."

I gritted my teeth, thanked him, and went back out to find Malo now in a full-throated argument with the attendant regarding her right to spit outdoors where she pleased. I took Malo by the arm as she was midsentence and pulled her away. "Come," I said. "Let's go."

"What!" said Malo, outraged. "Get your damn hands off me! I need to work up enough spittle to color this prude's eye!"

"Ana has left," I said, "and she apparently intends for you to track her. Can you catch her scent?"

"Eh? I mean . . . certainly, I can, if you give me a moment. What game is this she plays? I want to see the goddamn boat come in!"

"I've no idea," I said. "But let's find her first."

IT TOOK MALO no time to find Ana's scent—"The woman smells like an Old Town beach at low tide," she muttered—and we followed her trail west up a short set of cliffs overlooking Yarrowdale. Finally we came to a rocky outcropping, where a very nervous-looking medikker attendant was pacing back and forth. As I made the last step, I heard Ana's voice: "Ah! I believe we have been found. You are dismissed, sir! I appreciate your accompanying me on this lovely jaunt!"

"Praise Sanctum!" sighed the attendant, and he scrambled back down to the city.

I took in the scene. Ana sat beneath a short, crooked tree, dressed in her old black dress, her eyes bound. She faced out to sea with her head cocked and mouth slightly open, as if she was listening very hard and trying to catch a melody we could not hear.

"Ma'am," I said as I stepped over to her. "This . . . this all seems *extremely* unwise."

"Oh?" she said. "How so, Din?"

"Half the reason you were put in the medikker's bay was due to exhaustion, yes? And didn't that exhaustion come from too much exposure to too many environs?"

"That, and other things," she said. "But I did my math upon awakening and guessed that the hydricyst would be in today! Is that not so? I did not wish to miss it."

"A good point," said Malo. "And this *is* a fine place to watch."

"Ah!" said Ana, grinning. "Good morning, Signum Malo! How fares the noble kingdom of Yarrow?"

"Noble? Feh." Malo spat. "It has not been noble in living memory. But whatever it is now, it is all falling to piss and rubble."

"Oh?"

"Yes. First there was only one king, old and stupid. Now there are dozens, young and even stupider, all trying to kill each other. I pray they each succeed and empty the land of royalty."

"A very old story," Ana sniffed, "with a very predictable outcome. Thank you for helping Din find me! Yet I wish to ask, Malo—could you leave us for a moment? I have something that I wish to discuss with him."

Malo shrugged. "I shall go to the cliffs above you. The view is better up there, anyway."

I peered up the cliffs. "There's a great deal of seabird nests up there. They won't be pleased."

"I'll not let a bunch of fucking birds stop me," said Malo indignantly, and she scurried up the cliffs with the grace and speed of a mountain goat.

Ana patted the ground beside her. I sat, glancing at her sidelong. She seemed the Ana I'd always known: skinny, sharp, grinning, with her bone-white hair tied up in a messy bun. I wondered what to say and could think of nothing.

She broke the silence first: "Have you gotten my post while I rested, Din? What have I missed?"

"Mostly letters from various officials pleading for you to tell them what has happened here, ma'am. Others seem totally ignorant and ask you for advice on various matters."

"Dull," she proclaimed. "I shall deal with them in due time. What else?"

"Well," I said slowly. "It seems the Usini Lending Group has nearly collapsed, ma'am . . ."

"Ah! Has it?"

"Yes. And . . . I cannot help but feel that your hand is in that somewhere, ma'am."

"Me?" she said archly. "Oh, *I* did nothing, Din."

"Somehow I find that difficult to believe, ma'am."

"What could I do, for I was here in Yarrowdale the entire time! But . . ." Her grin broadened. "I will admit that there were many within the Iudex who have been looking *very hard* at the Usini Lending Group for some time. Lots of rumors about abruptly renegotiating agreements and harassing our officers, and so on . . . When you reported to me that you had experienced the same, well. I simply sent a few letters. A nudge, as it were, in the right direction."

"But why? You wished me to stay, didn't you? To turn away from the Legion, and remain your investigator?"

"Well, I promised you *two* revelations, boy," she said. "For one of them, you could not comprehend it if there were obstacles before your choice. I have removed them, so you may now choose freely and honestly. But, before I hear your choice, I must ask, Din . . . what does the ocean look like?" She flicked a hand at the sea before her. "Describe the sight for me. For I fear I shall never be so close to the sea again."

I eyed the endless, blank horizon. From here I could turn my head from side to side and see no works of humankind, save the Shroud, nor any speck of soil or stone. "It is rather . . . flat, ma'am."

"Flat? Is that the fullest extent of your poetic capacities?"

"I have no other word for it," I sighed. "It is enormous, and flat, and empty. And though I know it moves, the farther I look, the less movement I see."

"Ah," she said softly. "And yet we know it moves, in manners both huge and hidden, far beneath its surface. And we know, of course, what swims in its deeps."

A tremor in my belly. I looked down at the steady ground beneath me.

"It is good to place oneself before the vast expanse of this world," said Ana. "The ocean cannot tell the difference between a rich man and a poor one, nor one full of happiness, or despair. To those waves, all are so terribly small."

"Being an imperial from the Outer Rim," I said, "I need little help in feeling such a thing, ma'am."

"A good point." She cocked her head. "Hm . . . it all makes me wonder—perhaps that is why we invented them in the first place."

"Them?"

"Kings, of course. Perhaps we wished to make the ancient and divine mortal, to render the infinite in flesh and form. How reassuring that would be! And yet, a fool's game, as we have so thoroughly learned here. Our emperor wisely sleeps in his Sanctum, still and silent, hardly more than a spirit. We need no more kingly stuff than that! Not from the emperor, nor the kings of Yarrow . . ." She slowly turned her blindfolded face to me. "Nor anyone else."

I studied her and felt countless meanings hidden in these words. It was like so many great imperial things: so much was mystery, while the rest was politely unspeakable.

"How do you mean, ma'am?" I asked quietly.

"I mean, the Empire has granted our folk many blessings, Din," she purred. "Blessings of the flesh, the mind, the spirit. Any of these blessings might lead one to imagine that they are of regal element. And that is why we must have a watchman among us, to ensure that these folk never forget the truth."

"What truth?"

"That though a person's mind may be shaped differently, their hearts and souls are all too human. That makes them strong—but it also makes them weak. And petty. And predictable." She flourished a hand, like an actor performing a monologue. "I simply wonder—who shall that watchman be?"

Finally I could bear it no more. "Ohh, enough!" I said. "You can stop your lecturing, Ana."

"I beg your pardon?"

"You know what choice I've made. You knew it before you ever slept." I turned back to the sea. "I shall not go to the East. I shall stay with you, ma'am, and continue on in this strange work."

"Oh?" Ana said cautiously. "Truly? Why?"

"Because . . . what you said was true. I wish to keep an Empire worth defending." I eyed the rooftops of Yarrowdale, tiny and cheerful where they clung to the shore. "After all we saw here, that feels a hard fight. Perhaps even harder than what one might see at the sea walls. Though it does come with a sight less glory. That was the first of your revelations, yes?"

"True enough," she admitted. "You are a quick pupil. But I wonder . . . what would the person you left in Talagray think of this choice?"

I imagined him then: Kepheus, so tall and broad, yet always leaning crookedly against a wall or door, his shabby smile on his face, his eyes so understanding. It was he who'd spoken to me of service most of all, there in Talagray, yet only now, after I had been so long apart from him, had I come to truly comprehend it.

"I think he knows what I have chosen," I said quietly. "Wherever he may be."

There was a beat of silence. Then she reached out, fumbled to find me, took me by the hand, and squeezed it: the first time she had ever done so in my memory. "Then I thank you, Dinios Kol," she said quietly. "I hope I shall be an instrument of service to you, just as much as you are to me. And . . . I can hardly think of a better watchman than you. I shall keep you close—for though you and I are small, together we shall forge grand things indeed."

I bowed my head. I felt my heart almost burst with tension from so many things going unsaid in that moment. Was she what I suspected her to be? Was she asking, however indirectly, for me to watch over her, and ensure that her own mind did not go awry, just as had happened to Pyktis? Was this the role she had planned for me all this time?

But I knew she could not answer questions about that second revelation, or at least, she could not now.

"Thank you for the scarf, ma'am," I said softly. "It's very nice."

"Ah, that is good to hear," said Ana. "It is the least I could do, given how much I have put you through. Perhaps we need better allies in the Iudex, yes, Din?"

"Allies?"

"Yes . . ." She leaned toward me. "Do you know, there is an investigator I've aided in the Outer Rim canton of Ashradel who has lost four assistants in the past three years! A tragic thing, but perhaps not a surprising one, given that Ashradel is a terribly murderous place. Why, he asked me for assistance in finding a replacement just last month. So . . ." She gestured above us. "Tell me. How might she look in blue?"

I looked up at the cliffs. Malo sat perched on the edge of a rock dappled thickly with birdshit, chewing her hina root and squinting at the seabirds, who wheeled about her, shrieking angrily at her intrusion. One grew too near, and she flicked a pebble at it, striking it in the belly, and she laughed wickedly as the bird twirled away.

"I think I fear for the knaves and criminals of Ashradel, ma'am, if an investigator like Malo is to hunt them."

Ana laughed. "Quite so! I think she shall flourish there. Perhaps so much that our paths might cross again, someday."

Then a shout from Malo above: "To the east! It comes!"

"Ahh," said Ana with relish. "Tell me, Din! Tell me what it looks like, as the Fifth Empire begins!"

I shielded my eyes and squinted, parsing through the sunlight and the glittering seas. It emerged from the horizon, black and tall and shimmering with flags, bedecked with bombards and glistening bright, a ship larger than I could have ever conceived in all my days, a construction vast enough to split any wave and seek any shore.

I leaned close to Ana and began to speak.

AUTHOR'S NOTE

▲ ▲ ▲

The more I think of it, the more I feel there is perhaps no other genre of fiction more enamored of autocracies than fantasy.

Perhaps this is due to the fable-like roots of the genre, dating back to King Arthur and beyond: the endless search for a true and proper heir bearing the awaited divine blessings, the curse of the kingdom ending only when he—and it's almost always a *he*—is restored to the throne, and righteous restoration courses throughout the land.

Or perhaps our fascination with kings and autocracies is more innate. As Sir Terry Pratchett once put it, it's as if even the most intelligent person has this little blank spot in their heads where someone's written: "Kings. What a good idea."

Regardless, the second decade of the twenty-first century seems replete with examples as to why autocracies are, to put it mildly, very stupid. Our headlines are dominated by regimes with one nigh-all-powerful man at the top making any number of terrible choices, and then—to the bafflement of the entire globe—doubling down on them, thus inflicting massive suffering on his people. It seems the talents that make a man capable of navigating palace intrigue until he wins the throne generally don't coexist with the talents required for—or even a passing interest in—good governance.

In the decade or so before this inflection point, however, the story was very different. There was a dreadful murmuring around the globe suggesting that autocracy was not merely surging, but *better:* more efficient and effective than liberal democracies could ever hope to be.

"Wouldn't it be better," some began to mutter, "if we had someone in charge who didn't have to *listen* to so many useless little people?"

And it is a curious correlation that, during this moment of self-doubt, fantasy's fixation with autocracy not only grew in intensity, but grew stranger. For it was then that we saw fewer stories invoking a traditional, romanticized ideal of divine rule wielded by beneficent patriarchs, and in their place came a wave of fantasy that embraced if not celebrated the capricious cruelties of autocratic regimes.

And we loved it. We eagerly gobbled up tales of crude, primitive worlds where petty resentments, sexual sadism, and sheer stupidity regularly led to the torture, deprivation, and deaths of thousands. We delighted in the piques and feuds of aristocrats placed beyond the rule of law, and sat captivated as privileged princes indulged in murder, rape, and the sexual assault and torture of children, without even a gesture toward justice.

I suspect this was largely a function of our era. The 2010s were not only a time of surging autocracy, but also a moment of economic blight and rampant inequality. Perhaps the only escape we could imagine was one in which we could become one of the privileged princes we saw on the news every night, these boys who so blithely destroyed the pillars of society around us.

Yet if the 2010s awed us with the power of autocrats, the 2020s seem hell-bent to refute it. More and more, it becomes impossible to deny that autocrats—like any ruler—are but men, yet men with no obligation to listen to their people, and thus acknowledge reality. This, in turn, makes them fools: fools that are very difficult to dislodge from their thrones, true, but fools nonetheless.

Today's fiction seems more circumspect and more critical of the seductive powers of the throne and scepter. Perhaps the mood is shifting with the times; perhaps this is but a hopeful delusion. Regardless, I hope my own handful of words will contribute in their own small way, yet it's worth saying that the argument is not as clear cut as one might imagine.

When I first sat down to write this story, I made the unwise choice to depict the realm of Yarrow as a Dark Ages or medieval kingdom:

that is to say, squalid, filthy, and wretched. Disdaining such a thing was too easy, I realized. A wiser choice would be to not only have it resemble a kingdom of High Fantasy, aweing Din with its stone walls and armored warriors and high halls, but to weave imagery of High Fantasy autocracy throughout all the crimes of this story, from the king of Yarrow, to priestly Thelenai, to the pale king of the swamps.

Because all the characters in this story—like all of humanity, apparently—have a little blank spot in their heads that says, "Kings. What a good idea." The idea is powerful, and seductive, and should not be underestimated. To be a civilization of any worth, however, means acknowledging the idea—and then condemning it as laughably, madly stupid.

May we come to live in such a worthier world, and soon. Many thanks, as always, to my editor, Julian Pavia, and my agent, Cameron McClure, who aided me immensely in writing this. And much love to my wife and boys, and all the grandparents and friends who keep our family happy, whole, and functioning, for if we are not instruments in service to one another, then we are nothing at all.

—RJB
September 2024

ROBERT JACKSON BENNETT is the author of the Founders Trilogy and the Divine Cities Trilogy, which were both Hugo Award finalists in the Best Series category. The first book in the Divine Cities Trilogy, *City of Stairs*, was also a finalist for the World Fantasy and Locus awards, and the second, *City of Blades*, was a finalist for the World Fantasy, Locus, and British Fantasy awards. His previous novels, which include *American Elsewhere* and *The Company Man*, have received the Edgar Award, the Shirley Jackson Award, and the Philip K. Dick Citation of Excellence. He lives in Austin, Texas, with his family.

robertjacksonbennett.com